Praise for

DEATH, TAXES, AND EXTRA-HOLD HAIRSPRAY

"As usual, the pace is quick without being frenetic, and the breezy narrative style is perfection—fun and sexy without being over the top."   —*RT Book Reviews*

"This is a rollicking adventure that will have you rooting for the IRS for once—and you won't want to put it down until you find out how Tara will overcome all the obstacles in her way. Keep turning those pages—you'll love every second as you try to find out!"   — *Reader To Reader Reviews*

"If you've never read one of Diane Kelly's Tara Holloway novels, I strongly recommend that you rectify the situation immediately. The series has gotten better with every single installment, and I'd be shocked if you didn't see these characters gracing your television screen before too long (USA and HBO, I'm looking in your direction). Get on board now so you can say you knew Tara Holloway when."

—*The Season for Romance*

"Diane Kelly knows how to rock the romance, and roll the story right into a delightful mix of high drama with great characters."   —*The Reading Reviewer*

DEATH, TAXES, AND A SKINNY NO-WHIP LATTE

"Readers w   dred spirit to
Stephanie   f-deprecating
sense of hu   ng situations,
including   be muggers,
and head   bits, and the
nonstop a   standard plot
moving along at a good pace.   *RT Book Reviews*

St. Martin's Paperbacks Titles
by Diane Kelly

Death, Taxes, and a French Manicure

Death, Taxes, and a Skinny No-Whip Latte

Death, Taxes, and Extra-Hold Hairspray

Death, Taxes, and a Sequined Clutch
(an e-original novella)

Death, Taxes, and Peach Sangria

Death, Taxes, and Hot Pink Leg Warmers

Death, Taxes, and Green Tea Ice Cream

Death, Taxes,
and Green Tea
Ice Cream

DIANE KELLY

St. Martin's Paperbacks

DEATH, TAXES, AND GREEN TEA ICE CREAM

Copyright © 2013 by Diane Kelly.

For information address St. Martin's Press, 175 Fifth Avenue, New York, NY 10010.

ISBN: 978-1-250-02308-7

Printed in the United States of America

St. Martin's Paperbacks edition / October 2013

St. Martin's Paperbacks are published by St. Martin's Press, 175 Fifth Avenue, New York, NY 10010.

10 9 8 7 6 5 4 3 2 1

*To Donna, a super sister and good friend
all in one convenient package*

$\mathcal{A}$cknowledgments

Thanks to the best editor ever, Holly Ingraham, for helping me take my work to the next level. Working with you is such a pleasure!

Thanks to Eileen Rothschild, Aleksandra Mencel, and everyone else at St. Martin's who worked to get this book to readers. You're a wonderful team!

Thanks to Danielle Fiorella, Monika Roe, and Iskra Design for creating such fun and colorful covers for my books. You rock!

Thanks to my agent, Helen Breitwieser, for keeping my career moving forward. I appreciate all you do!

Thanks to my talented writing buddies, Trinity Blake, Celya Bowers, Angela Cavener, Hadley Holt, Cheryl Hathaway, and Angela Hicks, for your input, encouragement, and friendship!

Thanks to Liz Bemis-Hittinger and Sienna Condy of Bemis Promotions for your work on my Web site and newsletters. You always make me look good!

Thanks to Cynthia Gandy of the Poker And Literary Society book club for mentioning your stint as a Medicaid fraud investigator. You gave me a great idea for a subplot. And thanks to Kerrin Parris for hosting the PALS book club and introducing me to such a fun group of ladies!

A big shout-out to all of the wonderful writers of Romance

Writers of America, as well as the national office staff. RWA is an awesome organization! I am proud to be part of such a supportive, smart, and powerful group.

And, finally, much gratitude to my readers. Thanks to you I get to do what I love. I hope this book brings you lots of laughs!

chapter one

Sexnesia

"I don't know who I am anymore."

Okay, I know I sounded like a drama queen, but that was exactly how I felt. As if my sense of self, my identity as a butt-kicking federal agent, had been erased, replaced by an empty void. Since I'd been fired from my job as an IRS special agent a few days ago, forced to turn in my gun and badge, I felt like a mere stick figure, a black-and-white, two-dimensional version of myself. Like a hollow chocolate Easter bunny with the ears bitten off, no longer recognizable as a rabbit. Like a snowman that had melted and was now only a carrot and a soggy stocking cap sitting in a wet spot in the yard. But I suppose that's enough similes, huh? Let's just use southern shorthand and say that I felt like a sorry sack of shit.

My gumption was gone.

Nick rolled onto his side in the king-sized bed, propping his head on his elbow as he looked down at me with his whiskey-colored eyes. He reached out a strong, warm hand and stroked my cheek. "*You* may not remember who you are, but *I* do. You're Tara Holloway. You're smart, you're smart-mouthed, and you don't take crap from anybody. You can even be sweet when you want to be." He leaned his dark head in to nuzzle my neck, planting a soft kiss just below my ear. "You're also my woman."

And Nick was my man. He'd proved that multiple times over the past couple of days.

I snuggled up against him, reaching down to stroke him to arousal for the third time that day. Yep, I was using sex to help me forget my troubles, but when Nick drove himself into me he also drove every thought from my head. Well, every thought but the one that went, *Woo hoo!* He gave me sexually induced amnesia. Sexnesia. It's a recognized medical condition. Look it up.

Ready now, Nick obliged me once more, treating me to mind-blowing, thought-scattering sex. Nick was a fantastic lover, an athletic lover, one with strength and stamina and a primal, powerful, and possessive approach that might have offended a lesser woman. But not me. I viewed sex as part romantic interlude, part contact sport. Halfway through, I grabbed Nick by the shoulders, dug my nails into his flesh, and flipped him onto his back, taking possession of him, seizing control. I might only be five foot two, but I was feisty.

Nick looked up at me with half-closed eyes. A grin spread across his lips, exposing a slightly chipped tooth that, in its imperfection, only added to his raw masculinity.

I sat up straight, putting my hands on his chest for balance and straddling him, squeezing him tight with my thighs as if he were a bronc I was trying to break. I posted for a rhythmic few laps around the ring, then spurred my stallion to a full-fledged gallop. He reached out and cupped his hands around my hips, helping to stabilize me as he bucked, taking me for the ride of my life.

Yippee ki-yay!

As climax overtook me I arched my back, involuntarily crying out with desperation and pleasure.

Nick was that damn good.

Afterward, I melted, as if my bones had liquefied. If not for Nick's grip on me, I would've fallen sideways off the bed in a post-coital oblivion. He flipped me back over under him and issued a final, forceful thrust that finished him off.

He lay on top of me for several moments, until we'd both cooled down. His face buried in my hair, he said, "It goes against everything in me to say this, but I think we should put our clothes on and tackle this problem head-on."

"Party pooper," I said, though he had a valid point. We'd been in bed for forty-two hours straight, climbing out only to take a quick shower and nuke frozen dinners in the microwave. While sex could make me forget my problems, it couldn't make them go away.

How did these problems begin? With a runty pig of a man named Donald Geils who ran a strip club called Guys & Dolls. Nick and I had gone undercover inside the club, along with a local cop named Aaron Menger and Christina Marquez, a female DEA agent who'd become a personal friend after she and I worked some cases together. Our multiagency team had joined up to investigate allegations of prostitution, drug dealing, and money laundering at the club. I'd worked as a bookkeeper in the cash office, using my financial smarts to examine the numbers, determining that a produce company was supplying more than fruits and vegetables to Guys & Dolls and that a liquor distributor was Geils' primary customer for the crystal meth hidden among the limes shipped to the club.

Unfortunately, despite careful advance planning, the bust didn't go down as expected. Thanks to a break in a water main, the SWAT team wasn't in place when the shit hit the fan. I'd rushed back into the club and put a bullet into the foot of each of the club's bouncers who were attacking Nick. In the club's VIP room, I'd found Christina drugged, stripped half-naked, and covered in bite marks from a john poised to take full advantage of her. When Geils ran into the room and shot at me, I'd returned the favor by putting several bullets into Geils' leg.

So far, I probably sound like a hero, huh? But here's the problem. Those bullets I put in Geils' leg? Well, I didn't fire them one right after another. I paused between shots for a second or two, thinking what a bastard the guy was, how fun it was to give the pig-nosed prick a little justice.

Though they hadn't come right out and said so, I suspected it was those short pauses that gave my superiors at the IRS pause, made them think I should have stopped shooting. Geils had dropped his gun by that point and the SWAT team had arrived and stormed the club. In the minds of the internal affairs officer, the director of field operations, and George Burton, the overall head of criminal investigations based in Washington, D.C., there'd been no good reason for me to continue shooting. In my mind, there'd been no good reason to stop. Geils had arranged to have Christina drugged and raped, he'd allowed customers to physically abuse the dancers in the club, and he'd enticed dancers into using the crystal meth he dealt, leading at least one of them to become hooked. She'd nearly lost her life to an overdose, and she'd temporarily lost custody of her young daughter.

Don Geils had deserved every one of the bullets I'd put in his leg and dozens more. But the federal government wasn't happy with my performance. I'd become a liability to the department, and they'd let me go.

As much as I hated to admit it, part of me didn't blame them. If I were in their shoes, I might have made the same decision. It was hard to fault them, though I'd hazard a guess that each and every one of them might have reacted the same way I had if faced with such a situation. I was a human being, and I had a human response to an inhuman, inhumane situation. Still, without a job I felt as useless as tits on a boar hog.

Reluctantly, I climbed out of bed and retrieved my panties from the mouth of Nutty, Nick's geriatric golden retriever mix. The fabric was soggy with dog spit. Urk. Looked like I'd have to go commando. I slid back into stretchy yoga pants, a long-sleeved tee, and sneakers and pulled my chestnut hair back into a ponytail.

Nick dressed in his rumpled jeans and sweatshirt, and together we made our disheveled way to his kitchen.

Nick had recently leased a town house in my neighborhood, half a block down and on the other side of the street.

But while his floor plan was the same as mine, his décor was totally different. My living room, on the one hand, contained a tasteful, traditional tapestry sofa and chair set, with a cherrywood coffee table and accents. Nick's, on the other hand, held a masculine faux leather couch in dark brown, along with an oversized, overstuffed recliner in a manly block print of earth tones. His coffee table was an amorphously shaped slab of natural wood cut years ago from a fallen tree on his parents' farm near Houston. A television the size of a life raft hung on the wall. The only art in the room, if you could even call it art, was a poster from a fishing tournament held long ago in Galveston, the last Nick and his father had participated in before Nick's father had died from a heart attack. The two had taken second place with a thirty-six-pound yellowfin tuna.

Sorry, Charlie.

Nutty padded after us, following us into the kitchen and squeezing his way out of his doggy door. I peeked into the freezer. We'd pretty much depleted our options and were left with only a box of freezer-burned waffles and a bag of black-eyed peas, harvested from Nick's mother's garden. I let the black-eyed peas stay in the freezer. As is customary in the South, we'd eat them on New Year's Day for good luck.

While Nick went out front to collect the Sunday paper from the stoop, I slid six waffles into the oven to warm and retrieved the syrup from the pantry. There's no rule against eating breakfast at three in the afternoon, after all. Nick poured us two glasses of juice and we sat down at his dinette set.

Nick riffled through the *Dallas Morning News,* pulling out the sports page for himself and handing me the classifieds and a ballpoint pen.

I perused the want ads as I crunched my way through the freezer-burned waffle. A car dealership in the southwestern suburbs was looking for a person with financial experience to process auto loan applications. The pay was good, but the location was at least an hour's drive from my town house. Not exactly convenient. A fast-food outlet sought a person with payroll experience to work as an assistant manager. Not sure I wanted to go home smelling like grease, though the thought of unlimited free curly fries was definitely tempting. A hospital needed help in their insurance billing department. No thanks. The tax code was difficult enough. Trying to make sense of the goobledygook in multiple insurance policies would be a nightmare.

An ad in the construction section caught my eye. "Think I could handle a jackhammer?" It would be an awesome workout for my biceps. Plus, the thought of working out my frustrations on a piece of asphalt sounded enticing.

"A jackhammer would be loud. Wouldn't that rattle your nerves?"

True. Any stress relief the jackhammer provided would probably be offset by the irritating noise.

"Think the federal government would hire me back as a sniper for the CIA?" I was a sharpshooter after all, and I'd proved I had no qualms about putting a bullet in someone. Besides, I'd dropped hints to my dad that I wanted a rifle for Christmas, which was coming up in a matter of days. My personal gun collection contained a number of handguns but no longer-range weapon. Might as well round out the set, huh? Besides, given the current shambles my life was in, I was trying to avoid thinking of the present and had focused on the longer range.

"A sniper?" Nick said. "Nah. You wouldn't be able to kill anyone."

I sighed. Nick was right. As furious as I'd been at Don Geils, I hadn't even been able to bring myself to kill him. I would've been totally justified, too. After all, he'd shot at me first. Hell, in my training as a special agent I'd been taught to respond to lethal force with the same. If I'd done what I was supposed to do, if I'd shot the bastard dead, I'd still have my job. Instead, I'd let him live and gotten myself fired.

How that's for irony?

Nutty eased back through the doggy door, plodded over to his food bowl, and began crunching his kibble as Nick gestured to the newspaper in front of me. "Keep looking.

Tax season's coming up. I bet there's all kinds of jobs for preparers."

I made a gagging sound. *Blegh.* "I don't want to do tax prep." Not that preparing returns was bad work. It just involved a lot of sitting in an office, and I wasn't a creature who adapted well to captivity. Being a special agent had involved a significant amount of fieldwork, part of the reason why the job had been perfect for me. But I supposed beggars can't be choosers, huh? If I took a tax prep job, perhaps I could make do by going outside and taking a lap around the building every hour or so.

"Maybe you could just work through tax season while you look for something more permanent." Nick put the sports page down. "What about going back to Martin and McGee?"

I'd worked at the downtown CPA firm for four years before joining the IRS. The managing partner, Scott Klein, told me if I ever changed my mind about leaving they'd welcome me back with open arms. And why shouldn't they? I was a hard worker, skilled, reliable. I'd enjoyed many of my projects. The clientele at the firm had been varied and the work was interesting, a challenging combination of tax and consulting work. I'd felt trapped in my tiny cubicle before, but they'd promised me a management position with an office if I returned. Maybe it wouldn't be so bad.

"Good idea. I'll check in with Scott Klein in the morning." Even if I didn't intend to return to the firm permanently, they could surely use a hand during the upcoming spring tax season. Those weeks were insanely busy. It had been hard to even find time for a potty break. I'd learned to limit my liquids at the office and survived on potato chips, candy bars, and microwave popcorn from the vending machine.

I finished my waffle, stood, and took my plate to the sink. "Guess I'll head home now."

Nick rose from his seat. "Nutty and I will walk you home."

He clipped the leash on to Nutty's collar and the two followed me out the door and onto the sidewalk, Nutty's toenails clicking happily on the concrete.

Having Nick just down the block was wonderful. It made spending the night convenient and meant he was close by if I needed a jar opened or an errant bug corralled. I was available to feed Nutty or to take him for a walk if Nick was tied up with work. Yet, with our own places, we could maintain a modicum of independence, too.

It was the perfect scenario. At least for now. Someday, maybe even someday soon, I'd want more. My two closest friends had both recently become engaged, and my ring finger was beginning to feel a little bare. Still, Nick and I had only been dating a matter of weeks. It was much too soon to talk about marriage.

When we arrived at my place, Nick gave me a final soft kiss. He leaned his forehead against mine. "You know Lu's fighting for you, right?"

"Yeah. I know." My boss, Lu "The Lobo" Lobozinski, had been none too pleased that George Burton had demanded I be fired. After my hearing, when she'd met with the others privately, she'd argued on my behalf, insisted I was an essential asset to her department, but her pleas fell on deaf ears. She'd tried to console me by saying she'd keep up the fight, that maybe they'd change their minds once things cooled down, but frankly, I didn't hold out much hope. Hiring me back would be admitting they'd made a mistake letting me go, and who wants to admit they've made a mistake? Especially men. They seemed to fear that admitting an error would shrink their testicles.

If only there was a way I could prove, without a doubt, that they'd been wrong, that the agency needed my unique skills, that I wasn't the out-of-control agent they'd believed me to be.

I wasn't, was I?

Nick took my hand and pressed it to his lips now. "I'm not giving up hope yet."

I sighed. I didn't want to be a pessimist, but I didn't want to hang on to false hope, either. What good would that do?

My firing had come at a bad time, too. I'd just been assigned two great cases. Both involved transnational criminal organizations and posed the possibility of foreign travel. They'd been primo assignments, the kind of cases that didn't come along often. I'd been lucky to land the files, excited to embark on what would surely be complex and interesting investigations. Now they'd be in another special agent's hands.

I stepped back, careful not to step on Nutty lying sprawled on my doormat, and looked up at Nick. "Any idea who Lu gave my cases to?" It pained me to think of my cases being reassigned, of my coworkers vying for them like vultures pecking at the rotting carcass that had once been my career.

Nick shrugged. "Lu divvied them up all around."

"I'm talking about the two big ones. Tokyo Discount Telecom and United National Debt Recovery."

Nick diverted his eyes, taking a sudden interest in the Christmas wreath hanging on the front door behind me.

I crossed my arms over my 32As and narrowed my gray-blue eyes at him. "*You? You* took my cases?"

I wasn't so much mad at Nick as I was at the situation. The cases were some of the best to ever come through the office. Intriguing, intricate, high dollar. Sure to put an agent on the fast track for promotion.

The Treasury Department and its foreign counterparts were buckling down on transnational criminal organizations, called TCOs for short. These organizations engaged in all sorts of sordid activities, ranging from extortion, to illegal weapons trading, to drug and human trafficking. Some even traded illegally in endangered species or their parts, such as rhino horns.

The Treasury had designated a number of organizations and their members and was doing what it could to put an end to their violent, illegal reign, including freezing their assets and prohibiting persons in the United States from doing business with the TCOs. The U.S. government had recently imposed sanctions on members of the Brothers' Circle, a multiethnic crime syndicate composed of criminal groups based in former Soviet republics, the Middle East, Africa, and Latin America. The Treasury had also set its sights on the Japanese Yakuza criminal network, as well as its largest clan members, the Yamaguchi-gumi and Sumiyoshi-Kai families.

Of course the only way to successfully take down these groups was to work in conjunction with law enforcement in the countries where the organizations were based and operated. A multinational crime ring could only be defeated by a multinational crime-fighting force. As a girl who'd grown up in a small town in East Texas, I'd been proud Lu trusted me with cases of international importance.

"Tara, the cases weren't . . ." Nick trailed off. He'd probably been about to say the cases hadn't truly been mine, that they belonged to the IRS, but he apparently thought better of it. You can't fight an emotional reaction with logic. He took my hand again. "I'm sorry. It sucks."

I released a long breath. "I suppose if anyone had to get those cases, I'm glad it was you."

I'd already done some legwork on the cases. I'd spoken by phone with an agent from Immigration and Customs Enforcement about counterfeit electronics being shipped by Tokyo Discount Telecom. I'd also met with an assistant state attorney general about the collections fraud case. I'd been looking forward to working the investigations, especially because they'd involve foreign travel. The only international travel I'd done was an occasional trip to Mexico, standard vacation fare for Texans given the close proximity and relatively low cost. I'd been looking forward to visiting Asia. Now I'd be stuck at home.

Or would I?

"I'm going to Tokyo and New Delhi with you." The airfare would put a huge dent in my savings, but I had to go along. These cases were *mine,* dammit. I needed to see them through.

Nick dipped his head in acknowledgment. "Had a feeling you'd say that. Already bought your plane tickets."

The guy knew me well, huh?

"I'll pay you back."

"You'll do no such thing. We could use your help. Besides, I've got money in the bank and no one counting on me but a smelly old dog."

Nutty looked up on hearing the word "dog." Not realizing he'd been insulted, he wagged his tail, causing it to *thump-thump-thump* against my door.

"Thanks, Nick. So much." It was a generous, thoughtful gesture. I put my hands on Nick's cheeks and stood on tiptoe to give him a final peck and a tight, warm hug. Nutty received an ear ruffle and a kiss on the nose. "Bye, boy."

The dog replied with three wags of his tail and a *woof!*

chapter two

$\mathcal{D}$amaged Goods

I couldn't wait to visit Japan and India. When I was young, traveling from my small East Texas hometown of Nacogdoches to the big, bright city of Dallas had been like voyaging to Oz. And now I'd be going international! Who would've thought?

Tokyo would be a blast, with its interesting contrast of ancient traditions and modern technology and architecture. New Delhi would be a study in Eastern culture and philosophy. Wow. I'd be so worldly when I returned. I might have to stop drinking boxed wine and buying slightly irregular socks at the dollar store.

I spent a couple of hours Sunday evening performing research on the Internet, tracking down the hot spots to visit when I accompanied Nick on the trips.

As for Tokyo, the new Skytree was a must-see, of course. At 634 meters, it was the tallest broadcasting tower in the world and the second-tallest structure on earth, bested only by the Burj Khalifa, a skyscraper in Dubai. Tickets to the Skytree observation deck cost twenty-five hundred yen. I had no idea how that translated into U.S. dollars, but there was probably an app I could get for my phone that would do the math for me. Of course we'd take in a show at a Kabuki theater and visit one or more of the many gardens located around the city.

New Delhi boasted at least a dozen popular tourist spots, too. The Akshardham Temple with its musical fountain and lotus garden would be a spiritual place to visit. Lord knows my spirits were in need of a boost. Maybe if I had all of the Hindu gods pulling for me, too, things would turn around soon. The India Gate, a structure similar to the Arc de Triomphe in Paris, also went on my list. The Garden of Five Senses, with its cascading water and wind chimes, would be another great place to see.

I hoped the weather would be kind in both places. According to my search, the highs in New Delhi averaged just under seventy degrees Fahrenheit in January, while Tokyo averaged a high of fifty. Those temps would be manageable, especially if I bought that adorable cobalt-blue peacoat advertised in the Neiman Marcus catalog. I'd dog-eared the page. Not that I could justify the expense—I didn't have an extra $195 to drop on a coat, especially now that I was out of work—but a girl can still window-shop, can't she?

Monday morning, I pulled my red BMW convertible into the underground garage at the downtown bank building that housed Martin and McGee's offices. Following the sleek black Audi driven by my best friend, Alicia Shenkman, I circled down three levels. When she parked, I pulled into the spot next to her.

Alicia had been ecstatic yesterday when I told her I planned to return to the firm. The two of us had met back at the University of Texas in Austin years ago, in our first accounting class, and had been BFFs ever since. She'd recently moved into my town house with me, though she'd be moving out again once she and her fiancé, Daniel, exchanged vows in June.

Alicia stood behind her car, waiting for me. Her platinum

hair framed her face in a short, asymmetrical cut, severe yet sophisticated. Her suit, makeup, and nails were impeccable, as always.

My nails, on the other hand, were chewed down to nubs. My nail tech would surely flog me the next time I went in for a manicure. I wore a basic navy suit with loafers. No need for my cherry-red steel-toed Doc Martens at Martin and McGee. Nope, unlike my job with the IRS, a position with the CPA firm posed no risk that I'd need to kick someone in the nards or block a door with my foot. A shame really. When things got physical it could be kind of fun. Then again, it could be downright scary, too.

Alicia jabbed the elevator button and scrunched her shoulders, giddy with excitement. "It will be so great having you back! We can do lunch together, gossip with the girls over coffee, maybe even pull a prank on Nathan Jamison."

Nathan was an audit partner with whom I'd had a relationship years ago, just after I'd joined the firm. He'd led me on for weeks, then dumped me immediately once he'd bagged his prize. I'd been humiliated. Fortunately, I'd been able to even the score a few months ago when his clients, twin brothers, had been accused of securities and tax violations. But that's a whole 'nother story.

I wished I could be as excited as Alicia about my return to Martin and McGee. The place did have its perks—a competitive compensation package, free muffins on Mondays, name-brand coffee in its pots—but it was a tame place, a safe place. Though I'd sometimes feared the risks of my job as special agent, I'd thrived on them, too. And I missed carrying a gun. I felt underdressed without my Glock and holster. They were the ultimate female accessory.

The elevator dinged as it stopped on our floor. We stepped off and Alicia greeted the receptionist, whom I didn't recognize. Not surprising. The job was a springboard position for administrative staff. Most of the young women who started off at the reception desk ended up being promoted to an administrative assistant position after a few months.

"Tara's back!" Alicia called out in a singsong voice.

The young woman smiled, though I knew Alicia's words meant nothing to her. She had no idea who I was.

Alicia and I made our way down the hall, passing several of my former coworkers. Alicia informed everyone we passed that I was returning to the firm.

Several expressed excitement.

"We've missed you," said the young woman who'd occupied the cubicle next to mine. "Nobody's brought a beach ball to bounce around the cubes since you left."

Two of the guys who were the office pranksters caught us on their way out of the break room.

"I heard about the shoot-out at that strip club," one of them said. "How many people did you kill? Two? Three?"

I rolled my eyes. Once again the rumor mill had taken the truth and rolled it around until it didn't resemble the truth at all anymore. "Don't believe it. I didn't kill anyone. I just shot four men who deserved it, that's all."

The other guy snorted. "Oh. You 'just shot four men,'" he said, making air quotes with his fingers. "'That's all.'"

I didn't bother arguing the point further. Even I had to admit it sounded a bit extreme, especially in the tame environment of the CPA firm.

As the two walked on, Alicia turned to me. "I hope Mr. Klein will put you in the empty office on my hall."

"I'll request it."

Alicia gave me a hug as she reached the turnoff for her wing. "Let's do lunch, 'kay?"

"Of course."

"It's on me today!" she called over her shoulder. "Having you back here is cause to celebrate!"

I split off and headed down the partners' wing, where offices were bigger, the power was concentrated, and the ratio of penises to vaginas skewed significantly toward penises. You could almost feel the dollars adding up as I walked. *Cha-ching, cha-ching.*

When I reached Scott Klein's office, I peeked inside. He sat at his desk, mulling over the contents of a tax file.

I rapped on his door. *Rap-rap.*

He looked up, a flicker of surprise moving across his face before he offered me a smile and a welcome. He stood. "Hello there, Tara. Please don't tell me you're back to investigate another one of our clients?"

I raised a palm. "Not this time. I come in peace."

He offered a chuckle but hesitated a brief moment before offering me a seat.

Once I'd sat, he looked at me expectantly.

I smiled. "Good news. I've decided to take you up on your offer and return to the firm."

The smile faded from his face and he fidgeted in his chair as if suddenly uncomfortable.

He hadn't forgotten the offer he'd made, had he? Just in case, I figured I'd jar his memory. "You phoned me a few months ago, remember? You asked me how things were going at the IRS, and you said if I ever wanted to come back to Martin and McGee you'd have an office waiting for me."

"Yes. I remember." He exhaled a long, loud breath and slumped back in his chair, putting a mechanical pencil to his lips and chewing on it in a childlike action with which a psychologist would have a field day.

When Klein didn't continue, I said, "I'm no longer with the IRS. I know Martin and McGee can always use an extra hand during tax season, so my return will be good for both of us."

When he still failed to say anything, a sense of unease flared up in me. "I can start as soon as you like."

Ugh. I sounded desperate and I hated that. It was embarrassing. But why wasn't he saying anything?

"Tara, I . . . we . . ." His voice trailed off; then he seemed to gather his thoughts and his courage and sat up straight in his chair, leaning slightly toward me. "The firm can't take you back, Tara. Not under the circumstances."

"What circumstances?" Was the firm having financial trouble?

"We've all seen the news," Klein said. "We know you were fired from the IRS because you killed those people at the strip club."

I forced myself to remain calm. "I didn't kill anyone, Mr. Klein. I shot three bouncers who were attacking one of my fellow agents, and I shot the owner *after* he fired a gun at me. All of my shots were nonlethal," I said. "*Intentionally* nonlethal," I added a second later. I wasn't a crazed killer. I was saving the lives of my coworkers. Sheesh!

"Nonetheless," Klein said, "it wouldn't look good for the firm to have a person on staff who had been terminated from the IRS, especially when it's public knowledge. How would I explain that to clients?"

My anger got the best of me. "You could tell them I was doing my damn job; that's how you could explain it."

When he offered only a slowly shaking head in return, I realized there was no point in trying to continue the conversation. And again, I couldn't blame him. He had a lot of people counting on him and he had to do what was best for the firm.

I stood. "I understand. Thanks for your time." *You ball-less wimp.* Just because I didn't blame him didn't mean I couldn't mentally berate him. *Wuss! Chickenshit!*

Klein stood, too. "I'm really sorry, Tara."

I was sick of everyone telling me how sorry they were. A fat lot of good it did to have everyone feeling bad for me. I didn't like being the object of pity.

I raised a hand. "No need to be sorry. Martin and McGee was the first place I thought of. I'm sure I'll find another job soon." At least I hoped I would. The seven grand I had in savings would carry me for a couple of months, but it wouldn't give me time to dillydally.

Klein stepped around his desk, having apparently found his balls now. "I'd be happy to provide a reference for you."

I held out a hand. "Thanks. I appreciate that."

We shook hands and I left his office, taking a back way through the audit department so my former coworkers wouldn't see me slithering out in shame. I knew I probably should have given Alicia a heads-up, but I was afraid if I went to her office I'd end up in tears. I settled for texting her. *Make other lunch plans. I didn't get rehired.*

Her *WTH?* popped up a few seconds later as I stepped into the elevator.

I punched the button for the garage and sent a reply. *I'm damaged goods.*

chapter three

$\mathscr{S}$end Lawyers, Guns, and Money

When my cell phone bleeped a few seconds later, I didn't bother checking the readout. It had to be Alicia wanting the dirty details of my discussion with Scott Klein. I punched the button to accept the call and immediately began venting. "That's totally jacked up, right? I mean, who makes someone a job offer and then reneges like that?"

I heard only silence in response. Must be a bad connection. "Alicia?"

A male voice greeted me. "Is this Tara Holloway?"

"That depends," I said. "If you're trying to sell me aluminum siding, no. If I won the lottery, maybe."

The caller took a moment to digest my words. "I'm Troy Kerr, an assistant U.S. attorney."

A lawyer from the Department of Justice? He was probably calling about one of my former cases. "Sorry about that. I was expecting a call from someone else and didn't check the screen first. How can I help you?"

"I'd like to talk to you about Donald Geils."

"Sure. Are you helping Ross O'Donnell on the case?"

Ross was an assistant U.S. attorney who routinely represented the IRS in court. He'd been assigned to handle the
drug and money-laundering charges against Don Geils. The
DOJ had also considered bringing charges for assault on a
federal officer, but since I'd been undercover and Geils didn't
know I was with the IRS they didn't think the charges would
stick. The state prostitution charges would be handled sepa-
rately by the Dallas County district attorney's office.

"I'm not calling about the charges against Don Geils,"
Kerr said. "Those are being worked out."

"Worked out?" I asked. "You mean a plea deal?"

"Yes," Kerr replied. "Nothing's been nailed down yet,
but there's an offer on the table."

"How long will the asshole be in jail?"

"Fourteen years if the deal goes through."

Had I been the U.S. attorney assigned to the case, I
wouldn't have settled for anything less than eternity times
ten. But who was I to second-guess Ross O'Donnell's decision? After all, I didn't appreciate being second-guessed. I'd
be a hypocrite if I did the same to someone else. Besides, I
knew the Department of Justice was just as backlogged as
the IRS. Sometimes you had to move things along even if
the resolution was less than ideal.

Given that Lu had since reassigned my other investigations, it seemed Kerr should be speaking to the new special
agent on the case. "If you're not calling about Don Geils," I
asked, "what case are you calling about?"

"The potential charges against you."

What?

My heart performed a backflip in my chest. "Charges
against me?" The elevator door opened on the floor where I
was parked, but I was too taken aback to move. My throat
threatened to close up. "What are you talking about?" I
squeaked as the doors swung closed again and the elevator
started another ascent.

"Geils' attorney claims you used your weapon unneces-
sarily. I know the IRS terminated you after an internal affairs review of your actions. Given the circumstances, we're

considering excessive force charges. I'd like to meet with you in person and talk things over."

Stunned, I fell back against the wall and sank to the elevator floor. *Criminal charges? Against me?* But I wasn't a criminal! I was a crime *fighter,* for God's sake! I was one of the good guys!

Holy hell, what had my life come to?

Before I could say anything else, Kerr said, "I want to get moving on this. You and your lawyer swing by my office at ten o'clock Wednesday."

My lawyer? I hadn't hired an attorney to represent me in my internal affairs hearing and, in hindsight, that might have been a mistake. There was no way in hell I'd speak to the DOJ about potential criminal charges without legal representation. Still, it freaked me out to be in a position where I needed a lawyer to defend me. I'd always thought I'd be capable of defending myself.

"Okay," I managed, though my throat had constricted so tight I could barely breathe. The meeting with Kerr was only a little over forty-eight hours from now. I had to find an attorney to defend me, and I had to find him or her *fast.*

"One more thing, Miss Holloway."

"Yes?"

"We'd appreciate it if you'd stay in Dallas County. At least until we have time to make a decision on the matter."

Stay in the county? How dare this guy treat me like some lowlife poised to flee! Anger replaced my fear. "Christmas is in three days," I snapped. "I've made plans to visit my family in Nacogdoches." Not to mention my plans to travel with Nick to Tokyo and New Delhi. Dammit! This guy had me considering hari-kari.

Kerr paused a moment. "I suppose that'll be all right."

He *supposed* it was all right for me to spend Christmas with my family? What a Scrooge! I'd like to deck him in the halls, maybe shove a big old *bah* up his *humbug.* And the figgy pudding? Hell yeah, I'd bring it.

"I've also got trips planned to Japan and India," I said. "The plane tickets have already been purchased."

"Are the trips work related?"

Technically, they weren't. I no longer officially worked for the IRS, after all. In fact, my plans to remain involved in the investigations could get me in some hot water if the big-wigs up the chain at the IRS found out. But what could they do at this point? Fire me? Hell, they'd already done that. "Well, no. But—"

"Do I need to get an injunction, Miss Holloway?"

"An injunction?"

"A court order," he said, "preventing you from leaving the United States."

"You're kidding, right?"

His silence told me that no, he was not kidding. It also told me that yes, he was an a-hole.

Choking back my fury, I said, "You don't need to get an injunction. I'll stick around." I hoped the plane tickets were refundable.

"Good. Cooperation is in your best interest."

"See you Wednesday." I jabbed the button to end the call before I said something I'd regret, something like *go to hell, you peckerhead!*

What was I going to do? An attorney would cost big bucks, a scary thought given that I had no income and no-body in their right mind would hire me. I couldn't even file for unemployment benefits since my termination had pur-portedly been for cause. Only those laid off through no fault of their own were eligible for benefits.

I supposed I could hang out a shingle and go into business for myself, start my own tax practice. After all, I held a CPA license.

Whoa.

Wait a minute.

If I was convicted of excessive force, my CPA license would be at risk, too, wouldn't it? The Texas State Board of Public Accountancy wouldn't allow a convicted felon on their rolls. Ugh! If the board revoked my CPA license I'd be shit out of luck. I wasn't qualified to do anything else. My only jobs had been in the tax field. Well, other than my high school job at Big Bob's Bait Bucket. I'd sooner die than go back to sorting live worms.

So much was at stake. My identity, my livelihood, my personal freedom. I could find myself in prison! My cats would have to go live with my parents and I'd spend my best reproductive years behind bars. I'd die a bitter, barren woman.

The elevator opened on the ground floor and three women carrying paper coffee cups climbed on, chatting companionably. They glanced down at me sitting on the floor and became quiet, exchanging glances with one another before apparently deciding I was harmless and resuming their conversation. I stood, stuffed the phone into my purse, and rode up with the women to the fourteenth floor, envying their light-hearted chatter, tempted to climb off with them and start a new life here, become someone else. Other than making love with Nick, being Tara Holloway hadn't been any fun lately.

But no. I'd never run away from my problems before and, no matter how tempted I was to run away from them now, I had no choice but to deal with them.

Then again, it was only 450 miles to the nearest border crossing into Mexico and I loved me a good margarita. . . .

I punched the button to return to the garage. Numb with shock and fear, I stepped out of the elevator, shuffled to my car, and climbed in, sitting in the driver's seat and staring at the cement wall in front of me as I tried to think, to focus, to sort through the shit that had just been slung at me.

Who could help me?

Daniel.

Although Alicia's fiancé handled only civil matters, the law office he worked for was a full-service firm that employed dozens of attorneys. Surely Gertz, Gertz, and Schwartz had a criminal defense division.

I retrieved my cell phone from my purse, pulled up Daniel's work number on my contact list, and dialed him. The receptionist transferred me to his extension.

"Good morning, Tara."

I cut right to the chase. "I'm in big trouble, Daniel. The Department of Justice is considering an excessive force case against me for shooting Don Geils."

"Criminal charges?" His voice was incredulous. "Are you shitting me?"

"I wish I were."

He exhaled a long breath. "That's rough."

"Rough" was an understatement. I was in deep doo-doo here. Over my head. "I need a good defense attorney. A real ballbuster. Is there someone at Gertz you'd recommend?"

"Anthony Giacomo," Daniel said without hesitation. "The guy's somewhat unorthodox, but he's experienced and tough. Lots of hair on his ass."

Hairy assed, huh? Giacomo sounded like just the kind of lawyer I was looking for.

"His name sounds familiar," I said, searching my memory banks for information but coming up empty.

"He represented that woman accused of trying to electrocute her husband for the insurance money."

I remembered the case. The woman had taken out a $3 million life insurance policy on her husband shortly before tossing an electric bug zapper into the hot tub where he was relaxing. Fortunately for her husband but unfortunately for her, she'd misjudged the hot tub's distance from the socket and the zapper came unplugged as she hurled it. She should've used an extension cord. C'mon. Plan ahead, people! Giacomo had managed to get her off on a specious temporary insanity defense allegedly caused by a bad reaction to Chantix.

Given the attorney's high success rate, Daniel said Giacomo was in big demand and might not be able to take me on. Even more unfortunately, his rates ran four hundred an hour. Sheez, I'd spent less than that on my last laptop.

"Hold on a second while I buzz him and see if he's got time to meet with you."

I sat on hold, trying not to break down into tears like a

little girl. A minute later, Daniel returned to the line. "He can squeeze you in tomorrow morning at nine thirty."

"Great."

As if. Nothing in my life was great at the moment.

chapter four

When a Stranger Knocks

I drove home to my town house and went inside.

Anne, my creamy short-haired cat, didn't meet me at the door as usual. My fluffy brown feline, Henry, wasn't in his usual spot atop the armoire that housed my television, either. Rather, the two lay entangled in the middle of the floor. Annie lounged on her back on the rug, basking in the sunlight pouring through the front window. Henry lay draped over her, licking her under the chin and nibbling at her neck while she purred, her eyes half-closed in bliss.

I put my purse down on the table in the foyer and fisted my hands on my hips. "Is this what goes on when I'm at work? Kitty-cat porn?"

Anne looked up briefly, then dismissed me and returned her attentions to her lover. And to think all these years I'd thought the two had a platonic relationship. They'd done a good job of hiding their romantic involvement. Oh, well. They were both fixed. Might as well let them have their fun. I just hoped Henry didn't cough up a hairball later.

I walked to the kitchen and glanced at the clock. Ten

twenty-seven AM. Rats. Definitely too early to start drinking. Then again, mimosas were served at breakfast, right?

I poured myself half a glass of orange juice, opened the bottle of champagne I'd already bought for New Year's—*pop!*—and made myself a mimosa. I carried my drink back to the living room, kicked off my shoes, and plopped down on my couch. I laid my head on the back of the couch, eyes closed.

How the hell had everything gone so wrong?

A month ago my life was perfect. Nick and I had just begun dating and I'd wrapped up both the investigation against Don Geils and another against a group running a mortgage fraud scheme. I was flying high.

I should've known it was too good to last, that everything would come crashing down.

I suppose I should try to look at the bright side, though, huh? Having been fired, with no viable job prospects in sight, and now facing criminal charges, I'd surely hit rock bottom. At least I knew things couldn't get any worse, right?

My doorbell rang, followed by two loud knocks on the door. I dragged myself off the couch, went to my front door, and put my eye to the peephole. I couldn't see a thing. The festive holiday wreath hanging on my front door blocked my line of sight. Oops.

"Yes?" I called through the door. I'd watched *Oprah*. I knew not to open my door for strangers.

"Delivery for Tara Holloway," came a husky female voice.

I decided to take my chances and opened the door. At this point, an axe murderer would be a welcome sight.

Alas, no crazed blade-wielding maniac stood on my stoop, only an auburn-haired woman in a white oxford shirt and gray pants with a manila envelope in her hand. "Are you Tara Holloway?"

"That's what they tell me."

She handed me the envelope. "You've been served. Have a nice day."

I looked down at the envelope in my hand. "I've been *what*?"

No sense waiting for a response. The woman had high-tailed it back to her car and was climbing in, apparently not one for conversation.

I ripped open the envelope and pulled out the contents. The first page of the document contained a "Civil Action" case number and the caption DONALD J. GEILS, PLAINTFF, V. TARA HOLLOWAY, DEFENDANT. The document went on to inform me that Don Geils had filed suit against me for assault and battery. He'd requested compensatory damages in the amount of $2,842.39 for his health insurance deductible and out-of-pocket medical bills, along with punitive damages in the amount of $10 million dollars.

Holy mother of God.

My hand trembled as I read on. According to the summons, I had twenty-one days in which to file a response.

Oh yeah?

Well, I didn't need to wait twenty-one days. I responded right then, by flipping the bird at the process server's back window as she motored off, punctuating it with an emphatic, saliva-spewing raspberry. *PF-F-F-F-FT!*

Remember when I said my life couldn't get any worse?

I take it back.

chapter five

All Dressed Up and Nowhere to Go

For the first time in years, I had a weekday afternoon off with no plans. Frankly, I had no idea what to do with myself. It felt strange, as if I were playing hooky from school. Not that I'd know what that felt like. Okay, truth be told, maybe I would. Sometimes a teenage girl just needs a day off to go drink beer with friends in the woods. But surely the statute of limitations had run out on my occasional truancy.

Oh crap. I really *was* a criminal, wasn't I?

As upset as I felt, I was tempted to hop online and order that beautiful blue coat from Neiman's to cheer myself up. But no, I couldn't. Who knew when I'd find another job? And now I'd have a buttload of legal fees to cover.

Ugh!

I might not be able to go shopping, but I could go shooting. That would cheer me up.

At the bottom of my closet sat the trunk that housed my gun collection. I retrieved three of my handguns from the trunk, as well as several boxes of ammo. Nothing cleared my mind like hitting the firing range.

As I backed out of my driveway, it dawned on me that I was no longer eligible to practice at the law enforcement firing range. Luckily, I'd hit a public range on a regular basis when I'd worked at the CPA firm, particularly during the hectic spring tax season, so at least I knew where a shooting range was located.

I drove to the facility and went inside the building, which resembled a concrete bunker.

The attendant, a lanky man with a long, dark mustache somewhere between Fu Manchu and Yosemite Sam, looked up as I entered. "Hey there, Tara. Haven't seen you in months." He stood from his seat behind the counter. "I heard about that shooting at the titty bar. How many men was it you killed? Four? Five?"

I gritted my teeth. "None."

"None? The way the news reporters told it bullets were flying everywhere."

I didn't respond, afraid if I opened my mouth again I'd scream in frustration.

The attendant eyed me warily for a moment as if evaluating whether I posed a risk on the range. I must've passed muster, because he eventually handed me a stack of paper targets and let me into the secure area.

I slid into my noise-reducing headphones, prepared the target, and loaded a clip into one of my guns. I raised the weapon and took aim, visualizing Don Geils' face on the target.

Blam! Blam! Blam! Blam! Blam!

Damn, that felt good.

Blam! Blam! Blam! Blam! Blam!
Blam! Blam! Blam! Blam! Blam!

When I finished, the target was nothing more than confetti. I should've done the same to Geils back when I'd had the chance.

I loaded another target onto the clip, readied a smaller handgun, and let the bullets fly.

Pop-pop-pop-pop-pop!

I was beginning to relax a bit, entering that zen-like state that accompanied my acute mental focus. When I finished, I eyed my target. All shots dead center, as usual.

Maybe I could teach a firearms course or get a job as a sniper or mercenary. Surely Uncle Sam had some secret agents on his payroll who were needed to take out a target or two. Of course my skills with long-range weapons were a little rusty. I didn't own a long-range rifle and hadn't practiced on one in a while, since my job as an IRS special agent was unlikely to require long-range skills. If I didn't get one for Christmas, I'd borrow one of my father's hunting rifles when I went back home for the holidays, bring it back with me to bone up on my skills. I'm sure the deer population in East Texas would be glad to hear my father had one less rifle in his arsenal this hunting season.

As the end of the afternoon drew near, my shaking arms told me it was time to put the guns down, but the rest of my body told me it was time to go to the YMCA. Just because I was no longer a federal agent who needed to stay in shape for her job didn't mean I should let myself go, right? Besides, I'd eaten nine Oreos for lunch today. I'd better get a workout in before all those cookies settled on my ass and thighs.

I headed over to the Y and suited up in stretchy yoga pants, T-shirt, and sneakers. Grabbing my water bottle and a towel, I left the locker room and made my way to the machines.

My boss—make that my *former* boss—was seated on one of the Lifecycles. Lu wore pink tights under a purple leotard, with a gray off-the-shoulder sweatshirt topping things off. She'd bought the ensemble three decades ago, back when *Flashdance* was all the rage. Until I'd been fired, Lu and I had worked out together. She'd dropped quite a few pounds and, though still pear-shaped, didn't test the seams of her leotard like she had only a few weeks ago.

On the bike next to her sat her boyfriend, Carl. Carl wore a pair of too-short navy blue shorts trimmed in red, with knee-high white crew socks over equally white, spindly legs. His feet sported a pair of what were probably original

Converse All Star high-tops. Hard to say for sure since the shoe's style hadn't changed much, if at all, over the years. He wore a plain white undershirt, too. As usual, he'd glued his long, thinning hair in place in a crisscrossing basket weave pattern on top of his head, a style that always gave me the urge to whip out a pen and play tic-tac-toe on his scalp.

Despite Carl's fashion faux pas, you couldn't help but like the guy. He was genuinely nice, old-fashioned in a sweet and quaint way, and he was nuts about The Lobo.

When Lu noticed me, she waved me over to join them, hiking her thumb at the empty bike to her right. "Hop on, Holloway, and let's talk."

I greeted Carl and settled onto the bike, plunking my water bottle into the cup holder. I dialed up the mountain-climbing program and set off on my virtual journey. As angry and upset as I was, I could likely beat Lance Armstrong's record, even without performance-enhancing dope.

The Lobo cut her eyes my way. "I'm working on Burton and the DFO."

"Nick told me." I leaned forward to put more power into my pedaling and glanced Lu's way. "What do you think the chances are of me getting my job back?"

Her mouth, framed in bright orange lipstick, curved down in a clownish frown. "George Burton's never hired someone back after he's let them go."

"So it's hopeless." I fought the urge to kick the bike.

"There's a first time for everything," Lu said.

"Sure!" Carl called from his bike "Never say never!"

I suppose the guy meant to be supportive, but his overly cheerful attitude kind of made me want to pull his short shorts up his crack. Misery loves company.

Lu cut me a look punctuated with a flutter of her false eyelashes. "George Burton's never faced someone as determined as me to get an agent back on the payroll, either."

Lu's support was heartwarming. But what I needed was a way to make Burton and the director of field operations realize how much the IRS needed me.

I leaned forward for more leverage and huffed with exertion as the virtual route took me up a foothill. "I went by Martin and McGee this morning to see if I could get back on with them."

"And?" Lu asked.

"They said 'thanks, but no thanks.' "

She frowned. "That stinks."

"That's just the beginning," I told Lu, grunting out my words as I pushed down hard on the pedals. Might as well hit her with the civil suit first rather than the potential criminal charges. Better to ease her in. "I was served with a civil lawsuit today. Don Geils is suing me for ten million dollars." Actually he'd sued me for $10,002,842.39, but the medical insurance deductible and out-of-pocket expenses were negligible compared to the punitive damages.

Lu pursed her lips and forced a blast of angry air out her nose. "That rat. You should've killed him while you had the chance."

Carl dabbed at his pasty face with a towel. "There's no way on God's green earth that a jury in Dallas, Texas, would give that man a dime."

Okay, feeling less inclined to give Carl a wedgie now. He had a point. People in Texas tended to have little mercy on criminals. The state was the capital of capital punishment, leading the nation in executions. Heck, under the state's penal system children as young as fourteen could be certified as adults. Never mind that the kids might have yet to reach puberty. So, yeah, it was doubtful a jury would award a criminal a large civil settlement.

Nonetheless, I'd still have to file a response and deal with the nuisance suit. It was ridiculous, really. Even if Geils won the damn court case, he'd never be able to collect. I didn't have $10 million. Even with the equity in my town house and my retirement savings I was worth only forty grand at best.

But it wasn't so much the money that worried me. It was the fact that a jury could determine that I had, in fact, been unjustified in my actions, that I'd used excessive force, that I was no better than the slimeballs I'd pursued in my job. That would hurt far worse than the associated monetary penalty.

I looked pointedly at Lu. "A DOJ attorney named Troy Kerr called me, too."

"I know Troy," Lu said. "He's been a U.S. attorney for fifteen years or more. A real tiger. He'll be a good man to have on our side."

Only he wouldn't be on *our* side. Or at least not on *my* side. Lord, this was getting complicated.

Lu took a sip from her water bottle. "Is he helping Ross O'Donnell prosecute Geils?"

"No. He says they're considering criminal charges against *me* for excessive force."

Lu's orange-rimmed lips fell open and her feet stopped pedaling. The machine beeped and displayed the message WORKOUT PAUSED, chastising her for interrupting her exercise. "Kerr is coming after *you*?"

"Yep."

"This has gone too far!" Lu's face blazed, partially from exertion but primarily from anger. If flames had shot out of her nose I wouldn't have been surprised. "It's one thing for Burton to let you go, but criminal charges? I'm calling the DOJ right now and giving Troy Kerr a piece of my mind." With that she climbed off her bike and stormed to the locker room.

I continued to pedal as if my life depended on it, all the while praying Lu could convince Kerr he was off base.

The Lobo returned two minutes later, her scowl telling me she'd been unsuccessful. "Got his damn voice mail." She climbed back onto the bike.

"By the way," Carl said, addressing Lu now, "how did the interview go?"

Lu shot him a look before glancing my way.

It didn't take long for me to put two and two together. "You're interviewing for my replacement?"

Lu waved a dismissive hand. "I started collecting résumés weeks ago."

"But you didn't have an open position until I left."

She couldn't deny the truth. "Tara, you know better than

anyone how overworked my special agents are. I can't leave a position open indefinitely."

I couldn't take any more. I'd only made it halfway up the imaginary mountain, but my Tour de France was *fini*.

I snatched my water bottle from the holder, grabbed my towel, and hopped off the bike, heading for the locker room.

Lu leaped off her bike and hurried after me. "Tara! Hold up."

I'd retrieved my bag and was halfway out the main door when the attendant at the front desk called out to me, "Hey! That's our towel!"

I looked down at the white towel gripped in my fist, returned to the foyer, and tossed it into the bin.

Lu caught up with me and grabbed me by the shoulders. "I'm going to fight as hard as I can for you. You know that, right?"

I did know it. But I also knew that her efforts were likely to be futile.

Hot tears welled up in my eyes. The Lobo pulled me to her, and I melted against her, my head resting against her ample bosom while I sobbed and she patted my back and issued soothing sounds. We must have stood there for five minutes until I was all cried out. I knew nothing had been accomplished with my tears, but I felt better nonetheless. Embarrassed, silly, and childish, but better.

"Look," Lu said, releasing me as I straightened up. "I'm going to keep working on George Burton, but in the meantime I'll see what I can do about finding you another job. A few people owe me favors. No guarantees, but I'll do my best. Okay?"

"Thanks," I spurted on a final sob, using my hand to brush my tears away.

"Done crying?" Lu asked, tilting her head and looking into my eyes.

"I guess so." At least for now.

"Good. Because you need to buck up, girl. You've got some tough weeks ahead of you."

chapter six

*L*et's Roll

Nick texted me shortly after I arrived back home. *Can I take U 2 dinner?*

I texted him back. *Hell yeah.*

After the day I'd had, I needed a treat. Dinner and Nick would make two.

Nick arrived at seven. He'd changed out of his business clothes and into a pair of boots, faded Levi's, and a western shirt, topping it off with his white cowboy hat and duster. He gave me a soft kiss. "How was your first day back at Martin and McGee?"

I closed the door behind him. "They refused to take me back."

"What the hell? I thought the managing partner had issued you an open invitation."

"The invitation was revoked when I shot Don Geils."

Nick's eyes flashed with fury. "That's bullshit."

"Martin and McGee is the least of my problems right now." I picked the civil lawsuit paperwork up from the coffee table where Henry lay chewing on the edge of the document. I handed it to Nick. "Don Geils is suing me for damages."

"You've got to be kidding." Nick's eyes met mine before traveling down to the paperwork in his hand. He took a few seconds to read it, his hand fisting reflexively and crumpling the edge of the petition. "Ten million dollars? Geils got some fucking nerve. That bastard's life ain't worth a dime."

"I got a call from an attorney at the DOJ, too. They're considering excessive force charges against me."

Nick's jaw dropped, just as Lu's had. "That's ridiculous."

"Lu says the attorney's who's coming after me is really tough."

Alarm flashed in Nick's eyes. "Which attorney is it?"

"Troy Kerr."

"Dammit!" Nick spat. He glanced around as if looking for something to punch. Coming up short, he settled for crossing his arms over his chest. "He handled a couple cases for me a few years ago. The guy's a pit bull."

"Lu said the same thing." Well, Lu had said the guy was a tiger, but cat or dog, it was clear the guy was a hard-hitting lawyer. I began to tremble again. "I'm screwed, aren't I? Six ways from Sunday."

Nick grabbed me by the shoulders, leaned in, and looked me in the eye. He spoke slowly and softly, but with absolute conviction. "You'll get through this, Tara. *We* will get through this. *Together.*"

He pulled me to him and held on so tight I'd thought he'd crush me. I almost hoped he would.

After a moment, he released me and stepped back. "At least we have our trips to look forward to."

"I can't go. Kerr said he'd get an injunction to keep me from leaving the U.S. if I didn't voluntarily agree to stay here."

"That's bullshit!" Nick's nostrils flared and his eyes narrowed. "Kerr will be sorry he ever did this to you. Mark my words."

I hoped Nick was right.

A half hour later, the two of us sat side by side at a sushi bar a few blocks away. Since I wouldn't be able to go to Tokyo with Nick, I'd chosen Japanese food for dinner. Though Nick was primarily a meat-and-potatoes man, he didn't protest.

Nick picked up the order sheet, butchering the names of the offerings. "Eebie? Eye-nari? What the heck is this stuff?"

"Shrimp and tofu," I responded.

His lip quirked as he eyed the purple tentacle in the refrigerated case in front of us. "Is that thing staring at me an octopus?"

"Those are suckers, not eyes. Besides, you've had calamari. It's the same thing."

"No, it's not," Nick said. "Calamari is covered in batter and fried. The suction cups don't show. Besides, calamari is cooked. Most of this stuff is raw. This isn't dinner. This is bait."

"Trust me." I jotted our order on the sheet and handed it to the chef. "You'll love it."

Nick eyed the chef over the glass case. "Got any sushi made with fried catfish? Maybe some trout or bass?"

The chef laughed and pointed his knife at Nick. "You a funny man, mister redneck."

Nick frowned and turned to me. "I'm not totally clueless about the Japanese culture. I watched that 'Gangnam Style' video."

"You and a billion other people. Besides, that 'Gangnam' guy was Korean, not Japanese."

The waitress arrived to take our drink order.

"Sake," I told her. "And plenty of it." Enough to make me forget that today had been the absolute number-one shittiest day of my life.

After the girl left, Nick said, "I suppose you'll tell me I'm going to love sake, too."

"No," I said. "You'll hate it. The stuff tastes like battery acid, but it's strong." I had two pending court trials and an unemployment situation that I needed to forget about, at least for a little while. A few cups of sake should take care of the problem.

The waitress returned with our sake, setting the decanter between us and placing a small cup in front of each of us. Nick picked up the decanter and filled the two small glasses.

I raised mine in toast. "Bottom's up."

Nick chugged the sake. Though I waited for him to cringe, he didn't. Years of Tabasco sauce on his scrambled eggs had desensitized his throat and stomach. "Battery acid indeed," he said, affecting a snobby tone and holding his cup aloft as if he were a wine connoisseur. "With undertones of rubbing alcohol and notes of wart remover."

The sushi chef handed a large platter over the counter. I thanked him as I took it and set it on the bar between me and Nick.

Nick gestured to the platter. "What's the pink and green stuff?"

"The pink stuff is ginger." I'd never liked it. Too much like eating cold, boiled flowers. "The green stuff is wasabi. Don't use too much. It's really hot."

While I unwrapped the paper sleeve from my chopsticks, Nick opted for his fork, stabbing a blob of wasabi and maneuvering it on top of a piece of California roll.

"That's too much," I said.

"Nah." He scooped up the piece and forked it into his mouth.

I waited for his face to contort in agony or his eyeballs to pop out, but he merely gave a little twitch of his nose and swallowed. "Not bad. It's got a little kick to it."

A *little* kick? The stuff could clear even the most stubbornly clogged sinuses. Then again, the guy had a cast-iron stomach that could even handle my father's weapons-grade killer chili. A little wasabi was nothing compared to Dad's caustic concoction.

When Nick and I'd finished the sushi, we topped off the meal with bowls of green tea ice cream.

"Mm-m." The cold, creamy treat melted on my tongue. "I love this stuff." Not only did it taste good, it also was full of antioxidants. Good thing. Three cups of sake had left me feeling pretty oxidated.

When the bill was settled, Nick and I headed back to his truck. "That raw fish wasn't half-bad."

"Told ya."

chapter seven

You Get What You Pay for . . . Except When You Don't

Nick pulled out of the parking lot and headed in the opposite direction from my home.

"Where are we going?" I asked.

"Cell phone store. The owner asked me and Eddie to come by at closing time so we wouldn't disrupt his business."

Nick was taking a risk here. Since I no longer worked for the IRS, he shouldn't be letting me tag along. It was against policy. He could be reprimanded. Lu wouldn't give a crap, but if anyone up the chain found out they wouldn't be happy.

I reached over and gave his thigh an affectionate squeeze. "Thanks for taking me along."

Nick cut a meaningful glance in my direction. "I wouldn't have it any other way."

His words caused a warmth to spread through me, not unlike the earlier burn of the sake but much more pleasant.

A half hour later, we pulled up to a small store in a strip center off I-30. A sign over the doors of one of the shops read: "Westside Wireless." A smaller sign in the window indicated that the place sold both wireless phones and accessories.

Nick glanced over at another car in the lot, a plain white Ford sedan, clearly government issue. A fortyish Asian man with a head of salt-and-pepper hair sat behind the wheel.

"Is that Agent Tanaka?" I asked Nick.

"Yup." Nick raised a hand in greeting.

I'd spoken with the ICE agent by phone when I'd been assigned the case. He'd been wrapping up another investigation at the time but indicated he'd be ready to proceed on this case soon. Looked like *soon* had become *now*.

Agent Tanaka opened his door and climbed out. Nick did the same. I followed suit.

As we made our way to the sidewalk, Eddie Bardin pulled into the lot. Like Nick, Eddie was a senior special agent at IRS Criminal Investigations. He'd been both my mentor and my partner on numerous cases, teaching me the ropes. Too bad I'd become hopelessly entangled in those ropes.

Eddie stepped out of his car. He was tall, thin, and black, a conservative family man who was more Lacoste than LeBron. He was also a savvy, stellar agent. With his experience and my weapons skills, we'd made an unbeatable team. I missed working with him.

The four of us met on the sidewalk in front of the store.

After Nick and Eddie shook hands with Tanaka, Nick introduced me. "This is Tara Holloway."

Not *Special Agent* Holloway. I was a civilian now, titleless. Well, I was still the beer-chugging champ from my college dorm, but that was years ago and a half-dozen other girls had since won the annual award.

"Katsumi Tanaka." Tanaka spoke with neither a Japanese nor a southern accent, a clear indicator he'd practiced his English as a child. He looked me in the eye. "Agent Pratt told me what happened. Tough break."

As much as I hated my shame to be spread about publicly, the shooting was public knowledge thanks to the news reports and I knew Nick had to give the guy an explanation as to why the case had been reassigned from me to him. I couldn't fault Nick for that. He'd also have to explain why an agent who had been terminated from the IRS was along for the ride tonight.

"How many men did you kill at that bar?" Tanaka asked. "Six? Seven?"

"None," I said on a sake-scented sigh.

Nick cut his gaze my way before turning back to Tanaka. "Tara has been assisting with the transition of her cases. I figured it couldn't hurt for her to listen in tonight in case she has any ideas we don't."

Tanaka raised his palms. "No problem here. We can use all the help we can get. Tokyo Discount Telecom is hitting the industry hard. Complaints were recently filed with ICE in Los Angeles, Chicago, Miami, and a dozen other cities about counterfeit phones."

Nick raised a brow. "So this case may be even bigger than we thought."

Tanaka nodded. "In the millions of dollars already. Problem is, none of the victims can give us a good lead on anyone here in the states. A victim in Miami said the truck that delivered the phones to his shop had Texas plates, but that's all he could tell me."

We stepped up to the glass door. A personal check taped to the inside indicated someone named Scott Breckenridge had written Westside Wireless a check for $84.39 that was returned for insufficient funds. *Shame on you, Scott.* Of course I couldn't be too high-and-mighty. If I didn't get a job soon, I'd have trouble paying my bills.

Nick pulled the door open and we stepped inside. The owner, Kenneth McPherson, looked up from his seat on a stool behind the counter. He was a wide, heavyset man with reddish-brown curly hair. He looked like someone who'd be cast in the role of a king in a stage play.

He stood, his green eyes taking in the four of us. "Good evening. How may I help you?"

Eddie and Tanaka introduced themselves to the shop owner and shook his hand.

Nick extended a hand as well. "I'm IRS Senior Special
Agent Nick Pratt." He raised a hand to indicate me. "My associate, Tara Holloway."

Associate, huh? I liked it better when I was his partner,
but I supposed "associate" was as good a word as any. It
might imply I was still with the IRS, but, unlike Tanaka, this
store owner didn't need to know my sketchy history. And it
sounded better than Nick introducing me as his *little love
bunny.*

After introductions were completed, McPherson held up
a finger. "Give me just a minute to close up shop." He stepped
to the front door and locked it. He turned off the red neon
"Open" sign and pulled down the retractable blinds.

When he was finished, he stepped back behind the counter, reached down, and pulled out a box containing at least a
dozen cell phones. He laid them on the counter. "These are
the fakes I reported to Customs Enforcement."

Tanaka, Eddie, Nick, and I each picked a phone out of the
box. They looked like typical touch-screen-style smartphones and bore the logo of a name-brand electronics manufacturer.

Tanaka set his phone back on the glass countertop. "I was
told that the customers who bought these phones from you
had some problems with them."

"They didn't just have *some* problems," McPherson said.
"They had *every* problem. Dropped calls. Apps that wouldn't
work. Defective batteries. You name it. All of these phones
had problems during the first thirty days, so they were supposed to be covered by a manufacturer's warranty. But when
I sent the phones in for replacement, the manufacturer told
me they hadn't made the phones."

"Phony phones, huh?" I chuckled. Alone. Hey, I blame it
on the sake.

McPherson said he'd tried to call Tokyo Discount Telecom, the Japanese outfit he'd ordered the phones from, but
could only reach a voice mail. "I must've left twenty mes-
sages, but they never returned my calls. I sent them a dozen
e-mails, too. Nothing."

Tanaka cocked his head. "How did you first get in touch with Tokyo Discount Telecom?"

"I received a catalog in the mail," McPherson replied. "I normally like to deal in person with a local rep, but they offered much lower prices than any of the other wholesalers so I decided to take a chance. I ordered eight grand in phones and accessories from them. Now I'm stuck with a bunch of shoddy merchandise I can't sell. I'm a small businessman. An eight-thousand-dollar loss is a big hit for me to take."

McPherson pulled the catalog out from a drawer behind the counter and handed it to Tanaka. Tanaka thumbed through it, with Eddie, Nick, and me looking over either shoulder.

The last page of the catalog contained an order form with instructions directing the buyer to complete the form, scan it, and send it via e-mail to a specified e-mail address ending in ".jp" for "Japan." Payment was to be sent via PayPal to TDT at the same e-mail address. The e-mail address was not preprinted but, rather, had been stamped on the page. No doubt TDT changed its e-mail and PayPal accounts as they were closed down by the U.S. government, but it was easy enough to open another. Besides, it took weeks for customers to realize they'd been duped and for the accounts to be terminated. By then, TDT would have defrauded many more victims. An international phone number was also listed on the catalog but was handwritten.

The fact that business had been handled via e-mail could make tracking down the bad guys and bringing them to justice more difficult. Capturing a living, breathing person at a fixed business location was much easier than finding a criminal in the virtual world. What's more, proving who had accessed a computer and hit the keystrokes could be difficult.

These types of cases were often an exercise in futility and frustration. With Tokyo Discount Telecom based in Japan, its ringleaders operated beyond the reach of U.S. law enforcement. All agents could do here in America was put out fires after they'd already flared up and someone had been burned. Thus the need for agents to travel to Japan, dig up some dirt on the company, and convince Japanese law enforcement to take action on those in their country who ran the outfit.

"Did you file a claim with PayPal?" Eddie asked McPherson.

"I initiated a dispute, and Tokyo Discount Telecom denied that the products were fakes. When I tried to have the dispute escalated to a claim, I was told I'd missed the deadline. I'd had emergency gallbladder surgery and wasn't able to access my e-mails for several days, so I missed the notice."

"Who delivered the phones to you?" Tanaka asked.

While the headquarters of TDT might be out of U.S. jurisdiction, the local operatives would be fair game. Of course the shipping company might not have been a knowing party to the fraud. Heck, I couldn't tell these phones were fakes and I held one in my hand. If they weren't directly involved in the scam, how was a shipping company supposed to look at a bunch of boxes and know they contained counterfeit goods?

McPherson shrugged. "I can't say. The truck was just a plain white truck. I didn't foresee any problems, so I didn't think to get the license plate." He pulled out a bill of lading that listed the items delivered, but it contained no information to identify the shipping company that had delivered the goods.

We agents exchanged knowing looks.

"Looks like the delivery company took pains to remain unidentifiable," Eddie said.

Nick looked up from the paper. "Is your delivery bay out back?"

McPherson shook his head. "None of my products are large. Everything comes in through the front doors."

"Do you have security cameras?" Nick asked.

McPherson pointed to four cameras, one mounted in each corner of the rectangular shop. All of the cameras were angled to focus on activity inside the shop.

"Any cameras outside?" Nick asked.

"No."

I walked to the door, turned the lock, and stepped out front onto the sidewalk, looking up along the roofline for security cameras from the neighboring businesses that might have picked up the truck's license plate. Unfortunately, I saw none. Not surprising. The tenant to the immediate left was a barbershop, while the tenant to the right was a shoe-repair business, neither of which was likely a prime target for thieves. I went back inside. "Doesn't look like any of the tenants have outside security cameras that would have picked up a license plate."

Tanaka chimed in. "Was the deliveryman wearing a uniform?"

McPherson shrugged his meaty shoulders. "I don't recall."

Tanaka made a rotating motion with his finger. "Can you pull up the security tapes from your inside cameras?"

"Sure." While McPherson stepped behind the counter, logged on to his computer, and waded through the data looking for the footage from the delivery date, I wandered around the store, checking out the accessories. The place stocked dozens of phone cases, some plain and utilitarian, others colorful, with lots of personality. A red one with a cute cartoon panda caught my eye. I pulled the package off the hook to take a closer look.

"That's him." McPherson pointed at his computer screen before turning it to face the agents standing at the counter.

I stepped up next to Nick. The four of us watched as an Asian guy who appeared to be in his thirties rolled a dolly through the front door. Four unmarked cardboard boxes were stacked on the dolly. No way to tell yet whether the delivery driver's shirt bore a logo, since the boxes blocked his chest.

On the screen, we saw him speak with McPherson, then the two disappeared through a narrow door in the back wall that led to the storage room. They reappeared seconds later, the dolly empty now. McPherson stopped the footage and we all leaned toward the screen zeroing in on the delivery-man's shirt. Nope. No logo. Just a plain white cotton button-down.

Eddie exhaled in frustration. "Unfortunately, the tape gives us nothing more to go on."

While the men mulled over the situation, I whipped out a twenty and held up the phone case. "I'd like to get this."

After McPherson rang up my purchase and made change for me, I slid the old scuffed cover off my phone and put my new cuter cover on. Much better. The phone might look like it belonged to an adolescent girl, but it was bright and cheerful.

Nick turned to Tanaka and Eddie. "The deliveryman was Asian. You think that means he's in cahoots with TDT?"

Tanaka shrugged. "Maybe. Maybe not. It could just be coincidence."

We'd obtained all the evidence we could. We left the store with the catalog, leaving McPherson with our promise to let him know when arrests were made—assuming Eddie, Nick, Tanaka, and I could track down anyone involved.

We gathered in the parking lot to debate strategy.

Tanaka took the lead. "The MO here matches what I was told by the other victims. Orders by e-mail. Payments made online. It would help if we could nab someone here who might squeal."

"The delivery guy," Nick thought out loud. "We've got to track him down."

They couldn't very well have McPherson place another order. Since he'd already complained about the previous shipment and demanded a refund, TDT would know something was up if he ordered more merchandise.

"Have some phones sent to me," I suggested, partly to help out, partly to ensure my continued involvement in the investigation.

"Won't they be suspicious if an order is delivered to a home address?" Tanaka asked.

"I'll tell them I sell phones and accessories at Traders Village."

Traders Village was a year-round flea market in the neighboring city of Grand Prairie. My mother and I visited it at least once a year. The place sold everything from piñatas to purses, incense to Indian blankets, comics to computers.

Tanaka's head bobbed as he considered my suggestion. "That could work."

We followed Agent Tanaka back to the ICE office, where he, Eddie, and Nick set up new e-mail and PayPal accounts.

I thumbed through the TDT catalog, looking over their offerings. "These phone covers with the flowers are cute."

Eddie rolled his eyes. "It doesn't matter what we order. We're just trying to nab the delivery driver."

I supposed he had a point. Nick completed the form, ordering some of the less expensive items like car chargers, hands-free headsets, and skins, along with six dozen smartphones. When he was done, Agent Tanaka scanned the order form into his computer, attached the form to an e-mail, and sent it off through cyberspace to the criminals in Japan. He followed it up with a payment from the secret PayPal account.

Tanaka said he'd notify PayPal to close down TDT's account ASAP. Of course, the chances of recouping the funds McPherson and the other victims had sent were slim to none.

"I'll let you know when they provide me a delivery date," Tanaka told the rest of us. "We'll want to follow the delivery driver, see what we can find out."

"Sounds like a plan," Eddie said.

A plan that included *me*. It felt good to be part of the action, even if it was in an unofficial capacity.

chapter eight

Lawyer Up

The following morning, I arrived at Gertz, Gertz, and Schwartz twenty minutes prior to my 9:30 appointment. I checked in with the receptionist and sat down on a love seat in the foyer to wait.

While I sat, I read through the civil petition again. *Intentional assault and battery. Compensatory damages. Punitive damages. Ten million dollars.* I grew more angry, more anxious, as I flipped through each page. My stomach felt as if it contained a rabid rat gnawing on the insides, trying to eat its way out.

"Tara Holloway?" called a woman's voice.

I looked up to find a seasoned secretary addressing me from the doorway that led into the offices.

I raised my hand reflexively, as if I'd been called on in class. "That's me." I stuffed the petition back into my briefcase, stood, and walked to the door.

"This way, please," the woman said, her demeanor pleasant yet efficient.

I followed her through a virtual maze of hallways, passing offices that housed attorneys engaged in various law-yerly activities. Reviewing contracts. Arguing with opposing counsel on the phone. Reading case law online. Playing Fruit Ninja on their cell phone and watching dogs bark "We Wish You a Merry Christmas" on YouTube.

The secretary and I stopped at a large corner office.

"Have a seat," the woman said, gesturing for me to step inside. "Mr. Giacomo will be with you shortly."

I slid into the office and took a seat in an overstuffed gray chair. The secretary left the door open as she walked away.

I glanced around Giacomo's office. The walls were painted a soothing shade of pale blue and sported abstract paintings in muted shades on unframed canvasses. The whitewashed desk was relatively the size of a pool table, though only a laptop, a legal pad, and a potted ivy sat on its expansive surface. The padded gray seat behind the desk was so wide and tall it appeared more throne than chair. No family portraits graced Giacomo's desk or bookshelf, though I could hardly blame him for keeping his personal life pri-vate given that he represented thieves and drug dealers and murderers.

And me, of course.

Sigh.

The bookshelf held a number of anti-governmental tomes, John Grisham's *The Innocent Man,* Sinclair Lewis' *It Can't Happen Here,* and presidential candidate Ron Paul's *Freedom under Siege: The U.S. Constitution after 200 Years.* I stepped over and picked up a book by Kristian Williams called *Our Enemies in Blue: Police and Power in America.* The pages detailed horrific cases of police brutality, making me feel confused and uneasy.

Was I like those rogue cops? Had I hidden behind my badge and abused my power? It certainly didn't feel like it. But being prosecuted by the very government I'd once worked for stung like a swarm of killer bees. How could the govern-ment I'd once been an integral part of and the country I called home turn their backs on me after I'd risked my life for them? I felt betrayed.

An antique mantel clock sat on top of Giacomo's bookshelf, the hands moving with a *tick-tick-tick* that seemed to be counting down my last remaining minutes of freedom.

A moment later, Daniel appeared in the doorway. Daniel was tall, dark haired, and attractive in a clean-cut, boy-next-door-all-grown-up way. "Hey, Tara. How're you holding up?"

I slid the book back onto the shelf. "I feel like I'm going to lose my breakfast." Gross, but true. The Fruity Pebbles I'd eaten had become a fruity boulder in my stomach, a boulder sitting on top of a bubbling, acidic volcano.

Daniel rested a hand on my shoulder. "Don't worry, Tara. Giacomo will take the prosecutor to the mat."

Lord, I hoped so. If he didn't, I'd soon have a cellmate and an orange jumpsuit. "I appreciate you arranging this appointment."

"What are friends for?"

A man walked into the office with a dainty mug of steaming hazelnut-scented coffee in his hands. His black hair was cut short on the sides, his bangs, which he'd left a little longer, peeking out from under a green-and-red elf hat with a shiny silver bell on the tip. In addition to the holiday headgear, he wore a trendy gray suit with a fitted jacket and narrow legs, along with stylish square-toed dress shoes and a lavender shirt open at the collar. No tie. A small amethyst, apparently chosen to match his shirt, punctuated his right earlobe. He smelled good, a spicy, musky combination I recognized as the classic Calvin Klein Obsession for Men. His cheeks were soft and smooth, clearly the result of salon facials and expensive skin-care products. The fingers wrapped around the coffee mug were tipped with nicely buffed nails.

I wasn't entirely sure what to expect given Giacomo's alleged reputation as a hairy-assed criminal defense attorney, but the relatively hairless man standing before me certainly wasn't it. He looked like a Caucasian version of Prince from the *Lovesexy* album cover. He stood five foot five at most. He was thin and small boned, too. I'd bet the guy didn't weigh more than 140, if even that.

He was a runt. Then again, so was I. And my stature only

made me try all the harder. Besides, court battles weren't about brawn; they were about brains, fought not with muscle but with minds, through legal strategy, clever argument, and precedents. I tried to keep an open mind.

"Hello, Anthony," Daniel said.

"Daniel." Giacomo nodded, then jerked his head toward the door, the bell on the end of his hat giving off a *tinkle-tinkle* as he dismissed his coworker. "Git."

Daniel offered me a small wave and left.

The attorney turned to me now. His brown eyes bore a gleam of intelligence and determination that told me I was in capable, if well-moisturized, hands.

"Anthony Giacomo." He stuck out a hand barely bigger than my own, but he shook with a confidence that reassured me. He cocked his head. *Tinkle-tinkle.* "You look scared."

I managed a feeble smile. "Is that all? Because I'm absolutely terrified."

He set his mug on his desk and pointed a finger at me. "You need a hug." He proceeded to do just that, wrapping his arms around me and giving me three soft pats on the back. "There, there." He released me and stepped back. "I mentioned I charge extra for hugs, right?"

Despite the circumstances, I chuckled.

He gestured for me to take my seat as he slid into the enormous throne behind his desk. He took a sip of his coffee and held the mug two-handed in front of his chest. He arched a shaped brow. "So-o-o-o-o. Daniel tells me you're a federal agent who has found herself in some hot water."

That was putting it mildly. The water I was in was boiling. If I were a lobster, I'd be ready for melted butter and a fork. "I was fired from my job with IRS Criminal Investigations last week."

"Dish," he demanded. "Tell me everything, Miss Holloway. Every last, dirty, disgusting, lascivious detail."

Something told me I could trust this guy. I took a deep, fortifying breath and ran through the events of Geils' bust, starting with the undercover investigation at the strip club, moving on to the dancers abused by violent patrons, the drugs that led to a dancer nearly overdosing, and ending with me putting four bullets in the leg of the bastard who ran the place. I told Giacomo that Nick and I were dating, that Christina and I were friends off the clock, that I'd paused between each bullet I'd put in Don Geils' leg and contemplated what a total waste of flesh the bastard was.

Giacomo said little as I told him the story. He listened intently, occasionally running his eyes over me as if evaluating my posture, my body language, the tilt of my head. When I finished, he said, "I'll be darned. An honest client."

"I take it you don't get many of those?"

"I don't get *any* of those," he shot back. "I waste unbelievable amounts of time sorting through piles of poo, trying to find the truth."

His job didn't sound too different from being a special agent. The people we investigated often told us lies, too.

I cut to the chase. "What's the punishment for excessive force?" I asked, fearing the answer.

"Depends on the circumstances," the attorney replied. "A minor abuse against some thug would get probation, maybe a small fine. Something egregious, where an innocent victim is severely maimed or killed, could land a cop in jail for life."

Life? My insides turned to pudding. *Holy—*

"I'll need to gather some information from you." He shifted the coffee mug to his left hand, pulled a gold pen from the inside pocket of his jacket, and slid the legal pad closer so he could write on it. "Prior to the incident at the club, had you ever used your weapons on the job?"

"Yes." I gave him my long and complete history, including my shooting a box cutter out of the hand of an auto parts store owner intent on killing me, a later shoot-out at a private residence, moving on to my putting a bullet in a target's testicle, to a later incident in which I put one bullet each in a set of twins. I'd also been forced to shoot a rifle out of the hands of a crazy old coot who led a secessionist group, and I'd improvised a flamethrower with a lighter and a spray can to fend off another attacker. That one happened in my home, when I couldn't get to my gun, though the man who'd broken in and attacked me had been a target in a tax evasion case.

The attorney jotted down notes as I spoke. When I finished, he looked down at my long list of human targets, then up at me. *Tinkle-tinkle.* "This is quite a list. How many years were you with the IRS?"

I gulped back the lump in my throat. "Eight months."

"Eight *months?*" His eyes went from my face to his list and back to my face again. "You've been quite a busy girl, haven't you?"

What could I say to that? I simply shrugged.

"I assume there was some type of internal review each time you used your gun?"

I nodded. "My actions were deemed justified each time."

"Mm-hm. But not this last time?"

I forced a small smile. "Apparently not."

"Were you given a copy of the internal affairs report?"

"No. I didn't ask for one. I didn't see the need." Fired is fired, after all. The hearing had been bad enough. I didn't particularly want to relive the event by reading a summary of it.

"Get me a copy," he said. "In fact, get me copies of all of your internal affairs reports. I suspect the prosecutor will try to use them against you and I need to be prepared."

I nodded.

"I have a few more questions about what went down at the bar." He sipped his coffee before continuing. "At any time while you were in the VIP room with Donald Geils did you reload your gun?"

"No."

He jotted a note. "Did you empty your clip?"

"No." I'd been damn tempted, but I hadn't.

"Was the clip full?"

"Yes, but I fired only the seven bullets."

"Three in the bouncers, four in Don Geils," he clarified.

"Right."

Another note. "Did you attempt any fatal shots? Maybe aim for Geils' head or his heart, but he dodged the bullets?"

"No. If I'd attempted a fatal shot he'd be dead." It wasn't bragging. It was true. I'd been handling guns since my father gave me my first Daisy BB gun when I was just three years old. I'd learn to shoot a gun before I could ride a bike. "My bullets go exactly where I aim them."

"So I hear. Daniel says they call you the Annie Oakley of the IRS?"

"They do." At least they used to. I only hoped I wouldn't become known as the Annie Oakley of the Seagoville Federal Correctional Institution. "I was also called the Sperminator after I shot the target in the testicle."

The attorney hunched in phantom agony. "Let's not talk any more about that incident. It's just so . . ."

Apparently unable to find a suitable term, he fluttered his hands as if the motion could cause the very idea to dissipate. What was it with men and their family jewels? Women had mastectomies and hysterectomies all the time and you didn't hear us bellyaching about having our body parts ripped out.

Giacomo put his pen back to the paper, drawing a repeating circle as he looked past me to the wall, lost in thought. After a moment he stopped doodling, his eyes boring into me. "You enjoyed putting those bullets in that bastard's leg, didn't you?"

I closed my eyes as if unable to face the truth about myself. "Yes," I said weakly.

"You wanted him to suffer for what he'd done to your fellow agents, to those girls at the club."

"Yes."

When he asked no further questions, I opened my eyes.

With another *tinkle,* Giacomo turned away from me, looking out his window on to downtown Dallas as he mulled things over for another moment or two. When he turned back to me, he said, "This is how I anticipate the prosecution will spin things. They'll say there was no need for you to keep shooting Geils once he'd dropped his weapon and was too injured to flee. You were pissed at Geils for threatening your boyfriend and your friend and that's why you shot him multiple times. You intentionally retaliated against him. You took punishment into your own hands."

I supposed the guy was playing Devil's advocate in order to evaluate the case, but I didn't like it. There was some truth to what he said, a lot of truth in fact, but did that necessarily mean I had used excessive force? Did it mean I, like Geils, was a criminal? The mere thought made me sick.

Giacomo looked into my eyes. "Geils shot at you first. You had a legal right to kill the man."

I slumped back in my seat. "That's what everyone keeps telling me."

"So why didn't you?"

I looked Giacomo in the eye. "Honestly? I don't know. After he fired at me I turned around with every intention of shooting him in the head. But . . ." I looked down at my hands, clasped tightly in my lap, before looking back up at the attorney. "My hands seemed to have a mind of their own. They aimed for his leg rather than his head."

"So your actions were instinctive? You were acting on reflex? Impulse more than intent?"

I nodded. "I'd lost it by that point. Geils deserved to die, but I suppose on some subconscious level I knew I could let him live. I . . . I'm not sure I could live with myself if I ended a life. But holding back was hard. *Really* hard. A person has only so much restraint." Tears welled up in my eyes and I gulped back a sob. "Am I expected to be superhuman just because I'm a federal agent?"

A slow smile spread across Giacomo's lips. "You're pathetic."

What? Had this guy really just called me pathetic to my face? After I'd spilled my guts to him, opened myself up emotionally?

"You're nothing but a candy ass," he said. "You're not a tough federal agent at all."

I sat bolt upright in my chair. "Yes, I am!" Or at least I had been.

"No, you're not. Any other agent would've shot the guy

dead. But you couldn't bring yourself to kill a pimp and
drug lord who clearly deserved it."

I didn't want to be a criminal, but I didn't want to be a
chickenshit, either. Ugh!

"You didn't use excessive force." His eyes glimmered as
he continued. "In fact, I'd say you used woefully insufficient
force."

Oka-a-ay. Now I saw where he was going with this. I
took a deep breath and settled back in my chair.

He pointed his pen at me. "For the prosecutor to prove
you used excessive force, he has to show that you used force
beyond what a reasonable and prudent law enforcement
officer would have used under the circumstances. This is the
tricky part. A reasonable and prudent agent would have
blown Don Geils' head off or put a few bullets in his chest.
You didn't. The question is, if you did less damage than a
reasonable and prudent agent would have but continued to
put more bullets in the guy's leg once he seemingly no longer posed a threat, did you use excessive force or not?"

If that was the question, then . . . "What's the answer?" I
wanted this guy to tell me I wasn't guilty. I *needed* someone
to tell me I wasn't guilty.

Giacomo exhaled. "I could tell you what I think, but that's
not what really matters. It's what the jury will think that
matters. The prosecutor will focus on the minutiae. I'll convince the jury to take a step back and look at the bigger picture."

It would be like taking a photograph. But would the jury
use a wide-angle lens or a zoom?

Giacomo's eyes gleamed. "This trial will be a soap opera. Any jury would eat this up."

I didn't like the idea of being a spectacle, of my future
being played out like some kind of Broadway production or
reality TV show where the jurors could decide whether or
not to vote me off the island. But I supposed I didn't have
much of a choice. For better or worse, this was how the
American justice system worked.

He waved a hand dismissively, causing his hat to give off

another *tinkle*. "Of course I'm getting way ahead of myself here. This case hasn't even gone to the grand jury yet. Besides, once we speak to the DOJ the prosecutor might decide not to bring charges."

Dropped charges? That would be the best Christmas present ever.

Anthony took another sip of coffee. "Who's the prosecutor?"

"Troy Kerr."

"Kerr. Hm-m." Giacomo sat his coffee mug on the desk, twirling his pen in his fingers as he appeared to formulate his thoughts. "A case against a federal agent would send the message that Kerr is tough. Not to mention that a case against a federal agent is sure to be high profile and get him some attention." He stopped twirling the pen and pointed it at me. "One of the judges for the Northern District announced he'll be retiring in March. There will be a spot opening up on the bench here in Dallas."

My hand reflexively went to my chest. "What does that have to do with me?"

"Troy Kerr has had his eye on the bench for years." Giacomo jabbed the pen in my direction. "He's using you to get that judicial appointment he's been after."

Great. I'd become nothing more than a pawn in a game of courtroom chess over which I had no control. I felt like George Bailey in the early scenes of *It's a Wonderful Life* where his life was spinning into total chaos. "How does that affect my chances of getting the charges dropped?"

"Hard to say," Anthony said, the pen twirling again. "There's a lot at stake for Kerr personally. He's a competent enough attorney, but he hasn't handled any real newsworthy trials. He needs a big, high-profile case to pad his résumé, and the timing of your case would be perfect."

Perfect for him, maybe. As far as I was concerned, there was never a good time to be put on trial.

"On the other hand," Giacomo capitulated, "he's got a lot to lose if this trial doesn't go his way. His reputation could be irreparably damaged. He's taking quite a risk."

I felt like an unwilling player in a game of legal football, forced out onto the field without a helmet, mouth guard, or pads, with only Giacomo on my team, supporting me like a jockstrap, protecting me like an athletic cup.

I wondered if a guardian angel would come to help me if I wandered out onto the Margaret Hunt Hill Bridge, like the angel had helped George Bailey in the Christmas classic. I supposed I shouldn't count on it. Then again, maybe Giacomo would prove to be my guardian angel. I certainly hoped so. "Kerr wants to meet with us tomorrow at ten."

He frowned. "Christmas Eve?"

"It's not a federal holiday," I said.

"Hmph. Well, write me a retainer check for five grand and I'll be there."

Sheesh. Guardian angels don't come cheap, do they?

He cocked his head. *Tinkle-tinkle.* "I mentioned I charge extra on holidays, right?"

I chuckled.

"I'm not kidding this time."

Damn.

I made out the check, mentally cursing Don Geils all the while. At least I'd made some extra money while working for the jackass. Not anywhere near five grand, though. And I could forget the beautiful cobalt-blue coat from Neiman's. No way could I afford it now.

"I almost forgot," I said. "There have been some other developments." I dug in my briefcase and pulled out the petition I'd been served with yesterday. I handed it to the attorney.

Giacomo quickly scanned the document and tossed it aside. "Not a problem. Whenever there are parallel prosecutions—both a criminal and a civil case pending at the same time—the civil case is put on hold until the criminal case is resolved."

He went on to explain that the burden of proof in a criminal case, beyond a reasonable doubt, was higher than that required in a civil case, which required the plaintiff only to show it was more likely than not that the defendant had violated civil law. He noted that if I was found guilty in criminal court, a legal doctrine known as estoppel could prevent me from asserting my innocence in the subsequent civil trial.

My heart sputtered. "So if I'm convicted in criminal court, I'll automatically lose the civil case, too?"

Giacomo shot me a pointed look. "My clients don't get convicted."

I wanted to believe him, but I suspected he was only trying to build my confidence. No matter how much hair he had on his ass, no matter how smart the guy was, he couldn't guarantee we'd prevail. Only time would tell how things would turn out.

I stood to go, stopping at the door. "I know if my case goes to trial it will be up to a jury to decide whether I'm guilty, but I'd still like to know. Do *you* think I used excessive force?"

He offered a small smile and looked me directly in the eye. "No, Tara. I don't."

I felt a surge of relief. Looked like there was still a chance I'd make Santa's "nice" list this year.

chapter nine

*E*z Money, Difficult Case

I left Gertz, Gertz, and Schwartz with mixed feelings. I felt somewhat relieved that Giacomo now shouldered the burden of my defense, yet I knew I wouldn't be able to fully relax unless Troy Kerr agreed to drop the charges against me. And if Kerr didn't agree, I was looking at several weeks of intense anxiety until the trial. Then, what? Even if I was acquitted I still wouldn't have my special agent job; I'd still be unemployed. And if I was convicted . . . Ugh. I didn't want to let my mind even go there.

Oddly, a small part of me hoped Kerr wouldn't drop the charges. If a jury found, once and for all, that I hadn't used excessive force, that I was innocent, I'd feel vindicated, exonerated, blameless. I'd be able to forgive myself—if I had anything to forgive myself for—and the dark cloud hanging over me would dissipate.

If I was found not guilty, was there a chance the IRS would take me back? Make me a special agent again? I didn't let my mind linger on that thought long. The chances were slim to none. No sense setting myself up for more disappointment.

As I returned to my car, I received a text from Nick. *Lunch?*

Sure, I texted back. *Meet me in front of ur office in 5.*

I swung by the IRS office and picked him up at the curb.

"What sounds good?" he asked once he'd settled in the car and clicked his seat belt into place.

"Sushi."

"Again?"

I could eat the stuff for every meal and never get tired of it. I put on my sad face and batted my eyes at him.

"Okay," he said. "You win."

I knew where every sushi place in the Dallas area was located. I drove to the closest sushi bar, located near the Winspear Opera House, which, according to the sign out front, currently featured the *Nutcracker* ballet.

After miso soup, a seaweed salad, and a couple of California rolls, we topped the meal off with another round of green tea ice cream. I should try to find a store that sold the stuff. Now that I wasn't a special agent anymore, I wouldn't have to stay in shape. I could eat all the green tea ice cream I wanted.

Whaddya know? Getting fired had an upside.

After Nick paid the bill, we made our way back to my car and climbed in.

"Which way to EZ Funz?" I asked. Nick had mentioned he'd be making a stop by the place today and, being the upstanding American citizen I was, I volunteered to go along to help. I was going nuts without a job, without a sense of purpose. I wasn't the type of woman who could be happy lying on a couch sucking down bonbons all day.

Something was definitely wrong with me, huh?

Nick riffled through a file that had been mine mere days ago. The file contained documentation relating to an international debt collection fraud case that had made its way into the hands of the IRS in a roundabout way. Over the past two years, the Consumer Protection Division of the Texas attorney general's office had received a multitude of complaints against United National Debt Recovery. The collection agency had contacted thousands of Texas residents, demanding payments on loans the collection agency insisted were past due. The debtors, however, disputed the delinquencies.

Many of the victims had previously obtained small, unsecured loans from EZ Funz, an online lender headquartered in McKinney, a small city located a few miles north of Dallas. These particular complainants insisted they'd fully repaid the loans they'd received from EZ Funz. When the assistant state attorney general contacted EZ Funz, the loan company's owner corroborated his customers' claims. All of the victims had long since repaid their loans in full. No money was due.

Despite the fact that the people owed nothing further on the debts, United National's staff continued to relentlessly pursue them. The firm reported the debts as delinquent on the victims' credit reports, thus violating the Fair Credit Reporting Act and lowering the victims' credit scores. The collection agency's representatives phoned victims at all hours of the day and night, in direct violation of the both the Texas Debt Collection Act and the federal Fair Debt Collection Practices Act, which allowed calls only between 8:00 AM and 9:00 PM local time. United National also phoned the victims' neighbors and relatives, alleging the victims had failed to repay their loans, disparaging the victims' reputations and causing them untold embarrassment. According to the victims, each of the callers had a distinct Indian accent.

The collection agency sent letters to the victims' employers, threatened to file theft and fraud charges against the victims themselves, and threatened to seize the victims' property even though such seizures violated state law. Texas had been settled largely by deadbeats fleeing creditors in the Northeast and, as a result, the state property code contained fairly liberal exemptions to protect debtors from pauperism. United National had no court judgments against the victims and, even if it had, it couldn't seize assets that did not secure the loan and were legally exempt. Making such false statements was another violation of the Fair Debt Collection Practices Act.

The amounts alleged to be in arrears were relatively small, most in the one- to two-hundred-dollar range. Though the debtors had proof they'd paid their loans on time and in full, United National refused to back off. To the victims, a couple hundred dollars seemed like a small price to pay to stop to the harassment and buy some peace.

The assistant AG had completed a preliminary investigation, determining that the collection agency had failed to post the required ten-thousand-dollar bond with the Texas secretary of state and that Darshan Sundaram, the man who had filed the assumed name certificate for United National, held no Texas driver's license or identification card, owned no real estate in Texas, and appeared to be untraceable. The business address listed for United National was a fictitious address that didn't actually exist. Sundaram and United National were operating out of the shadows.

Each of the victims had been instructed to make their payments directly to specified accounts at local banks. The AG's office contacted the banks and closed the accounts, though in each instance the vast majority of the funds had already been transferred out of the accounts to another bank in India. As new information poured in, the AG repeatedly closed accounts, but Sundaram maintained a number of accounts at different banks and when one was closed he'd simply use another. Typical MO for this type of crime. Some of the accounts were in neither Sundaram's name nor that of United National but were in the names of other Indian citizens and collection companies, indicating Sundaram was merely the tip of the iceberg in a much larger scam.

None of the addresses the collection agencies provided to the banks were legitimate. Unless a victim who'd made payment to a particular account reported it, it was impossible to tell how many of the accounts remained open. It was also impossible to tell how many bogus collection agencies and people were involved.

In addition to closing the bank accounts, the AG also terminated the local phone numbers used by the collection agencies. Like the bank accounts, though, it was primarily an exercise in futility. The government would terminate one telephone account only to have someone open another immediately thereafter. Still, it kept Sundaram and his cohorts on the run. When the crooks tired of the game of cat and mouse, the collection agency began using Internet calling services based in India. The Texas AG's office had no authority to order a foreign phone company to shut down its services to a particular customer. What's more, without knowing all the names of the people and collection agencies involved it was impossible to completely close the illegal enterprise down. The best law enforcement could do was chase after the bad guys and put out small fires.

When the state AG's office learned that Sundaram and his cohorts had operated similar scams in other states, too, it booted the case up to the Federal Trade Commission, which had nationwide authority. Unfortunately, the FTC had more easily catchable fish to fry. They'd put some effort into locating Sundaram and the others in his crime ring, but they had no better luck than the state AG's office. Given that the funds had been transferred to Indian bank accounts, the FTC speculated that the operation was now being primarily run from abroad. Trying to enforce U.S. law against an outfit operating overseas would be next to impossible.

When the FTC hadn't been able to make progress, the case had been punted over to the IRS as a potential tax evasion case. It was no big surprise when I'd searched the tax filings and found no tax return had been filed by Sundaram or United National Debt Recovery. In addition to the individuals they'd victimized, they'd also defrauded Uncle Sam.

As I headed up the on-ramp for Central Expressway, Nick found the address for EZ Funz, plugged it into his phone's GPS app, and gave me turn-by-turn instructions.

When we reached the red dot on the screen, we found ourselves in a small business park. The building was two-story white stucco with a minimum of landscaping, a low-rent venue for businesses with no need to impress clients, nothing like the quaint nearby square in old downtown McKinney.

Nick and I stepped inside the double glass doors and consulted the building directory. The sign indicated our destination, suite 103, was to our left.

The glass door to suite 103 was locked, though we could see a young Hispanic woman with a headset sitting at a desk inside the space. A quartet of cubicles sat behind her, followed by an open door that led into an office.

Nick whipped out his badge and held it up as he rapped on the glass. "We're from the IRS!" he called loudly. "We need to see Mr. Bower!"

The girl came to the door, turned the knob, and let us in. "Wait here, please. I'll get Mr. Bower for you."

There were no chairs, so we remained standing while the girl stepped to the back office. She returned with a graying sixtyish man in navy pants and a green sweater covered in small fabric pills.

"You're with the IRS?" the man asked.

Nick nodded and held out his hand. "Senior Special Agent Nick Pratt." He then introduced me. "My associate, Tara Holloway."

There was that word again. "Associate." A vague moniker, but it sounded far more professional than introducing me as his *orgasm provider*.

"Come back to my office," Bower said, indicating the way with a tilt of his head.

We followed him past the cubicles, where two young women and two young men sat processing loan applications and payments.

Bower's office was spare and tidy. He had a large, cheap desk with a desktop computer and multiline phone resting on it.

He gestured to a couple of vinyl chairs and Nick and I each took a seat.

"I know you've already spoken with the AG's office and

the FTC," Nick said, "but I'd like to get the rundown again. Sometimes one agent picks up on something another didn't."

Bower lifted his chin in acknowledgment. "Okay. So here's how we operate. At EZ Funz we do all of our loans online. The maximum loan is a thousand dollars and we require a short payback period, one to six months depending on the circumstances. Most of our clients have decent credit but low-to-moderate incomes."

The company filled a critical niche, making short-term loans to people who found themselves in a temporary financial bind. Bower noted that he'd spent decades in banking, first as a personal loan officer and later in commercial lending. After the financial crisis, he'd been let go by the bank as they consolidated their branches and cut back on staff. Given his extensive experience in the loan market, he decided to start his own company.

"I was approached a while back by a representative of United National Debt Recovery. An Indian guy. He wanted to buy our client list and contact information for the purported purpose of offering larger, secured loans for cars, appliances, that type of thing."

"Sounds reasonable." Nick shifted in the uncomfortable chair and leaned forward. "When this deal was being worked out, what type of research did you do into United National?"

A cloud passed over Bower's face as he lifted a shoulder. "None. I had no reason to suspect the guy was some kind of con artist." He crossed his arms over his chest, a clearly defensive gesture. "It's not my fault if the guy used the information for improper purposes."

Nick raised a palm to let Bower know we weren't here to nail him, we just wanted information that might help the IRS nail the assholes who were ripping people off. "We're just trying to find the people who are running this thing. That's all."

Several days ago, before I'd been terminated, I'd tried the callback number the collection agency had provided to some of the victims. I'd reached a call center in India. The staff at the call center refused to disclose who they worked for. Heck, maybe they didn't even know. One had gone so far as to tell me that she didn't get a paper paycheck or direct deposit of her earnings but was paid in cash. One hundred and twenty-five rupees per hour.

Bower threw up his hands. "I'm as upset about the situation as you are. Probably more so. I'm running a legitimate business here. Whoever has done this has ruined the name of EZ Funz. We get four or five calls a day from previous clients who have been contacted by that damn collection agency and are ready to tear us a new one. My employees spend lots of time dealing with upset clients and gathering up information to show their loans were paid off. I can't even begin to tell you how many complaints I've dealt with through the Better Business Bureau, too. Our rating has gone down from an A to a C minus as a result of all the reports. Business is down forty percent, too."

Bower, too, had become a victim.

"Do you have a copy of the information you sold to United National?" I asked.

"I can get it for you," Bower said. "It's basically a list of every client through July seventeenth of last year."

He summoned his receptionist and asked her to download the data to a thumb drive.

"How did Sundaram pay for the data he purchased from you?" Nick asked.

"Wire transfer."

"What was he like?" I asked, more out of personal curiosity than any sense the information would help us locate the man.

Bower lifted the shoulder again. "He seemed like a nice guy. I even took him to lunch at Rick's Chophouse after we negotiated the deal."

"Who paid for lunch?" Nick asked.

"I did. He ate like he was starved. He said he'd stayed at a bed-and-breakfast and that he'd overslept and missed the breakfast."

Nick and I exchanged glances. Knowing where Sundaram

stayed when he was in town could help us track him down. Then again, it could be a dead end. If the guy was smart, he'd stay at different hotels so he'd be harder to trace. Still, neither the AG's office nor the FTC had pursued this angle.

Nick turned back to Bower. "Did he say which bed-and-breakfast?"

There were several situated throughout McKinney's Historic District.

Bower looked down in thought for a moment before turning back to us. "I don't think he said. If he did, I don't remember."

It wasn't much, but at least we had a new lead now.

chapter ten

Who's the Fairest
of Them All?

We thanked the man and headed out to my car. I handed Nick the keys. He drove while I searched the Internet on my phone, finding a half-dozen bed-and-breakfasts in McKinney. I directed Nick to the one nearest our current location.

The first B and B was gorgeous, an enormous three-story gray Victorian with burgundy trim, a wraparound porch and balcony, and a cupola on the third floor. We pulled into the gravel lot and parked.

The porch creaked as we stepped onto it. A hand-lettered calligraphy sign in the front window read: "*Come on in.*" So, we went on in.

We found the proprietors, a fiftyish couple, in the home's front parlor. The woman lay sprawled on a velvet-covered fainting couch reading a racy romance novel with a bare-chested man on the cover. Her husband stood on a stepstool nearby, replacing bulbs in a Tiffany light fixture. Unlike the fictional hero on the book, he was fully dressed.

"We're from the IRS," Nick said, flashing his badge. "We

need to find out if a certain person stayed here on or around July sixteenth of this year."

The woman lifted a finger, not taking her eyes off the page. "Gimme a second. They're almost done screwing."

I glanced around while Nick and I waited for the characters to climax. A tall, wide bookshelf behind the fainting couch was loaded with books at least two layers deep. Romances. Mysteries. Thrillers. A few classics sprinkled here and there among them in no particular order. A small orange tabby had curled up for a nap in the gap between *Pride and Prejudice* and what appeared to be an erotic tome titled *Every Inch of You.*

The woman finished the scene, sighed, and closed the book, depositing it on an antique table next to her chair. "All right. Let's check those records."

She led us to a small desk, where she sat down and logged in to a laptop computer. She punched a few keys to pull up the information. "We had a couple of guests around that date," she noted. She rattled off their names. "Morton. Schuster. Vreeland." None of them sounded remotely Indian.

"No Indian man?" Nick asked.

The woman shook her head. "It doesn't appear so."

"How did the guests pay for their stay?" I asked. There could be a chance Sundaram had provided a false name and passed himself off as an ethnicity other than Indian. After all, actors did it all the time. They even had a term for it. "Racebending." Though he wasn't African-American, Fred Armisen did a great Obama impression on *Saturday Night Live.* Rashida Jones, who was the daughter of a white mother and black musician Quincy Jones, played an Italian-American woman on *The Office.* Sacha Baron Cohen played a variety of repulsive European assholes, though in retrospect they were all white repulsive assholes, so maybe that didn't prove my point.

The woman checked her records. "All of the guests around that date paid with credit cards."

Hm-m. If Sundaram had used a false name, I might've expected him to pay with traveler's checks or in cash. Then again, he could have used a stolen credit card or a counterfeit one.

"Any problems with the credit cards?" I asked. "Identity theft? Fraud?"

"No. No problems."

We thanked the woman for the information and continued on our rounds. Unfortunately, we had no better luck at the next two B and Bs.

It was after five o'clock and dusk settled in. The streetlights flickered on as we drove to the fourth bed-and-breakfast. The place was a sunny yellow one-story with white gingerbread trim and scalloped shingles on the gables. Cute. Quaint. Homey.

The sign out front read: "The House of the Seven Fables—Bed, Breakfast, and Boarding." An orange pumpkin-shaped horse-drawn carriage stood in the yard to the right of the center walkway, as if waiting for its horse and driver to take Cinderella to the ball. Centered in the left half of the front yard was a black iron gas lamp on an eight-foot post. Given that the lamp contained an electric lightbulb rather than a gas outlet, it couldn't be an original. Nonetheless, it added to the old-fashioned look of the place.

As we watched, a blond woman in a puffy baby-blue dress opened the door, stepped out onto the porch, and crouched to plug an extension cord into an outlet on the wall next to the front door. *Bling!* The house exploded in so many lights it appeared to be on fire.

Nick gave a whistle. "Holy moly. Did Clark Griswold decorate this place?"

I blinked in a desperate attempt to focus. My retinas felt fried.

When I could finally see clearly again, I noted that the house was completely outlined in large red lights, including the four dormer windows adorning the roof. Icicle lights hung from every eave. Multicolored strands were wrapped around the porch rail, while the bushes sported solid blue. The black iron lamppost in the front yard served as the central support beam for a dozen strands of green lights that angled out from the top, forming a conical Christmas tree of lights. I could only imagine what the owner's electric bill would look like.

Blinking against the brilliance, we stepped onto the porch, pulled open the screen door, and rapped on the front door. Our knock was answered by the woman who'd been on the porch a moment before.

Whoa. She could be Cinderella's doppelganger.

The woman's teased blond hair was topped with a rhinestone-studded tiara. Along with the puffy blue dress she wore a sparkling necklace, long white gloves, and Lucite heels, probably the closest thing she could find to glass slippers. A drooling, droopy-eyed basset hound with a big red bow around her neck shuffled past the woman and onto the porch, sniffing my loafers and Nick's boots, leaving a smear of saliva across Nick's left toe.

"Hello there," the woman said. "Welcome to Seven Fables. Are you two looking for a room?"

Nick cut me a grin that said her suggestion sounded like a good one.

"We're here on official IRS business," I told her. At least Nick was. I was merely here as a busybody, butting in where I didn't belong. But hey, that had never stopped me before.

"IRS?" the woman asked, looking from me to Nick.

Nick flashed his badge and introduced himself, offering his hand.

I merely told the woman my name and bent down to pet the dog. "Hey, pooch."

The woman introduced herself as Cindy (*seriously?*) Allen, her dog as Anastasia, and shook Nick's hand. Anastasia offered me her paw, which I shook, too.

"To what do we owe the pleasure of this visit?" Cindy asked.

Nick slid his badge back into his shirt pocket. "We're trying to locate someone who may have been a guest here back in July. On the sixteenth to be precise."

A nervous look skittered across her face. "Is there a problem?"

"Possibly," Nick said. The number one rule in investigating a case was to provide information on a need-to-know basis only.

"Oh . . . well . . . okay," Ms. Allen said, obviously wanting more details but at the same time realizing she wasn't likely to get them. "Come back to my office."

She led us into a foyer papered in a gaudy rose print and through a set of French doors into her office. Anastasia shuffled after us in a graceless short-legged, side-to-side gait.

"Your decorations are wonderful," I told the woman. "It must've taken you forever to string all those lights."

"Thanks," Cindy said, "though I can't claim the credit. My handyman service hangs lights in their off-hours."

She stepped over to an antique roll-top desk, pulled an old-fashioned ledger book out of the top drawer, and set the book on the desk. She eased the glove off her right hand and flipped through the pages until she found the date we were looking for. "I had four guests on July sixteenth. Two couples, the Fenwicks and the Garrisons."

Nick's shoulders slumped. "So no one by the name of Darshan Sundaram, then."

Her eyes brightened. "Oh, Mr. Sundaram isn't a guest here. He's a boarder. I treat my boarders like family."

Nick and I exchanged another glance. I wondered if she'd want Sundaram in her family once she learned he was a wanted criminal. Then again, Cinderella had always had family issues. Still, a wicked stepsister or two were nothing compared to a wanted felon.

"Is Mr. Sundaram here now?" Nick asked.

I hoped he was. Nick and I could take him down, quick and easy. I felt myself begin to buzz with anticipation.

The woman closed her ledger book. "No. I haven't seen him in a week or so. He keeps a room here for when he's in town, but I don't always know when he's coming."

She went on to tell us that Sundaram had boarded at her place for a couple of years and always paid his rent in advance. "I'm hoping he'll come back soon," she said. "His mail is stacking up."

My ears perked up. "He receives mail here?"

"Why, sure," she said. "It's one of the services I provide to my boarders." She looked from me to Nick, a frown creasing her brow. "What sort of business do y'all have with Mr. Sundaram, anyway?"

Nick went ahead and told her about the illegal activities, about the call center in India, the fraudulent demands on people who'd already made good on their loans.

As he detailed Sundaram's indiscretions, the woman's frown became less defensive and more skeptical. "And you're sure it's him? He's always seemed like such a nice man. Very polite, impeccable manners. I find this hard to believe."

Nick showed her a copy of the assumed name certificate with Sundaram's name and signature on it. She eyed the signature for a moment, then reached back to a bulletin board behind her and pulled off a postcard featuring an Indian elephant.

"Sundaram sent you a postcard?" Nick asked.

Ms. Allen nodded. "I asked him to. I collect stamps from around the world. See?" She pulled a large scrapbook out of the desk and turned the pages, showing us stamps from various countries around the world. Still, we'd come to track down Sundaram, not to discuss her hobby as a philatelist, a word that I'd always thought sounded far more naughty and sordid than the concept it represented.

"Let's compare the signatures," I suggested, trying to get things back on track.

Ms. Allen laid the postcard and assumed name certificate side by side on the desk. Sure enough, the name Darshan was spelled the same on both the postcard and the certificate, from the excessively round *D* to the swoop following the *n*. Same with the last name. The final *m* in Sundaram was also followed by a distinctive swoop.

"I can hardly believe it." She looked up from the documentation, her eyes wide, incredulous. Once the truth sank in, though, she became royally pissed. "I run a nice place here. I'm not running a halfway house for criminals. The nerve of that man."

"Any chance we can take a look at his mail and his room?" Nick asked.

Allen owned the place. She could agree to let us execute a search without a warrant. Of course she could also refuse and force us to seek a court order. I mentally crossed my fingers.

"Of course."

Phew.

She led us down a long hallway papered in a different gaudy floral print, this one featuring pink poppies. We passed a room bearing a plaque that read: *The Rip Van Winkle Room,* complete with a set of nine pins and an antique liquor jug. I glanced into Sleeping Beauty's Bed Chamber and noted an assortment of spindles displayed on the dresser. I hoped none of the guests would prick themselves on a spindle and die. The Princess and the Pea Room featured a bed with three mattresses stacked on top of one another and a wooden stepstool to climb up into the tall bed. A potted pea plant grew in a window box sitting on the inside windowsill.

We stopped at the end of the hall, at the closed door of a room identified as the Snow White Suite. The keys on Cindy's ring jingled as she sorted through them.

"Here we go." She slid a key into the lock and pushed the door open. "The mail's in the chamber pot." She gestured to a large white ceramic pot with daisies painted along the outside.

The room boasted not only a small bushel basket filled with red wax apples but also seven garden gnome statutes, probably the closest thing she could find to dwarves. An enormous bejeweled oval mirror was hanging, of course, *on the wall.* Sundaram could hardly be called the fairest of them all, however. What he'd done to his victims was very *un*fair.

Cindy left Nick and me to scour the room, searching for clues.

Nick gestured around at the gnomes, all of which were smiling. "Those things are creeping me out. It's like they're watching us."

I got the same feeling. Eerie.

While Nick checked the dresser drawers, I pulled the mail from the chamber pot, trying not to wonder whether the thing was a kitschy reproduction or an original antique that might have actually been used. Ew.

Sundaram had several pieces of mail. Most were standard sales circulars and charity solicitations, though a few of the items were more personal. An invitation from an upscale jewelry store inviting him to a private showing for preferred customers. The most recent issue of *Entrepreneur* magazine. That one earned a snort from me. The final piece was a past-due notice from a local gym, notifying him that his automatic monthly payment had been rejected due to the account being closed. If he didn't make good on the payment and late charges within ten days, he'd lose his membership privileges and his account would be turned over to a collection agency. How's that for irony?

In some ways, the fact that banking and communications were done electronically made things more difficult, since there was no paper trail to follow, only a path of electronic fairy dust. On the flip side, if an electronic trail could be found it could be easy to obtain a wealth of information in one fell swoop. It was too bad we didn't know Sundaram's e-mail address. Access to his in-box could provide us all sorts of clues, break the case wide open. We'd mined all sorts of critical data in earlier cases via e-mail accounts. If we could figure out what Sundaram's address was, the office tech guru, Josh Schmidt, could hack the account in no time.

I noticed a notepad on the bedside table, pulled a mechanical pencil from my purse, and ran it back and forth across the pad to see if a phone number or name Sundaram had jotted down might magically appear, like in the movies. Unfortunately, the only thing that popped up was a doodle of a bow-wearing basset hound, and a poorly drawn one at that.

A search under the bed turned up a herd of dust bunnies and a single brown dress sock.

"Wait a minute," I said when we stood. I gestured to one

of the gnomes on the dresser. "Didn't that gnome used to be farther back?"

Nick stepped over, bent down, and looked the gnome in the eye, pointing a finger in his face. "Stay put, you little freak."

Using his phone, Nick snapped photos of the jewelry circular, the letter from the gym, and both the label and publisher information page of the magazine. "One last place to look," he said, stepping over to the bed and putting his hands under the mattress to lift it.

I walked over next to him as he raised the mattress.

All we found underneath was a copy of *Hustler.*

Holding the mattress up with one hand, Nick picked the magazine up with the other. "I'm obligated as a special agent to perform a thorough investigation," he said, his lips spread in a roguish grin. "I'll need to look this over page by page."

"Like hell you will." I slapped the magazine out of his hand. The force sent it sailing to the box spring, where two small blue booklets slid out of it. Passports.

A-ha!

I grabbed one while Nick grabbed the other. We opened them to the identification page and held them up. Both contained pictures of what was clearly the same man, though he was clean shaven in one and had a full beard in the other. The name on one read: *Krishnan Gupta.* The other read: *Sanjay Bhattacharjee.*

"Multiple aliases," Nick said, thinking aloud.

We'd assumed Sundaram was the tip of the iceberg in a large transnational criminal organization, but given these aliases he might be a whole iceberg onto himself.

Nick slid the passports into the inside pocket of his jacket.

We left the room and returned to the front of the house. Ms. Allen sat in the small but comfy parlor now, one foot propped on an embroidered footstool, the other, now barefoot, rubbing her dog's belly as she lay on her back on the rug. "All done?"

"For now," Nick said. "Let us know if Sundaram returns, okay? And don't let him know we've been by."

"Of course."

"Any chance you've got a photo of the guy?" I asked.

"I sure do." She stood from her chair and retrieved a photo album from a bookshelf. "Here's one I took at Thanksgiving."

The photo showed several guests gathered around a large oval table. A roasted turkey languished on a platter in the middle of the table, surrounded by heaping bowls of mashed potatoes, green beans, cranberry sauce, and rolls. At the end of the table sat a surprisingly buff Indian man who appeared to be around his mid-thirties. Looked like he'd been hitting the gym regularly, at least before his payment had been declined.

Nick asked Ms. Allen if he could take the photo with him.

"Be my guest," she said.

"Any chance you've got an e-mail address for Mr. Sundaram?" I asked. "Maybe a cell phone number or home address?"

She shook her head. "Sorry, but no on all accounts. Since he always paid in cash, I didn't see any need to keep tabs on him."

After we returned to Nick's truck, we headed for the gym, which was only a mile away on the highway frontage road. While I waited in the foyer, watching a couple of twentyish men try to outdo each other on the weights, Nick spoke with the assistant manager and secured his agreement to notify Nick if Sundaram showed up at the club.

"Did they have an e-mail address?" I asked Nick as we returned to the car.

"Nope," he said. "I get the impression Sundaram avoided giving that out at all costs."

"What about a phone number?"

"He left them the number for Seven Fables."

Damn.

The jewelry store, located a couple miles down the freeway, had already closed for the night. We looked through the windows to see if anyone might be about, but the interior darkness was broken only by the flashing red beacon of the alarm system.

With all leads exhausted for the time being, we headed back to Nick's house for our own private holiday celebration.

chapter eleven

$\mathcal{C}$hristmas Comes Early

Although Nick and his mother had come to my parents' house in Nacogdoches at Thanksgiving, they planned to visit Nick's aunt and uncle in Houston for Christmas. I would've liked to have Nick with me for the holidays, but he was an only child and I knew he wouldn't want his mother making the four-hour drive to Houston on her own.

Tonight Nick and I would have an intimate celebration, just the two of us. We drove back to Nick's place to exchange gifts, making a quick stop at my town house so I could pick up Nick's present.

Nutty greeted us at Nick's door, sniffing intently around our ankles, apparently scenting Anastasia. His tail wagged as he sniffed. Maybe we should introduce the two of them. Anastasia wasn't much to look at, but then again, Nutty had cataracts, so what did it matter? Besides, beauty was only fur deep.

Nick knelt down and ruffled Nutty's ears. "She wasn't all that pretty, boy. Stubby legs and long ears."

"Don't sell Anastasia short," I said. "At least she knew how to dress." The bow had been a cute touch.

While Nick let Nutty out back for a potty break, I grabbed Nick a beer from his fridge and fixed myself a cup of instant cocoa.

The three of us convened a few minutes later in the living room. I took a seat on the couch and Nutty climbed up next to me.

Nick retrieved two gift bags and a large wrapped box from under the small artificial tree and set them on the coffee table. "Ladies first."

Who was I to argue? The first bag was tall and narrow. I reached inside and pulled out a bottle of one of my favorite wines, a sweet orange moscato. "Yum." Maybe if I drank the whole bottle myself I could forget about my situation.

The second bag contained a kit for making sushi. The supplies included a bamboo rolling mat, a small rice paddle, two sets of chopsticks, two dipping-sauce dishes, and two chopstick rests. I wasn't much of a cook, but since sushi didn't need cooking maybe I could pull it off. Sushi was more about assembly. That I could do.

Now for the box. The box was wrapped in the Neiman Marcus signature wrap, complete with a shiny star-shaped trinket. My heart began to pitter-patter in my chest. I looked up at Nick. "Neiman's?"

He grinned. "Go ahead. Open it."

I tore through the wrap and lifted the lid off the box. Inside was the beautiful cobalt-blue peacoat I'd *oohed* and *aahed* over with Alicia when I'd received my catalog in the mail. Nick must've consulted my best friend for gift ideas. I couldn't help myself. I squealed like a pig. "Nick! I love it!"

I leaped from the couch to give Nick a big hug and a warm kiss. Nick picked up the coat, held it open, and helped me into it. *Mm-m.* I rubbed my cheek against the lapel. The garment was soft and warm and comforting, a nice designer piece to add to my mostly clearance-rack wardrobe. It had definitely been time for an update. The only other winter coat I owned was a sporty bright red nylon model I'd had since high school.

I lifted my shoulders, snuggling into it. "How do I look?"

Nick's eyes locked on mine. "You look beautiful," he said. "But it has nothing to do with the coat."

Aw-w-w . . .

His sweet words earned him another kiss, this one warmer and deeper. After a moment, I reluctantly pushed him back.

I held out the two small boxes containing his gifts. "Your turn."

Nick opened the first box to find a Japanese language program on CDs. "Japanese, huh?"

"I figured you could listen to it on your drive to Houston."

"Good idea," he said. "The only Japanese I know is '*domo arigato,* Mr. Roboto.' That won't get me too far. I better at least learn 'please,' 'thank you,' and 'how many yen does this cost?' "

He opened the second box to find a two-tone leather western-style belt in black and brown with a shiny buckle and engraved pewter accents.

"Fancy," he said. "I'll be the best-dressed cowboy in Tokyo."

"You'll be the *only* cowboy in Tokyo." Or maybe not. I supposed someone had to round up the cattle for the Kobe beef. Still, I had a hard time picturing a Japanese man dressed in boots, jeans, and a cowboy hat.

Nick put the box down on the coffee table, stood, and unbuckled his relatively plain tan belt, sliding it from the waist of his navy dress pants. He removed the buckle he'd had on, a gold-tone piece featuring a pair of pistols, their barrels crossed to form an X.

"Let me help with that." I stepped over to him and slid the leather strap out of his hands. His shirtfront vibrated with the pounding of his heart as I eased the end of the new belt through the loops on his jeans, wrapping my arms around his waist and pressing myself up against his chest as I worked the belt around him. Who would've known it could be so sexy to put clothes *on* someone?

When I finished, I took a small step back and tucked two fingers into his waistband behind the buckle. "There," I said softly, giving his fly a little tug. "Nice and snug."

Nick put a finger under my chin and raised my face to his. "I know which reindeer you are," he said. *"Vixen."* His lips quirked in a sexy grin. "The only thing that could make this better was if you took the belt back off right now and joined me in some reindeer games."

So I did.

Nick picked me up and carried me to his bedroom, where we made love once again. This time, though, he took his sweet time with foreplay, jingling my bells, dashing through my snow, providing me some much-needed holiday cheer before stuffing my stocking. I won't share all the sordid details, but suffice it to say that *I came a-wassailing.*

chapter twelve

$\mathcal{B}$anging Dicks

The next morning was Christmas Eve. Though it wasn't an official federal government holiday, Nick had elected to use one of his accrued vacation days. I woke to find him already dressed. He pulled a couple of pairs of boxer briefs from his dresser and tossed them into a duffel bag before zipping it.

He gestured to the nightstand. "I poured you some coffee."

Rubbing my eyes, I sat up and slid my legs over the side of the bed. I took the mug and sipped from it. He'd added gingerbread creamer. *Yum.* He'd bought the stuff just for me. The thought warmed my heart while the coffee warmed my tummy. I drank it while he finished packing; then I slipped back into the clothes I had on last night.

I drove my car up the street to my place while Nick followed in his truck. He walked me to the door. On the porch he took my hands in his and squeezed them. "Let me know how things go today."

"I will."

He'd offered to postpone his trip to Houston for a few

hours in case I needed moral support after the meeting with Troy Kerr, but I assured Nick I'd be fine. No sense letting my problems get in the way of his Christmas plans with his family.

He gave me one last, soft kiss before heading back to his truck.

As I stepped inside, I was hit with a lonely quiet. Since Alicia and her fiancé were Jewish, they'd taken advantage of the holiday to head for the ski slopes in Taos. It must be nice to be free to leave the state. I already felt like a prisoner. Though since my cell comprised nearly 269,000 square miles of Lone Star State soil, I supposed I couldn't complain much.

After showering, I dressed in a chocolate-brown suit accessorized with a salmon-pink scarf, hoping to appear professional yet feminine. Maybe Troy Kerr would go easier on me once he saw me and realized I was a petite woman. Not that I wanted sympathy just for being small and/or female, but at this point I'd take anything I could get that might help convince Kerr not to bring a criminal case against me.

I met Anthony Giacomo at his office a half hour before our scheduled meeting with Troy Kerr. Giacomo had ditched the Santa hat today and replaced the amethyst in his ear with a small silver hoop.

He closed his door after I stepped into his office. "Take a seat. Time for your pep talk."

I slid into one of his wing chairs and he took a seat in the other, angling it to face me. His gaze traveled over me. "You look great, by the way. Love the scarf."

"Thanks."

"All right, here's the plan." He leaned toward me, his forearms resting on his knees. "I'll do the talking, try to convince Kerr that taking this matter to trial would be a colossal mistake. No matter how tempted you are to speak, don't say anything. We want to feel him out, force him to show his hand, but keep him guessing about our strategy. Got it?"

"Okay," I said. My voice sounded tentative and unsure. Ugh. That's what I got for wearing plain white cotton little-girl panties today. I made a mental note to buy some leopard-print underwear for the trial. Nothing like racy panties to give a girl some confidence.

My attorney reached out and took my hand. "I know you're scared, but you can't show it. Prosecutors are like wild dogs. If Kerr smells fear, he'll pounce on you and shred you limb from limb."

Wonderful.

Giacomo looked me in the eye. "You are a tough, strong woman, Tara. A smart woman. While we're meeting with Kerr, this is what I want you to think. 'Kiss my lovely little ass, Troy Kerr.' Can you do that?"

I smiled. "Yep. I can do that." Heck, I'd already been thinking that very thing.

"Great." He gave the back of my hand a pat and stood. "Let's move out."

We rode the elevator down to the parking garage and climbed into Giacomo's car, a two-seater Jaguar F-Type V8 in lunar-gray metallic paint. The car looked like something James Bond would drive. Anthony opened my door for me, then circled around the back to the driver's side. Once inside, he cranked the engine and cranked up the stereo.

Holy crap!

My hands reflexively moved to cover my ears as the speakers spewed the most obnoxious death metal music ever made. With all the screeching and banging, it sounded as if the lead singer had stuck his head in a garbage disposal.

Giacomo laughed. He yelled over the shrieking voice, "Let me guess! You were expecting Michael Bublé or Celine Dion?"

It wasn't so much that I was stereotyping Anthony. It's just that the guy had ears. Seriously, could he not hear this nerve-shattering cacophony? I'd bet this was the band the CIA used to break prisoners.

"Who *is* this?" I hollered.

Giacomo held up the CD cover. *Attila.* I'd never heard of the band. With any luck, I'd never hear them again, either. The blood vessels in my temple threatened to burst.

"Isn't this song great?" he asked as he slid his card through the reader to exit the garage.

"It sure is something!" I hollered over the music. *Something god-awful.*

Fifteen minutes and one shattered eardrum later, we were sitting in a small conference room at the DOJ office, the same room I'd sat in when going over the paperwork in previous cases with Ross O'Donnell. I was used to being on the same side as the prosecutor. It felt odd to be in here defending myself. Odd and wrong.

A moment later, Troy Kerr entered the room. He was fortyish and formidable, standing well over six feet, with broad shoulders and a solid physique. His black hair bore just enough silver to give him a look of seasoned respectability. If I didn't have the urge to leap across the room and wrap my fingers around his throat, I might even say he was attractive.

His blue eyes touched briefly on me but didn't linger long enough for me to get a read on him. When he spotted Giacomo sitting next to me, a flicker of apprehension crossed Kerr's face, so quick and subtle I might not have noticed had I not been watching him so intently. As I was nearly deaf now thanks to the scream-o music, my other senses were heightened. Hm-m . . .

Kerr nodded in greeting and extended his hand. "Anthony. Good to see you again."

Giacomo rose slowly, reaching out his hand to take Kerr's. "Troy. Always a pleasure," he said in a tone indicating their interactions were anything but. I stood when Giacomo turned to me. "My client, Tara Holloway."

I shook Kerr's hand and nodded but said nothing. *Pucker up and kiss my lovely little ass, Troy Kerr.*

When we were all seated, Kerr glanced again at me before he addressed my attorney and began banging his dick on the table, metaphorically speaking. "As you know, your client shot a man multiple times in the leg during an arrest."

"Mm-hm."

"Four times to be exact. Most of the shots being fired after the victim no longer had a weapon." *Bang. Bang.*

Giacomo banged back. "And?"

Kerr stiffened. "And that's not how a member of federal law enforcement should have handled the situation."

Jackass. What did he really know about these situations? Had he ever risked his life by going undercover among criminals, hoping not to be discovered? Had he ever stared down the barrel of a gun wondering if it would be the last thing he'd see? Had he ever been shot at? Of course not. For the first time, I found myself with penis envy. I wanted a dick to bang, too.

Giacomo steepled his fingers but said nothing. He merely stared at Kerr as if waiting for him to say something of any significance.

Kerr shifted in his seat, apparently uncomfortable to be carrying the entire conversation on his own. "I can't let this type of abusive behavior slide."

"Of course not," Giacomo said, a knowing smile spreading his lips. "Not when there's a place on the federal bench up for grabs."

"This isn't about me!" Kerr barked, though the red flush exploding on his cheeks said otherwise. "This is about justice."

"Justice?" Giacomo *tsked* and shook both his head and a finger. "Now-now, Troy. If this were really about justice, none of us would be sitting here."

Kerr's cheek twitched as he clenched his jaw. "I have a duty to make sure the laws are upheld and to prosecute those who break them, no matter who they are." His dick banging had become tentative now, his voice softer, his arguments flaccid.

Giacomo remained silent but lifted a skeptical shoulder.

Kerr tried again. "If we let our law enforcement run roughshod over our citizens, then we're no better than a third-world government."

Giacomo raised a credulous brow. "You're comparing Miss Holloway, a woman who put her life on the line every day serving the American people, to some power-hungry

African warlord?" My attorney snorted. "That's not merely over-the-top, Troy. It's over-the-top and back again."

I remained quiet, though my mind was shrieking louder than Attila's lead singer. *Kiss my lovely little ass, Troy Kerr! Smooch away!*

Enraged by Giacomo's composure and losing his own again, Kerr said, "It takes courage to do what's right, you know."

"It certainly does," Giacomo replied. "And *'discretion is the better part of valor.'* "

Flustered, Kerr threw up his hands. "Cut to the chase, Anthony. What are you saying?"

Giacomo offered a small smile belied by his incendiary gaze. "What I'm saying, Troy dear, is that using my client as a pawn in your political game would be a very unwise move."

Kerr sprang up from his seat and jabbed a finger in my direction. "She shot a man four times in the leg! This is a cut-and-dried case of excessive force."

Giacomo ducked his head and quietly gazed up at Kerr until the man realized he was standing and reclaimed his seat. "In the legal world," Giacomo said, "nothing is ever cut-and-dried. You know that as well as I do. Besides, you know my track record."

The hangdog expression on Kerr's face told me that he was indeed familiar with Giacomo's courtroom successes. Perhaps that explained the flicker of concern I'd seen skitter across his face earlier.

"Miss Holloway didn't break the law," Giacomo said. "She did the world a tremendous favor by taking a pimp and drug dealer off the streets."

"A jury would never see it that way."

"Mm-m-m . . ." Giacomo cocked his head. "You sure about that? Sure enough to bet a place on the bench?"

"Absolutely," Kerr spat, though there was uncertainty in his eyes.

Ha!

"Be patient, Troy," Giacomo said. "A bigger, better case will come along in a year or two. You can make your mark then."

Now it was Kerr's turn to be silent. I hoped he was thinking about dropping the charges. *Please, Troy. Please,* I mentally begged. *No ass kissing required. Heck, I'll even kiss yours!* I wanted this over. Now. I wanted to get on with my life.

Giacomo continued, lowering his voice, speaking softly and soothingly like a parent attempting to placate a child. "This case will be headline news, Troy. When you lose at trial, everyone will know. You'll forfeit any chance of a judicial appointment. Who wants to put a loser on the bench?"

Kerr broke eye contact with Giacomo and looked away for a long moment before turning back. "Look," he said. "I've got Geils' attorney breathing down my neck, insisting I do something about this."

"So, what?" Giacomo said. "You're going to let his attorney push you around?"

"I don't let anyone push me around," Kerr said, a distinctively defensive tone in his voice. So we were back to the dick banging. Great.

"That's not what it looks like," Giacomo said. "It looks to me like you're letting his attorney call the shots."

Kerr seemed at a loss, as if realizing that, no matter what he did, it might look as if he'd given in to one side or the other. "I'll take it to the grand jury," he said, "let them decide whether this case should go to trial."

"That's a coward's way out," Giacomo volleyed. "You can choose not to pursue this."

As I'd learned during my tenure with the IRS, a case only went to trial if both the grand jury deemed there to be sufficient evidence to warrant a trial and the prosecutor chose to pursue a case. A grand jury was presented only with evidence against the defendant. No exculpatory evidence would be introduced and, in fact, neither the defendant nor the defense attorney was permitted to attend the proceedings. The threshold for determining whether to proceed to trial was quite low.

Kerr glared across the table. "I'm not a coward."

Giacomo sighed. "Ah, but you are. A regular old yellow belly. A wimp." He paused for a brief moment before hammering the point home. *"A pussy."*

Kerr's face contorted in rage. "And what would you know about pussies, you little—!" He stopped himself just in time and turned his head away as if to avoid the stench of his words.

Giacomo laughed as he stood. "Expedite the proceedings. Miss Holloway doesn't need this silly matter hanging over her."

That's for sure.

Kerr nodded. "I'll put the case first on the list for Friday."

Giacomo gestured for me to follow him out. At the doorway, he turned back to Kerr. "If you happen to grow a pair, Troy, let me know."

With that, we went out the door.

chapter thirteen

$\mathcal{N}$aughty or Nice?

We passed Ross O'Donnell on our way out of the building. He took me aside. "For what it's worth, Tara, I think Troy Kerr is out of line."

Gee. Dirty news travels fast, huh?

"Thanks, Ross." I appreciated his support, especially when I knew he was taking a chance offering it to me. After all, Kerr was one of his superiors at the Department of Justice.

Once Anthony and I were seated again in his Jaguar, he turned to me. "Kerr's nervous. That's clear."

Nervous or not, an attorney with a personal stake in the outcome of a case was likely to work harder on it, give it his all. Still, I knew Giacomo had done his best to convince Kerr to drop the charges. Now it was up to the grand jury. At least I'd only have to wait two days for their decision. Thank heaven for small favors.

So many thoughts were running through my head that I hardly heard the shrieks of the metal band as we drove back to the law office.

* * *

When I returned home, I packed, took a shower, and dressed in fresh clothes, then loaded my cats up with food, water, and fresh litter. I gave Henry a scratch behind the ears and Annie a kiss on the head. I turned the thermostat down to sixty-five degrees. Who knew how long I'd be out of work? Might as well start watching my bills. Besides, the cats wore fur coats and if they got cold they could curl up together and keep each other warm or snuggle under the blankets on my bed, which I'd left unmade.

I slid into the beautiful new coat Nick had given me, tossed my overnight bag and gifts into the trunk of my BMW, and headed out. I tried not to think of all my problems as I drove. It was all so overwhelming. No job. Criminal charges pending. A $10 million civil lawsuit. My sense of self still all discombobulated.

Ugh. Some season of cheer and goodwill this was turning out to be. Merry nothing.

As I left downtown and entered the eastern suburbs, my eyes spotted a shopping mall. I exited the freeway and pulled into the parking lot, circling up and down the rows in a desperate search for an empty spot. Looked like there were lots of last-minute shoppers.

My favorite niece, Jesse, had a particular Breyer horse on her list, a limited-edition holiday-themed collectible model decked out in glittering bridle and a saddle with a poinsettia leaf underlay. None of us in the family had been able to find it. All of the online outlets had been out of stock, as were the five malls I'd previously visited in my search. But if there was any way I could spare my niece disappointment, I would. Even if it meant fighting an insane holiday crowd at the mall. Just because my Christmas sucked didn't mean hers should, too.

A parking spot finally opened up on the outermost row. I waited for it and pulled in as soon as the minivan pulled out, beating out a Lexus whose driver had sped up in the other lane in the hopes of stealing the spot from me. The woman driving flipped me the bird even though the spot was clearly rightfully mine. What a Scrooge.

I climbed out of my car, thankful I had my new coat to keep the chill at bay, and made my way inside. The place was packed, frenzied shoppers rushing around like fire ants from a mound that had been poked with a stick. I weaved my way through a blockade of strollers in front of a children's clothing store and ventured farther in.

In the center of the mall sat Santa's village, a semi-circle with a painted north pole backdrop, outlined with artificial pine trees and oversized gift boxes topped with bows the size of basketballs. In the center sat Kris Kringle himself, decked out in his bright red suit and black boots, his booming laugh echoing off the second-floor walkway. The strains of a caroling quartet entertained those waiting in line to see the right jolly old elf, and I laughed when I saw him, in spite of myself.

I bypassed Santa's village and gave the carolers a smile and nod, aiming for the teeming toy store across the way. Boy howdy! The fire marshal would be none too happy with this crowd. I sucked in my gut and squeezed past frantic shoppers, winding my way up and down the aisles, past dolls and action figures and board games, until I located the Breyer horse display.

Score!

A frazzled employee was putting out new stock as shoppers milled around him, jostling his elbows as he placed items on the shelves. My eye caught one of the collectible horses in his stash and it had Jesse's name on it. I snatched the toy off the cart and cradled it to my chest as if it were the Holy Grail. "Thanks! Merry Christmas!"

I weaved my way to the cash register and paid for the purchase, trying once again not to worry about my rapidly dwindling bank account. My shopping mission accomplished, I headed back into the main part of the mall. As I approached Santa's village, my feet slowed of their own will, then stopped moving altogether. I stood and stared at the man playing Santa as he spoke with a small brown-haired boy perched on his lap. When the boy finished rattling off his long list of Christmas wishes, Santa lifted the child off his lap and set him on the floor, offering the mother a warm smile.

This whole mess with Don Geils was driving me crazy. Shooting him in the leg multiple times made me look bad, I knew. But a woman has only so much restraint, and I'd already foregone killing him. All of that repressed energy and emotion had to go somewhere. And, come on, I was only human, after all. Still . . .

I had to know.

Was I naughty? Or was I nice?

Only one person could tell me for sure. And that person was wearing a red suit and hat trimmed in white faux fur and sitting in a big chair forty feet away from me.

I stepped into line behind a dozen mothers with young children, some eager to see Santa Claus, some a little more timid. A smiling red-haired elf in short green overalls, tights, and fuzzy boots escorted each child to Santa's large padded seat and helped them up to his knee. Another elf snapped photographs, which, according to the nearby sign, could be purchased for the "lo-ho-ho price of just $9.99!" Nearby, the carolers belted their way through "Angels We Have Heard on High" and "Joy to the World" before segueing into "Up on the Housetop."

As the line inched forward, I began to feel increasingly ridiculous. A few of the mothers gave me odd looks, trying to figure out why a woman in her twenties with no child in tow was in line to see jolly old Saint Nicholas. The carolers continued their crooning, circling around the village, singing about roasting chestnuts, one-horse open sleighs, building snowmen in meadows. My favorite was "Carol of the Bells." Too bad I couldn't just throw my cares away like the lyrics suggested.

When I reached the front of the line, the elf greeted me with a, "Hi-ho there!" A raging blush heated my face. This was crazy. Nuts. Certifiable. Embarrassing! The guy on the decorated chair was nothing more than an actor, a worker paid to impersonate Father Christmas.

What did I really think he could offer me?

The elf motioned for me to follow her. "Right this way, please. Santa's been waiting to see you."

I took a couple of steps and stopped. "Um . . . I've changed my mind," I told the elf. "Lost my mind" was more like it. I didn't need to see Santa. I needed to see a shrink.

"Come on up!" Santa called from his seat, waving me forward.

I pointed to my chest.

"Yes, you!" he called, waving again. "It's been a long time. Let's catch up."

I glanced behind me, noting the expectant faces on the children waiting in line. What would they think if I walked away from Santa? I couldn't turn my back on him. I had no choice but to continue on my way.

The parents and children stared as I slowly made my way up to Santa. When I reached him, my eyes gave him a once-over. This guy's beard looked real, as did his chubby belly. No pillow there. He might ought to cut down on the milk and cookies before he had a heart attack. His nose was red, like a cherry. Heck, this Santa even had dimples. How merry!

"Right here, young lady." He patted his thigh. "Have a sit."

Maybe it was the Christmas spirit, maybe it was the residual effects of last nights' sake, or maybe it was the fact that I longed to once again be a young girl whose biggest problem was trying to keep her church clothes clean. Whatever the reason, I climbed up onto Santa's lap and sat. To my surprise, my embarrassment fled and I felt a sense of comfort and security I hadn't felt in a long time. I fought the urge to lay my head on his shoulder.

The man offered an understanding smile. "Life's been treating you rotten lately, hasn't it?"

"You know about that?" What was he, a psychologist? Then again, I suppose it didn't take a genius to figure out that an adult wanting to sit on Santa's lap was going through a rough patch.

"Of course I know. I'm Santa. Like the song says, I keep an eye on you when you've asleep. I watch you when you're awake, too."

I chuckled. This guy was good. Probably had some formal theater training.

He narrowed his eyes at me. "You know, since I see you when you're asleep, I know you don't always sleep alone. Some nights you don't even sleep in your own bed."

I stiffened. Was this Santa a pervert? But when I looked in his eyes I noticed they twinkled with merriment, not lust.

I looked down at the floor, then back up at him. "Am . . ." My God, this was crazy. Wasn't it? But I had to know. "Am I on your 'naughty' list?"

He laughed, and his belly shook like a bowlful of jelly. Or like an oversized Jell-O shot. "Don't worry. If everyone who fooled around ended up on my 'naughty' list I'd be out of business."

So Santa believed in moral relativism, huh? Good to know.

"It's not about . . . *that*," I said. "There was something else I did, something I'm not sure about." If I told this guy I'd shot someone several times, would he push me off his lap and call mall security to haul me away?

He ducked his chin and gave me a knowing look. "I know all about it. Not to worry. You did what you had to do. You made my 'nice' list again this year."

Relief surged through me. "I did? Are you sure?"

He laughed again. "Of course I'm sure. I made the list myself. Checked it twice. Trust me, you're on the 'nice' list."

That was just what I needed to hear. My mouth curved up in a broad smile. "Thanks, Santa."

"There's a name at the top of my 'naughty' list that I think you'd recognize, though."

"Is it Donald Geils?"

He wagged a finger. "Now, now. Santa's lists are confidential trade secrets." He followed his words with an exaggerated wink that I took to convey the message I'd been right. Don Geils was on the "naughty" list.

Santa gave me a reassuring pat on the back. "Now, what would you like for Christmas?"

"How about a new job?"

"That's the first time I've heard that one," he said. "I'll work on it. Now smile for the camera."

I turned and grinned at the photographer.

When I stood, Santa gave me a pat on the shoulder and a candy cane.

I stuck the peppermint stick in the pocket of my coat. "Thanks, Santa. I'll leave you some milk and cookies on the hearth."

"Milk?" He made a face. "How about something stronger?"

"You got it."

I left feeling my spirits buoyed for the first time in days. I also left with the photo. Why pass up such a *lo-ho-ho price*, right?

chapter fourteen

Home for the Holidays

I pulled into the drive of my parents' ancient Victorian farm-house early that afternoon. The old house had a lot of charm. It also had a lot of spiders, a mouse or two, drafty windows, and noisy pipes.

I tried to focus on the charm.

Mom's decorating skills rivaled those of Cindy Allen, though where Cindy opted to decorate with lights my mother opted for garlands. The entire front porch was wrapped in greenery accented at precisely measured intervals with bright gold bows. The wreath on the front door was made from fragrant pine boughs stripped from one of the many trees that grew on the property. I had no doubt the tree itself now stood in the living room near the fireplace, covered with homemade ornaments and tinsel and topped with the glitter-covered cardboard star I'd made in second-grade Sunday school.

Mom and Dad met me in the drive, along with a small pack of friendly, tail-wagging dogs who made their home in the heated barn along with a couple of goats and Dad's tractor.

Like me, my mother was petite, with chestnut hair. Dad, on the other hand, was broad shouldered and square. While I hadn't gotten my physique from my father, he had given me his gray-blue eyes. He'd also taught me everything he knew about guns and that I should knee a boy in the crotch if he got too handsy.

Dad gave me a peck on the cheek and grabbed my overnight bag. "Glad to have you home."

My mother likewise gave me a peck, following it up with a tight hug that told me she'd been worrying about me. When I'd phoned my parents about the potential indictment, they'd been outraged. Justifiably so, if you asked me. When Mom finally released me, she held me by the shoulders and ran her eyes over me. "What a gorgeous coat!"

"Nick gave it to me for Christmas."

"Neiman's?"

"Yep."

"Shoo-ee," Dad said. "That coat must have cost a fortune. If that boy is spending that kind of money on you, he's got it bad."

Nick was hardly a boy, but yeah, I hoped he had it bad for me. I certainly had it bad for him.

The two helped me carry in my bags and gifts. As expected, the fresh-cut tree stood in its proper place, anchoring the large room with a festive presence. The smells of roasting beef, squash casserole, and yeast rolls mingled with the scent of pine in the air. My stomach growled in reply. *Rr-rowr-r.*

After stashing my gifts under the tree, I headed upstairs to my old bedroom to unpack. I'd just gotten settled in when the noises of my two brothers and their families arriving filtered up the staircase. If I didn't think I'd get caught, I would've slid down the banister like I'd done when I was young. Rather than risk my mother taking a wooden spoon to my hide, I settled for trotting down the steps.

My favorite niece, Jesse, stood at the bottom, dressed in her pink cowgirl boots and a green hand-me-down boys' coat that had once belonged to her older brother and was still a size too big. Not that she'd care, being the tomboy she was. I swooped her up in my arms and covered her tiny freckled face with kisses. She giggled and squirmed all the while.

My older and more girly nieces, Emma and Olivia, each received a hug and a kiss on the forehead.

I greeted my nephew Cole by pulling him down in a headlock and ruffling his hair. "Hey, squirt." I released him and grabbed Hayden. "Other squirt."

My sisters-in-law garnered hugs rather than noogies, while my brothers each received the usual punch in the arm.

Once everyone had wriggled out of their coats, Mom called us all to dinner. "Wash up! It's ready!"

The twelve of us gathered around the dining room table. We took one another's hands as Dad led us in a quick blessing. Several sets of eyes glanced my way when my father asked the man upstairs to help me through my current trials and tribulations. The minute the prayer ended, we dropped hands like they were hot potatoes and reached instead for the real hot potatoes. I sent the squash casserole around to my right, accepting a bowl of cranberry sauce from my sister-in-law to my left.

The table was quiet for a minute or two as we dug in.

"Delicious, as always," Dad said after he'd sampled a bite of everything on his plate.

My brothers grunted in agreement while the rest of us murmured various sentiments of appreciation.

We engaged in chitchat over the meal, the family catching me up on the local gossip and the kids' latest escapades. Hayden had his first crush on a girl in his class, which had to be true given how adamantly he denied it after his mother spilled the beans. Olivia got to sing a solo in the school choir concert. Jesse was sent to the principal's office for calling a boy a doo-doo head.

She crossed her little arms over her chest. "He pulled my hair first but the teacher didn't see him."

I reached out and tweaked her cheek. "Life isn't always fair, little one."

It sucked, but it was true. And the world was full of doo-doo heads.

When dinner was over, the women cleared the table, stored the leftovers in the refrigerator, and washed the dishes. The men removed the leaf from the dining room table and hauled in cut logs for the fireplace, stacking them on the hearth.

Mom wiped her hands on her apron and glanced at the clock on the oven. "Church starts in twenty minutes. We better get moving."

I rode to the church in my father's truck, sitting between my parents just as I'd done since I was little. My brothers and their wives followed in their cars.

The church parking lot was full, and we had to park on the adjacent horse pasture. The inside of the church was just as packed, parishioners sitting butt cheek to butt cheek on the pews. Jesse sat on my lap, swinging her feet in her pink cowgirl boots and unintentionally kicking me in the shins, trying her best not to fidget but failing miserably. I'd been the same way at her age. The promise of Christmas presents was too much to bear.

When the final "amen" was spoken, we made our way to the foyer, where Mom presented our pastor with a tin of her homemade pecan pralines.

He took one bite and declared them "sinfully delicious."

We returned to my parents' house. While my mother poured mugs of mulled wine and cocoa in the kitchen, the children scrambled about and divvied up the gifts, piling them in front of each family member, each exclaiming when they happened upon one with their name on it.

Mom returned with a loaded tray. Everyone grabbed a mug, settled back in their spots, and waited for my dad to give the signal. "On your mark, get set. . . ." Dad grinned as he tortured the children by making them wait.

"Go!" Jesse hollered, refusing to wait any longer.

We tore into our gifts like rabid wolves into a fresh kill. I scored a cuckoo clock for my kitchen, a box of peanut brittle, a bottle of vanilla-scented hand lotion, and a new scratching post for my cats. Jesse had fashioned me a colorful necklace out of yarn and painted macaroni. I slipped it on over my head. "Thanks, sweetie! I'll wear it every day."

Jesse beamed with pride. She ripped into my gift next, squealing when she realized it was the horse she'd been begging for. She launched herself at me, arms splayed wide in a full-body hug. When she realized I'd also bought her the barn and corral, purchased before I'd been fired, of course, she gave me another hug. "You're the best, Aunt Tara!"

When the gifts were all unwrapped and the paper had been collected and disposed of, the adults sat around the room chatting while the kids played with their new toys. My brothers and their wives talked about their kids and their jobs, carefully tiptoeing around the subject of my dismissal from the IRS. The matter was like an elephant in the room. And not just any old elephant. Like Dumbo, with giant ears, a yellow hat, and a ruffle around his neck.

I suppose I could've broken the ice by broaching the subject myself, but I wasn't much in the mood to talk about my job situation anyway.

When the children began to yawn and fuss, my brothers gathered up their families and a final round of hugs and kisses were distributed. I stepped onto the porch and watched them pack up and leave, jealous of the relatively simple lives they led. Maybe I should move back to Nacogdoches, get a simple bookkeeping job somewhere in town. I'd left my hometown to find excitement and, boy, had I found it. Gotta be careful what you wish for, huh?

After everyone had gone home, Mom and I washed, dried, and stowed the mugs. We left the remaining mulled cider in the Crock-Pot to keep warm overnight. The stuff only got better the longer it simmered, and we could finish it off tomorrow.

Mom gave me a hug before heading off to her bedroom. "Night, honey."

"Night."

I started upstairs to my bedroom but only got halfway before turning around and going back to the kitchen. I retrieved two of Mom's pecan pralines and put them on a plate. I ladled up a fresh mug of mulled cider from the Crock-Pot. I took them into the living room and left them on the hearth for Santa. I wasn't sure whether it was a good idea to serve alcohol to a man who'd be pulling an all-nighter flying a toy-filled sleigh, but surely his magical flying reindeer would make sure they stayed on course. Besides, it's not like the FAA would pull Santa over and arrest him for sleighing under the influence.

I went up to my room. My phone, which was charging on my dresser, bore a text message from Nick. *Nutty and I miss u.*

I typed in a reply text. *Back at ya.*

After brushing my teeth and changing into my faded flannel pajamas, I lay in my childhood bed, staring up at the ceiling, wondering where I'd be next Christmas Eve.

Would I be lying in this bed again? Or would I be lying on a thin mattress in a federal penitentiary, singing carols with my cellmate? If I was convicted, where would I end up? Would I be put in a club-fed-type low-security facility with tennis courts and art classes? Or, since the charge was excessive force, would I be considered a violent offender and thrown in the high-security clink with armed robbers and murderers?

So much for visions of sugarplums dancing in my head.

I slept fitfully and didn't venture downstairs until ten the next morning. I padded down in my pj's and a spare pair of ratty slippers I kept at my parents' house. My mother's smile and the smell of cedar logs burning in the fireplace greeted me.

"Hungry?" Mom asked, pulling out a chair for me at the dinette.

I slipped into the seat. "Hard to believe after all the pie I ate last night, but yeah."

My parents had already eaten their breakfast, though my mother had saved me a plate. She warmed it for me now in the microwave. While I ate, she puttered around the kitchen, sweeping the floor, wiping down the windowsills, straightening the pantry.

After sitting in the pot for four hours the coffee had grown bitter, but I poured a cup and drank it anyway. When I finished eating, I rinsed my dishes and stuck them in the dishwasher, then joined my father in the family room.

I glanced over at the hearth. The plate I'd left for Santa contained only a couple of praline crumbs and the mug was empty. Huh.

My dad sat kicked back in his recliner, nursing his own mug of leftover mulled wine. I plunked down on one end of the couch and Mom brought me a mug, too. Maybe these Christmas spirits would lift my spirits.

I stretched my feet out toward the fireplace, basking in the warmth from the burning logs. Since my brothers had married, they spent the first half of Christmas day at their own houses, then ate supper at the homes of their in-laws. Christmas day was quiet, just me and my parents. I kind of liked having my mom and dad to myself. What I didn't like was having time to think about my problems.

I sipped the mulled wine as I mulled over my predicament.

"You look worried," my mother said from her chair.

"So do you." I took another, bigger sip of the cider.

She sighed. "I am. But remember, honey. What doesn't kill us makes us stronger."

"I didn't kill Don Geils," I said, "but I certainly didn't make him stronger." After all, it's not like the bullet holes I put in his leg would fill in with titanium.

Mom narrowed her eyes. "Are you sassing me?"

I raised my mug of hot wine. "I'm a little too old to have my mouth washed out with Ivory soap."

"Don't be so sure."

"Sorry." Really, she was trying to be supportive. When would I learn to keep my mouth shut?

"Have you checked your stocking?" Dad asked.

I glanced over at the fireplace where my stocking hung. The solitary stocking was a long red one my mother had crocheted for me when I was a kid. Sure enough, the stocking bore telltale bulges. I set my mug on the coffee table and pulled my stocking from the hook on the mantel. The fire warmed my back as I took a seat on the hearth.

Reaching inside, I pulled out the loot. A bottle of Chanel No. 5, my signature scent. A blue scarf my mother had knitted for me. A Ken doll and a plastic egg of Silly Putty. Holy crap! Had my mother known I'd used the putty to make a penis for my Ken doll when I was young? How embarrassing!

I looked up to find her watching me.

"Is that a Barbie doll?" she asked.

I turned the front of the box her way. "Ken," I said. I held up the Silly Putty. "This, too."

She frowned. "How on earth did those things get in your stocking?"

"You didn't put them there?"

"No."

My father raised his palms in a declaration of innocence.

If neither of them had put the toys in my stocking, then who did? Could the toys really have been from Santa? Or had they been put in my stocking by my brothers as a joke?

I pushed the ridiculous thoughts out of my mind. Of course it had been my brothers. Right?

The final item in my stocking was a box of ammo. I checked the box. "These bullets are for a long-range rifle."

Dad reached behind the couch and pulled out a long, rectangular box. He held it out to me, offering me a grin at the same time. "Here you go, hon. Merry Christmas."

I took the box from him and opened it. Inside was a Winchester Super X rifle, an autoloading repeating model with a gas-operation system to reduce recoil. "Hot damn!"

Nothing like some firepower to lift a girl's spirits.

Dad stood from his chair. "What say we give it a try?"

He didn't have to ask twice. I ran upstairs and changed into a pair of jeans, a sweatshirt, and an old pair of ropers I found in the back of my closet. What the hell. I was so excited I slid down the banister.

Spying me from the kitchen, my mother put her hands on her hips. "What have I told you about sliding down the railing?"

"Sorry!" I dashed past her and out the back door.

Dad was already waiting for me on the porch. "I've attached a scope and set up some targets."

We went out the gate that led from the backyard into the hayfields. Dad had posted a target on a round hay bale four hundred yards away. He'd brought one of his own long-range rifles with him, too.

I loaded my new gun, stepped into place, and gathered my focus, aiming for the bull's-eye. Yep. Got it in sight. I squeezed the trigger. *Bang!*

Dad raised his field glasses to his eyes.

I looked up at him. "How'd I do?"

"See for yourself." He held the glasses out to me.

I squinted through them. Not only had I hit the bull's eye; I'd hit it smack center. I may have lost my job and my sanity, but I hadn't lost my marksman skills. Maybe I could get a job with the rodeo, do a show like Annie Oakley used to do, shoot an apple off the top of someone's head. I doubted such a gig would pay much, though. Heck, I'd probably have to send around a hat for tips. Someone would try to stiff me; I'd shoot him and end up right back where I was now.

Dang.

chapter fifteen

𝒮ayonara

I drove back to Dallas early the day after Christmas, leaving before sunup with a thermos full of coffee and a couple of Mom's greasy homemade biscuits. No time to stay and enjoy them with an artery-clogging covering of gravy. The grand jury would be back at work today, deciding my fate. I could only pray they were feeling kind and forgiving this morning.

I fretted anxiously the entire drive, nearly chewing a hole in the inside of my cheek constantly checking my cell phone to see if I'd missed a call or text from my attorney. What if the grand jury decided there was enough evidence against me to proceed to trial? I was no stranger to the courtroom, of course. I'd testified a number of times in tax cases. But I'd never been the one on trial. All of those procedures and processes designed to protect the rights of the accused had once seemed to be nothing more than unnecessary and annoying legal hoops we'd been forced to jump through to nail the bad guys. Now, however, those protections felt flimsy and fragile.

I'd always had faith in the judicial system. But could I count on it now?

Even after sunrise the sky remained gray and dark. A light rain fell from the sky, occasionally changing to sleet when I drove through a colder, open area. The dreary weather fit my mood perfectly. With any luck, I'd hit a patch of ice, slide off the road, and enjoy a quick death.

Ugh.

I really needed to stop thinking like that.

Nick, too, had risen with the sun to head back from Houston. He was flying out in the afternoon for Tokyo, and this would be our last chance to see each other until he returned on New Year's Eve. Nick couldn't have picked a worse time to be out of the country. Not that he'd picked the time, but still. I needed him here. I was terrified. So terrified I felt frantic and nauseated, as if I'd drunk ten *venti* full-caff lattes.

I made a brief stop at my place to check on the cats, then walked down to Nick's place. The *pings* and *pops* coming from the engine of his pickup truck told me he'd just arrived home. The motor hadn't had time to cool yet.

I knocked on his door and he opened it immediately.

"Any word yet?" he asked by way of greeting, his face drawn.

"Not yet."

He stepped back to let me into his foyer. "Maybe no news is good news."

I bent down to greet Nutty with an ear ruffle. "I hope you're right."

I'd brought back some of my mother's leftover Christmas roast and made the three of us an early lunch of roast beef and mayonnaise sandwiches. Nutty finished his in four bites. For an old dog with nubby teeth and bad gums he still had quite an appetite.

When we'd finished eating, I reached into my purse and pulled out the envelope containing the eight-by-ten photograph of me with Santa. I handed the paper sleeve to Nick. "For you."

He glanced at the photo studio's logo on the envelope and raised a hopeful brow. "Boudoir photos?"

"Not exactly."

He slid the picture out, took a look, and gave me his chipped-tooth grin. "I don't know. Seeing you sitting on Santa's lap still turns me on. Is that weird?"

"Lord, yes." I gave a mock shudder.

He walked over to his fridge and affixed the photograph to the front of it with a promotional magnet from a real estate agency. "So? What did you ask Santa for?"

"A new job."

"Darn," Nick said. "I was hoping you'd asked him for some lace panties."

"Nah. Nutty would just chew them up."

"True."

I stood to put our plates in the dishwasher. "Guess what? Santa told me I made his 'nice' list."

"See?" Nick replied, reaching out to chuck me under the chin. "I told you not to feel guilty about shooting Geils."

"Santa may not have a problem with it," I said, "but there's no guarantee a jury will feel the same way."

"Maybe you can get Santa to testify on your behalf as a character witness."

If only.

"How did it go with *Entrepreneur* magazine?" I asked, knowing Nick had planned to call the publisher to determine whether Sundaram had used a credit card to pay for his subscription. If Nick could obtain a valid credit card number, he could have the card activity traced.

"No luck," Nick replied. "Sundaram used a debit card linked to a bank account that was closed months ago."

"Darn. Well, maybe another lead will turn up soon."

We rounded up Nutty for the ride to the airport. He liked riding in the car, sticking his head out the window and barking at passing cars for fun. Of course we had to crank the heater up full blast to combat the frigid air flowing in. At least the rain had broken temporarily.

On the drive over, my cell phone rang. I yanked it from the cup holder where I'd stashed it for easy access in anticipation of my attorney's call.

I looked down at the readout. "It's Eddie," I said, handing

the phone to Nick. The roads were slick. No sense taking unnecessary chances by also talking on my cell phone.

Nick punched the button to accept the call and put Eddie on speaker, holding the phone up where the mic could pick up my voice.

"Hey, Eddie!" I called out.

All I got in reply was the soft sounds of him chatting with his wife and one of his daughters asking if they could stop for pizza.

"Yo. Eddie. You there?"

Still nothing.

"Eddie Munster. Eddie Van Halen." I raised my voice and hollered, "Eddie spaghetti!"

Nutty pulled his head back into the car and joined in, giving a loud, *Arf!*

Still nothing.

Nick jabbed the button to end the call and set the phone back in the cup holder. "Eddie told me Sandra was getting him a new phone for Christmas. He must've butt-dialed you."

"Is Eddie taking your same flight to Tokyo?" I asked.

"Eddie's not coming."

"Really? Why not?"

"Too busy with new cases. We're all swamped. Besides, Lu didn't feel like she could justify the cost of sending two agents to Japan and India. We drew straws and I got the travel."

I knew I had no right to feel hurt, but I did. I needed Nick here now, with me, supporting me. I'd only face criminal charges once.

At least I hoped it would only be once.

"When did y'all decide this?"

Nick looked my way and, as if reading my mind, answered, "Before you heard from Troy Kerr. If we'd known what you'd be going through now, Eddie would've taken the trips. I don't like leaving you all alone in the middle of all this shit."

"It's okay. The shit will still be here when you get back." It might even be deeper by then. "Did you listen to the Japanese CDs on your drive?"

"Sure did," Nick said. "Not sure it did me much good, though. The language seems to be all vowels. *Ah. Eh. Uh. Oh. Ooh.* It sounds like you when you're having an orgasm."

"Nick! Jeez!" My cheeks flared up like a barbecue grill.

He cut me a grin. "Hey, I never said I didn't like it. It's nice to know my efforts are appreciated."

At the airport, Nick held me in a long hug, his face buried in my hair. "I wish you were coming with me."

"Me, too."

"I bet I could find some lifer in the prison who'd be willing to shank Geils in the shower. Want me to look into it?"

"The same thought crossed my mind." While I was sitting in church during the Christmas Eve service, no less. I probably should have been ashamed of myself for that, but I wasn't. I was ashamed at not feeling ashamed, though, so that should count for something, right?

Nick stepped back. "I'll be looking forward to seeing you on New Year's Eve."

"I've got a new dress." I'd bought it before I'd been fired. It was a gorgeous evening gown in a shimmery golden fabric.

"Can't wait to see you in it," he said. His lips spread in another grin, this one more subtle, more sexy. "Can't wait to see you out of it, either. I've got plans that'll put you on Santa's 'naughty' list next year for sure."

Mm-m . . .

Nick made me promise to text him the instant I learned the grand jury's decision. With one last warm kiss, he climbed out of my car and grabbed his suitcase from the backseat. He gestured through the glass for me to unroll the window. When I did, he leaned back in and gave me a wink. "Sayonara."

chapter sixteen

$\mathcal{S}$anta Comes Through

I pulled the collar up on my new coat as I exited the airport. The day was colder than a witch's tit and still drizzly. Uneven patches of ice had begun to form on the road and sidewalks. If this winter weather kept up, Traffic Control would have to commandeer a Zamboni from the Galleria's skating rink.

As I walked through the short-term parking lot, trying to remember where the heck I'd parked my car—level three? Four?—my cell phone bleeped. I yanked it from my pocket. The screen read: LOBO. Damn! Not that I wasn't happy to hear from my former boss, but waiting to find out the grand jury's decision was killing me.

I jabbed the button to accept the call, noting it was time to replace my Christmas manicure. The candy cane stripes on my fingernails had been cute, but the edges were now chipped. Besides, I wanted to get a glamorous and sexy style for New Year's.

"Hey, Lu."

"Come see me!" she barked. "I got a job for you."

"You do?" My heart whirled in my chest like a figure skater executing a camel spin. "George Burton changed his mind?"

"Slow down there. I said I've got 'a' job for you. I didn't say it was your old job."

My spinning heart went off-kilter and fell to the frozen ice, momentum causing it to career into the wall like an Olympian who'd just lost all hope of a medal. "What is it, then?"

"Come into the office and we'll talk about it."

I drove to the IRS building, circling the lot until I reached my usual spot next to Eddie's minivan. The parking place was occupied by a mid-sized white SUV with stick-figure decals on the back window indicating a man, a woman, three boys, and a dog. Hm-m . . .

I drove on until I found a narrow spot under a tree. As I climbed out of my car, the crows perched on the now-leafless tree cackled with birdie laughter. I knew what their caws meant. *Hey, dumb ass! Thanks for parking your car here so we can crap all over it.* If I'd had my gun, I would've scared them off with a warning shot. Without my gun, I had to settle for calling, "Shoo!" and flapping my arms ineffectually. One had the nerve to dive-bomb me.

Before setting off, I cast them a final glare. "Jerks."

I went inside, stopping at Security and having to wait in the longer civilian line rather than the shorter, expedited employee lane. When both me and my purse had been scanned and found to pass muster, I rode up in the elevator to the Criminal Investigations Division.

Ding! The doors slid open and there I was. Back home, in a sense. Except now I was only a guest here, no longer a permanent resident. What's that old saying? Oh yeah. "You can't go home again."

I hate that old saying.

I stepped out and headed down the hall. Viola eyed me over the top of her bifocals and computer monitor as I approached. "Good morning, Tara."

I stepped up to her desk. "It's great to see you, Vi."

"You, too." She angled her head to indicate Lu's door, which was cracked open a couple of inches. "Go on in. She's waiting for you."

"Thanks."

I rapped on the door to announce my arrival and proceeded inside. The Lobo sat behind her massive desk, enjoying a pink-frosted donut.

Busted.

"What happened to the diet?" I asked.

She tossed her free hand in the air as she took another bite. "Between the pumpkin pie and Christmas cookies, I blew it. I'll start again after New Year's." She motioned for me to take a seat and I slid into one of her wing chairs.

She ran her eyes over my coat. "Nice. Is that new?"

"Christmas gift," I said.

"From Nick?" she asked.

I nodded.

She leaned back in her chair, a frown dragging her orange-painted lips downward. "That boy hasn't been the same since you've been gone."

Nick was hardly a boy, but I knew Lu used the term as a sign of affection rather than an insult. "What do you mean?"

She took another bite of donut. "He's off his mojo."

I wasn't sure exactly what she meant by that, but I'd already gotten myself fired. The last thing I wanted was to jeopardize Nick's job, too. "He'll adjust," I said. "I'm sure he'll be back on his mojo soon."

"I hope so," she said. "Things are busier than ever around here. I need all my agents to be at their best."

I mentioned the pending order from Tokyo Discount Telecom, the delivery that was to take place at my town house. It didn't seem fair to keep the information from her.

Lu considered the situation for a moment. "I suppose it can't hurt if all you do is accept some boxes. No sense in me throwing a monkey wrench in things."

Lu popped the last piece of pink donut in her mouth, pulled a sticky note off the pad on her desk, and held it out to me.

The note contained the name *Clyde Hartford* and an address in Fort Worth, a city thirty miles to the west of Dallas. Fort Worth, the official "Gateway to the West," was known for its historical stockyards, Billy Bob's country-western nightclub, and the National Cowgirl Museum and Hall of Fame. Though looked upon by some as Dallas' less sophisticated country cousin, Fort Worth was actually a thriving cultural center, featuring the world-renowned Kimbell Art Museum and Bass Hall, an ornate white stone theater downtown. The city's Colonial Country Club hosted an annual golf tournament that drew visitors from all over the globe. I ventured west to Fort Worth on occasion for a concert or when Alicia dragged me to an art exhibition.

"Clyde and I go way back," Lu said. "We worked together in the audit department for years before I transferred to Criminal Investigations. He's the head of the Fort Worth audit office now. I gave him a call and he says they can use you over there."

Several thoughts went through my head. The first was, *Do I want to work as an auditor?* The second thought was, *Don't be an idiot! Your mortgage is due in a matter of days, and you'll be left with just enough in your bank account to survive a couple of months. Take the job!* My final thought came out of my mouth. "Is George Burton okay with this?"

Lu pursed her lips. "I had to work on him, remind him that this agency invested thousands in your training. But he said as long as we don't put a gun in your hand you're welcome to come back to the IRS."

I had mixed feelings about Burton's comment, but I wasn't about to pass up this opportunity. Not only would it get my foot back in the door, it also might help with my criminal case. The fact that the IRS hired me back would make me look like less of a pariah. Auditing might not be so bad. It would be more routine work, surely less stressful. That was a good thing, right? Then again, I thrived on stress. I got a charge out of knowing my targets were bad guys, looked forward to taking them down, playing real-life cops and robbers. Still, just like Nick would have to get used to me not working in Criminal Investigations, I'd have to adjust, too.

"Did you mention the civil lawsuit and the excessive force case?" I asked.

"Of course I did." Lu pursed her lips again, though this time her eyes blazed with mischief. "Then again, I might've forgotten." She winked a false eyelash at me.

My heart sank. I couldn't let Lu get herself in trouble over me. "Lu, I can't let you—"

She cut me off with a karate chop motion of her hand and a pointed gaze. "You're not trying to tell me what to do, are you?"

"I wouldn't dare," I said. "But—"

"But nothing!" she barked. "I feel partly responsible for your predicament. If I hadn't assigned you to that damn case none of this would have ever happened."

I opened my mouth to protest further, but her narrowed eyes told me I'd best remain silent.

"You put your life on the line for this agency. Getting you a transfer to the audit department is the least I could do." Lu ran her tongue over her orange lips, removing the remnants of pink frosting, then dabbed at her mouth with a napkin. "Clyde says to head on over Monday and he'll get you set up."

The Lobo had put herself on the line for me when she'd asked Clyde to give me a job and sought approval from George Burton. I wouldn't let her down. I stood to go. "Thanks, Lu. I really appreciate this."

"You're welcome," she replied. "Now scat. I've got work to do."

After I left Lu's office, I figured I'd poke my head around and say hello to some of the other agents, let them know I'd landed on my feet. Or, more precisely, that I'd been hauled back to my feet by Lu.

I headed down the hall, stopping between Nick's office and the one directly across the hall that used to be mine. With Nick in Tokyo, his office was empty and dark. My office, however, was lit and occupied. Sitting at my desk was a thirtyish black guy with short hair, a green-and-brown-striped tie, and a gold band on the ring finger of his left hand. On my bookshelf—make that *his* bookshelf—stood a framed portrait of him with his wife and three sons, ranging in age from toddler to 'tween. Situated around the family portrait were framed photos of his oldest son with a shiny trombone, the middle son in a basketball uniform, and the youngest on a wooden rocking horse.

Seeing my replacement in my office was like being hit with an emotional wrecking ball. I'd held out hope that one day I'd return to criminal investigations. Heck, The Lobo had kept Nick's office vacant and waiting for him for three whole years while he'd been a wanted federal fugitive in forced exile in Mexico. But she'd put the new agent in my office, a sure sign she didn't truly expect me to come back.

Time for me to face facts, huh?

The agent looked up from his laptop, his intelligent brown eyes assessing me. "Can I help you?"

"Um . . . sorry. I didn't mean to interrupt you. This used to be my office."

He stood. "You're Tara Holloway?"

I nodded.

"I heard what happened." He cocked his head. "Why didn't you just kill the guy?"

If I heard that question one more time I'd tie a cinder block around my waist and throw myself into the Trinity River. I clenched my teeth to keep from screaming, hoped my grimace could pass for a smile, and shrugged.

He opened the top drawer of his desk, pulled out a silver pen, and offered it to me. "I found this yesterday behind the filing cabinet."

I took the pen from him. Engraved on the side was *IRS Special Agent Tara Holloway*. My parents had given me the pen as a gift when I successfully completed special agent training earlier in the year. The pen had disappeared a couple of months ago. I must've set it on top of the file cabinet and it rolled off behind it.

"Thanks," I said. "I'd been wondering where this went."

He held out a hand now. "I'm William Dorsey. I transferred from the Tucson collections office."

"Collections, huh?" That meant he was a rookie special agent, just as I'd been when I started with the IRS this past spring. I shook his hand. "What did you think of the special agent training?"

He groaned. "It kicked my ass."

I didn't want to like this guy, but I couldn't help myself. He seemed genuine and friendly. Besides, it wasn't his fault I'd been fired.

"Well . . . welcome to Criminal Investigations. I hope you'll be as happy here as I was."

Oh, Lord. I blinked back tears as I rushed out of the office. Leaning against the wall in the corridor, I fought to regain my composure. *Deep breath. Deep breath. Okay. Good.*

I continued down the hall, stopping briefly to greet Josh Schmidt, the office's technical expert, before moving on to Eddie's digs.

Eddie was on his phone as I stepped into his doorway, but he gave me a wave in greeting and gestured for me to come inside. Like Agent Dorsey, Eddie was black and married with children. A pang of jealousy sliced through me when I realized Eddie would probably prefer William as a partner. The two of them had much more in common than Eddie and I ever had.

"Exactly," Eddie said into his phone. He paused a moment. "I can give you until the third, but that's it." Another pause. "Okay. I'll keep an eye out for the paperwork." He hung up his phone.

"Fun case?" I asked.

He tossed the file into his in-box. "Not at all. Sorry about the butt dialing, by the way."

I shrugged. "No biggie." I slid into one of his wing chairs. "I met William Dorsey. He seems like a nice guy."

"He is," Eddie said. "Much nicer than you ever were."

"Ass."

"He can't handle his Glock as well as you, though."

"Neither can you."

Eddie raised a brow. "Now who's being an ass?"

Touché.

Eddie tilted his head. "What brings you by?"

"Lu called me in. She pulled some strings and got me a position with the audit department in Fort Worth."

Eddie leaned back in his chair, folding his hands across his ribs. "Auditing in Fort Worth, huh? The commute will suck, but otherwise that could be an okay job."

It *could* be an okay job. The problem was, I didn't want an okay job. I wanted an exciting job, one where I could put bad guys out of business, where I could be a hero of sorts. "I guess I just thought that . . . you know . . . maybe some-day . . ."

I didn't finish my sentence, but I didn't have to. Eddie knew exactly where I'd been going.

Eddie sighed and rubbed a hand across his forehead before looking me directly in the eye. "Tara, as much as I hate to say this, I think it's best if you let go of your hopes and move on."

I knew Eddie wasn't trying to hurt me. He was only trying to be honest. Still, his words were like a punch to my gut.

"I came to the same conclusion myself when I saw Dorsey in my office." I stood to go. "The grand jury is meet-ing as we speak, deciding whether to indict me."

Eddie groaned. "No shit?"

"No shit."

"Let me know how that turns out the minute you know something." Eddie stood now, too. "And stay in touch, okay?"

"Sure. Maybe I'll come across some good cases I can send your way."

We stared at each other for a moment, unsaid words pass-ing between us. In the few short months Eddie and I had been partners, we'd been through a lot together. I'd been slashed by a nut wielding a box cutter. Eddie had been shot in the head. A violent target had threatened Eddie and his family, forcing them into hiding. Terrorists had come after Eddie and me with explosives. Together we'd taken down an abusive tax preparer who called herself the Deduction Diva and had come after us with a letter opener. Frankly, her enor-mous breasts had been more scary than the blade. They'd been like the Grand Tetons coming at us in an avalanche of flesh. Eddie and I might not be partners anymore, but the bond we'd formed working together was still intact.

I stepped to the doorway, stopping to look back. "We had some good times, didn't we?"

"The best," Eddie said. "Take care of yourself, okay?"

I pretended not to notice the slight crack in his voice. "I will."

chapter seventeen

$\mathcal{T}$ruth and Consequences

As I exited the IRS office, my cell phone bleeped. I checked the readout. *Hairy Ass.*

It was the moment of truth.

Light-headed with emotion, I punched the "accept" button. "What did the grand jury decide?" I was too anxious for niceties.

The caller turned out not to be Anthony Giacomo but his secretary. She said that Anthony wanted to see me as soon as possible.

My pulse kicked into double time as I repeated the question, hoping she could provide me an answer. "The grand jury. What did they decide?"

"He didn't say."

Damn!

I ran to my crow-crap-covered car, hopped in, and activated the wipers to remove the white droppings impeding my vision. Stupid birds! I drove the few blocks to the skyscraper that housed Gertz, Gertz, and Schwartz. Tires squealing, I whipped into the garage, parked, and leaped from my car as if I'd been ejected. I sprinted to the elevator. I jabbed the "up arrow" button eleven times in quick succession—like that was going to help anything—and climbed on, silently cursing each person for whom the car stopped on my way up.

I dashed across the foyer of the firm to the receptionist's desk, hovering over her as she buzzed Anthony's office. She looked up at me as she spoke to him. "Tara Holloway is here to see you." She paused a moment. "I'll send her back."

I didn't wait for her to give me the okay. I shoved open the glass doors leading back to the offices and raced down the hall, nearly colliding with a clerk pushing a mail cart.

"Sorry!" I called back over my shoulder as I hurried on.

Momentum nearly carried me past Giacomo's office, and I grabbed his doorjamb to slow myself, spinning halfway around as I entered his office.

I grasped the back of his wing chair, holding on tight, my fingers digging into the fabric. "What did they decide?"

From his throne behind his desk Anthony offered a placating smile. "Take a seat, Tara."

I stepped around to the front of the wing chair and dropped into it. My knees quivered and my hands shook like an addict coming off a bender.

Anthony leaned back and put his palms together as if he were praying. "The grand jury voted to indict you."

Holy shit. I was going to be put on trial.

Fireflies darted around in my peripheral vision. My lungs began to spasm and I gasped for breath. *Uh-huh-uh-huh-uh-huh!* Sheez. I sounded like Nutty after he'd struggled up the stairs.

Anthony came around his desk, put a hand on my back, and forced my face down between my knees. "Take deep breaths, Tara. Everything is going to be fine."

Easy for him to say. He wasn't the one facing the possibility of several years in prison. Win or lose, he'd still collect his fee, he'd still have his freedom. Then again, I should cut the guy some slack. He'd agreed to see me on short notice and the timing of my case was obviously screwing up his holiday vacation plans.

I forced myself to take full, slow breaths. A couple of minutes later, when the fireflies had flown off, I sat up.

Anthony leaned back against his desk in front of me. "The threshold for going to trial is extremely low, Tara. We talked about that. Remember?"

Of course I remembered. But when he'd mentioned it I faced only the possibility of being indicted. Now I was facing the reality of it. It was no longer a question of "if" I was going to trial; it was a question of "when." I supposed I'd been hanging on to some shred of hope that the grand jury would decide to give me a break. Didn't they know I was on Santa's "nice" list?

Anthony reached out and put a hand on my shoulder, looking into my eyes. "We'll win at trial, Tara. Don't you worry."

Don't worry? my mind shrieked. *Are you crazy?*

He walked back around his desk. "We'll need to be in court first thing Monday morning for your arraignment. We'll plead not guilty, of course. I expect the judge will require only a small bail, if any, and will release you on your own recognizance, but there's always the outside chance the judge will order you to be immediately arrested. You should arrange for someone to take care of your bills, check your mail, that type of thing."

Despite my best efforts to stay calm, I began to tremble again.

"I know this is frightening for you," my attorney said, "but I've been through this hundreds of times before. It's standard procedure."

I closed my eyes and put my hands over my face for a moment, giving myself one final moment to freak out before forcing aside my terror and summoning my courage to replace it.

I was Tara Holloway, dammit. I was no stranger to conflict and adversity. Hell, I'd faced down money launderers, drug dealers, and murderers and lived to brag about it. A federal criminal trial? Ha! This was nothing. Small potatoes compared to what I'd dealt with.

Nerves settled and resolve mustered, I opened my eyes. "All right. Where do we go from here?"

"We start preparing for trial." He situated his legal pad and held a pen, the fingers of each hand pinching a respective tip. "I need a list of people who would make good witnesses on your behalf. The local cop who worked the case with your team. The other federal agents who were on duty that night. Your supervisor at the bar who phoned you when the fight broke out. What was his name?"

"Merle Vasilakis. You can reach him at the Guys and Dolls Dinner Theater."

Anthony jotted notes, adding phone numbers as I provided him with both Nick's cell and home numbers and scrolled through the contact list on my cell phone to find numbers for DEA Agent Christina Marquez, Lieutenant Aaron Menger of Dallas PD, and Guys & Dolls.

When Anthony finished writing the numbers down, he looked up at me. "Their prime witnesses are likely to be Don Geils and the officer who led the SWAT team. They might even call Wesley Prescott since he was in the room when the shooting occurred."

With the help of Geils and his bartender, Prescott had drugged Christina with a glass of tainted champagne and dragged her into the strip club's private VIP room, where he planned to do unspeakable things to her while she lay unconscious, unable to defend herself. By the time I'd made it to the room, the sick bastard already had removed her blouse and covered her with bite marks.

Anthony continued. "Since Christina was unconscious, she won't be able to testify to what exactly happened in the VIP room. Besides Geils and Prescott, you were the only other one there. I don't normally like to put my clients on the stand, but, depending on how things go at the trial, you might have to testify in your own defense."

I forced down the fist-sized lump that had formed in my throat despite the courage I'd attempted to summon. I'd testified in tax fraud cases before, so I knew the drill. Still, serving as a witness against some jackass who'd cheated the government and serving as a witness in my own defense would be two totally different things.

"We'll run through some practices to prepare you," Anthony said. "You'll do great."

I hoped so. Everything was riding on this trial.

My freedom.

My future.

My relationship with Nick.

This trial had the potential to change the entire course of the rest of my life. If I was convicted, the state board of accountancy would yank my license, and then what? I'd never work in accounting again, yet I wasn't qualified to do anything else. Who would hire a convicted felon? If I was lucky enough to even find a job after I was released from prison, I'd end up doing some type of unfulfilling, menial work, like picking up garbage or stocking shelves at night at a discount store, where the manager would ride herd over the "violent felon" they'd hired.

"What about your boss at the IRS?" Anthony asked.

"Lu?" I thought for a moment. "She's always been supportive. She's fighting for me to get back my job in Criminal Investigations and got me reassigned to the audit department in the meantime." But if The Lobo testified on my behalf in court, would that mean she'd have to address my history with the service? The many times I'd used my gun? Wouldn't that hurt my case? Still, it was my attorney's job to collect as much information as he could, talk to every potential witness, before deciding how to present my defense. It couldn't hurt for him to talk with her. I provided him with her phone number, too.

He made a final note before setting his pen down. "I have to warn you," Anthony said. "Now that Kerr has decided to go forward with this trial, he is going to milk this case for all it's worth. This trial is going to get a lot of media attention. If any reporters corner you, smile and tell them your attorney has advised you not to speak about the case until you've been acquitted. Got that?"

I nodded. It was all I could do. That lump in my throat had swelled to the point that I feared my esophagus might explode.

"The media will probably try to catch you going into work, and they'll surely try to catch you at home. Do you have somewhere you can hide out until this blows over?"

I nodded again. I could stay at Nick's. It was only a half block down from my town house, but if I drove into the neighborhood the back way and parked in his garage I could likely avoid detection.

Finished, my attorney stood and came around the desk, taking my hand in his and holding it up in an act of strength and solidarity. "We are going to give Troy Kerr the fight of his life. When we're done, he'll be sorry he ever messed with either of us."

I forced a smile.

"Keep your chin up, okay?"

I swallowed the lump. "I'll do my best."

chapter eighteen

The Show Must Go On . . .
and So Must I

With a final reassuring pat on the back, my attorney passed me off to his secretary. The woman prepared a power of attorney giving my parents the right to manage my financial affairs in the event of my incarceration. She asked to see my driver's license, jotted down the number in her public notary book, and stamped the document with her official notary seal. After sliding the paperwork into a manila envelope she held it out to me. "Here you go."

"Thanks." I returned to the elevator and stepped into the car. When I reached the garage, I shuffled forward like a zombie, my mind in a haze.

I needed Nick. Now. But he was up in the air somewhere, flying to Tokyo. Damn! Now I knew how Brett felt when I hadn't been available for him when he needed me.

I texted Nick the news in two succinct words. *Indicted.*%$&!

I phoned Christina. Might as well warn her that she'd be contacted by Giacomo to testify in the case. Unfortunately, I only got her voice mail. I left a quick message.

I phoned Eddie next. "The grand jury indicted me. I'm going to trial on excessive force charges."

"Oh, hell, Tara. That's screwed up."

"You're telling me."

He was silent a moment as he processed the information. "What can I do to help? Can I testify on your behalf?"

Though Eddie hadn't worked the investigation at Guys & Dolls, as my partner on numerous previous cases Eddie knew better than anyone how I operated under pressure. He'd seen me shoot a box cutter out of the hand of a target who was attacking me. Eddie knew I exercised remarkable restraint given the violent criminals we faced on a regular basis.

"Would you?" I asked. Eddie's testimony could be critical in getting me a shorter sentence if I was convicted.

"Of course. Give me your lawyer's number."

I rattled off the phone number.

"Have you told Nick yet?" Eddie asked.

"I texted him. He's on his flight to Tokyo as we speak."

"He'll go ballistic," Eddie said.

"Would you tell Lu for me?" I wasn't up to telling her about this latest development. I knew she'd be concerned about me, but I felt guilty. She'd hired me, convinced the audit department to take me on now. How would my actions reflect on her?

"Be glad to," Eddie said.

When I phoned my parents with the news, the quaver in my mother's voice told me she was fighting sobs but trying to stay strong for me.

"Don't worry yourself over this, hon," she said, though obviously she was worried herself. "Everything will come out at trial and you'll be exonerated."

I wished I could share her faith.

My father declared my indictment a travesty of justice and a waste of taxpayer money. "I don't know what that prosecutor is thinking, taking you to trial. I have half a mind to call our congressman."

I convinced him that making the call would only make

matters worse. Besides, though I appreciated his concern, I was much too old to have my daddy fighting my battles for me. Nevertheless, my parents insisted on driving out to Dallas to support me.

"We'll hit the road Sunday just as soon as we get out of church," my mother said.

Nick called soon after while he was on his layover at LAX. "This is bullshit, Tara. Pure bullshit!" His words were tinged with equal parts anger and frustration, though his tone softened a moment later. "How are you holding up?"

"As well as can be expected, I guess." Hearing Nick's voice made his absence more acute. What I wouldn't give to have his strong arms around me right then. But no sense putting the guy on a guilt trip. "My arraignment is Monday morning. Anthony said it's unlikely I'll be denied bail, but you'll come visit me in jail if I am, right?"

"Hell yeah," Nick said. "I'll bake you a cake with a file inside."

"Make it chocolate," I said. "With sprinkles on top."

As I hung up the phone, it hit me that if I was convicted and sent to jail Nick would be forced to put his life on hold, too. He'd already lost three years when he'd been in forced exile in Mexico. It would be unfair to expect him to wait for me. I had no right to ask that of him. But the thought of him moving on, of him falling in love with another woman . . . Hell, they might as well execute me.

Early that evening, I tried making sushi with the kit Nick had bought me for Christmas. Of course I was too lazy to make a trip to the grocery store, so I improvised with things I found in my fridge. The roast beef sushi wasn't bad, though the hot dog sushi was a wretched combination. Fortunately, Nutty made short work of it when I fed it to him. Not a picky eater, that dog. Henry watched from the kitchen doorway, a look of disgust on his face that I'd let a dog into my house. At least Henry'd grown accustomed enough to having Nutty around that he no longer hissed incessantly. Annie still gave the dog wide berth, though Nutty had no interest in chasing her.

Around seven, the walls began to close in on me and a sense of loneliness permeated every cell of my body. All of my friends were tied up with holiday visits and Alicia wouldn't be back until later tonight, so I was on my own for the evening. I took Nutty back to Nick's place so he could use the doggy door to relieve himself during the evening, and decided to drop by Guys & Dolls and see the show. My former supervisor, Merle, now owned the place, along with his new wife, Bernice.

The last time I'd been to the club was the night of the shooting. A mix of feelings hit me as I pulled into the parking lot.

Fear.

Anxiety.

Disgust.

Horror.

Rage.

But no guilt.

I *wasn't* guilty, was I? I hadn't overreacted the night I'd shot Don Geils. In fact, I'd exercised control by holding back and only shooting him in the leg.

Santa was right. I belonged on his "nice" list.

Maddie, the former stripper who now worked as a fully clothed hostess, let me in for free. Every ticket had been sold, but she rounded up a barstool for me to sit on along the back wall. Probably a fire code violation, but what the heck.

I gave the young woman a smile. "Thanks, Maddie."

She smiled back. "Enjoy the show."

When they'd taken over the club after Geils' arrest, Merle and Bernice had removed the stripper poles from the stage and hauled off the nude statuary, though they'd left the black-and-gold art deco furniture and accents in place. Without the bare cleavage bouncing all about, the club now had a classy, retro feel to it.

While they'd been running *Mary Poppins* for a couple of weeks now, tonight's performance was a variety show featuring an assortment of local talent including singers, a magician, a comedian, and a tap-dancing trio. For the closing number, Bernice, a former Vegas showgirl and exotic dancer of indeterminate age, took the stage in a champagne-colored evening gown the same shade as her carefully coiffed locks. A gray-haired man in a tuxedo took a seat at the black baby grand piano at the back of the stage. Bernice stepped up to the old-fashioned standing microphone and launched into a stunning and emotional rendition of Etta James' song "At Last." As Bernice sang the final stanza, she gestured for her new husband, Merle, to join her onstage. Merle, who could pass for an aged Charlie Brown with his bald head and boxy build, blushed as his bride serenaded him.

It had taken decades for the two to make their way to each other, but I had no doubt nothing would ever again keep them apart.

When the show was over, the crowd leaped to their feet and gave Bernice a well-deserved standing ovation. She responded with a smile and curtsy, then turned to Merle and gave him a big kiss on the cheek.

As the crowd gathered up their things and strolled out, Merle and Bernice wandered over my way.

"Great show," I told them, fighting a smile when I noticed the red lipstick smudge on Merle's cheek. "There was something for everyone."

"It's sold out every night," Bernice said. "We can hardly believe it."

I offered them a smile. "Congratulations. You deserve every success." After putting up with Don Geils, hell, the two should get a medal.

"I'm sorry you lost your job," Merle said.

"Losing my job was only the beginning. Don Geils has filed a ten-million-dollar assault and battery case, and the Department of Justice is bringing excessive force charges against me."

Bernice's eyes popped wide and Merle's jaw went slack. "You're kidding, right?" he asked.

"I wish I were."

"Unbelievable." He shook both his head and a clenched fist. "I'd love to punch that jackass right in the nose." He unclenched his fist, reached out, and put a supportive hand on my shoulder. "If there's any way I can help, Tara, you let me know."

"Would you testify on my behalf? About what happened that night?" Merle was the one who'd summoned me when all hell had broken loose in the club. Though I'd been working undercover as his assistant, he'd clued in that there was more to me than met the eye.

"Of course I'll testify," he said.

"Thanks, Merle. I gave your name and number to my attorney. He'll be in touch soon."

"Any luck finding a job yet?" Merle asked. "I'd be happy to hire you back on here as a bookkeeper if you need work."

"Thanks, but my boss at the IRS got me on with the audit department in Fort Worth."

Merle ducked his chin in acknowledgment. "Just know that if you ever need work, there will always be a place for you here."

I gave him a grateful hug. Unlike Scott Klein with his empty promises, I had no doubt Merle would keep his word. If I ended up with a conviction on my record, I'd take him up on the offer.

chapter nineteen

Hiding Out Stinks

My cell phone bleeped as I drove home. Alicia, back from her ski trip. I put her on speaker.

Her voice was frantic. "What's going on? I drove to your town house and there are four television vans on the street and reporters in your yard."

"The grand jury voted to indict me."

"That's ridiculous!"

She'd get no argument from me. "Was Trish LeGrande at my place?"

"Front and center."

Figures. What a bitch, that one. "Did you go inside?"

"Are you crazy?" Alicia replied. "I drove on by and got the hell out of the neighborhood. You're not inside the house, are you?"

"No. I caught the show at Guys and Dolls. I'm on my way home."

"Thank goodness. What should we do?"

"We'll hide out at Nick's."

Of course I'd have to hop the fence and sneak in my back

door to feed my cats, but given that I'd been a less-than-perfect teenager, climbing a six-foot wooden fence posed little challenge. Heck, I could do it barefoot with a cup of beer in one hand and not spill a precious drop. If those reporters wanted to catch Tara Holloway, they'd have to try a little harder.

Fortunately, when we'd exchanged house keys Nick had also given me his spare garage door opener. I sneaked into my neighborhood by the back route and hid around the corner, out of sight of the reporters, while I activated the door. Once the interior light turned off a minute later, I zipped around the corner, up the drive, and out of sight. I heaved a sigh of relief as the door slid closed behind me.

Once inside, I opened the front door, leaving the porch light off, and motioned to Alicia, who waited in her car at the curb. She slid quietly out of her car and scurried inside.

"How long are you going to have to hide out here?" she asked, her eyes wide.

I shrugged. "Until they go away. My attorney advised me not to talk to them."

We greeted Nutty and fed him a can of wet food for dinner. After, we went upstairs and into Nick's spare bedroom, leaving the light off as we went to peek out the window.

"Holy crap!"

Alicia hadn't been kidding. Three TV vans remained parked on the street in front of my house, while the driver of another van, the one from Trish LeGrande's station, had the audacity to park in my driveway as if they belonged there.

"Jerks." I raised a middle finger at them. It was too dark and I was too far away for them to see it, but it made me feel better nonetheless.

While Alicia told me about all the fun she'd had on her ski trip, I cooked up a couple of fried baloney sandwiches for dinner and we ate them with a handful of barbecue-flavored potato chips.

"I'm no longer an unemployment statistic," I told her as we took our plates to the sink. "The IRS hired me back as an auditor."

Her lips quivered, as if not sure whether to form a frown or a smile. "How do we feel about this?" she asked, ready to support me whichever way I went.

Hell, I wasn't sure whether my new job was a good thing or not, either.

"We feel good that we will be getting a paycheck," I replied. "But we are sad that Lu has already hired a replacement for me in Criminal Investigations."

Alicia cringed. "Oh no. Really?"

"He's moved into my office, put family photos all over my bookcase." I pulled the engraved pen out of my purse on the counter. "On the bright side, he found my pen."

"Well, there's that. . . ." Alicia eyed me. "You gonna be okay?"

I shrugged. "What choice do I have?"

After dinner, we sprawled out on Nick's couch with Nutty between us. I scrolled through the recorded shows on Nick's DVR. *Duck Dynasty. Call of the Wildman. Hillbilly Handfishin'.* Jeez. And I'd thought Brett's golf tournaments were boring. Then again, I suppose these shows were the male version of mindless drivel, the kind of show where a person could just turn off their brain and be entertained by people who lived an entirely different lifestyle. Kind of like a guy's equivalent of *Sex and the City*.

"Thank goodness for pay-per-view," Alicia said. We dialed up a recent movie that both of us had wanted to see but hadn't had the time to catch.

I peeked out the upstairs window again at 9:30, knowing Trish would have to be back at the station for her ten o'clock broadcast. Sure enough, the van from her station was gone, though the other three TV vans remained. Tenacious twerps.

I riffled through Nick's closet until I found a dark Dallas Mavericks hoodie. I slipped it on, crammed my keys into the pocket, and retrieved a flashlight from his garage. Quietly I exited his front door, leaving the porch light off, and slinked around the corner, doing my best to stay in the shadows.

Uh-oh. My best may not have been good enough. The

engine and lights ignited on one of the vans and it pulled away from the curb, the motor roaring as it rushed my way.

Shit!

I broke into an all-out run, making my way onto the next block in mere seconds. I grabbed the top of a wooden privacy fence and scaled it, half-dropping, half-falling to all fours on the other side, praying I hadn't landed in the yard where the Doberman lived. I got lucky. My efforts earned me only a vacant stare from a lazy Pomeranian lying on a padded chaise lounge, enjoying the cool evening air.

My breaths came so fast and loud I was sure everyone in a five-mile radius could hear me panting. Through the narrow break between the fence slats I saw the van slowly make the block. The driver turned around at the end and inched their way back around the corner, probably scanning the yards for any sign of that questionable shadow they'd spotted earlier.

Since I'd had to hop the fence sooner than intended, I was four town houses down from mine and had to scale several more fences before landing in my backyard. My efforts earned me three splinters and a stubbed toe, but at least I'd made it home.

Inserting my key into the back door, I glanced right and left to make sure nobody was watching me over the fence. The coast seemed clear.

I dashed inside, scaring the bejeebers out of Anne, who emitted a hiss that escalated to a howl.

"It's me, Annie baby," I whispered.

Though my words stopped the howling, the poor cat nonetheless darted off to parts unknown. I turned on the flashlight to light my way, grabbed the bag of kitty kibble from the pantry, and filled the cat bowl. Just to be safe, I retrieved an aluminum pie pan and filled that, too. Who knew when I'd be able to get back in here? If there had been any way to manage their carriers, I would've taken the cats down to Nick's with me.

As I was filling their water bowl, Henry sauntered in, his

furry tail swishing, and gave me his usual look of conde-
scension before he began crunching the food.

I ventured upstairs next, where I cleaned out the litter
box and packed a suitcase for myself. Comfy pajamas, work
clothes, jeans, sweaters, shoes, toiletries, curling iron, and
hair dryer. As I went to close my closet, my eyes landed on
the locked trunk that contained my guns.

Maybe I was just rattled knowing my place was under
surveillance, but something told me to take a weapon with
me. I retrieved the case that contained my new long-range
rifle, as well as the red Cobra pistol I'd purchased recently at
a pawnshop. Boxes of ammo made their way into my suitcase, too.

Sufficiently outfitted now, I lugged the suitcase downstairs. I went over to where Henry now lay on top of the TV
cabinet and gave him a scratch under the chin. Anne peeked
out from under the couch and scurried over. I picked her up,
cradled her in my arms, and buried my face in her fur. She
rewarded me with a comforting purr. At least she still thought
I was worthy of her love.

What if the judge didn't release me on bail Monday? Tonight could be the last time I'd see my beloved cats for years.

The thought both made me want to cry and instilled a
new sense of determination in me. I wasn't about to let Don
Geils make a fool of me or allow Troy Kerr to use me for political gain.

If those two jackasses thought they'd get the best of Tara
Holloway, they'd better think again.

I set Annie on the couch and sneaked back out my patio
door, waddling to the fence with my heavy suitcase gripped
in both hands. I counted—*one, two, three!*—and heaved it
over my back fence with all my might into the yard behind
me. It landed with a *thud*.

I placed a foot on the crossbeam and hauled myself up,
throwing first my right leg, then my left over the fence and
sliding down the other side. My landing was much softer
than my suitcase's had been.

The soft glow from the low-wattage patio light didn't

reach to the edges of the postage-stamp-sized yard, so I was able to stick to the perimeter and remain in darkness as I sidestepped to the gate. I reached for the handle and found it thankfully unlocked. I hurried through, closing it behind me, cringing when the loud *click* of the latch connecting cut through the late-evening quiet.

I wobbled to the sidewalk with my suitcase, extended the handle, and rolled it as fast as I could behind me down the sidewalk. The wheels sounded like a Roller Derby bout in the tranquil night. A couple of times I hit uneven pavement and the bag teetered, threatening to career out of control, but I was able to right it. I made my way around the corner and stopped at the fence to peek down my street. The van was back in its earlier position.

I wasn't sure what to do now. Given that the driver had spotted me sneaking through the shadows earlier, there was no way he'd miss me pulling a suitcase across the street. There was no way I could roll the darn thing across a lawn, though, and carrying the heavy thing and moving quickly would be impossible.

I was debating what to do when a car came from behind me, its high beams illuminating the night like a spotlight. A-ha! The headlights would temporarily blind the driver or force them to avert their eyes, giving me a narrow window of opportunity to make it across the street.

As soon as the car turned the corner, I took off, sprinting with my bag behind me, the suitcase going temporarily airborne as I cut it too close and had to yank it over the curb next to Nick's driveway. Luckily for me, the car with the high beams was going slow. I made it onto the porch in record time.

Unluckily for me, I wasn't the only one on the porch. A small, furry black-and-white animal was nosing around the casement. My first thought was that the creature was a cat, but when he raised his head I realized I'd been mistaken. When he turned and raised his tail I realized I was up shit creek without a paddle.

I dove sideways on top of Nick's holly bushes, the prickly

leaves biting into my skin. The skunk, having sprayed me, my suitcase, and most of Nick's porch, sashayed away as if he didn't have a care in the world.

"Ohgodohgodohgod!" I cried under my breath as I stood up, instinctively putting my forearm to my nose to protect it from the smell. Big mistake. The hoodie was drenched in the skunk-butt juice.

My eyes watered so much I thought they'd float right out of my head. Snuffling came from the threshold as Nutty sniffed from the inside. The poor dog emitted a whine as he inhaled the acrid skunk smell.

Alicia cracked the door. "Tara?"

I pushed the door open and dragged my suitcase inside. "I got skunked."

"Oh, God! That smell!" She backed up involuntarily, putting her hand over her mouth and nose.

I rushed to the laundry room, yanked off my clothes, and stuffed them into the washer. Wearing nothing but my panties, I crossed my arms over my boobs and rushed upstairs and into the hottest shower my skin could handle.

Fortunately, my clothing had absorbed most of the spray and twenty minutes later I emerged from the shower into the steamy bathroom smelling less like skunk and more like a teenage boy, thanks to Nick's Axe body wash. Gotta say, though, I can see why the stuff was so popular. It smelled damn good. It must have pheromones in it. I was tempted to ask myself on a date, buy myself a nice dinner, maybe try for second base.

I found a striped T-shirt in Nick's drawer and slipped it on. The thing fit me like a dress, hanging down to mid-thigh. It might not look so great, but at least it covered my private parts.

I returned downstairs. Nutty had fled out his doggy door for the fresher air out back, but Alicia was still inside.

"Here." She held out a pair of rubber gloves she'd found under Nick's kitchen sink and I put them on to inspect my suitcase. While the bag was ruined, the suitcase had been treated with Scotchgard, creating a moisture barrier that had protected my clothes inside. I carefully pulled out my clothing and took it upstairs, returning to put the suitcase in a plastic garbage bag before adding it to the can in the garage.

My first instinct was to open the windows to let the foyer air out, but I was afraid doing that would only let more skunk smell in. Besides, it was only in the forties outside. Much too cold to leave a window open. We settled for lighting a scented candle, hoping the match wouldn't cause an explosion. Once I mopped the tile in the entryway and Alicia had hosed off the porch, either the smell had dissipated or we'd grown so used to it that we couldn't tell anymore.

Nick's second bedroom had yet to be furnished, so Alicia opted to sleep on the couch. I opened the back door and urged Nutty to come back inside with me and upstairs. I helped him up onto Nick's bed, climbed in next to the dog, and wrapped my arms around him. He didn't smell as good as Nick, though he was just as warm and his kisses just as loving.

chapter twenty

$\mathscr{P}$leading for Mercy

A peek through the window blinds confirmed that the TV vans were back at my place Saturday morning. Or perhaps they'd never left. Jackasses. Here I was, spending what might be my last weekend as a free woman for years, and already I felt like a prisoner.

Of course my friends would have none of that, being the awesome women they are. Christina swung by in the early afternoon, pulling her Volvo up to within inches of Nick's garage door. She texted me to let me know she was in place. *Elvis is at the building.* There was probably no need for code given that she was sending a direct text, but it seemed appropriate given that we were sneaking around.

Alicia and I raised Nick's garage door a couple of feet, shimmied out through the opening, and duckwalked to the back door of Christina's car so the news crews couldn't see us. We climbed into the backseat and curled up the best we could on the floorboards until she'd backed out of the drive and made it a few blocks away.

"Where to?" she asked once I'd climbed over the seat and buckled myself in front.

"Where else?" I said. "Neiman's." Now that I'd have a job again, I could afford to treat myself to a little pick-me-up.

We spent the afternoon browsing and trying on clothes at Neiman Marcus.

I tried on a white blouse with a lacy collar and faux pearl buttons. "What do you think about this?" I asked my friends, turning to and fro so they could get the full effect. "Does this top say 'innocent' to you?"

"Definitely," Christina said. "You look downright virginal."

When our shopping excursion was complete, Christina and Alicia took me out for more Japanese food, plum wine, and green tea ice cream, their treat. Like I said, awesome women.

The news crews were still camped out on my lawn when my mother, father, and brother Trace arrived at Nick's place on Sunday afternoon.

"We'll get rid of 'em," Dad said from the front doorway, motioning for Trace to follow him.

Mom, Alicia, and I watched from the upstairs window as Dad and Trace got back into Dad's truck, drove down to my town house, and ordered the news van out of my driveway. As they climbed down from Dad's pickup, the reporters gathered around. With his broad shoulders, no-nonsense demeanor, and my formidably sized brother to back him up, Dad quickly convinced the reporters that it was in their best interests to scram. Within five minutes, the crews were gone. Maybe I did still need my daddy to fight some of my battles, after all.

Monday morning, I opened my underwear drawer and looked over the selections, trying to find the best pair of big-girl panties I owned. I snatched a pair of black satin panties trimmed with red lace. If that didn't say "big girl" I didn't know what did. I dressed in my new blouse and my best business suit, slid into a pair of feminine yet professional pumps, and topped things off with the gorgeous new coat Nick had given me for Christmas.

Since I hadn't gotten my old job back, it would be a lie to say I felt like a million bucks. But I felt like at least five hundred grand, maybe even five-fifty. Not too shabby.

Although my parents wanted to come along to provide moral support, I convinced them not to attend my arraignment, afraid having mommy and daddy in tow would make me look less professional. After all, this was federal criminal court, not a trip to the principal's office. Besides, I didn't want Troy Kerr to realize how terrified I was. Of course my trial would be a different matter. I'd definitely want them in court with me then.

I retrieved the manila envelope containing my power of attorney and held it out to my mother.

Her head angled as she took it from me. "What's this?"

"A document giving you legal authority to manage my finances if I end up in the slammer."

"Oh, honey," my mother said. "Don't even think like that!"

"Better to be prepared, just in case. You've always said as much."

She couldn't deny it.

The two of them walked me to my door.

"Call us the minute you know something," Dad said.

"I will." I accepted their hugs and kisses and set off for downtown.

I met Anthony Giacomo at his office at 9:30.

"Did you see the news?" he asked.

"No." I hadn't watched the news all weekend, afraid the reports about my pending trial would pysch me out.

"Good."

"That bad?"

"Scandals sell," was all he said.

Looked like the reporters had played the case up for all it was worth.

We walked over to my arraignment together. Anthony gave me another pep talk on the way.

"I've spoken with several of the potential witnesses on the phone," he said. "Sharp bunch. I'm going to meet with each of them in person and run through their testimony, make sure they are fully prepared for the trial. I'm also going to the jail to meet with Don Geils. I want to get a feel for the guy."

"He's a disgusting pig. Save yourself a trip to the jail and just roll around in a hog wallow." I really shouldn't insult swine so. Contrary to popular belief, pigs were actually intelligent, clean creatures. Geils was anything but.

Giacomo cut his eyes my way. "Any idea what his weaknesses might be? Any sore spots that might set him off?"

Over the weeks I'd worked at Guys & Dolls, I'd come to know Don Geils better than I would have wanted. "He's rude. Egotistical. Self-centered. Cheap, at least where others are concerned. Doesn't like to have his authority questioned."

"Uck." Giacomo made a face. "I hate him already."

We reached the courthouse and made our way through the security checkpoint. My stomach began to flutter, but the sensation felt more like bats dive-bombing for insects than butterflies.

"Which judge is the case assigned to?" I asked as we stepped onto the elevator.

"Judge Trumbull."

I groaned.

"Problem?"

"It's just that she handled a lot of the cases I worked on in Criminal Investigations. I hate for her to see me like this."

"No need to worry," Anthony said. "Trumbull's been around the block a few times. She knows to keep an open mind."

"She's also a liberal. What effect do you think that might have on the case?"

"It's true that she does lean left," he said, "but I think that's because one of her breasts is larger than the other."

I'd noticed the same thing myself. Her chest looked like

the lopsided udders on our nanny goats back home. Still, the fact that what my attorney said was true didn't lessen the surprise of hearing him say it out loud. "Anthony!"

He grinned. "Only trying to get you to lighten up. I've told you not to worry."

"I'll stop worrying once this whole damn nightmare is behind me."

He stepped out of the elevator and I followed him.

"Do you think we should request a change of venue?" I asked. If we asked for the trial to be moved, maybe we'd get a more pro-government judge.

"Look," my attorney said softly, glancing around to make sure no one of any importance could overhear us. "I know Trumbull's not always the government's best friend, but she's fair. Besides, she adores me. But who doesn't?"

Anthony shot me a wink and pulled open the door to the courtroom. As we walked in, my eyes immediately spotted Eddie seated in the third row. He glanced back and motioned with his hand, indicating he'd saved seats for us. When we reached the bench, he scooted over so that my attorney and I could sit along the aisle.

"What are you doing here?" I asked as I slid onto the bench next to Eddie.

"I came to support my partner."

I felt my eyes grow misty. "Thanks."

He shrugged. "Besides, it was a good excuse to get out of the office."

Typical man, trying to hide his mushy feelings.

I introduced him to Anthony. Though they'd already spoken on the phone, this was the first time they'd met in person.

My eyes scanned the crowd, finding Troy Kerr leaning nonchalantly against the far wall, his arms crossed over his chest, a single manila folder in his hand. The way he stood there as if he were lording over the place irked me. *Sit your ass down!* I wanted to scream.

My eyes found Trish LeGrande's butterscotch-blond hair next. She'd pulled it up in a sophisticated twist. She sat between two male reporters, chatting without a care in the world. I made a mental note to toss some rusty nails into my driveway in case she and her TV van returned today.

At the bailiff's direction, we all stood as Judge Trumbull entered the courtroom. Alice Trumbull was a full-figured woman with gray hair, loose jowls, and a no-nonsense demeanor. She was also a woman with a pair of ankle-high fuzzy booties on her feet, complete with pom-poms. I couldn't much blame her. The temperatures had taken a dive since New Year's. From what I could see when her robe flounced around her, she was also wearing a pair of soft cotton sweatpants under her robe.

Trumbull called the first matter to her bench. Two attorneys stepped up in front of her and proceeded to squabble for ten minutes about whether bail should be revoked for a defendant who'd sent a text to a witness he'd been ordered not to contact. The defendant claimed he sent the text in error and that it was intended for someone else. Trumbull found in favor of the defendant but warned him that if any further mistakes were made he wouldn't be given the benefit of the doubt.

My case was the second matter called.

Eddie grabbed my hand and gave it a quick squeeze as I stood.

Ignoring Trish's gaze, I held my head high as I made my way to the bench, Giacomo following me. Troy Kerr stepped up on the other side of my attorney a moment later.

Judge Trumbull looked down at me. "Hello there, Miss Holloway."

"Good morning, Judge Trumbull."

"This is quite a mess you've found yourself in." Though she arched inquisitive brows, the eyes underneath shone with compassion.

"Quite a mess," Troy Kerr agreed.

"Oh, pish-posh." Giacomo waved a dismissive hand. "It's just a little bitty mess and I'll get her out of it before you can say 'acquittal.'"

Trumbull chuckled. "Good to see you again, Tony."

Anthony put one arm in front of him, crooked the other

behind his back, and performed a slight bow. "Always a pleasure, madam."

The attorneys engaged in some short preliminaries before Trumbull shifted her focus back to me and the paperwork in front of her. "In the matter of *The United States versus Tara Holloway,* how does the defendant plead?"

She looked from Giacomo to me.

I looked her directly in the eye. "Innocent."

She offered a slight smile. "I'll put you down for a 'not guilty.'" She made a notation in her file before turning once again to the attorneys. "Bail?"

Kerr stepped forward. "Miss Holloway is accused of using excessive force against a target in a tax investigation. She shot the victim four times in the leg, three of those shots being fired after he was relieved of his weapon and lay defenseless and bleeding. This is a violent and serious crime, Your Honor. Although she's been relieved of both her government-issued Glock and her position as a special agent, it's come to my attention that the defendant has a concealed-carry license and owns a virtual arsenal of personal weaponry."

Gee. How, exactly, did that come to his attention? Maybe because he had a law clerk check the registry?

Kerr glanced my way before returning his attention to the judge. "Bail of fifty thousand would be appropriate in a case like this."

Fifty grand? Was this guy nuts? The bond would cost me seventy-five hundred dollars—money I didn't have at the moment. Not since writing Giacomo the check for his retainer and buying this new blouse, which looked totally cute on me, by the way.

Trumbull turned to my attorney. "Any response?"

"Besides my eye roll?"

"Yes. Something verbal we can put in the record."

"As you wish. Fifty thousand is ridiculous. Miss Holloway is no more a threat to anyone than I am. Had she wanted to use one of her personal weapons, she's had ample opportunity already."

Trumbull looked to me again. "You promise to behave?"

I raised three fingers. "Scout's honor."

Judge Trumbull notated her file again. "I'm going to let the defendant go on personal recognizance. No bail."

Thank goodness. The last thing I wanted to do was have to pawn my guns or borrow bail money from my parents. How humiliating would that be?

"I'm assuming you all want this resolved as soon as possible?" Trumbull asked.

All of us at the bench murmured in agreement. I wanted it resolved quickly so I could either get on with my life or begin serving my sentence. Giacomo wanted it scheduled so he could accumulate more billable hours. Kerr wanted it to move along so he could land that judicial position when the federal judge retired in March.

"Okey doke," Trumbull said. "Let's get this trial on the calendar."

She asked how long the attorneys expected my trial to last. They agreed it would take one full day, maybe two. Ironic that it would take hours for the attorneys to present evidence and the jury to make a decision about an event that had lasted only ten seconds, tops.

"You're in luck," Trumbull said. "One of my other scheduled cases worked out a plea deal. We can start this trial in three weeks."

I realized that was a quick period, but it still felt like forever to me. I had twenty-one more days to agonize over my fate, to worry, to fret. By then my stomach would have dissolved in acid erosion.

Nevertheless, I thanked the judge. She looked down and gave me a pitying smile.

Ugh.

I didn't want pity.

I wanted *justice.*

chapter twenty-one

$\mathcal{W}$estward Ho-Hum

Trish and the other reporters dashed after us as my attorney, Eddie, and I exited the courtroom. Whaddya know? I had paparazzi. Now I knew how the Kardashians felt. I only hoped my photo wouldn't end up on the front of the *National Enquirer* above the caption WORST BEACH BUTT EVER! Maybe I should cut back on the green tea ice cream.

Trish attempted to shove her microphone in my face, but my attorney stepped between us.

"We appreciate this opportunity to speak to the media," he said, "to discuss my client's innocence. Though other commitments require us to scurry along, rest assured I will see that Tara Holloway receives the justice she deserves." He raised a hand and flashed a smile, like a president exiting a media conference. "Thanks, folks!"

Trish frowned as Anthony put a hand on my back and hurried me along.

Eddie parted ways with us on the courthouse steps. My attorney and I continued on to the lobby of his office building, where he stepped onto an elevator going up and I took one going down to the garage.

My mind spun as I walked to my car. *Released on my own personal recognizance*. What the hell does "recognizance" even mean?

Once in my car, I circled up out of the garage, paid the attendant the ten-dollar charge that had accrued, and took aim for Fort Worth.

As I headed west on Interstate 30, I tried my best to muster up some excitement about my new job as an auditor. No way could this new job be as thrilling as being a special agent had been. I suppose I'd be no different from most people now. After all, few people really enjoyed their work, right? Most simply put in their time, took home their paychecks, and lived for the weekends. I'd become one of them. A nine-to-fiver. A drone. A working stiff.

I stopped for an early lunch at a Chinese fast-food place on my drive, eating my vegetable lo mein and egg roll in a corner booth in the back. As I ate, I wondered what type of food they served in prison. It was doubtful the menu would have much variety. How would I survive without sushi and lo mein noodles and naan and green tea ice cream?

When I finished eating what I could force past the lump in my throat, I cracked open my fortune cookie and unfolded the white paper slip inside. *You will reach new and unexpected heights.* Huh. I was definitely experiencing some new and unexpected lows. I wondered what kinds of new and unexpected heights I might reach.

I crunched my way through the cookie, followed it with a breath mint, and tossed out my trash.

A short drive later, the skyline of Forth Worth appeared in the distance. The city was smaller than Dallas, with a population of 750,000 compared to the 1.2 million people in Dallas. Forth Worth had far fewer skyscrapers, but it also had less traffic.

I exited the freeway and drove past the convention center and Water Gardens to the IRS office on Taylor Street. I parked in the underground garage, made my way through the security checkpoint, and rode up to Clyde Hartford's office. His administrative assistant was away from her desk, so I knocked on his door frame. He summoned me in.

Clyde had thick dark-gray hair, and wiry brows that could really use a trim. The things looked like they were trying to reach out and grab me. But he also had a wide smile and a warm temperament. "Welcome to Cowtown, city slicker." He motioned for me to take a seat.

I slid into a chair. "I appreciate you offering me a job, Mr. Hartford."

"No need to thank me," he said. "Lu says you're a hard worker and smart as a whip. As many audits as we've got pending, I could use ten of you." He leaned forward across his desk. "I gotta know, though. Lu told me what happened. Why on earth didn't you just kill the guy?"

I made a mental note to buy some rope and a cinder block on my way home later, but for now I forced a smile. "Death would've been too good for him." Hey, not a bad line. I'd have to remember it for next time.

Hartford gave me a quick primer on office procedures, then stood and led me to a bank of six cubicles down the hall. Though Christmas was over now, a green garland and a strand of multicolored lights still draped the cubes, a sign that my new coworkers had some personality. Good to know.

After briefly introducing me to the only other auditor who was in the office today, a round, middle-aged woman with white-blond hair, he stopped at the last cubicle. "Here's your spot." He gestured to a tall stack of files piled on the modular desktop. "There's a few cases to start with."

A few? The stack was three feet high!

"They're all small-business cases," he said. "Figured those would be more up your alley."

"Thanks."

He gestured to another file folder sitting by itself to the side. "All of your employment-related forms are in that folder. Once you get those filled out, drop them on my assistant's desk."

"Will do."

After my new boss left, I dropped my purse in the bottom drawer, took a seat in the rolling chair, and pulled myself up to the desk. I looked around me, feeling like a soldier stuck in a foxhole. I fought the feeling of entrapment the small space gave me, forcing myself to power through.

"Hey, you look familiar."

I looked up to see my new coworker eyeing me over the top of the cubicle wall that separated the two of us. She probably recognized me from the newscasts and newspapers. My photograph had been shown all over the Dallas–Fort Worth metroplex.

She squinted at me. "You're that special agent who was in the shoot-out at the topless bar, aren't you?"

No point in denying it, though I was sick and tired of the shoot-out being the event that defined me. "Yep," I replied. "That was me."

"Wow." Her eyes went wide now. "How many people was it you killed? Eight? Nine?"

I closed my eyes and counted to ten before opening them again. "None."

Her light brows drew together. "None?"

"None."

"Huh." Disappointment dulled her eyes. "Guess I'll let you get to work." With that, her face disappeared from view.

I opened the personnel file first and spent a half hour filling out the documentation. Name, address, Social Security number, phone number. It probably wasn't legal to list my cats, so I designated my parents as the beneficiaries of my life insurance policy. I signed various acknowledgments regarding the allowable and prohibited uses of government property, the same forms I'd signed when I'd joined Criminal Investigations.

Once I'd completed all of the personnel forms, I carried the file over to Hartford's assistant. He took them, input some information into his computer while I waited, and issued me both a laptop and a key for my new G-ride.

Properly equipped now, I returned to my desk and began to look through the audit files.

Though many people feared an audit, audits were actually quite rare. The IRS audited only 2 to 3 percent of taxpayers each year. An individual taxpayer would be selected for audit if the revenues reported on the tax return were less than those reported on W-2s or 1099s. A business taxpayer would be selected for audit if the return's Differential Income Factor or DIF score, which evaluated income relative to expenses, exceeded certain thresholds. I could tell you what those thresholds were, but then I'd have to kill you. Neither of us wants that, right? To encourage accurate reporting by taxpayers, a certain percentage of returns were also selected randomly for audit. It was kind of like playing spin the bottle with Uncle Sam, but without the kiss and risk of herpes transmission.

There were three types of audits. The simplest was a correspondence audit in which a taxpayer would provide requested documentation and information via mail. The second type of audit was a field office audit, where a taxpayer would meet with the auditor at the IRS office to review documentation and discuss the return at issue. The third type of audit was an on-site audit, which involved the auditor going to the taxpayer's home or place of business to perform an extensive review. Sometimes what began as a correspondence or field office audit would evolve into an on-site audit if the auditor discovered widespread inaccuracies or if the person being audited was particularly attractive. Hey, I'm not saying I'd ever do it. You just hear things.

Working my way down from the top of the stack, I performed triage on the files, separating them by the size of the business, then by level of complexity. Some of the files were new cases. Others were audits already in progress that had been reassigned to me.

A large dental practice on East Rosedale had been randomly chosen for audit. I set that file in the priority stack. A quick glance at the file told me the practice was highly profitable. The return didn't raise any immediate red flags. I could probably work through that case in a day or two and impress my new boss with my productivity.

A file for Cowtown Candy Company also caught my attention. Though the company's gross revenues had been increasing by leaps and bounds, its net profits had been on the decline due to rising costs. The business owners might be able to explain the situation, though things seemed a bit questionable at first glance. The auditor who'd initially been assigned to the file had planned on merely performing a correspondence audit and had sent a request to the company last month for data regarding some of the expense accounts. There was no data yet in the file, though the company had three more days until the deadline. Although my initial impulse was to set the file aside with a note to myself to follow up in a week, my plans changed the instant I saw the signature line on the tax return.

Chloe Marie Aberdeen-Jennings, CFO.

My blood heated instantly to its boiling point. Chloe "Dean's List" Aberdeen had been my secret archrival back at the University of Texas, the Washington Redskins to my Dallas Cowboys, the Angelina Jolie to my Jennifer Aniston, the grilled steak-Gruyère panini to my fried baloney on white bread sandwich. All of the other students had adored Chloe. I did, too, at first. She was delightful and enchanting, with the tall, trim physique, thick dark hair, and innocent doe eyes of Anne Hathaway. As far as I was concerned, she had Anne Hathaway's acting skills, too, though everyone else believed Chloe's charm was natural and genuine rather than affected.

But I knew better.

She was too perfect to be real.

Chloe had always been one step ahead of me. If it took me two hours to complete my accounting exam, it took Chloe only one hour and fifty-nine minutes. If I was in line at the counselor's office trying to snag that last spot in the cost-accounting class, Chloe was right in front of me, exclaiming with glee when she got the seat, leaving me to suffer through the class in summer school. And if that hot blond guy who'd flirted with me in Accounting 101 had thought I was cute, the minute Chloe Aberdeen floated through the door I was nothing more than a frustrated blur in his peripheral vision.

Chloe had always worn revealing, form fitting clothing, though she'd managed not to look slutty because of clever pairings. She'd wear a low-cut tank top, but it might have a cartoon of a kitten lying on its back in the sun with the logo *I♥SUNSHINE!* Rumor had it that though she'd dated enough boys to fill a fraternity house, she never let any of them past first base. Chloe Aberdeen had been a virginal vixen, defending her hymen until she scored the hyphen and became Chloe Aberdeen-Jennings. Of course, her refusal to put out made her a conquest the boys wanted all the more, each sure he'd be the one to finally break through her defenses.

Here I was, faced with a chance to finally have one up on Chloe. God help me, but I was going to take it. As beaten-down as I'd felt lately, I needed this.

I picked up my phone and dialed the number for Cowtown Candy Company. "Chloe Aberdeen, please," I said when the receptionist answered.

"May I tell her who's calling?"

"Tara Holloway. I'm an auditor for the IRS."

Thirty seconds later, Chloe came on the line. "Good morning," she said in her perfectly polite, perfect diction. "Chloe Aberdeen-Jennings speaking."

On hearing her voice, a hot blush of shame rushed to my face, the absurdity and immaturity of my seeking revenge on Chloe hitting home. This was silly, stupid, petty. So what if Chloe Aberdeen was prettier, smarter, and richer than me? I still had a lot going for me. Well, not so much at the moment. But usually I did.

"Hi, Chloe. It's Tara Holloway. From U.T." I figured I'd tell her I ran across her name in the file and was calling to catch up. I'd let her mail in the requested documentation as planned. No need to put her through an on-site audit, right?

Seven seconds of silence came over the line, as if this truly were a game of spin the bottle and I was the greasy-haired kid with BO whom she didn't want to kiss.

"We had some accounting classes together," I said to jog her memory. Five classes to be exact. I'd sat directly in front of her in Managerial Accounting. She'd looked over my head for four months straight.

More silence.

"You lived two doors down from me in the dorm freshman year?" My room had been right across from the elevator, the constant *dings* and chatter as girls climbed on and off the elevator driving me nuts as I tried to study. Chloe's room, however, was at the end of the hall, in a nice, quiet corner where she not only had privacy but also an extra window that looked out over the campus and provided a spectacular view of the university's signature tower in the distance.

"I'm so sorry," Chloe cooed through the phone, "but I can't seem to place you."

Can't seem to place me? I'd shared my notes with her numerous times when she'd missed class, including one time when she'd purportedly been fighting a short bout with the flu. Odd that she'd been tagged in Facebook photos at a Taylor Swift concert that same night. I'd shared my mother's pecan pralines with Chloe when Mom had sent me a tin in the mail. I'd even helped Chloe carry her heavy things out of the dorm on move-out day. Or, more precisely, I'd helped the fraternity boys who'd been helping her. Later, when I'd needed help with a box of books, she'd begged off, claiming she had an appointment at the hair salon. I'd seen her half an hour later hanging with friends at a coffee shop on the Drag, her hair looking the same as ever. Gorgeous, sure, but not freshly coiffed. Meanwhile, I'd tripped down the stairs with the box of books and skinned my knee.

Those old feelings of resentment came rushing back.

Time for a change of plans.

Whether she wanted to or not, Chloe was going to kiss me. Metaphorically speaking, that is.

"I'm an auditor with the IRS now," I told her. "I need to meet with you tomorrow afternoon to discuss the candy company's tax returns."

"Gosh, it's short notice," she replied. "I have a full calendar the next few days." She spoke with the conviction of a woman who was used to getting her way.

"No problem," I said with the conviction of a woman who might soon be convicted. "I don't need your time, just access to the Cowtown Candy Company's financial records."

She was quiet again for a moment. "Let's reschedule for after the new year. I'm sure you can allow that. After all, we're old friends, right?"

Nice try. You had your chance. The only thing I'd let you kiss now is my ass. "So sorry, Chloe, but my calendar is really busy, too." With civil and criminal trials looming, I was indeed busy. "I'll be there at one thirty. If you aren't available, have someone else who's familiar with the accounting system there to meet me, okay?" I ended with a quick, "Great-thanks-bye!" before she could offer further protest.

Neener-neener.

chapter twenty-two

Who's Calling?

I snuck out of my cubicle at four thirty, hoping not to get caught by my new boss and to beat the rush-hour traffic on my new thirty-five-mile commute. What I wouldn't give for some decent public transportation. But given that I lived in Texas, where cars and oil are king, I was shit out of luck.

I stopped for gas on the way home. I'd need a full tank for my new, long commute. The temperature hovered in the fifties and the station's drive-through car wash was open for business. Fortunately, it was one of those no-touch types that could accommodate my convertible. No way would I let the bombardment of bird crap continue to defile my sweet red baby.

As I drove into the bay, I was tempted to put the top down and see if the high-pressure water could wash away my worries. If only.

A few minutes later, my Beemer and I emerged from the car wash and continued on our way back to Dallas. I arrived home, reemployed and crap-free. What's more, no reporters surrounded my home today. Things were looking up. Looked like those big-girl panties were working their magic.

Alicia lay on the couch, the remote in her hand as she surfed through the evening news and pre-prime-time sitcom reruns. No doubt Martin and McGee was experiencing its usual end-of-year doldrums, the downtime before spring tax season. Alicia had probably spent the workday sitting at her desk shopping for after-Christmas sales on the Internet. Once the new year arrived, tax season would kick in full force and she'd be working late every night. Those crazy hours were definitely one thing I wouldn't miss about Martin and McGee. Of course being a special agent had meant working crazy hours, too, but by and large they'd been much more fun hours.

"I put a frozen lasagna in the oven," Alicia said, glancing up from the television. "It'll be ready in twenty minutes."

"Great," I replied, unbuttoning my new coat. I hung it on a padded hanger in my coat closet, shut the door, and kicked off my pumps, walking into the living room and flopping down into a chair.

Alicia sat up. "How was the audit department?"

I made a "so-so" sign with my hand. My new boss seemed nice enough and the cases I'd been assigned weren't bad, but I could do without the confining cubicle. "Guess who I'll be auditing."

"Chuck Norris?"

"No." Too bad. That could be fun. Maybe he'd give me some tips for hand-to-hand combat.

"Don Henley?"

"Nope." Again, too bad. Who wouldn't want to meet one of the Eagles?

"Selena Gomez?" Alicia asked, naming yet another celebrity who allegedly lived in Dallas.

"Chloe Aberdeen," I said lest this back-and-forth continue all evening. More precisely, Chloe Aberdeen-Jennings. Chloe had married into the wealthy Jennings family, owners of Jennings Prefabricated Buildings, Incorporated, which operated a chain of outlets in Texas, Oklahoma, and Arkansas. Jennings Prefab sold a wide range of structures, from small backyard toolsheds to enormous airplane hangars. My dad had bought his barn from their East Texas store in Lufkin. I'd seen Chloe's wedding announcement in the newspaper a few years ago. It had been one of those pricey quarter-page spots that included a detailed description of the bride and how she looked "absolutely enchanting in an ivory gown of Chantilly lace."

Pf-ff-t.

"Chloe?" Alicia's face brightened. "I haven't seen her in ages. She was so pretty. Remember her hair? It was always so shiny. And that dimple? Adorable! She was so friendly, too. Everyone liked her."

"I didn't."

Alicia rolled her eyes. "You didn't like her because she was smarter than you."

"No, she wasn't." *Yes, she was.* Not only did she turn in her tests before me, she also always scored a point or two higher than I did, no matter how hard I studied. I wasn't normally a competitive person, striving only for my personal best rather than comparing myself to others, but it irked me that everything seemed to come so easily to Chloe. It didn't seem fair.

Alicia sipped her wine. "You can't deny she was very sweet."

"Oh, she was sweet all right. But I still say it was an act."

Alicia ignored my lies and pettiness, because that's what friends do. They allow each other an annoying flaw or two. Take me, for instance. I was able to ignore the fact that Alicia thought Chloe Aberdeen was all that and a bag of chips when Chloe was really just a phony, manipulating people with her winning smile and long, batting eyelashes.

"I'm going to change." I climbed off the chair and went upstairs, as much to get out of my work clothes and into my pajamas as to put an end to the one-person meeting of the Chloe Aberdeen fan club. If I had to listen to any more of my best friend singing Chloe's praises I would puke.

As I changed, Nick phoned me from Tokyo with an

update on the TDT investigation. He and Agent Tanaka had met with representatives of Japan's tax department and their National Police Agency. Though the Japanese authorities had initially been skeptical of the accusations and were hesitant to acknowledge that one of their citizens was involved in an extensive counterfeit products scam, they'd come around once Nick and Tanaka showed them one of the counterfeit phones and provided them with a copy of Tokyo Discount Telecom's catalog, e-mail address, and telephone number.

"The Japanese agents ran a search," Nick said. "TDT isn't registered to do business in Japan."

"That's suspicious."

Nick agreed. "We're going to do some snooping to figure out who runs the show here." Once they knew who was involved, they'd perform surveillance to determine whether the parties were knowingly involved in illegal activity or were merely pawns for someone further up the criminal food chain.

Nick said the Japanese authorities discovered that the phone number McPherson had provided belonged to a mobile phone rather than a landline. Japanese law enforcement used a process called multilateration to determine the location of the cell phone, which appeared to be moving along with the person who possessed it. In a city as large and crowded as Tokyo, hitting a moving target, especially with a margin of error of fifteen to twenty meters, was damn near impossible.

"We came close in Shibuya," he told me. "But not close enough."

From my research, I knew that Shibuya was a crowded commercial district often referred to as the Times Square of Tokyo due to its bright lights and abundance of entertainment venues. Unfortunately, given that the area was packed with Japanese teenagers, young adults, and tourists, all of whom seemed to be talking, texting, or taking pictures on their cell phones, law enforcement hadn't been able to pinpoint the phone and its user.

"We're still working on it," Nick said. He sent me a photo

of himself with the bright lights of Shibuya behind him. He also sent one of himself at the base of the Tokyo Skytree.

"Cool." I tried really hard not to be jealous that he was halfway across the world working a kick-ass case. I tried and I failed. Envy ate at me. I should be in Tokyo, too, enjoying *kappa maki* and green tea ice cream, not stuck here assigned to audit Miss Perfect and waiting on a tasteless frozen lasagna to finish cooking. Damn, that Don Geils! I'd love to stuff his mouth full of wasabi and poke his eyes out with chopsticks. Then he'd really have a case for excessive force.

Just after Nick begged off, my cell phone bleeped again. It was Eddie calling. "Hello?"

All I got was the muffled sounds of girls giggling and Eddie hollering, "Look out for the tickle monster!"

Ugh. "You butt-dialed me!" I yelled into the phone. No response. Apparently my words were butt-muffled. I hung up and texted him. *Dude. U butt-dialed me 2x. Learn how to lock ur keypad.*

chapter twenty-three

*M*y First Audit

Tuesday morning, I pulled into the compound that contained the headquarters and manufacturing facilities of Cowtown Candy Company. The building sat at the front of a twenty-acre tract of land directly north of Fort Worth. The two-story structure had been painted in a white-and-black simulated cowhide motif. Parked along the side were a fleet of small delivery trucks also painted in black and white, the fronts bearing brown eyes, pink noses, and upturned lips. The side mirrors were fashioned to resemble cow ears. The Cowtown Candy Company's logo was painted on the side, the company's name spelled out in script made to look like rope.

Fifty yards behind the expansive manufacturing facility sat an old-fashioned red barn. A small herd of Holsteins milled about the acreage, pulling up grass to snack on. One cow had backed up to a gnarled tree stump and was rubbing her hip against it, scratching an itch.

I parked in the small front lot next to a bluish-silver Town & Country Limited minivan, the most expensive minivan on the market. Two child car seats were buckled into the seats on the second row, one an infant-style seat, the other a toddler-sized model. I had a sneaking suspicion the car belonged to Chloe. Most of the other cars were aging sedans and small commuter-type vehicles likely belonging to the employees who worked in the manufacturing department.

I opened the glass door that led into the foyer. Unlike the outside, the foyer was painted in a soft pink, though the floor was black-and-white checkerboard tile. A desk with a computer, a three-line phone, and an empty chair greeted me. A small silver bell sat on the desktop, along with a folded paper placard that read: *Ring bell for service.*

I slapped the bell. *Ching!*

"I'll be right with you!" called a female voice through an open door to my right.

A few seconds later a young woman ventured out of the supply closet carrying a ream of copy paper. She wore black pants and a shirt in the same faux cowhide as the building and trucks. The shirt bore the company's embroidered logo on the chest. "Sorry to keep you waiting. The printer ran out of paper."

"No problem," I said. "I'm Tara Holloway from the IRS. I'm here to see Chloe."

While I stood at the desk, the girl plopped into her rolling chair, picked up the telephone receiver, and punched two digits. "There's a Tara Holloway from the IRS here to see you." She listened for a second, said, "Okay, thanks," and returned the receiver to its cradle. "She'll be right with you."

I took a seat on a plush pink wing chair to wait, using the spare moment to send Nick a text. *Miss u.*

A second later, I sensed the infuriating fabulosity of Chloe's presence. I looked up to find her standing in the doorway that led back to the factory floor and offices. She was as pretty as ever, her dark hair and fair skin glistening under the fluorescent lighting. She wore a fashionable long-sleeved sweaterdress in a feminine and pure cream color. The dress was formfitting enough to show off her perfect figure yet covered enough skin to nonetheless seem modest. An enormous diamond glittered on her left hand.

She batted her big brown eyes at me, her lashes fluttering like butterfly wings. She offered a smile, flashing that dimple that others found adorable. As for me, though, I didn't find her dimple to be at all adorable, nor was it merry like Santa's. Rather, it seemed to me more like a magician's trick designed to distract you, to entice you to divert your eyes while the deception was performed. Then again, maybe I was being overly dramatic.

"Hello there." She stepped forward, extending her hand. "It's nice to meet you, Tara."

I didn't bother pointing out that she wasn't *meeting* me, she was *seeing me again*. Still, the second I took her hand I realized the feelings I'd had back in college had been nothing more than jealousy. That dimple was indeed adorable. Chloe'd had it all. Still did, apparently. Who wouldn't be envious? But I should be above all that now. I'd been foolish and immature to come here seeking to settle the score when, really, there was no score to settle. So she'd been a little immature and self-centered back in college. Who hadn't? Besides, that was all in the past. We were adults now. I should let it go, right? I'd just take a quick look at the company's accounting records and go.

I shook her hand. "I appreciate your cooperation."

"Of course," she said. "Though I'll have to be leaving soon and hand you off to my brother. He's the chief operational officer, but he can get you into the accounting system."

"Jeremy works here, too?"

She batted her eyes again. "You know Jeremy?"

Jeremy had been a year ahead of us in college, a marketing major. As with Chloe, everyone liked Jeremy, but for entirely different reasons. Jeremy was a cutup, always ready to share a joke or a pitcher of cold beer. Unfortunately, the cutup wasn't cut out for college. He'd slept through class after class, forgotten to turn in his assignments. He was infinitely creative, but the more regimented business school environment didn't work for him. He'd dropped out halfway through his junior year.

"Jeremy and I had a management class together." When he bothered to show up, that is.

"Oh," was all she said before turning her back to me. "This way. The offices are upstairs."

She led me into the large manufacturing facility. The smells of warm chocolate, vanilla, and sugar sweetened the air. A dozen workers in cowhide-print jumpsuits, latex gloves, and white hairnets milled about the stainless-steel machinery and conveyer belts like Oompa-Loompas, checking the finished products for defects before they were sent on to the packaging department.

Chloe led me up a metal staircase onto a catwalk that spanned a section of the factory. I wondered if the catwalk was the *new and unexpected heights* foretold by my fortune cookie. Ten feet below stood large open vats of melted chocolate in milk, dark, and white varieties. The surface of each pool of chocolate swirled slowly, stirred by an internal mechanism. I fought the urge to dive over the edge and into a vat. I might've done it if I could have decided which of the three was the most enticing.

The catwalk ended at a hallway leading to the administrative offices. The first door on the right bore a nameplate that read: *Dennis Aberdeen.* The door was partway open, and a white-haired man sat inside, his back to the door as he spoke on the phone.

Chloe's office was next door. Her office was beautiful and appeared to have been professionally decorated. The walls were painted a soft mauve color. Her desk was one of those broad types that was really more like a table. The wood was rich, with reddish hues and gold leaf accents, the legs curved, giving it a fancy, feminine appeal. A matching credenza graced the side wall, forming an L-shaped workspace. An antique glass-front bookshelf took up a large part of the front wall, its shelves filled with books on accounting and finance as well as assorted antique candy dishes. The bookshelf was flanked on each side by wooden four-drawer file cabinets. Two wing chairs upholstered in plum-colored suede faced her desk, a dainty round table between them.

Gee. If I hadn't thought my tiny cubicle sucked before, I sure as hell did now.

A wide plate-glass window looked out from Chloe's office over the production floor. If I had to stare down at those vats of melted chocolate all day I'd weigh three hundred pounds.

A large family portrait, one of those photos that were transferred to canvas, hung on the wall over the credenza. They were the epitome of the perfect American family, an attractive husband and wife with a baby and a toddler, both miniature Chloe clones with her same dark hair, same innocent doe eyes, same left-sided dimple. Chloe's husband was good-looking, too, with dark-blue eyes and light-brown hair cut short. The four wore white in the portrait, which made their features pop.

"Your girls are cute," I said, motioning to the portrait.

Chloe glanced over at the picture and smiled. "I've been blessed." Her eyes moved to my coat now. "Is that coat from the Neiman's holiday catalog?"

"Yep." Page 164 to be exact. "My boyfriend bought it for me for Christmas." I might not be married with the requisite 2.1 children and a house in the suburbs, but I did have a hot boyfriend who spoiled me and my two cats were sort of like kids—kids who shed and cough up hairballs.

"How nice." Chloe gestured for me to take a seat. Once I had settled into a wing chair, she picked up her audit notice and blinked her eyes at me. "I'm a little confused here. The audit notice I received only asked me to mail the documents in."

"Right," I said. "They're due in the IRS office in two days. I figured I'd save you a trip to the post office." As if. "Or perhaps you've already sent them?"

Chloe hesitated a brief moment. "Well, no, I haven't sent the paperwork yet. Like I mentioned on the phone, my schedule has been crazy."

I glanced down at the desktop calendar. Other than an

appointment to take "Taffy" to the groomers and several evening holiday parties, the days appeared wide open.

Chloe followed my gaze. "I only jot reminders there," she said. "It's not my complete schedule."

"If you have the paperwork printed, I can run through it here in just a few hours."

Chloe's eyes batted again, though this time they looked less like fluttering butterfly wings and more like angry fly-swatters seeking a bug to squash. "I'll get Jeremy to pull it together for you." She picked up her phone and punched in a couple of digits. "Can you come to my office? I've got an IRS auditor here who needs to see some of the records." She paused a moment, her eyes cutting from me to the bookcase behind me. "We'll talk about that later." She set the phone down gently, though with the tight grip she had on the thing I'm surprised it didn't implode in her hand.

A moment later, Jeremy traipsed into the room, as loose limbed and jovial as always. He was dressed in the same black-and-white cowhide jumpsuit as the production staff. "Hi there." He stuck out a hand, flashing the Aberdeen dimple that graced his cheek, too. "I'm Jeremy Aber—" He stopped himself and cocked his head, squinting his brown eyes at me. "Wait. I know you. Tara . . ." He snapped the fingers on his extended hand three times in quick succession. *Snap-snap-snap.* "Hall? Hallsworth? Hallingford?"

"Holloway."

He raised his index finger in the air. "That's it! Tara Holloway. You once bested me at darts at the Crown and Anchor." The extended arm now wrapped around me in a friendly hug, pulling me up from the chair. "How the hell have you been?"

"I've been great." What a lie, huh? "As for the darts, you might have stood a chance of beating me if you'd been able to stand up straight."

He chuckled as he released me. "Yea-a-ah. Kind of hard to aim a dart after four beers and two shooters."

Chloe watched the two of us, her expression impassive. "I need to get going. Sure you can handle this, Jeremy?"

He groaned and threw his head back. "Yes! I can handle printing out some documents." He looked down at me and draped an arm around my shoulders. "Come with me, old buddy."

chapter twenty-four

$\mathcal{P}$our Some Sugar on Me

Jeremy led me down the hall to his office. His space was much smaller and windowless, with cheap, functional, put-it-together-yourself furnishings. Unlike Chloe's tidy office, Jeremy's appeared to have been ransacked by monkeys on meth. His desk was covered with colorful drawings of candy wrapper mock-ups, as well as balled-up drafts that had been rejected. Two of the drawers on his filing cabinet hung open, papers sticking out at odd angles, preventing the drawers from closing. A bulletin board behind his desk was covered with photos of a pretty young blond woman and a dark-haired boy who also had the Aberdeen dimple. The boy appeared to be about six years old.

When Jeremy saw me looking, he removed a thumbtack and handed me a photo of himself, the woman, and the boy. "That's my wife and son. They totally rock!"

"You're married? And a father?" He'd been such a goofball in college, it was hard to think of him in those grown-up roles.

"I know, right? Who would've thought it?" He grinned.

"Of course my wife only married me 'cause I knocked her up. Best mistake I ever made."

Now it was my turn to laugh. "She's very pretty. And the kid's a cutie pie."

Jeremy looked down at the photo and beamed before tacking it back to his board. "So what have you been doing since college? Catch me up." He had no wing chairs, but he pushed his rolling chair over to me and hopped up onto his desk, crossing his legs to sit Indian-style amid the paper carnage.

I told Jeremy about the years I'd spent at Martin and Mc-Gee. "It wasn't a bad job, but I had a hard time being cooped up in a cubicle."

"I hear that. So then you became an auditor for the IRS?"

I hesitated a moment, unsure whether I wanted to go into my questionable work history. But looking up at Jeremy, at his friendly, nonjudgmental face, I decided to open up to him. Heck, the guy had made dozens of mistakes himself. He'd understand. I told him about my track record in criminal investigations, about all the attacks I'd endured, about the shooting at Guys & Dolls.

"I heard about the bust at the strip club on the news. Holy shit, that was *you*?"

"It was me all right."

"How many people did you shoot in that raid? Ten? Eleven?"

At least he hadn't accused me of killing anyone. "Four," I replied. "Three bouncers and the club's owner."

Jeremy shook his head slowly. "So they bumped you over to audits?"

"Yep. They don't trust me with a gun anymore."

"It could be worse," he said sympathetically. "My father and Chloe don't trust me with a stapler."

I picked up one of his drawings to take a look. "It must be nice being part of the family business." Especially when the family business was candy.

He hesitated a moment before responding. "Let's just say it has its ups and downs. Hey, why don't I show you around?"

"I'd love that."

We left Jeremy's office and went back down the hall, passing Chloe's now-closed door. Dennis Aberdeen was off the phone now and glanced up as Jeremy stopped in his doorway. Now that Dennis was facing us, I could see that he had a white goatee and the same brown eyes as Jeremy and Chloe. Dennis had the Aberdeen dimple, too. He reminded me of Kenny Rogers.

Jeremy took a step into his father's office and held out his arm to indicate me. "Dad, this is Tara Holloway."

Mr. Aberdeen rose from behind his desk and stepped around to shake my hand. "Hello there. You're the auditor from the IRS?"

"That's right."

"You'll have an easy time of it. I'm sure Chloe kept impeccable records."

I'd figured as much myself. She hadn't graduated with honors because she cut corners.

Jeremy crooked his arm around my shoulder again and pulled me closer with his elbow. "Tara's also an old friend of mine and Chloe's from college."

Dennis rocked back on his heels, his face softening a touch. "Don't that beat all."

"Chloe and I lived in the same dorm freshman year and had several accounting classes together." Not that Chloe remembered any of that. "Jeremy and I were in Marketing together."

"Tara beat me at darts once, too," Jeremy added.

Dennis cut his son a look. "If you'd spent more time in the library and less time at the pubs, you might have managed to graduate."

The arm Jeremy had wrapped around me stiffened. I was about to point out that I'd spent plenty of time in Austin's bars and still managed to earn my degree, with honors no less, but I realized that wouldn't really help Jeremy's case.

Dennis turned back to me. "Looks like you've done well for yourself."

That was up for debate. Luckily, he didn't wait for a response.

"Chloe's been quite a success, too," Dennis said. "She spent three years working for one of those big CPA firms in Oklahoma City, learning the ropes, before coming back here and taking over as chief financial officer two years ago. She's a financial whiz, that girl. Made a killing last year in the stock market, even in this economy. She and her husband have a beautiful home in Southlake, two girls, the whole nine yards." He beamed with pride.

"Jeremy's son sure is a cutie, too," I said.

"Can't argue with you there," Dennis said. "I only hope that boy will have more sense than his daddy."

I glanced over at Jeremy, noticing the tightness in his neck and jaw. "Let's take that tour," I suggested. I turned back to Dennis. "Nice meeting you."

We made our way back over the catwalk and down the stairs. Jeremy led me past the vats of delicious-smelling melted chocolate, warning me to be careful of the hot metal. He took me up and down the factory floor, introducing me to the workers, all of whom he knew by name. He snatched candy samples off the conveyer belts as they went by, handing them to me to try.

"I'm not supposed to accept anything from a taxpayer," I said.

"I'm not offering this candy to Tara Holloway the IRS auditor," he said. "I'm offering it to Tara Holloway my old college buddy. Besides, you can hardly call me a taxpayer. I haven't filed a return in five years." He flashed the dimple to let me know he was joking.

According to the information I'd found in the file and gleaned from some quick research, Cowtown Candy Company had been in business for thirty years. While it had been a relatively small operation for more than two decades, the company had made a major expansion several years ago. The company had also gone organic and acquired its own herd of milk cows. It was then that the company acquired its fleet of bovine-themed delivery trucks. Until that time, the company had primarily sold chocolate truffles and the typical assortment of candies at its boutique stores, located in Fort Worth's suburban malls. During the expansion, the company added a variety of unique western-themed candies, opened a large ice cream and candy store in the historic Fort Worth stockyards district, and began offering tours of its factory and dairy facility to tourists and schoolchildren alike.

Jeremy handed me a package of Licorice Lassoes. A white label on the package read: *Warning! Eating Licorice Lassoes can make you tongue-tied!*

"Let me guess," I said. "You came up with that line?"

Jeremy grinned. "You got me."

Next he handed me a Happy Hen, a yellow marshmallow chick perched on a trio of colorful jelly beans in a nest of green-colored coconut. He followed it up with a bag of Pink Piggy Popping Gum, ordinary pink bubble gum formed in the shapes of little pigs. The company also manufactured yellow lemon pellets in a drawstring pouch labeled *Chickenfeed*. The coup de grace—or should I say *poo* de grace?— was the Cowtown Cow Patty, an amorphous dome of fudge that came in both plain and walnut varieties.

"Here," Jeremy said as he handed me a cow patty. "Eat shit."

Although he also treated me to some of the company's classic offerings, such as a white chocolate raspberry truffle and a chocolate-covered cherry, I had to admit the more upscale candies lacked personality.

"Want to be my guinea pig?" he asked.

"Guinea pig?"

"My taste tester. I've got a new product in development." He led me through a swinging door into a kitchen where three workers milled about. A large bin of candy corn sat in the middle of the table. On a tray next to the bin sat what appeared to be ears of corn in varying sizes, all made with candy corn.

"What a great idea!" I said. "Who came up with it?"

"I did," Jeremy said. "All of the new candy concepts were

mine." He handed me a sample of each type. "Try these. Give me your honest opinion."

The first ear had a nougat center; the second was held together with firm caramel, the final with a crisp, cookie-type core.

"I like the first one best."

"That was my favorite, too."

"What else are you working on?"

"A new kind of jelly bean called a Goat Eye." He pointed to a mock-up on the table. The drawing was of a golden jelly bean bisected horizontally with a thick brown line.

"What flavor is it?"

"Butter rum and root beer," he said. "It's a surprisingly good combination."

We continued on to the packaging department, where the candies were sorted and placed in cowhide-print boxes for shipping. He grabbed a jacket off a peg near the exit door and slid into it. "Come meet the cows."

We made our way outside into the brisk afternoon. Despite the fact that the sun was shining, the temperature hovered in the mid-forties. I was glad for the warm coat Nick had given me.

Jeremy and I walked across the parking lot and through a gate that led to the barn and pasture. Given that the wind had picked up, the cows had decided to huddle in the heated barn.

Jeremy introduced me to the cows, scratching them behind the ears as he did so. "Ladies, meet Tara. Tara, this is Barbara, Elisabeth, Joy, Sherri, and Whoopi."

I raised a brow. "Whoopi?"

"I let my son name them. My wife's a stay-at-home mom. She's hooked on *The View*."

One of the cows nuzzled my hand and I gave her a scratch under the chin. She lowed in gratitude. *Moo-o*.

Given the small dairy operation, it couldn't be very cost-effective. "Wouldn't it be cheaper to buy your milk from a supplier?" I asked.

"It would be less expensive," Jeremy agreed. "But this way I know the cows are treated right." He turned to one of the big beasts. "Right, Babs?" He gave the cow a kiss on the nose.

Our tour completed, Jeremy led me back inside. He returned the jacket to the hook, and I followed him back upstairs to his digs at the end of the hall.

"Okay." He clapped his hands together. "The American people don't pay taxes to Uncle Sam for you to shoot the shit with old friends, you know. What would you like to see?"

I pulled out the audit notice. "I need to take a look at the expense accounts for utilities, maintenance, raw materials, salaries, phone, mortgage payments—"

Jeremy threw his hands up in surrender. "Okay! Okay! Enough already!" He gestured for me to sit in the rolling chair, stepped behind it, and called out, "Vroom-vroom!" as he steered me in a fast, roundabout course ending behind his desk. He picked up a few of his sketches-in-progress, then ran his arm over the desktop, knocking the wadded-up paper balls to the floor. He punched a few keys on his computer keyboard and angled the screen my way. "There. You've got full access to the accounting system. Have your way with it. But please, be gentle and don't forget to call afterward."

"Thanks." I set my briefcase on the now-clear desk and opened it, removing a legal pad and a thumb drive. "You okay with me copying the computer files?"

"Why not?" He kicked aside a couple of the paper balls. "I'll be back in a few. I need to check on a shipment. A dude ranch in Bandera ordered three thousand cow patties. Can you believe it?"

"That's a shitload."

He pointed a finger at me. "Now I remember why I liked you."

After Jeremy headed out, I pulled up the expense files and quickly perused them on the screen. Nothing immediately caught my eye, other than the already-noted fact that some of the costs seemed to have increased significantly from previous years.

I delved a little deeper into the utility accounts, checking to see if there had been a change in providers that might

explain the increase. Nope. Cowtown Candy Company had
been with the same provider since the expansion. Of course
it was possible the rates had increased. I made a note to take
a look at the bills.

I took a look at the maintenance costs next, noting they
had increased a couple of years ago when an outside janitorial firm was hired. The bills seemed a bit high to me, over
eighty thousand a year, but the building was large and I supposed it wasn't easy to clean floors made sticky with sugar.
If the bill also included mucking the barn, eighty grand was
a steal.

The largest increase in expenses was manufacturing. Although sales had increased by leaps and bounds over the past
few years, the increase in profits had been more than eaten
up by increased costs for raw materials such as cocoa, sugar,
nuts, and Red Dye No. 3. The increase could likely be explained by the company's decision to use only more expensive organic ingredients, but I'd need to verify if such was
the case.

The salaries account had increased quite a bit, too, though
the reason for the increase was immediately obvious. They'd
added three new members to their sales staff, all of whom
were paid generous salaries. The increase in sales required
increased production, which necessitated more factory
staff, too.

Looking over the salary data got me wondering. How
much was Chloe paid? Although auditors weren't supposed
to dig through taxpayers' accounts willy-nilly and I would
have no grounds for reviewing her personal tax return, there
was nothing to prevent me from accessing her salary information as part of the audit. In fact, I'd be remiss if I didn't
do a thorough analysis, right? I owed it to Uncle Sam, to
honest taxpayers.

Aw, who was I trying to fool.

I was being nosey.

I ran through the list of subaccounts labeled with each
employee's name until I found the one for Chloe Aberdeen-
Jennings. I clicked on the account.

Holy guacamole!

Chloe was pulling down just over ten grand in each of her twice-monthly paychecks. Only five years post-college and she was earning a quarter-million dollars a year. She wasn't just one step ahead of me now. She'd leapfrogged me and reached a level of financial success I'd likely never achieve. Not that success should necessarily be measured in dollars. Still, it stung. I'd been paid a respectable amount as a special agent, but nowhere near $250K annually. And I hadn't been sitting on my ass in a cushy chair in a cushy office in a cushy candy company. I'd been out fighting bad guys, putting my safety and life on the line.

Tempted to put my fist through the computer screen, I backed out of the account. Just below Chloe's name were salary accounts for Dennis and Jeremy Aberdeen. Curious, I clicked on those.

Dennis earned less than half as much as Chloe, only $110 grand as chief executive officer, and a large part of his salary was paid in the form of a bonus based on net profits. Hm-m. The situation smacked of income shifting, a way for Dennis to reallocate income that should be his to another family member. Income shifting was always a potential issue in family-owned businesses, where older family members who no longer had the need for a high income and might have fewer itemized deductions to offset their salaries often paid their children excessive amounts. The excess salaries were essentially gifts, though, of course, the families never reported them as such for tax purposes.

Still, I wasn't sure whether to raise a stink about the issue. If the extra income was a gift, it would be nontaxable to Chloe and potentially taxed to her father. No sense putting a burden on him and giving her a break. Besides, with her husband's salary and the money they'd made trading stocks she was likely already in the highest tax bracket. Reallocating the funds would only complicate matters and wouldn't yield any more money for the government coffers.

I exited Dennis's account and clicked on Jeremy's. He was paid twenty-five hundred dollars every two weeks, putting his annual salary at sixty-five thousand dollars. Nothing to sneeze at, but nothing to write home about, either. After all, he'd been at the company longer than Chloe and, from what I could see, worked really hard, juggling several roles. While Chloe seemed to be getting a bump up in pay for working at the family business, Jeremy could likely be doing just as well, if not better, elsewhere. He certainly deserved more than a quarter of his sister's salary. I wondered if he was aware of the disparity. Given his aversion to numbers, maybe he'd never taken a look at the accounting system.

Having poked around sufficiently in the salaries account, I moved on.

The mortgage account had increased quite a bit. Building such a large facility had been costly, of course. But mortgages were normally a set amount each month. Why had their annual totals risen so much? I checked the dates. Sure enough, two payments had been made last December, one seventy-eight-hundred-dollar payment representing the installment due that month, the other seventy-eight hundred dollars a prepayment for January. Nothing unusual about that, especially when personnel might plan to be on vacation over the holidays and would not be in the office when the bill came due at the beginning of January. Just to be thorough, I checked this year's records.

"Huh." Oddly, another mortgage payment had been made on January 3. I scrolled down to see the payments that had been made this month. Again, two payments had been made. One for the current month, the other for January. The same thing had been done in the preceding year. It didn't make sense that thirteen mortgage payments had been made during both of these years. Of course, the mortgage company would have simply applied the extra payments to the mortgage account. Still, it surprised me that Chloe would have made such a mistake. She was a financial whiz, after all. I jotted another note to take a look at the mortgage documentation.

Jeremy returned just as I was wrapping things up. "How's it looking?" he asked.

"Pretty good," I said. "But I'll need to take a look at the utility bills, invoices for the manufacturing materials, and mortgage statements. The bank statements, too." Might as well do the job right, even though I fully expected the additional information to put my questions to rest. "Can you get those documents for me?"

Jeremy's brows drew together. "I'm not sure where Chloe keeps the hard copies. Let's try her office."

I followed him down the hall to the closed door. He rapped on it twice, but there was no response from within. He tried to turn the knob only to find the door locked. Stepping next door, he rapped now on the door frame of his father's office. "Tara needs to take a look at some of the bills and invoices. Do you have a key to Chloe's office?"

"I believe so," Dennis replied. He reached into a drawer and pulled out a key ring, carrying it over to us. Most of the keys were labeled with small stickers that read: *Shipping, Barn, Front Door,* et cetera, but none of them were identified as the key to Chloe's office. He stepped over to Chloe's door and tried each of the unlabeled keys. None of them fit. "Well, darn," he said. "Doesn't look like I've got a copy of her key."

"Tell you what," I said. "How about I come back when Chloe will be here and take a look then?"

"We'll be closed tomorrow and the day after for New Year's Eve and New Year's Day," Dennis said, "but we'll be open again on Friday."

"Great," I said. "I'll be back then."

I left with a thumb drive loaded with financial data and a briefcase loaded with candy. All in all, not a bad afternoon.

chapter twenty-five

$\mathcal{I}$nbound

I spent the rest of the day in the audit office, looking over paperwork. At 6:00, I crept east on I-30, surrounded by thousands of equally frustrated drivers fighting the urge to bang their heads on their steering wheels. I might have if not for the fact that I was high on exhaust fumes. A sign on the side of the road read: "MINIMUM SPEED 45 MPH." Yeah, right. My speedometer had yet to reach 20.

On my drive home, I stopped by the grocery store for cereal, bread, and toothpaste. All that sugar I'd consumed this afternoon had me fearing cavities. I picked up some staples for Nick, too, knowing he'd be in need of some fresh food when he returned from his trip. I also picked up another bottle of champagne for tomorrow's New Year's Eve celebration, since I'd used part of the original bottle to make mimosas and the remainder had since gone flat.

Nick would be flying home tomorrow. I couldn't wait to see him. The time difference between Dallas and Japan had made it difficult for us to talk much on the phone, and texting was a poor substitute. I couldn't wait to hear his voice, to see him, to feel his arms around me again. With my criminal trial looming over me, I hadn't been able to relax. Nick would be able to distract me from my woes. So would celebrating the new year at Wolfgang Puck's Five Sixty restaurant and bar atop Reunion Tower.

No sleeping in for me on New Year's Eve. December 31 wasn't a federal holiday, either, and I had no accrued vacation time. Rats.

Nutty had left a puddle on the kitchen floor near the back door. I couldn't blame the poor dog. His ancient bladder could only hold out so long in the morning and I didn't have a doggy door for him to let himself out.

I cleaned up the puddle, fed the dog and my cats, and fixed myself a bowl of Fruity Pebbles. Alicia wandered down a few minutes later and started a pot of coffee.

"I can't wait until tonight," she said as she plopped down in a chair at the table to wait for the coffee to finish brewing.

"Don't forget our manicure appointments today."

"How could I? After pulling my ski gloves on and off all those times my nails are a wreck."

"Oh, boo-hoo," I replied, casting her a look. "At least you were allowed to leave the state."

She reached an arm across the table and squeezed my hand. "It'll all work out, Tara. You've got to trust that it will."

"I'm trying." I wasn't totally succeeding, however.

I spent five hours at the audit office, close enough to a full day. Besides, everyone else had sneaked out early, including Clyde Hartford.

In the afternoon, I met up with Alicia at my favorite nail salon. The technician removed my Christmas-themed polish, shaped my nails into soft curves, and applied a glittery, glamorous gold coat. Alicia opted for silver.

"Thanks." I paid the tech for my manicure, adding a few extra dollars to my tip. My holiday spirit hadn't quite yet evaporated, despite the circumstances I found myself in. Besides, my mood had been buoyed by the fact that I'd get to spend the evening with Nick, surrounded by our friends and in a gorgeous new dress to boot. No sense letting a looming criminal indictment spoil what might be one of my last fun, free nights for a while.

Alicia headed back to my town house while I drove to the airport. I parked in short-term parking. It might have made more sense to pick Nick up at the curb, but I didn't want to wait a second longer to see him than I had to.

I made my way to the baggage claim area, reading a romance novel I'd downloaded to my cell phone while I waited. The star-crossed couple could never seem to get things right. At least I didn't have that problem. Then again, if I ended up in prison could I really expect Nick to wait years for me until I was released? He'd already had to put his life on hold when he'd been in forced exile in Mexico. Would he be willing to do that again, for me? And would I want to know that I might be holding him back from a chance at happiness with someone else?

Ugh.

I stuck my phone in my purse as weary travelers began to filter through the revolving door and into the baggage claim area. I stood on tiptoe, trying to see over the heads of the gathering crowd. I watched as each person emerged from the door.

Nope.

Nope.

Nope.

Nick!

The instant the door spat him out I hurled myself at him. He dropped his carry-on bag to the floor and wrapped his arms around me, enveloping me in warmth, comfort, and the conflicting smells of citrus-based soap and stale, recycled airplane air.

He kissed the top of my head and released me. "Lord, it's good to be home."

Agent Tanaka followed soon after, though I greeted him with a mere nod and a, "Welcome home."

The three of us moved along to keep from blocking the other travelers eager to reconnect with their loved ones. I looked up at Nick as we stopped next to the baggage carousel. His hair was mussed, as if he'd been sleeping on the plane. His eyes carried bags nearly the size of his luggage. His cheeks bore a five o'clock shadow, or, given that he'd flown in from Japan, maybe it was actually a 10:00 AM shadow, Tokyo time.

He grabbed his suitcase as it came off the belt. We said good-bye to Tanaka and headed out to my car. Nick climbed into the passenger seat and laid his head back against the headrest, his eyes closed. "Stick a fork in me. I am done."

"You're still up for tonight, right?" I needed tonight. I needed some fun to take my mind off my troubles.

Nick forced his bloodshot eyes open and glanced my way, noting the anxious look on my face. "Of course. I'd never leave my woman disappointed."

Nick updated me on the Tokyo Discount Telecom case as I drove. While the Japanese officials had finally pinpointed the person in possession of the cell phone used to accept orders for the business, they realized the twentyish young man involved was merely a low-level chump. Rather than bring him in for questioning, they'd decided to follow him for a few days, trace his movements and calls to determine who else was involved. No sense putting the ringleaders on alert and giving them a chance to disappear if they could be tracked down and arrested in a larger sweep. They'd agreed to keep Nick and Agent Tanaka informed of their findings, and our agents agreed to return the favor. The only thing we could do now back here in Texas was wait to hear when the order of counterfeit phone parts would be delivered to my town house so we could follow the truck back to its source.

I drove Nick back to my place, where we rounded up Nutty before walking down the street to Nick's digs.

"I'm starved and I'm tired," Nick said as we stepped inside. He cut me a grin. "I'm also dirty and in desperate need of some good lovin'."

"Clean up and get in bed," I told him. "I'll make fried baloney sandwiches and then we'll see about the lovin'."

He gave me another kiss on the head before heading

upstairs. "Give some to Nutty!" he called back over his shoulder.

As if the dog would let me ignore him.

Nick's shower kicked on with a hiss overhead as I heated a nonstick pan and added a pad of butter. I slung three slices of baloney into the pan, tearing another into bite-sized portions that I fed to Nutty. He wagged his tail and woofed for more. I pointed the spatula at him. "Watch your manners."

The shower turned off as I slapped the meat onto slices of white bread spread with mayo. I added a pickle to the plate along with a big blob of store-bought potato salad and poured Nick a refreshing glass of lemonade to round things out. Nutty followed me upstairs, still woofing for more baloney despite my repeated assurances that he'd grow a fat ass if he didn't watch his calories.

When I reached Nick's bedroom, I found him flopped facedown and sideways on his bed, the white bath towel he'd wrapped around his waist gaping to reveal part of one firm and irresistible butt cheek. My hands full, I lifted a foot to nudge his exposed rear. "Sit up, cowboy. Got your lunch ready."

His only response was a shuddering breath before he broke into an all-out snore.

Dang.

Nutty looked up at me, wagging his tail back and forth.

"Okay, buddy. It's all yours." I set the plate on the floor. Nutty devoured the sandwiches, though his sniff of the potato salad told him to give it a pass. I drank the lemonade myself.

I folded the bedspread down over Nick so he wouldn't be cold and climbed onto the bed next to him. This wasn't at all how I imagined our reunion, but how could I fault the guy? He was wiped out. Besides, we had a late reservation at Five Sixty. Why not let him get in a couple hours of shut-eye before an evening of fine dining, dancing, and celebration?

I lay snuggled up against him for a few minutes, thinking, worrying, and wondering, until deciding I might as well take my new rifle to the range and get in some practice. Lying next to Nick with him completely naked was only making me hot and bothered.

"New gun?" asked the attendant at the range as he took in my shiny new long-range rifle.

"Christmas present from my dad."

"You're a lucky girl. That's a nice piece."

Only the best for Daddy's girl.

I headed out onto the rifle course, tugging my knit cap down farther on my head as I went. I'd left the coat Nick had given me at home and traded it for the old puffy bright red jacket my father had made me wear for safety when we'd done shooting practice in the woods at the back of our property in Nacogdoches. The neighbors who owned the property behind us sometimes leased their acreage to deer hunters. Didn't want to risk being mistaken for Bambi.

I set up my targets and took a few warm-up shots. Oh, who was I fooling? I didn't need to take any warm-up shots. I hit every one of them dead center.

I quickly ran through two full boxes of ammo. Not cheap, at over a dollar a bullet, but I'd needed this. Besides, Dad had sent me home with an entire case of ammunition in a special dry-storage box. It would take me months to get through all of it.

When I turned to go back inside, a couple of men who'd been watching me tipped their baseball caps.

"You're one hell of a shot," one of them said. "Former military?"

"Nope," I said. "Former IRS special agent." My heart twitched at the word "former."

"IRS?" His face scrunched in confusion. "I didn't know IRS carried guns."

"Special agents do," I said.

"Want to shoot some skeet with us?" the other asked. "Maybe you could give us some pointers."

My arms and shoulder muscles had already grown weary, but I was never one to back down from a challenge. "I'm game."

We moved over to the skeet range, where I easily put the two men to shame. To their credit, they didn't seem to mind being bested by a woman. I gave them some pointers, advising the first to loosen up his shoulder, the second to widen his stance. When we finished, they thanked me and even paid for my gun rental and ammo.

By the time I returned home, evening had set in. I glanced down the street and noted Nick's place was still dark. The guy must still be sleeping.

Upstairs, I showered and fixed my hair, swooping it up into the best updo a nonprofessional could manage and shellacking it with the contraband Chinese hairspray Lu had given me a few months ago. The caustic stuff could stop a train. I reserved it for special occasions but kept it handy in case of an alien invasion. I layered on the makeup, applying a generous swipe of gold eye shadow, glamming it up for this special night.

My face and hair complete, I unzipped the nylon bag containing my gown and gently slid it off the hanger. The dress was divine. The fact that I'd scored it on sale made it that much better. I gingerly stepped into it and eased it up over my hips. The ruby drop earrings Nick had given me when we first began dating found their way to my ears, completing the ensemble.

Alicia came over from her room across the hall. My roommate was decked out in a silvery-gray dress with a stiff bodice, the skirt hanging just above her knees in front but swooping down to mid-calf in the back. She'd put some loose curls in her normally straight, angular hair, and they curved around her ears and chin in a beguiling way.

She stepped up next to me and we checked ourselves out in my full-length mirror.

"Damn, girl," I said in my best street-tough voice. "We look fine!"

After expressing sufficient mutual admiration for each other, Alicia and I parted ways. I went downstairs to phone

Nick while she returned to her bedroom to search for her evening purse.

The phone rang five times before going to voice mail. "This is Nick Pratt. I can't take your call—"

I hung up and dialed again. Still no answer.

I called up to Alicia to let her know I was going down the street to check on Nick. I grabbed the bottle of champagne and my purse and set off down the sidewalk in my beautiful gown and stilettos, way overdressed for a neighborhood stroll.

Nutty raised his head from the couch as I walked into Nick's place.

"Hey, boy," I said. "Where's your daddy?"

The place was silent. I ventured upstairs to find Nick sprawled on his bed, his eyes closed. This time, he lay completely naked, the towel having come undone and fallen off the side of the bed. He had one arm flung over his head, the other lying crooked beside him.

"Nick?" I whispered.

No response.

I tried again. "Nick?"

Nothing.

I sighed and sent Alicia a text. *Have 2 cancel. Nick's beat.*

I set the champagne down on the night table and eased out of my dress, finding a spare hanger in his closet to hang it up. I looked down at myself, now wearing a pink push-up bra, lace panties, and the sparkly stilettos.

Nick had no idea what he was missing.

I slipped out of my shoes and bra. Rather than retrieving my red nightie from the dresser, I snatched Nick's white T-shirt from the chair where he'd tossed it and slid it on over my head. The shirt smelled like Nick. If I couldn't actually have him wrapped around me, at least I could pretend.

I climbed into bed, picked up his remote, and turned the television on low, trying to combat my sense of disappointment and loneliness by engaging in a virtual celebration. I popped open the champagne and drank it straight from the bottle as I scrolled through the channels. A local station broadcast the "Big D NYE" festivities from Victory Park, an open space near the American Airlines Center that served as a gathering point for various celebrations. A local country-western band performed cover songs on a wide stage, to the delight of the crowd, who raised fists and sang along. They looked like they were having a great time. Dang.

I supposed tonight was par for the course. After all, fighting crime wasn't exactly a nine-to-five job. Serving in law enforcement wasn't just a job; it was a calling. A calling that required occasional sacrifices.

For the first time, I wondered if the sacrifices were too great.

chapter twenty-six

*N*ew Year, Same Old Worries

I woke on January 1 with a slight headache. That's what happens when a woman drinks an entire bottle of champagne all by herself.

I climbed out of bed, snagged a couple of aspirin from the medicine cabinet in Nick's bathroom, and went to the kitchen for a glass of water. Nutty heard me inside and squeezed back in through the rubber flap of his doggie door.

"Hungry?" I asked him.

He wagged his tail as if to say, *Silly you! I'm always hungry!*

I scooped a cup of kibble out of the bag in the pantry and poured it into his bowl. He sniffed it and looked up at me.

"Oh, all right, you spoiled thing." I opened the fridge, retrieved a slice of baloney, and tossed it into his bowl, earning a happy tail wag in reply. "But tomorrow you start a diet."

I had no idea when Nick might wake, but I knew he wouldn't mind being greeted by a full breakfast. I went all out, fixing home fries, biscuits and gravy, sausage patties, and scrambled eggs. The breakfast of champions. Champions with high cholesterol and heart disease. I also warmed up some of the black-eyed peas for good luck.

Nick wandered downstairs at noon to find me lounging on the couch with Nutty watching one of the day's many college bowl games. He ran a hand over his stubbly cheeks. "Tara, about last night. I am so sorry—"

I raised a palm. "It's okay. Not your fault. Besides, there's always next year." Assuming I wasn't in prison, of course.

"Something smells delicious."

"There's a plate for you in the microwave."

He stepped over to the couch, his eyes now clear and bright, the bags having packed up and moved on. "There's something else I'd rather take a bite of first." He bent down, eased the T-shirt I was wearing off my shoulder, and put his mouth to my neck.

Mm-m . . .

He pulled away—damn him!—and walked over to the suitcase he'd left in his foyer yesterday. He flipped the bag onto its side, unzipped it, and removed a plastic bag and a slightly crushed, slightly crumpled gift-wrapped box with Japanese characters on the outside. He carried the box over to the couch and held it out to me. "Here. I got you a little something on my trip."

I took the package from him and ripped into it. Inside was a gorgeous red silk kimono embroidered with light-pink cherry blossoms. "I love it!"

Nick sat down next to me and gestured to the box. "There's more."

I riffled through the tissue paper and found a traditional Japanese fan.

Nick shot me a wink. "You'll need that fan when I'm done with you."

The final souvenir in the box was a white ceramic cat with a raised paw, looking as if it were ready to bitch slap someone, the same type of figurine seen in many Japanese restaurants.

"The store owner called him a *maneki neko*," Nick said. "It's supposed to bring good luck."

I could definitely use some of that.

He handed me the plastic bag next. "These are for your nieces and nephews."

I looked inside to find three small black-haired female dolls dressed in traditional Japanese garb as well as two colorful kites shaped like fish.

"Wow, Nick." He'd gone above and beyond with these gifts. What a sweet, thoughtful gesture. "They'll love them." I gave him a big kiss.

"Check out this little souvenir I bought for myself." Nick returned to his suitcase and pulled something else from the bag. It was a long, thin, slightly curved blade with a black handle and a dragon encircling the guard.

I stood and walked over to him. "Is that a samurai sword?"

"Yup. Had a hell of a time getting it through customs. Had to play the federal agent card." He gripped the sword and held it over his shoulder in a striking pose. "How do I look?"

Sexy as hell. "Almost perfect. All that's missing is a black bun on top of your head."

"Guess I'll have to grow my hair out."

Nick lowered the blade, sheathed it, and stared at me for a moment. "I really missed you in Japan, Tara. It went beyond missing *you.*" He put a hand on the back of his neck, a gesture I'd come to realize meant he was serious, upset, thinking hard. "I miss *working* with you."

With complementary skills, Nick and I had made an amazing team. While he had the muscle to make taxpayers think twice about giving us trouble, I had the gun skills to hit a target on the first try. In addition, though we both had good investigatory skills, we tended to approach cases from different angles, taking different tacks, increasing our chances of success. In the few short months we'd worked together, we'd taken down a man running a gambling and credit card fraud scheme and laundering his illegally earned funds, a minister who'd been stealing from his church, an abusive tax preparer who also operated a deer-processing and taxidermy business, and Don Geils and his minions. We'd even put an end to a cockfighting ring.

We challenged each other, brought out the best in each other.

An uncomfortable realization dawned on me then. Much of our relationship had developed around our jobs as special agents. Although we enjoyed doing the usual things together—dinner, movies, and whatnot—what we both enjoyed most was working together to take down bad guys. We bonded while strategizing, planning, and pursuing, then achieving satisfaction with a takedown. Without that connection, without that thrill of a joint pursuit, was there enough left to keep us together?

I had to admit that I found Nick most attractive when he was in action, putting himself at risk for the good of our country. It was selfless, heroic even. I knew he felt the same way about me. Could he still feel that way about me if I was no longer a special agent? How would I feel about Nick if he weren't a special agent? It was hard for me to say. So much of how I felt about him was tied up in his work, because his work was what defined him. My work had once defined me, too.

I had no idea what defined me now. I hoped it wasn't the fried baloney.

I forced the negative thoughts aside. Nick had done nothing to make me doubt whether he still cared about me. He'd merely said he missed working with me. With my emotions on edge lately, I was simply overreacting. Right?

Nick's cell phone blared his current ringtone, Tim McGraw's "Truck Yeah." Nick handed the sword to me, scooped his phone off the coffee table, and checked the readout. He punched the button to take the call. "Senior Special Agent Nick Pratt."

I looked the sword over, admiring it, as Nick began pacing in the room. I'd always been a gun girl, but I could see the allure of a blade. Not only would the wielder need good aim, they would also need physical strength and agility.

Maybe I could take up fencing now that I'd be working regular hours.

"He did?" Nick said into his phone. "When was that?" He paused a moment. "Did he come by the gym in person?"

He paused again as I slid the sword back into its sheath and laid it on the couch.

"Great," Nick told the caller. "Let me grab a pen and paper so I can get that number from you."

Raising a finger to let Nick know I was on it, I scurried into his kitchen, found a pen but no paper in his junk drawer, and returned to the living room, where I tore a piece of gift wrap from the crumpled mess on the couch. Nick motioned for me to take dictation for him. As he repeated a sixteen-digit number, I wrote it down. "Thanks. If Sundaram shows his face at the gym, your staff knows to call me, right? Without alerting him?" Another pause. "I appreciate that."

Nick ended the call and I held up the paper. "Credit card number?"

"You got it. Sundaram's come out of the woodwork. He's updated his credit card number with the gym. He must be planning on coming back to the U.S. soon or he wouldn't have provided them a new card number."

The gleam in Nick's eye told me that, despite Lu's concerns, he still had some mojo left. I was as excited as Nick that he had a new lead.

He rounded up his laptop and logged in to the IRS system. He gestured to the computer. "Get the bank info while I call Ross."

Looked like we were working together again, even if it was in an unofficial capacity.

I turned Nick's laptop to face me and entered the credit card number Sundaram had provided to the gym. The first few numbers indicated it was a MasterCard. The next six digits would identify the bank that had issued the card. "It's a Chase account," I said when the data popped up on the screen.

Nick nodded to me before speaking into his phone.

"Ross, hey. Sorry to bother you on a holiday, but I need a hot-watch warrant ASAP."

A hot-watch warrant required a bank to provide law enforcement with a play-by-play account of activity on a credit card. With that information, we would be able to track Sundaram's movements and, with a little luck, track him down for an arrest. I'd never been involved in a hot watch before. I hoped my auditing job wouldn't get in the way.

Nick shared the details of the investigation with Ross, leaving out the fact that I had accompanied Nick to the boardinghouse, jewelry store, and gym. He answered a few questions, then discussed the procedure for getting the hot-watch warrant on a federal holiday. From Nick's end of the conversation, I gleaned that Ross could get in touch with the judge who was on call to handle emergency matters, though with the banks also closed today Nick wouldn't be able to deliver the warrant anyway. He'd have to wait until tomorrow, and he'd have to make it quick. He was scheduled to fly out to New Delhi in the early afternoon.

"Great," Nick said to Ross. "I'll swing by your office first thing in the morning."

He ended the call and immediately dialed Eddie to give him the update. "You'll have to handle the hot watch until I get back from India." He paused a moment. "If you're tied up, maybe Dorsey can help out."

William Dorsey had been a special agent only a matter of days and was already getting to handle a hot watch? No fair! And though I could count on Nick and Eddie to include me in the investigation, the new guy might be a rule follower and refuse to let me in on things. Ugh!

When Nick ended the call, he raised an excited fist. "We're closing in. I can feel it!"

I forced a smile.

Did that "we" still include *me*?

I spent the rest of the day hanging at Nick's place, watching him unpack the suitcase he'd taken to Japan and refill it with fresh clothes for his trip to India tomorrow.

"How's William doing?" I asked, my curiosity and envy getting the best of me.

"Dorsey?" Nick said, glancing my way. "He's a smart guy, but he's not up to speed yet. Things are really bogging down."

Part of me was sorry to hear about their backlog, but another part of me was glad they felt my absence.

We made love in the late afternoon. Nick was a man who kept his promises. I definitely needed that fan to cool off after the things he did to me.

We had an early dinner at an Indian restaurant. Nick wanted an introduction to Indian food so he wouldn't be at a loss when he arrived in New Delhi. We started off with an appetizer of vegetable samosas, enjoying *saag paneer* and naan for the meal and rice pudding for dessert. Nick seemed less resistant to the Indian food than he had been to the sushi, probably because the naan resembled the more familiar tortilla. He picked the raisins out of his pudding, though. I hadn't realized he wasn't a fan of the shriveled suckers. Guess you learn something new every day.

He dropped me off at my place, saying good-bye with a hug and kiss. "I'm not sure when I'll be back. I'll be in touch."

All I could do was nod.

When he walked away, I closed the door behind him and leaned back against it, my eyes closed. In hours, Nick would be back up in the air, on his flight to India. It felt as if everything in my life were up in the air at the moment.

I only hoped it wouldn't all come crashing down.

chapter twenty-seven

$\mathcal{S}$wish and Spit

Friday morning, I made the drive over to Fort Worth in record time. The traffic was light, many people opting to add a day of vacation to their holiday rather than return to work on a Friday. Not me, though. I'd started from scratch with the auditing department and had not yet accrued any vacation time.

When I arrived at Cowtown Candy Company, the receptionist told me Chloe wasn't in. "One of her daughters is sick. Ear infection."

It would've been nice if Chloe had bothered to let me know so I wouldn't have wasted my time driving over here.

The receptionist summoned Jeremy, who appeared in the foyer moments later, Dennis trailing after him.

Jeremy apologized on behalf of his sister. "Sorry, Tara. I figured Chloe would have called you."

"She was probably too worried about her baby to think about anything else," Dennis said. "She's a very dedicated mother."

I made sure the two had my phone number in case of future problems. "I'll come back on Monday."

I drove over to the audit office and made my way up to my cage—I mean cubicle. Only one other auditor was in the bank of cubes. He must've been out of vacation time, too. An episode of *The Big Bang Theory* played on his smartphone while he looked over a spreadsheet. Nerds unite! I introduced myself and continued on to the small square that was my designated workspace.

After plopping my butt down in the chair, I pulled the Rosedale Dental file from the stack and looked things over. The previous auditor who'd been assigned to the file had reviewed documentation provided by the practice, including earnings and service-related expenses, such as toothbrushes, mouthwash, and nitrous oxide.

Unlike Cowtown Candy Company, which had unusually high expenses relative to their income, the dental practice's expenses seemed unusually low compared to the revenues. Their CPA might have accidentally left some of the costs off their return, or they might have neglected to provide him with complete data. Might as well follow up, huh? Though, really, someone *over*paying their taxes wasn't nearly as much a problem as those who underpaid.

There was always the chance the return was correct, too. Though the earlier auditor had compared the data of this practice to dental industry standards, this practice could be especially cost-effective, particularly because it was a large practice in a lower-income part of town. Or perhaps they charged higher than average rates. That could explain things.

I dialed the dentist office and spoke with the bookkeeper who'd sent the documentation, notifying her that I'd be coming by their office on Monday.

"Is there a problem?" she asked.

"Nothing major," I said. "I just wanted to get out of the office." I chuckled, but she remained silent.

She really needed to lighten up.

"The ratio of revenue to expenses seems to be better than usual," I explained.

"The doctors keep a close eye on the bottom line," she said, a defensive tone in her voice.

Good thing I was used to being treated like this or I might have taken personal offense.

"Well then," I said, "my visit shouldn't take long." With that, I ended the call.

I selected another file involving a suburban trophy store operated by a married couple. The two certainly wouldn't win any awards for their bookkeeping. The records they sent over were disorganized and incomplete. Their record-keeping system seemed to consist of jotting down notes on gum wrappers and sticky notes. How the heck could they even tell how their store was doing?

Back at the audit department, I sat at my desk, staring at the wall of my cubicle, wishing I had a magical time machine that would fast-forward me through the next few weeks until after my trial was over. How would it turn out? Then again, maybe I could use that time machine to go back to that fateful night at Guys & Dolls. If given a second chance, I'd put a single bullet right between Don Geils' eyes. Then I'd still have my job as a special agent, still have my freedom, still have my gumption.

I'd have a different identity, though.

Killer.

I forced myself to look over another file or two, but I couldn't concentrate. The numbers danced around on the pages, taunting me. If I was convicted, how many years would I serve in prison? Two? Three? Four? More? How old would I be when I was released? Thirty? Thirty-one? Thirty-two? Older? What were my odds of winning in court? Twenty-five percent? Fifty percent? Seventy-five percent?

With Nick in India, my weekend was relatively uneventful. I found myself bored, anxious, antsy, like a kid with ADHD. Maybe I should get myself tested.

I phoned Eddie on Sunday afternoon to check in. "How's the hot watch going?" I asked. "Any action?"

"Still cold," he said. "The card hasn't been used yet."

"Maybe things will pick up soon. Sundaram might rent a car or make a stop at Starbucks."

"I hope so," Eddie replied. "I don't know how else we're going to track that guy down. He could be anywhere in the world right now."

Heck, for all we knew Nick could pass him on the street in New Delhi. Sundaram would be much more difficult to spot in a country full of Indians.

"Let me know if you hear something," I said.

"You know you don't even have to ask, right?" Eddie said.

"I appreciate that." It was big of Eddie to keep me in the loop. But he had my same work ethic, my same dedication to duty. He knew my termination was killing me. I hoped William Dorsey realized what a wonderful partner he had in Eddie.

When I climbed out of the shower Monday morning, my cell phone screen indicated a voice-mail message waited for me. I put the phone on speaker and listened.

"Hi, Tara. It's Jeremy Aberdeen. We just got a call from Chloe that her daughter is still sick. Okay if we postpone things until tomorrow?"

Sheez. My nieces and nephews had suffered ear infections as babies, and while they'd run high fevers and shrieked in agony at first, they'd recovered fairly quickly once the antibiotics took hold. I was beginning to think Chloe was jerking me around.

Was there something in those records she didn't want me to see?

I had a hard time believing it. I mean, Chloe came from a well-to-do family and had married into one that was even weller-to-do. She was paid a pretty penny to serve as CFO of the candy company, and per her father, she'd also made a killing in the stock market. She had no need to cook the books.

Right?

Still, I wanted to get this audit wrapped up.

I punched the button to call Jeremy back. I reached his voice mail. He was probably out messing with the cows or taste-testing a new product in the candy lab. Maybe he'd decided to expand on their popular cow patties and develop a whole line of chocolate-flavored animal scat. Piggy Poo. Donkey Doo. Ewe Ew.

At the tone I left a message telling him I'd be in first thing tomorrow.

I swung by the audit department in Fort Worth to pick up the Rosedale Dental files and arrived at the dentist office fifteen minutes later. The practice was housed in its own freestanding one-story building, between a thrift store and a fast-food chicken joint. The brick was painted a nice, shiny white, though the exterior was marred along one side by graffiti—a crudely drawn open mouth with crooked teeth over the words "BITE ME." Lovely. The chicken place had been hit harder. Their graffiti read: "ALL YOU CAN EAT FRIED PECKERS $1.99."

The sign in front of the dental office corroborated the information I'd seen in the file. The practice was operated by four dentists, three men and one woman, Drs. Barrett, Gore, Paulsen, and Walendzik. The W-2 information I'd seen indicated they employed twice as many hygienists, as well as four full-time office staff to handle appointments, billing, and bookkeeping.

I reached the front glass door and held it open for a black man with a walker making his way out. The man was grizzled and gaunt, stooped and shuffling. A bright yellow helium balloon advertising *Rosedale Dental* was tied to his walker with white curling ribbon. Looked like he'd been a good boy today.

"Bye now, Mr. Tillotson!" called the receptionist. "See you in six months."

"If I'm still alive," he replied jovially, giving her a wave before turning back to me. "Thank you, young lady." He gave me a wide smile that said not only was he friendly, but also he had just ten remaining teeth, all in front. Four on the bottom, six on top.

If you've got 'em, flaunt 'em.

Once he'd *klunk-klunk-klunked* his way out the door, I

stepped inside and over to the counter. "Hello," I said to the tiny fortyish redhead working the desk. "I'm Tara Holloway with the IRS. I was told to ask for Patricia."

"Right. She's expecting you." The woman picked up her phone. "Let me buzz her." She punched a four-button sequence, held the receiver to her ear, and said, "Hi, Pat. The IRS agent is here to see you." She listened for a moment, said, "'Kay," and hung up her phone before looking back up at me. "She'll be right up."

I stepped aside to wait and glanced around. Three people sat in the waiting room, two women, one man. All of them were elderly and dressed in the well-worn attire of those in the lower income brackets.

A moment later, a woman with large features and dark hair styled in a female version of a buzz cut pushed open the door. She looked over at me. "Miss Holloway?"

"That's me."

"Come on back."

I passed through the door and followed her down the hall past a series of open doors through which I could see patients reclined in the examination chairs. The sounds of swishing and spitting, gagging and gargling greeted me, along with the antiseptic smell of medicated mouthwash.

Patricia led me to an examination room at the very end. "You can work in here." She gestured to a computer on the counter. A rolling stool sat in front of it. "I've got the accounting records pulled up. Buzz me if you need anything. I'm at extension two-six-three-two." With that she left, closing the door behind her.

I sat my purse and briefcase on the counter, plunked my butt down on the stool, and spun myself around as if Rosedale Dental were Disneyland and the stool were the teacup ride. Hey, life's tough. You have to grab joy where you can find it.

Once the stool stopped spinning, I looked around. The exam room was typical. A set of sanitized tools sat on a paper-covered tray. A ceiling-mounted maneuverable light hung over the reclining chair. A box of latex gloves sat on the countertop. Metal canisters of oxygen and nitrous oxide stood in a special place under the cabinet.

Turning to the computer, I spent several hours looking over the expense data, running a trend analysis on my laptop, stopping only to step next door for lunch. Contrary to the graffiti on the building, the place offered no $1.99 all-you-can eat special. A side salad, two biscuits, and a soda cost me $5.39.

Toward the end of the day I finished with the expenses and decided to take a look at the revenue accounts. The practice's biggest source of income by far was Medicaid payments. Heck, they'd received half a million in benefits in the last year alone. The place had four dentists, sure, but that amount of money had to represent a high volume of procedures. Then again, what did I know about dentistry?

Still, something told me to take a closer look.

I pulled up the records for the most recent payments from Medicaid. A $40 payment for a routine cleaning for a Ruth Knowles. A $260 payment for a root canal for Camille Swearingen. A $300 payment toward a crown on a molar for an Alexander Tillotson.

Wait a minute.

Wasn't Tillotson the last name of the man who'd been leaving when I arrived? The man with only ten teeth left in his gums?

HIPPA protected patient records and I had no right to access them, at least not without a court order. Luckily for me, I could glean the information I needed from the billing files, which were organized by the names of the patients.

Pulling up the billing files, I ran down the list, searching for the name.

Tibbets.

Tillman.

There it was. *Tillotson.* Only one patient with that last name was listed. Alexander.

Why the heck had they ordered a crown for a molar when Alexander Ten-Teeth Tillotson had none? Had it been a mistake?

I jotted down his home address, as well as the names and addresses of several others for whom Rosedale Dental had billed Medicaid for crowns.

I gathered up my things and made my way to the front. I passed Patricia's office but noticed she was on her phone. I asked the receptionist to let Patricia know that I'd be back tomorrow afternoon.

In the parking lot, I climbed into my car and typed Alexander Tillotson's address into my GPS.

Time to play tooth fairy and pay him a visit.

chapter twenty-eight

House Calls

Alexander Tillotson lived in a small subsidized apartment three blocks from the dental office. He was more than happy to let me take a photograph of him standing in his front hall with his mouth hanging open. In fact, he insisted I take several more, putting one hand on his hip, the other behind his head in a pinup girl pose.

For someone who probably had trouble chewing meat, he was quite a ham.

I slid my cell phone back into my purse. "Thank you, Mr. Tillotson. I appreciate your cooperation."

He grabbed the handles of his walker to steady himself. "What did you say you needed the photos for again?"

"I'm auditing the dental practice. I just need to verify some of the procedures that were billed to Medicaid."

"Well, sure," he said. "They bill my cleanings every six months."

That wasn't all they'd billed. "Did you ever receive anything from Medicaid showing Rosedale Dental had billed for other procedures?"

He looked up in thought before looking back at me. "Come to think of it, there was a time a while back I got something in the mail about a cap or crown or something."

"Did you ask Rosedale Dental about it? Maybe call the Medicaid office?"

"No. I didn't get billed for nothing myself and I guess I forgot about it until just now. Should I make a call or something?"

"Not necessary," I said. "I'll see to it. You take care now."

I returned to my car and spent the next two hours visiting with four other patients of Rosedale Dental. All of them were happy to show me their teeth. One of them even showed me his appendix-surgery scar and an impressive plantar wart on the bottom of his foot that was roughly shaped like the state of Texas.

Only one of them actually had the crown that Medicaid had been billed for.

Patricia would definitely have some explaining to do tomorrow.

The highlight of my day was a quick phone call with Nick that evening.

"How are things going in New Delhi?" I asked.

He groaned in frustration. "Not good. I spoke with an agent of the Indian equivalent of the FBI. He asked me a lot of questions but made no promises. He acted as if this whole debt collection fraud could be nothing more than a miscommunication."

"As if you'd travel all the way to India without conducting a preliminary investigation." Sheez.

"It wouldn't surprise me one bit if the guy is over at the call center right now meeting with Sundaram, or Gupta, or Buttafuoco—"

"Bhattacharjee," I corrected. "Buttafuoco was that creep who cheated on his wife with that young girl who later shot his wife in the face."

"Oh yeah. That was some crazy shit, huh? Anyway, I'd

bet my left nut the official I spoke with is over at the call center right now soliciting a bribe."

"Why your left nut?"

"The right's my favorite."

I pondered what Nick had just told me. Not the BS about his favorite nut, but about the Indian government official possibly accepting a bribe from the target. Damn. That could effectively put an end to the case. If the target learned the U.S. government was on to him, he'd lie low, maybe obtain yet another alias before returning to America, or maybe not return to America at all.

Bribes, though commonplace in many third-world countries, had no place in the American economic system. To prevent those doing business in the United States from gaining an unfair advantage over those competing honestly under free-market rules, Congress had enacted the Foreign Corrupt Practices Act, a broad law that imposed potential felony punishment on anyone engaging in business in the United States who had unduly influenced a foreign official for business gain. India was known as a country where practices such as bribery were common and merely considered a cost of doing business.

Despite the fact that the law was in place, obtaining evidence of its violation was next to impossible. The exchanges often took place in the foreign countries and involved cash or property transactions that were difficult, if not impossible, to trace.

"What's your plan from here?" I asked.

"I'm supposed to follow up with the guy tomorrow and find out if the Indian government is going to cooperate."

"Good luck."

"Thanks," Nick said. "I'm going to need it."

chapter twenty-nine

$\mathcal{L}$aughter Isn't Always the Best Medicine

Jeremy phoned me again Tuesday morning.

"Let me guess," I said. "Chloe's baby is still sick."

"Unfortunately, yes," Jeremy said. "Chloe's down with the flu now, too. I told Chloe I'd swing by her house to pick up the key, but she didn't want to risk passing the flu on to me."

"Gee. How thoughtful," I snapped, out of patience now. Come hell, high water, or health issues, I had a job to do. It was ridiculous that Chloe seemed to be the only one in the company with access to her office and the hard copies of the financial records. Then again, family-owned businesses didn't always follow the best practices.

"Don't worry, Tara," Jeremy said. "Chloe's sending her husband by with the key today."

Oh. Now I felt a little bad for snapping at Jeremy. "All right. Call me when it gets there, okay?"

"Sure thing."

I drove through a coffeehouse and bought a skinny no-whip latte, knowing I'd need a little caffeine boost to be at my best when I confronted Patricia about the botched billings at Rosedale Dental.

As I drove west, sipping my drink, I wondered about the extent of the Medicaid fraud. Did Patricia know what was going on? Maybe. Maybe not. After all, she'd probably trusted the doctors to properly input the procedures in their hard-copy paperwork, right? Were all of the doctors involved? Again, maybe or maybe not. I had no way of telling from the billing accounts which doctor had treated the patients I'd visited with last night. I hadn't thought to ask them at the time. It had been early evening by then and my brain had started shutting down for the night. Oh, well. I could find out today.

I tossed back the last of my drink in the parking lot of Rosedale Dental, watching as a schoolkid emerged with a blue balloon tied to his wrist. He yanked on the string, making the balloon bob and weave in the air.

I climbed out of my car and went inside. The first thing I did was make a trip to the bathroom. I'd ordered a *venti* latte, but I apparently had only a nineteen-ounce bladder. Another minute and I'd have been in trouble.

The receptionist buzzed Patricia, who led me back to the same room at the end of the hall where she'd taken me yesterday.

I sat down on the stool, foregoing the teacup spin today, and got right down to business. "I've discovered a major problem."

Standing over me, she tilted her head, her face drawing inward. "In the bookkeeping?"

"The billing," I said. "Specifically the Medicaid billings."

A dark cloud seemed to pass over her face. Did this mean she knew something? Or did she simply not appreciate having her staff or record keeping criticized?

I handed her a list of the four patients I'd visited with last night for whom Medicaid had been wrongfully billed for crowns. "Can you tell me which doctor treated these patients?"

She looked down at the list in her hand. "Let me go get that information for you. I'll be right back."

She left the room, closing the door behind her. A couple of minutes later, my cell phone rang. The readout indicated it was Eddie.

I jabbed the button to accept the call. If his butt had dialed me again, it would soon receive a personally delivered message from my foot. "Hey, Eddie."

"Hey." Given that he was on the line, it looked like this was an intentional call. "Nick tells me his trip to India might be a bust."

"Yeah," I said, keeping my voice low so those in the adjacent rooms wouldn't be able to hear. "He called me last night, too. Sucks, huh?"

"Sure does. Luckily, we just got a hit on Sundaram's credit card here."

"You did?" Instinctively I stood up, as if ready to go after the guy. Old habits die hard. "Where?"

"Restaurant in San Francisco," Eddie replied. "A pancake house. Of course by the time Sundaram paid he was on his way out the door of the place, but we've got agents there on standby in case he uses the card again for lunch or dinner or checks into a hotel tonight."

The news was both good and bad. Good that a potential target had been sighted. Bad because it would suck if Eddie, Nick, and I had done all the work on the case and another agent would get the thrill of making the bust. There was nothing more satisfying than slapping handcuffs on a target after a successful investigation. It was like a work-related emotional orgasm.

"I wonder if he might have a room at a boardinghouse in San Francisco, too." I might not be officially assigned to the investigation anymore, but that didn't mean I couldn't offer suggestions.

"Good point," Eddie replied. "I'll make some calls today, look into it."

Our conversation shifted from his work to mine. I told him about my current case at Rosedale Dental, that I was waiting to find out which doctor or doctors had been behind the scheme to rip off Medicaid.

"No kidding?" Eddie chuckled. "No matter where you go, trouble just seems to find you."

What could I say to that? It was true.

The door opened and Patricia stepped in, followed by three men and one woman who I assumed were the dentists.

"I've gotta go," I said into my phone.

"Call me back as soon you're done there," Eddie said. "I can't wait to hear how this goes down."

I glanced down as I slid my phone into my pocket. When I looked back up, I found the five of them surrounding me like a street gang in blue scrubs.

Instinctively I reached for the hip holster that was no longer there. Damn! "What the—"

A latex-gloved hand clamped over my mouth from behind, cutting off my speech. If I'd had my Glock, these dentists would've had holes in them no amount of amalgam could fill. Without my weapon, though, I was in serious trouble.

The man behind me crooked his other arm around my neck, cutting off my air supply as he began dragging me backward. The others shuffled along with us like a mobile human cage entrapping me.

Panic seized me like a body-shaping undergarment. I opened my mouth and bit down hard on the hand that covered it, not stopping until I bit through latex, tasted blood, and hit bone, enjoying the oh-so-lovely scream of the doctor behind me. *Neener-neener.* I fisted my right hand, enclosed it with my left for extra leverage, and forced my elbow back with all my might into his soft gut.

The cry ended with an *oomph* as he released me.

Momentum carried me stumbling backward until I fell onto my ass on the floor. Before I could holler for help, the others pounced on me.

I'd been instructed in evasive maneuvers in my special agent training, but no matter how well trained I was, five against one was simply insurmountable odds. Still, the fact that I'd surely be bested by this squad of deviant doctors wasn't going to prevent me from giving these assholes the fight of their lives.

I could only wonder, though. Was I fighting for mine?

Exactly what did the doctors plan to do with me?

They grabbed my arms and tried to grab my legs as well. I managed to kick one of them in the nose, another in the mouth, and the woman in the ear before they dragged me into the examination chair, which Patricia had reclined.

The dentist I'd bitten sprawled across my legs and torso, pinning me to the chair, while the other two male doctors ripped yards of dental floss from the plastic containers in their hands and tied my forearms to the chair's armrests and my lower legs to the bottom of the chair. The female doctor stood next to my head, trying to force the mask for the laughing gas onto my face. I whipped my head side to side, screaming for someone to call the police.

Dear God! Please let someone hear me!

My arms and legs were immobile now, thanks to twenty yards of waxed, mint-flavored floss. One male doctor put a palm on my forehead, another on my chin, forcefully holding my head still despite my efforts to turn my face. I might not be able to open my mouth, but that didn't prevent me from telling them exactly what I thought of them through my clenched teeth. I used a number of words that would have shamed my instructor at Miss Cecily's Charm School.

My cursing ceased and I looked up in shock and horror as the female doctor strapped the nitrous oxide mask to my face.

Could a person overdose on laughing gas?

Would their evil faces be the last things I'd ever see?

chapter thirty

*N*o Laughing Matter

I woke to the feel of a hand gently slapping my face.

Eddie's concerned voice came through a haze, as if he were far away. "Tara? You okay?"

Okay? Of course I was okay. In fact, I was feeling groovy! Hahaha!

I giggled as my eyes fluttered open. Eddie, William Dorsey, and a female paramedic hunkered around the chair, looking down at me.

"She's coming to," Eddie said. "It's about time." He stood and stepped back to let the emergency medical technician tend to me.

Waking up more fully now, I tried to push the mask off my face.

"No, no," the woman said. "This is oxygen. You need it."

I took deep breaths and closed my eyes, trying to will the fog in my head to clear. In a moment or two, I felt mostly myself again. I opened my eyes and struggled to sit up in the seat. Big mistake. Nausea rolled through me. I turned my head just in time to prevent from urping latte all over myself. Instead, I urped it all over Dorsey's tassel loafers.

Oh, well. I'd always thought tassel loafers looked pretentious.

Eddie yanked a couple of latex gloves from the box on the counter. "Here you go, buddy." He handed them to William, who slid them onto his hands before removing his shoes.

I looked up at William. "Sorry."

He raised his palms. "Not your fault."

The paramedic crouched down next to me with a small penlight. "Let me take a quick look in your eyes."

"Okay."

She held open the lid on first my right, then my left, eye. "Looking good." She instructed me to remove my blazer and pushed up the sleeve of my sweater, affixing the Velcro blood pressure cuff to my arm. She squeezed the rubber pump. *Kshh-kshh-kshh.* Eyeing the readout, she said, "Your blood pressure's normal now. That's good."

She whipped out a cold stethoscope next and stuck it down into the V of my sweater, the cold of the metal making my nipples pucker in response. Her gaze locked on her sports watch as she counted my heartbeats. "Your heart rate is fine, too." She stood. "Overexposure to nitrous oxide can cause nerve damage and paralysis. Too much can be lethal. You're lucky you've got your partner looking out for you." She hiked a thumb at Eddie.

I turned my gaze on him.

He shrugged, as if saving my life were a routine matter. Of course, for the two of us it kinda was. "I got a bad vibe when you didn't call me back. I tried Rosedale Dental's number five times and nobody answered, so I called Fort Worth PD and asked if they could do a courtesy drive-by."

A male cop stepped forward, a white police-style motorcycle helmet in his hand. "I swung by and found a note taped to the door that the practice had closed due to an 'unexpected emergency.' Your car was still in the lot. I peeked in the windows and saw you tied to the chair."

I looked down at my arms and legs, noting the floss had dug wrinkles into my clothes. Someone had cut the floss off me and it lay in piles on the floor around the chair.

"What about the dentists?" I asked. "And the book-keeper? They're the ones who tied me to the chair."

"We've sent officers to each of their residences and put out an APB on their license plates. No word yet."

The cop pulled out a notepad and asked me a few questions. When he finished, he slid the pad back into his pocket, activated a button on his shoulder-mounted mic to update Dispatch, and stepped to the door. "We'll be in touch when we find the doctors and their staff."

"Thanks." Was it wrong of me to hope they'd find them at the bottom of the Trinity River?

The paramedic had me stand and perform some basic physical maneuvers to make sure I was okay. When I'd passed muster, she packed her things back into her bag. "You're good to go."

I thanked her as well.

It was three in the afternoon by then. I called my new boss and told him what happened.

"Are you for real?" Hartford asked.

"Yep."

"I've worked for the IRS for decades and nothing even remotely like this has ever happened to any of my staff."

What could I say to that? "I bring out the crazy in people."

I was still feeling a little queasy, so Hartford suggested I take the rest of the day off.

On the way out, Eddie grabbed a bright yellow helium balloon from the half dozen tied to the receptionist's chair. "Here you go," he said, handing the string to me. "A souvenir."

"Yay."

William and Eddie had driven over from Dallas in Dorsey's car, so Eddie drove me back to my place. We went inside, where I tied the balloon to the back of a kitchen chair. I reached into the fridge and pulled out a beer for

Eddie, then fried us up a couple of baloney sandwiches. The only thing I'd had all day was the latte and, like I mentioned earlier, it hadn't exactly stuck with me.

"Not bad," Eddie said after he'd taken a bite. "Who would've thought white-trash food would taste so good?"

"I'd be happy to share the family recipe for squirrel stew."

His lip curled in disgust. "I'll pass on that. But thanks."

Eddie's cell phone chirped and he took the call. From his end of the conversation I gleaned that the IRS office in San Francisco had sent an agent out with a photograph of Sundaram to make the rounds of boardinghouses. He'd hit pay dirt at a rooming house in the Pacific Heights neighborhood. Sundaram maintained a prepaid room there under yet another alias—Neelam Rangarajan.

Unfortunately, the pay dirt turned out to be dust in the wind. The landlord noted that the man he knew as Rangarajan had packed up and left that morning without saying where he was headed. A search of the room turned up no useful evidence. Like Cindy Allen, the landlord promised to let agents know if the man returned.

A few minutes later, Eddie's wife swung by to pick him up and take him home.

I walked him to the door when she arrived. "I'd be dead if it wasn't for you, Eddie."

Again, he shrugged. "You've had my back before. Isn't that what partners are for?"

I looked up into his brown eyes. "We're not partners anymore."

"I seem to keep forgetting that."

I hated to ask, but at the same time I wanted to know. "Working with William. What's that like?"

Eddie looked down for a moment in thought. "Well, he's smart. Determined. Knows the special agent manual backward and forward. Likes to talk sports."

"Sounds like the perfect partner."

"He is," Eddie said. "That's why I can't figure out why I miss working with you."

I replied with a friendly punch in the arm.

"Take care of yourself," he said.

"I will."

After Eddie left I lay down on the couch with Nutty beside me. It wasn't until I woke early that evening that I realized I hadn't heard from Jeremy.

I retrieved my cell phone from my purse. I'd missed a call from him that came in at two, when I'd been lying unconscious in the dentist chair. I listened to the voice-mail message.

"Hi, Tara. It's Jeremy. Listen, Chloe called and said her husband's having car trouble. Dad and I realize this is dragging out far longer than necessary and we don't want to put you out any more. He's going to head over to Chloe's house this evening for the key. We'll have it for you first thing tomorrow morning."

Looked like I'd finally get my hands on those hard copies. A child's illness was one thing, but now car trouble, too? Call me suspicious, but the repeated excuses felt like delaying tactics.

Now, more than ever, I was curious to see what was in those records.

chapter thirty-one

$\mathcal{B}$ad Credit

I arrived at Cowtown Candy Company at nine o'clock sharp Wednesday morning, ready to get to work. Chloe still hadn't returned. No big surprise there. The receptionist paged Jeremy for me. He led me upstairs to the offices.

We found Dennis standing in front of Chloe's door, a screwdriver in his hand.

Jeremy's brows angled in confusion. "What are you doing, Dad?"

He gestured to Chloe's door. "Fixing to take this door off its hinges."

Anger heated the blood in my veins. "I take it you didn't get the key last night?"

Dennis cut an apologetic look my way. "I drove by Chloe's house, but she wasn't there when I arrived. She'd gone out with some of her former sorority sisters to a play in Dallas. She must've forgotten I was coming."

A play? What happened to her flu?

"Was her husband home?" I asked.

Dennis nodded. "Yes, but he didn't know where the key was."

"Shouldn't he have had it? According to Chloe, he was supposed to bring it by yesterday."

Dennis shook his head. "Seems she'd forgotten to mention it to him."

The oh-so-perfect Chloe had supposedly forgotten not only to give her husband the key but also that her father was coming by to get it? I didn't believe that for a second. Any of it.

"Wait a minute." Jeremy looked even more confused. "Chloe called me yesterday afternoon and said he couldn't bring it by because he was having car trouble."

Dennis lifted a shoulder. "There must have been some miscommunication." He looked back at the door. "At any rate, I'm sure I can get this door off if you'll bear with me a moment."

I reached into my purse, retrieved my wallet, and whipped out my Neiman Marcus credit card. "I've got an easier solution."

Dennis raised a palm in invitation. "Be my guest."

I stuck my card between the door and the frame, pushed it hard against the mechanism, and gave it a forceful flick while turning the knob.

Click.

We were in.

"You learn that trick at the IRS?" Jeremy asked.

"No," I replied. "From a friend in high school." Back then I hadn't had a Neiman Marcus card and had to use my driver's license. That little trick had enabled me to spring several of my friends from house arrest to sneak out after curfew.

I stepped into Chloe's office and flipped on the light. The men followed me in.

"I'll check this filing cabinet," Dennis told his son, gesturing to the one on the left of the bookcase. "You check the other."

Dennis and Jeremy began pulling out the drawers one

by one and looking at the file tabs on the hanging folders inside.

Dennis read the names out loud for my benefit. " 'Insurance Policies.' 'Equipment Warranties.' 'Property Tax Statements.' "

None of those were the items I needed.

Jeremy did the same on his side. " 'Store Leases.' 'Furniture.' 'Light Fixtures.' "

Nope. Nope. And nope.

The two continued to rattle things off until Jeremy opened the third drawer down.

"There's not much in this one."

I stepped closer and looked. Sure enough, the drawer contained far fewer files than any of the others. More suspiciously, the exact files I needed were missing.

Jeremy looked from me to Dennis. "It looks like some of the files have been removed."

"Maybe Chloe took some work home with her," Dennis suggested.

I had a hard time believing she'd just happen to take home the same files that I'd need to complete the audit. Besides, if that were the case, why not just say so?

"Call her," I insisted. "Ask her where the files are."

Dennis stepped over to Chloe's desk and dialed her home number. He blushed slightly and turned away when he obviously reached her machine. He left a quick message and tried her cell. Same result. He left a voice mail.

He turned to me, seeming at a loss for words. No problem. I had plenty to supply.

"One way or another we need to get that documentation. Are you a signer on the checking account?" I asked.

Dennis nodded. "I was the one who originally opened the account years ago. We added Chloe when she came on board as CFO."

"Same for the mortgage accounts? Utilities? Manufacturing supplies?"

He nodded again.

"Let's go straight to the source, then." I instructed him to give the bank, the mortgage company, the utilities, and the suppliers a call and ask for duplicate statements and invoices.

As long as I was at it, I figured I might as well have him get invoices from the janitorial service, too. I'd thought their fees seemed somewhat excessive. It couldn't hurt to take a look.

"I'd like to see copies of the statements from the janitorial service, too."

Dennis cocked his head. "We don't use an outside janitorial service. We've got a full-time employee here during business hours to take care of the cleaning, and a part-timer in the evenings."

"Not according to the accounting records." Now I knew for certain. Something was definitely up.

Dennis clearly had conflicting feelings. His eyes flashed with alarm, though he also crossed his arms over his chest, as if rejecting my insinuation. "What are you saying, Ms. Holloway?"

I gestured to the computer on Chloe's desk. "Log in to the accounting system and I'll show you."

Dennis hesitated a brief moment before he made his way around his daughter's desk, sat down, and booted up her system. Once the sign-in screen popped up, he logged in and clicked on the icon for the company bookkeeping.

I stepped up next to him, Jeremy taking a spot on the other side. I motioned to the screen. "Scroll down."

Dennis moved the cursor down through the accounts.

"There." I pointed. " 'Janitorial Service.' "

Dennis clicked on the account to open it and leaned toward the screen, lines forming across his forehead. "I don't understand. What is this?"

Jeremy leaned in, too.

I hated to be the one to break it to them, but they needed to know. "That data shows that eighty grand was paid to Squeaky Clean Custodial Service."

Dennis sat back, his face tight, perplexed. "Never heard of them."

Jeremy turned to his father. "Dad, this doesn't look good."

The throbbing vein in Dennis' neck told me he was becoming agitated. He threw up a hand, cutting Jeremy off before he could say more. "Before you go off half-cocked, Son, you need to remember this is Chloe we're talking about. She knows how to handle basic bookkeeping. She's a CPA, for God's sake! It's her financial expertise that's keeping this company afloat." He lowered his voice and muttered, "All you've done is cost this business money, what with your pet cows and edible bullshit and all those other ridiculous ideas."

Maybe it wasn't my place to butt into their dysfunctional family matters, but enough was enough.

"Jeremy's 'ridiculous ideas' are what's enabled this company to hang on," I said. "Particularly the 'edible bullshit.' You realize his cow patties are bringing in major moolah?"

Dennis looked up at me. "What do you mean?"

I motioned for him to let me have the chair. After we'd swapped places, I generated a report showing sales figures for each type of candy the company produced. While the traditional candies on which the company had been built continued to enjoy steady sales, Jeremy's cow patties, Licorice Lassoes, and Chickenfeed topped the sales charts. Orders were increasing exponentially.

"All of the old-fashioned candies combined don't match the cow patty sales." I gave Dennis a moment to digest that information before I pointed at the screen. "Numbers don't lie, Mr. Aberdeen. Jeremy's a marketing genius."

Dennis stared at the screen for a moment or two. He glanced over at his son, then back at the screen, his expression incredulous, as if he seemed to be seeing his son in a different light, as if the black-and-white figures in front of him told him things about his son he'd been unable to see otherwise.

Sure, Jeremy was a college dropout who'd knocked up his girlfriend and had a shotgun wedding. Yep, his shaggy hair was always in need of a trim. He might even have dozens of goofy ideas. But he also had some damn good ones. He was one sharp candy-coated cookie. It was time someone in the family started paying attention.

Dennis reached over to the keyboard and hit the button to print the report. He stood up straight and looked Jeremy in the eye. "I don't know what to say, Son, but that I'm sorry. I've obviously been selling you short."

Jeremy could have gloated. He could've gotten angry. He could've done what I would've done in his position and put a finger up to his father's cheek and shouted, *In yo' face!*

But Jeremy did none of those things. Because while no one else in his family might have realized his value, Jeremy had. So had his wife. And apparently that was all that really mattered to him.

I picked up my things and stepped to the door. "See you two tomorrow."

chapter thirty-two

$\mathcal{D}$eath by Chocolate

I spent the rest of the day at the IRS audit department office in Fort Worth, caged in my cubicle, reviewing paperwork sent in by a company that made engraved monuments and headstones. Talk about dull. Much more of this and they'd be inscribing a stone for me. *Here lies Tara Holloway. She died of boredom.*

Nick phoned me from the airport in New Delhi that night.

"I've gotten nowhere here," he said. "The local officials won't cooperate at all. This whole trip has been a waste of time and money."

I was sorry to hear his trip had been a bust, but I was also glad to know he'd be home soon. I had been awfully lonely without him, even with Nutty to keep me company. "I can't wait to see you," I told Nick. What's more, Giacomo wanted to meet with Nick to go over his testimony in my upcoming trial. "Were there any more hits on the hot watch today?"

"One," Nick said. "Eddie texted me about it and I told him I'd give you the news. Sundaram rented a car in San

Francisco for a one-way trip. Guess where he's supposed to turn the car in?"

My ears pricked up. "Dallas?"

"You got it."

A-ha! "So he's headed this way. When is he scheduled to turn the car in?"

"He left the date open."

"Have you contacted Cinderella to let her know to keep an eye out for him?"

"Eddie has."

I felt my adrenaline surge. I missed the rush that came with a successful bust. I'd hoped to bust the doctors at Rosedale Dental, but we all know how that turned out, don't we? Fort Worth PD had called me earlier to let me know they'd apprehended Patricia and two of the doctors, but the other two were still on the loose. Dr. Paulsen had apparently tried to hide in his attic, but a police dog had easily sniffed him out. The bloody finger had given him away. *Neener-neener.*

Still, Sundaram was on his way. It shouldn't be long now. . . .

Thursday morning, when I arrived at Cowtown Candy Company, Chloe's Town & Country minivan was parked in the lot. Whaddya know. Looked like she'd finally decided to grace us with her magnificent presence.

The receptionist was at her desk, looking not merely like the cat that swallowed the canary but more like the lion that had swallowed the ostrich. She pointed to the ceiling. "You can go on up. They're waiting for you."

"Thanks." I stepped past her, through the door that led to the manufacturing facility and administrative offices, and started up the metal staircase. I was halfway across the catwalk when Chloe appeared at the other end.

"Whoa." I hardly recognized her. Rather than her usual perfectly coordinated outfits, she wore sneakers, a pair of grungy, wrinkled yoga pants, and a faded sweatshirt. Her normally lustrous hair stuck out at crazy angles all over her head as if she'd simply rolled out of bed this morning and forgotten to brush it. She wore not a molecule of makeup. Without the usual eye shadow, mascara, liner, and blush, she was surprisingly plain.

Her eyes blazed with vengeance. Even the dimple, which was usually so adorable, seemed to look like a flaw today, a chink in her armor. "How dare you!" she shrieked.

I stopped in the center of the catwalk. "How dare I what? Do my job?"

She headed toward me, stomping so hard the catwalk shook.

The employees on the production staff stopped working and looked up at us.

As Chloe continued to approach, I found myself instinctively reaching for my pepper spray, once again coming up empty. The Lobo had confiscated my spray along with my badge and Glock when she'd been forced to fire me.

Dang.

But no need to worry, right? I mean, this was Chloe "Dean's List" Aberdeen I was dealing with. She wouldn't do anything crazy or violent. She was probably just blowing off steam.

I held my ground as she came closer, though I set my purse and briefcase down to have my hands free, just in case. Instinctively I turned sideways to make myself a more narrow target, squatted into a fighting stance, and raised my hands in front of my chest, ready to fend off an attack if necessary.

When she was a mere five feet from me, she stopped. She glared into my eyes with a rage so raw, so intense, I found myself inching backward.

"Aa-a-a-a-h!" She let out a scream like something released from the gates of hell, ducked her head, and hurled herself at me, coming at me like a human cannonball.

On the narrow catwalk, there was nowhere for me to escape to. She collided headfirst with me, the top of her skull in my gut, knocking me back on my butt and forcing the air from my lungs.

She pounced on me, slapping at my face, grabbing at my

hair, clawing my cheeks. "You bitch! You nosey fucking bitch!"

I twisted to the side and threw her off balance. On her knees, she struggled to a stand. But I was faster. On my feet again, I held up fists to protect my face and scrambled backward, trying to reach the stairs to escape.

Chloe launched herself at me again and the next thing I knew we were wrestling in a standing position as if we were playing a game of chicken—without the swimming pool or anyone on our shoulders, of course.

Jeremy and Dennis appeared at the other end of the catwalk.

"Chloe! Stop!" Jeremy yelled.

She didn't listen. Hell, as crazed as she looked right now, she probably didn't hear him.

Jeremy and Dennis rushed toward us.

My training gave me an advantage, and I managed to force Chloe against the rail. Pushing her back against the banister for leverage, she kicked out with both feet, hitting me in the chest and knocking me backward.

Oh, hell no.

This woman would not best me again.

I grabbed her legs as she kicked out again and forced them upward. She teetered on the railing, on the verge of falling backward over the side. She shrieked, reaching out and grabbing the lapels of my new coat as momentum carried her over the rail.

The force yanked me to the rail, bending me in two over the bar. Holy shit! With her height and curves, Chloe outweighed me by a good twenty pounds. No way could I support her weight. If she didn't let go of me, she'd pull me over with her. I gripped the bar with one tight fist, clawing at Chloe's hands with the other. "Let go of me!"

Chloe hung from me for a split second, kicking her feet in the air in a desperate attempt to find leverage. Then the laws of physics took hold and Chloe dragged me over the railing with her.

chapter thirty-three

*H*ave Mercy

Looked like that fortune cookie knew its stuff. I'd reached unexpected new heights, all right.

KERPLUNK!

And now I'd reached unexpected depths in an enormous vat of dark chocolate. Headfirst, no less.

The thick, warm, suffocating liquid surrounded me. I'd heard of death by chocolate, but I don't think this was really what they had in mind.

The good news was that the melted chocolate broke our fall. The bad news was that, in my panic, I'd sucked the thick, warm chocolate into my mouth and lungs. I fought my way up through the heavy liquid and surfaced, sputtering and coughing.

Fortunately, the vat was only four feet deep, so I was able to stand. I wiped the thick goo from my eyes to see Chloe doing the same.

"Call me a bitch, will you?" I seized her arm, twisted it up behind her, and put my palm on the back of her head, dunking her face-first into the chocolate. It would serve her right if she drowned.

"Stop!" Jeremy hollered from the catwalk above. He took off running, his footsteps *clang, clang, clanging* on the metal as he raced down to the first floor.

Dennis was frozen on the catwalk, his mouth gaping, his eyes wide in disbelief.

A rounded stirring blade at the bottom of the vat brushed up against my ankle and I lifted my leg to let it pass.

By the time Jeremy reached us, I'd let Chloe come up for air. Given that I faced an excessive force trial, I figured killing her might not look too good. Still, I had her arm crooked up behind her and a tight grip on her hair to keep her immobilized.

Several employees had gathered around, unsure what to do. Thankfully, one of them had the sense to turn off the heat and the stirring mechanism.

Jeremy ran up, grabbed a large wooden paddle off a hook nearby, and held it out. "Grab this, Tara!"

I let go of Chloe, gave her a forceful shove between the shoulder blades, and took hold of the paddle, using it to leverage myself up and over the side of the vat. No easy feat given my clothes and hair held what felt like fifty additional pounds of melted chocolate.

Chloe draped her arms over the edge of the vat and hung her head, sobbing now, her tears making rivulets in the chocolate mask coating her face. "I'm sorry!" she cried. "I'm so sorry!"

Dennis hurried down the steps and rushed over, helping Chloe out of the vat. She slipped as she tried to climb out, twice falling back before finally managing to emerge. She stood hunched over next to the vat, her hands on her thighs, melted chocolate dripping from her to form a pool around her soaked sneakers.

Flinging wet chocolate from his hands, Dennis turned to me. "Are you all right, Miss Holloway?"

I was fine, though I couldn't say the same for my brand-new coat, the beautiful one Nick had bought me for Christmas, the one with the *Dry clean only* label.

A half hour later, after rinsing off the best I could in the ladies' room and changing into a cowhide-print jumpsuit Jeremy had rounded up for me, I sat in Dennis's office. Chloe sat in the other wing chair, still crying uncontrollably. Jeremy had pulled his rolling desk chair into the office and sat between me and Chloe, as if ready to protect me should his sister go berserk again. Dennis sat behind his desk, staring at his daughter as if she were a complete stranger. At this moment, I supposed she was.

Dennis handed me a stack of paperwork, including invoices, bank statements, and utility bills, all of the documentation I'd asked for. I thumbed quickly through the material. The increase in electric bills was explained by a switch to an environmentally friendly green plan, though there were sticky notes on pages showing that Chloe had diverted the extra mortgage payments and fraudulent janitorial fees to her personal bank account, along with tens of thousands of dollars in payments allegedly made to suppliers.

"You stole from this company," Dennis said to his daughter, his voice more incredulous than accusing. "You stole from your own family. How could you do that, Chloe?" The hurt and betrayal he felt were etched on to his face, his dimple drooping, the dent in his face nothing compared to the hole in his heart.

"I wanted you to b-b-be proud of m-m-me!" she stammered, gulping air between her sobs. "I wanted you to think everything was f-f-fine." After a few seconds, she finally got her sobbing under control. She took a breath to calm herself. "I only intended to borrow the money, Dad. I planned to pay it back. Really!" She sounded desperate now, desperate for her father to believe her. She gestured to the computer. "If you look in the system you'll find a spreadsheet under the file name 'Company Loans.' "

Dennis maneuvered the mouse, hit a few keys, and pulled up the document. I stepped over and took a look over his shoulder. Sure enough, each payment Chloe had received from the company was documented by date and amount. She'd even tacked on interest at 10 percent and tracked the total accumulated outstanding balance.

She sniffled again and dabbed at her nose with the tissue. "I was going to pay it all back as soon as we got on our feet again."

"On your feet again?" Dennis asked. "What are you talking about?"

Over the next fifteen minutes, I learned everything there was to know about the Aberdeen family, the skeletons in their closets, their interpersonal dynamics, the full extent of their dysfunction. Seemed young Chloe had clued in early on that Jeremy was a disappointment to her father. Being a daddy's girl, she didn't like to see her father upset and did her best to make up for Jeremy's perceived shortcomings by being as perfect as possible herself, always pleasant and polite, pretty and punctual. It was a habit she'd developed as a young child, a role in the family that had, in some ways, been thrust upon her.

Problem was, life isn't perfect and neither was Chloe.

That alleged killing she'd made in the stock market had actually been the opposite. She'd lost hundreds of thousands of dollars investing in a start-up company that had seemed like a sure thing but later went belly up. Her husband had been ousted from his job at Jennings Prefab a year and a half ago when he missed the deadline for submitting a bid to supply portable buildings to the Fort Worth school district. The flub cost the company half a million dollars in potential profits and was the last straw in a long line of blunders made by a sleep-deprived father with a colicky baby.

Chloe worked the crumpled tissue in her hands. "He's sent résumés out all over Dallas and Fort Worth but hasn't gotten a single call."

Their exclusive lifestyle necessitated two good salaries and, with only one of them bringing home the bacon, their financial woes began to snowball. They fought to keep up appearances in their upscale neighborhood while also dealing with a costly foundation repair on their house and Chloe's husband's battle with depression.

"We've talked to an attorney about filing bankruptcy," Chloe said, out of tears now, though still sniffling. "We've also been going to a marriage counselor. All of this stress has been hard on our relationship." She looked down at her lap for a moment before forcing herself to look back up at her father. "I'm sorry, Dad." She turned to me. "Tara, I'm sorry about . . ." She waved her tissue around as if not sure how to encapsulate in words what she'd put me through. She finally settled on, "Everything."

Dennis was quiet a moment before releasing a long breath. "I wish you'd told us what was going on, Chloe. We could've helped you out." He tilted his head. "You be honest with me from now on. You hear me?"

She nodded.

Dennis glanced at Jeremy before turning his attention back to Chloe. "I've been way too hard on your brother all these years. We may not see eye to eye or go about things the same way, but he's a good kid." Dennis told Chloe about the data I'd given him that showed Jeremy's candy concepts were the company's best sellers.

Chloe's lip quivered as she turned to her brother. "Oh, Jeremy, I wished I'd noticed. I've been so wrapped up in all of my problems I never thought to analyze the sales data."

Jeremy raised a forgiving palm. "It's all right."

Dennis shifted his focus from his children back to me. "We've got a fine mess to deal with, Miss Holloway. Where do we go from here?"

I mulled over my options.

Option one, I could be a hard-ass, hit the company with a variety of penalties, seize their assets to satisfy their tax debt, and refer Chloe for criminal prosecution. The crazy woman could have killed me earlier. If not for that vat of chocolate breaking our fall my neck would likely be broken now.

Option two, I could go easy on them, work out a payment

plan to ensure all taxes were paid and that both the company and Chloe stayed in compliance from here on out.

Sure, Chloe had done some bad things, some wrong things. She'd gone whacko earlier when she'd attacked me, her emotions taking over.

But I, too, had been there, done that.

Chloe didn't need a criminal record bogging her down. She needed a second chance.

Here I was, finally in a position to expose Chloe Aberdeen to all the world for the phony she was, and I wasn't going to take it. I was going to show some mercy toward her. Besides, Dennis and Jeremy had done their best to cooperate. They hadn't been parties to Chloe's fraud. No sense punishing them for her actions.

Maybe Anthony Giacomo was right. Maybe I wasn't as tough as I thought I was.

"Replace my coat and we'll keep what happened today between us. I'll work up the numbers and send y'all a bill. If you're not able to pay the taxes all at once, an installment plan can be worked out."

"That's it?" Dennis asked, his brows raised hopefully.

"That's it."

Chloe thanked me in a soft, teary voice. "I did remember you, Tara," she admitted. "I'm sorry I pretended like I didn't."

A-ha! But I supposed that was all water under the bridge now, huh?

"You were always smart and thoughtful and willing to lend a hand." She looked at me with eyes filled with remorse. "I kind of hated you for that."

Though her words sounded harsh, I knew she meant the comment to be a compliment of sorts. Who would have guessed it? Chloe Aberdeen had been jealous of *me*.

She dabbed at her eyes again. "I'm sorry I didn't tell you. I was afraid, I guess. I knew you'd figure out I was a fraud."

"We all make mistakes," I told her. Hell, I knew that better than anyone.

The situation thus resolved, Dennis shook my hand and Jeremy walked me out to my car.

I looked down at the jumpsuit. "I'll get this back to you."

"Keep it. It's cute on you." Jeremy stepped over and gave me a warm hug. "Give me a call sometime when you're free. We'll have a rematch at darts."

chapter thirty-four

The Hot Watch Heats Up

"What in the world are you wearing?" Clyde Hartford stopped as I came up the hallway in the black-and-white jumpsuit. "And why does your hair look gooey?"

"I fell off a catwalk at the candy company and ended up in a vat of chocolate," I said, making a very long, very complicated story as short and simple as possible.

"Lu warned me you'd be a handful." He shook his head as he headed back to his office.

I plunked down on my rolling chair in my cubicle. I would've loved to go home for a shower and shampoo, but by the time I drove to Dallas and back half the day would be gone. With my days as a free woman potentially numbered, I didn't want to have to make up any more lost time.

I couldn't wait for Nick to get home tonight. I knew he'd probably be tired again, but at least I'd get to curl up next to him in bed. I might only have a couple more weeks with him. I wanted to make the most of every day, every hour, every second.

I spent the afternoon looking over the accounts receivable for Corner Pocket, Inc., a store that sold pool tables. Unfortunately, it sold them on credit to an exceptional number of deadbeats. The store had taken a large write-off that triggered the audit, but after I'd examined the ledger it seemed the deduction was legit. I was on the fence about some travel deductions that seemed to be part business, part personal, but decided to let them slide. They weren't significant and a good CPA or tax attorney might find a way to justify them. I wrote up a clean audit report and called the business owner to tell him there'd be no tax assessment.

Rather than accepting my findings graciously, he ranted about how the IRS had wasted his time with the audit. "It took me four hours to print out all of that data the IRS demanded. Used up a full ream of paper and two printer cartridges. My time's important, you know. It's harassment is what it is! It's like the Spanish Inquisition. You auditors—"

I'd had enough of this guy and his yapping piehole. "You want me to take a closer look at those travel expenses?"

That shut him up.

On the way home from work that evening, I stopped by an Asian grocery and picked up a half gallon of green tea ice cream. After the day I'd had, I needed a treat.

At my town house, I stuck a frozen pizza in the oven to cook while I went upstairs to bathe. I had to turn my shower massager to sandblast mode and lather, rinse, and repeat twice to get all of the heavy chocolate out of my hair, but finally I was clean again. It made me sad to see all of that chocolate going down the drain. What a waste.

Alicia arrived home from work just as I was taking the pizza out of the oven.

"I made dinner," I told her.

"Good," she said. "I'm starved."

Over dinner, I told her what had taken place at Cowtown Candy Company.

"What?" Alicia's eyes widened as she held her pizza poised for a bite. "Chloe stole from her own father?"

"Borrowed without asking, I guess." I shrugged and pointed my fork at Alicia. "I hate to say I told you so—"

"No you don't. You love to say 'I told you so.'"

It was true. I liked being right. "Whatever. But I was right about Chloe."

"Okay. You win. Now what's for dessert?"

"You've got two choices. Green tea ice cream or chocolate poop."

She made a face. "I'll go with the ice cream."

Nick had taken a shuttle to the airport when he left for New Delhi, but I picked him up at DFW that evening. He looked even more beat this time than when he'd returned from Tokyo. Two international trips in one week had really taken their toll.

As he exited the revolving door leading from the airport's secure area into the baggage claim, he offered me a weary smile and a warm hug. He buried his face in my hair. "Lord, I've missed you." He sniffed. "Did you get some kind of chocolate-scented shampoo?" He stepped back and eyed the old coat I was wearing. "And where's the coat I bought you?"

"It's a long story," I said. "I'll tell you on the drive home."

Nick managed to stay awake on the ride this time, listening to my story. "Boy howdy," he said when I finished. "How is it that you're a magnet for every kook out there?"

Given my history, the question probably wasn't intended to be merely rhetorical. Still, there was no good answer for it. Why *did* I seem to bring out the inner nut job in my targets? Was it just bad luck, or was there something more to it? Did I give off some kind of pheromone or something?

We reached Nick's town house and went inside. Nutty was thrilled to see Nick, wagging his tail so hard it threatened to come loose.

Nick got down on his knees and wrestled with his old dog, who offered a playful growl in return.

While Nick went upstairs to take a quick shower, I warmed him up some of the leftover pizza I'd brought with me and retrieved a beer from the fridge. Ten minutes later, he was seated at the kitchen table, digging in, while I opened yet another gift bag full of goodies he'd brought me. This one contained jasmine incense, a trio of bangle bracelets, and a pair of red curly-toed shoes embellished with fake jewel accents.

I stood and slid my feet into the shoes. "I feel like a magic genie."

"Good." Nick cast me a predatory grin. "'Cause I've got several wishes I hope you'll grant me."

I cut him a grin right back. "Don't you have to rub my lamp first?"

Nick moaned. "Darlin', I'll rub anything you ask me to."

He finished his dinner, held out his plate while Nutty licked it clean, and stuck it in the dishwasher. He headed straight toward me, picked me up, and slung me over his shoulder. "Come on, woman. Let's get started on those wishes."

Brr-r. Brr-r. Brr-r.

The vibration of Nick's cell phone woke us at 7:15 the next morning. Nick grabbed it from the nightstand and checked the readout before accepting the call. "Eddie. Hey."

I snuggled closer to Nick, laying my head on his chest, partly because it felt good and partly because I was being nosey and hoped that by moving closer I'd be able to listen in on the conversation.

"He did?" Nick said. "Well, he ought to be here in Dallas any time then." He paused a moment. "All righty. See you at the office."

I sat up as Nick ended the call. "Is that about Sundaram?"

"Yup," Nick said. "He just used his card at a convenience store in Vegas."

He was headed this way, obviously, though there was no way of telling how long he might stay in Sin City.

"Someone's checking the boardinghouses in Vegas, right?"

"They've already sent an agent out to make the rounds."
"Good."

Nick looked down at me. "I'm scheduled to meet with your attorney this afternoon to talk about my testimony."

"Ugh." I sat up and threw the covers back as I climbed out of bed. "Did you have to remind me about the trial?"

"Sorry," Nick said. "I just thought you might like to know."

We got out of bed and began our day. Luckily, it was Friday. Thank goodness. It had been a long, hard week. I needed some fun.

Nick and I made the most of the weekend. Though neither of us came right out and said it, we both knew this might be one of our last weekends together for a long while.

We went to see a movie, out for dinner, dancing at a country-western bar. With my life spinning out of my control, it was nice to feel Nick's strong arms around me, guiding me in safe, controlled turns as we twirled our way around the floor. We made love so many times I lost count. I found myself wondering how long a prisoner was given for a conjugal visit. Fifteen minutes? Thirty? A full hour? Would there be time for foreplay, maybe a cigarette afterward? Not that I smoked, but I might be able to trade the cigarette for something else, like a shiv made from a toothbrush.

On Sunday evening, just as I was about to head back to my town house, Nick's cell phone rang again. He glanced at the screen and looked up at me, a flash of excitement in his eyes. "It's Cindy Allen."

My heart kicked up to a thousand RPMs. A call from Cindy could only mean one thing. Sundaram, or whoever the hell he was, had returned to Dallas.

Nick took the call. "Hello, Miss Allen." A pause. "He did?" Another pause. "Uh-huh. My partner and I will be there ASAP. Thanks."

As soon as Nick ended the call, I squealed in delight and clapped my hands. "Let's go get him!"

We hopped into Nick's truck. I drove so that he could call

Eddie on the way. Given that Eddie lived in the northern suburbs, he'd likely arrive at the House of the Seven Fables before us. "Wait for us around the corner," Nick told Eddie. "We don't want to take any chances that Sundaram might see you waiting and drive off."

Nick had run a search under all of Sundaram's aliases and found no guns registered in any of the names. That didn't mean much, though. Not all guns sales were registered, and we had no idea whether Sundaram might have additional aliases. It was always best to assume the worst, that a target could be armed and dangerous.

I drove as fast as I dared to McKinney. We drove slowly down the street behind the house, noting only one car parked in the B and B's back lot. A silver Ford Taurus with California plates and a rental car sticker on the back windshield.

Bingo.

We found Eddie parked on a side street. He hopped into Nick's truck with us, and I drove around the corner to the front of the bed-and-breakfast. It was early evening now and dark outside. Only the porch light was on at Seven Fables. The gas lamp sat dark upon its post.

A white king-cab pickup with a handyman logo was parked in the driveway of the house. Two men worked their way down the front porch, unwinding the strands of Christmas lights from the railings and packing them into cardboard boxes. They'd already removed the lights from the roof. All that remained was the strands of green lights angling down from the top of the gas lamp. Like the lamp, the strands were not lit.

Nick phoned Cindy from the street. "Can you come to the door to let us in? I'd rather not knock and risk alerting Mr. Sundaram."

With that, Nick ended the call.

While Nick exited the driver's side, Eddie and I slid out through the passenger door and walked up the sidewalk.

Cindy opened the front door as we stepped onto the porch. "He's in his room," she whispered. "The door's closed."

Eddie, Nick, and I played rock-paper-scissors to see who

would go inside, who would stay out front, and who would watch the back door in case Sundaram made a run for it. Chances were the guy would surrender willingly, but we'd learned to hedge our bets.

Nick won round one and would be going inside. I won round two, which gave Eddie the back door and me the front.

"Good luck," I told Nick as he headed in.

I waited on the porch for several minutes, making small talk with the men taking down the lights. A brisk wind kicked in, and I started to shiver in the frigid air. What the heck was taking Nick so long?

chapter thirty-five

The Night the Lights Went Out in Dallas

I stepped off the porch. Maybe a little exercise would warm me up.

I paced back and forth on the sidewalk in front of the bed-and-breakfast, flapping my arms around myself, my steamy breath visible in the air. Several more minutes passed. By this time, the guys from the handyman service were nearly done removing the lights from the railing. One of them crouched at either end of the wide porch, unwrapping the last strands.

I stopped at the end of the walk that led to the porch and stared at the house, wishing I had Superman's X-ray vision so I could see what was going on inside. Was Nick talking things over with Sundaram, negotiating a peaceful surrender? Or were they grappling in the Snow White Suite while Grumpy, Sleepy, Sneezy, Dopey, Bashful, Happy, and Doc looked on?

Bam!

The front door swung open, hard, the panel slamming back against the house, causing the windows to shake.

What the heck?

A naked and dripping and nicely built Indian man ran out onto the porch. Looked like those workouts had paid off. Through the open door, I could see both Nick and Eddie in pursuit, the two of them elbowing each other aside in their attempts to the be one to nab Sundaram. Men. Sheesh. Always so competitive.

With a quick glance behind him, Sundaram leaped over the two steps that led down to the sidewalk and headed toward me at an amazing speed, his exposed junk flapping with his efforts.

Normally, I'd pull a weapon to encourage an uncooperative target to rethink his attempt to escape. At the moment, though, I had no weapon to pull. Instinctively I spread my arms out to each side and bent my knees a little. It was the same stance I used to help my father round up a stray barn chicken.

The man careened to his right to avoid being clotheslined by me. In the dark and in his haste, he didn't see the remaining strands of holiday lights affixed to the gas lamp. He ran right through the strings, the first hitting him across the throat, the next across the belly, the third across his calves, tripping him.

"Yi-i-i!" He fell to the ground and rolled to the side in an attempt to free himself from the unexpected web of lights. Unfortunately for him, his twisting and turning only managed to entangle him further. Even his junk was tangled in lights now.

Nick reached out to try to grab the guy's legs, but the man kicked Nick's arm away. Eddie had no better luck trying to seize an arm, especially since it was dark in the yard.

Cindy stepped onto the porch, reached back inside to flip a switch, and an instant later the flickering electronic flame in the gas lamp ignited. The switch for the gas lamp apparently also controlled the outside outlet. The Christmas lights wrapped around Sundaram came to life, bathing him in an eerie green glow.

Zap!

A shower of golden sparks shot out from a frayed spot on the strand of lights.

Zap! Zap!

More sparks sprayed out of the cord, like a defective firework going off on the ground.

Zap-zap-zap!

Sundaram shrieked and began to twitch on the ground as electricity surged through his wet body. His junk continued to flap as he twitched.

"Uh-oh," Eddie said. "This isn't good."

From her porch, Cindy put her hands over the mouth and issued a stifled scream.

Nick ran back to the porch and yanked the cord from the socket. "Call an ambulance!"

Cindy nodded frantically and ran back inside to get her phone.

Eddie and I stood over the Indian man as he continued to convulse involuntarily at our feet.

"Should we do something?" I asked.

"I don't know," Eddie said. "If we touch him will we get electrocuted, too?"

"I have no idea." I'd always stunk at science.

One of the workers rushed over and pulled the strands of lights from Sundaram. Nick went back into the house, returning a moment later with a crocheted blanket. He draped it over the wet man, probably as much to cover his still-twitching junk as to prevent him from freezing to death.

I looked up at Nick. "I take it he was in the shower when you went inside?"

"Yeah," he replied. "Taking his sweet time about it, too. When he came out of the bathroom and saw me, he ran for the back door."

Eddie chimed in now. "He ran back inside when he saw me waiting and headed out front instead."

The earsplitting peal of the emergency siren grew louder as the ambulance approached, setting the neighborhood dogs to howling. *Aroo-o! Aroo-o!*

As the vehicle pulled to a stop at the curb, the driver cut

the siren but left the lights on, the spinning beams flashing across the houses, lighting the street up like a nightclub. The only things missing were overpriced drinks and a throbbing bass line.

The back doors swung open. Two male EMTs hopped out of the bay and rushed over to Sundaram. While one of them checked his vital signs, the other returned to the ambulance, pulled a rolling gurney out of the back, and pushed it up over the curb and into the yard.

Sundaram put a hand to his head and groaned as the paramedics gingerly maneuvered him onto the mobile bed, rolled him over to the back doors, and eased him inside the vehicle.

"You covered the travel," Eddie told Nick. "I'll take it from here."

Eddie bade us good-bye and hurried back to his van. He followed the ambulance as it drove off. He'd keep watch at the hospital until Sundaram was released into the custody of law enforcement.

One of the handymen tossed the defective strand of lights into a large trash can at the curb; then the two of them climbed into their truck and drove away. Nick and I thanked Cindy Allen for her help in rounding up Sundaram. At that point, all she could do was nod in bewilderment.

The House of the Seven Fables had a new story to add to its book, this one true. And while Sundaram would surely disagree, I'd say this story had a happy ending.

chapter thirty-six

$\mathcal{M}$y Last Supper

The remaining days before my trial passed both much too slowly and much too quickly.

Dr. Walendzik had turned herself in to Fort Worth PD, while Dr. Barrett had been apprehended at the airport, attempting to board a flight to Ottawa. The dentists and their bookkeeper faced charges of Medicaid fraud and assault on a federal employee. The dental board had suspended all of the doctors' licenses.

After Sundaram was arrested here, Nick spoke with a different agent in India and was able to convince the government to close down his call center in New Delhi. With so much business moving overseas, the government there was trying to clean up its reputation. The earlier agent who'd refused to take action was bumped down to an administrative position.

Tokyo Discount Telecom e-mailed me to say that my shipment of phones would be delivered soon. The date was on a Saturday at the very end of January, the weekend after my trial was scheduled to begin. I'd suggested to Eddie and

Nick that they arrange with one of the female special agents to take my place in case I was convicted and couldn't be at my town house to accept the delivery. Though they assured me they had no doubts I'd be exonerated, I had a sneaking suspicion that Eddie had gone ahead and made arrangements to have one of the other women on standby.

My stomach was in knots, my nerves on edge. As hard as I tried to concentrate on my audit work, all I could think about was the pending trial. I made little progress on my caseload. Fortunately, my new boss cut me quite a bit of slack. I supposed he figured I wouldn't be deadweight to his department much longer. Either I'd win my case and be up to speed soon or I'd lose my case and be off to jail.

I spent several hours with Anthony Giacomo going over not only my potential testimony but also that of my other witnesses. He'd clearly put a lot of thought and preparation into his questions and strategy. I only hoped it would be enough to convince the jury not to convict me.

My parents arrived in Dallas on Friday night so they could spend the weekend with me before my trial began on Monday. Having them around was comforting, though I still had trouble sleeping. Too much on my mind.

Sunday evening, Nick took me, my parents, Alicia, and Christina out to dinner, my choice of restaurants. After all, it was my last supper of sorts. I picked my favorite sushi place, savoring each delicious bite, basking in the burn of the wasabi in my sinuses, the harsh sensation forcing me to live in the moment.

Mom tried some for the first time, coughing and sneezing and grimacing. She chugged half a glass of water. "Dear, Lord! That stuff almost killed me."

"Remember, Mom," I said, repeating the words she'd told me at Christmas. "What doesn't kill us makes us stronger."

She pointed her chopsticks at me. "Do I need to get the Ivory soap?"

Dad stabbed a piece of giant clam with his fork and held it up in front of his face. "Remind me what I'm eating here?"

I rolled my eyes. He was as bad as Nick had been the first time I'd brought him here. "It's clam, Dad."

He grunted. "They don't look like this when they're floating in chowder."

Mom and I indulged in a bottle of plum wine. After two glasses, my nerves had settled a bit. I raised my glass. "To truth, justice, and the American way."

If I could have only one of those things, I'd settle for justice.

Nick clinked his bottle of Sapporo beer against my wineglass. Though he smiled at me, his jaw was rigid. Everything that had happened the last two months had been hell on me, but I wasn't alone. It had been hard for Nick, too. He didn't like to see me worry, and he sure as hell didn't like not being able to do anything about it. Nick was a man of action, a man who liked to be in control. Unfortunately, everything was out of our hands. It would be up to the attorneys, witnesses, and jury to determine my fate.

We wrapped the dinner up with bowls of green tea ice cream. I wondered how long it might be before I'd enjoy the treat again.

When we returned to my place, everyone went inside while Nick and I stood on the porch, merely staring at each other. Everything and anything we could say to each other had already been said, several times over. Finally, he stepped toward me and pressed his lips lightly against my forehead. I wrapped my arms around him and held on for dear life.

My mind briefly toyed with the idea of the two of us running away together, hiding in the woods somewhere in East Texas, living off the land and off the grid. Nick knew how to fish and I could probably forage for berries or raise vegetables or something. But no. A life on the lam would be no life at all. I'd miss my cats, shopping at Neiman's, eating sushi and green tea ice cream. Besides, after all these seasons of watching Ted fall in love with virtually every woman in New York City on *How I Met Your Mother,* I wanted to see him finally meet their mother, dammit!

After a few moments I released Nick, turned, and went into my place without another word.

My former boyfriend, Brett, phoned that evening to wish me luck at the trial. Though we'd both moved on to new relationships with people better suited for us, we'd always have a soft spot in our hearts for each other.

"I heard about the shooting and the trial on the news," he said. "I also heard about the incident at the dentist office."

"Yeah," I replied. "I've been extra busy lately."

We shared a chuckle.

"I'll be rooting for you, Tara," he said softly.

"Thanks, Brett. I appreciate that."

When we ended the call, I went upstairs to get ready for bed. My mother grabbed me in a tight hug after I bade her and my father good night in my bedroom. "Keep the faith, honey. It's going to all work out."

I might've been more convinced if I didn't hear her burst into a sob the instant I closed the door behind me.

I slept in my guest room with Alicia that night. She'd suggested she stay with Daniel at his downtown loft apartment, but I'd insisted she remain at my place. I needed her now more than ever. She was my best friend, the sister I'd never had, a shoulder to cry on. A skinny, bony shoulder, but a shoulder nonetheless.

"I'm scared," I told her after we'd turned off the lights.

She turned her head on her pillow, her face lit softly by the night-light. "You'd be stupid not to be." She propped herself up on her elbow. "But you've got the best attorney money can buy and a lot of good witnesses to testify on your behalf. When this trial is over, I'm taking you on a spa day. We'll do facials, massages, get our nails done. The whole works."

"Thanks. You're a good friend." Once she'd closed her eyes, a tear escaped the corner of my eye and rolled down my cheek, leaving a warm, wet trail.

chapter thirty-seven

Twelve Angry Men . . . or Seven Women and Five Moderately Irritated Men

I spent ten minutes the next morning hovering over the toilet with the dry heaves. Real attractive, I know. But between my nerves and the adrenaline, my system was on overload.

My mother had cooked me a full breakfast with all of my favorites. Fried eggs, biscuits and gravy, cheese grits, and home fries. Unfortunately, I couldn't eat a bite. I refused the coffee, too. Didn't need caffeine making me any more anxious than I already was.

"You need to eat something, sweetie," Mom insisted.

I pushed the food around on my plate and crumbled up the biscuit to make it look like I'd taken a few bites. My father wasn't fooled. He eyed me over the top of his coffee mug but said nothing. Alicia, on the other hand, was a nervous eater. She scarfed down three biscuits, a huge bowl of grits, and two servings of home fries. Maybe next time I cried on her shoulder there'd be a little more meat on it.

Nick swung by to pick me up in his truck. My parents and Alicia followed us to the courthouse in my dad's pickup. Scott Klein had been none too happy that Alicia had requested time off in the middle of tax season, but when she told him why she needed to be out of the office he'd acquiesced, even told her to wish me luck on his behalf. Klein might not have hired me back, but he was still a nice guy at heart.

Nick and I said little on the drive over to the courthouse, both of us absorbed in our thoughts. We parked and inched our way through the long line at the security checkpoint. Several of the people in line with us held a jury summons in their hand. I eyed them as discreetly as I could. Would one or more of them be who would determine my fate?

I'd been warned by Giacomo to say nothing in the elevator, halls, or bathroom that could potentially be overheard, and I'd passed this instruction on to Nick, Alicia, and my parents. The five of us rode the crowded elevator up to Judge Trumbull's courtroom in silence.

We were early, and people were just beginning to trickle into the room. Trumbull's black female bailiff sat in the witness-box, reading the *Dallas Morning News*. My trial was covered on the front page, my photograph in full color next to a photo of Don Geils. They say everyone gets fifteen minutes of fame. I'd gladly give my fifteen minutes to someone else.

Giacomo stood at the defense table, his briefcase open in front of him as he removed file folders filled with paperwork.

My father's eyes narrowed as he sized up my attorney, taking in the fuchsia-colored dress shirt and polka-dot tie he wore with his black suit. "This is the hairy-assed lawyer you told me about?"

I gave my dad a pointed look. "Reserve judgment until you see him in action."

I led my parents up to the defense table and introduced them to Anthony.

Giacomo was nonplussed by my dad's assessing look. "Don't you worry, Mr. Holloway. I'm going to take very good care of your daughter. We'll wipe the floor with Troy Kerr and Don Geils."

Dad shook his hand. "That's what I needed to hear."

My father gave me a kiss on the cheek and my mother squeezed my hand before they stepped away and slid onto the bench in the front row where Alicia was already seated. Nick's mother, Bonnie, entered the room, gave me a small wave, and took a seat on the bench with my parents and best friend.

Nick leaned in to me and whispered, "Remember. You're Tara Holloway. Don't take any crap from anybody." He chucked my chin, gave me a soft smile, and took a seat next to his mother.

I eased myself into a wooden chair at the defense table. It felt weird to be sitting on this side of the room. I used to think this side was for losers, bad people, people who deserved to rot in jail.

My perspective had definitely changed now. Things were not quite so black and white on this side of the room.

The benches began to fill. Several reporters, including Trish LeGrande, filed in, followed by Lu, Eddie, Josh, and Viola. Each of my coworkers came over to offer me words of encouragement, as did Merle and Bernice.

Christina entered the room and also came up to the table. She leaned in and gave my hand a squeeze. "When this is over," she said, "the margaritas are on me. Top shelf."

Giacomo looked up at her. "Me, too?"

Christina nodded. "Of course."

Lu lingered after the others had taken their seats. She laid a piece of paper on the defense table and bent over us, speaking in a low voice. "Troy Kerr sent me a personal invitation."

I leaned in and took a glance at the document. It was a subpoena ordering The Lobo to appear in court today to testify on behalf of the prosecution.

What?

How could that be? Lu had agreed to testify on *my* behalf.

I looked from Lu to Giacomo. "What does this mean?"

Did Kerr plan to use my former boss against me? Had she

said something during her interview with the prosecutor that could damage my case?

"No worries," Giacomo said. "Kerr needs Ms. Lobozinski's testimony to authenticate the internal affairs report, that's all."

I hoped that was all. I didn't think I could bear it if Lu helped put me behind bars, even if it was against her will. I adored the crotchety old broad.

Lu looked from Giacomo to me and shot me a wink with her false eyelashes. "Knock 'em dead." With that, Lu picked up her subpoena and took a seat in the gallery next to Viola.

The last person to enter the room was Troy Kerr. He strode in, his briefcase in one hand, a cell phone in the other, the phone pressed to his ear. As much as I hated to say it, he looked confident, intelligent, ready for battle. He nodded to Anthony before slipping into his place at the prosecution table.

Giacomo draped an arm around my shoulder and huddled close, whispering in my ear. "Pay close attention to everything the witnesses say," he instructed me. "Help me help you. If anything they say isn't one hundred percent correct, you let me know." He slid a pen and notepad onto the table in front of me. "Keep your demeanor attentive and professional. Be especially careful how you look at Don Geils. The jury will be watching you."

In other words, behave as if I were being viewed under a microscope. Great. As if I weren't nervous enough already.

A couple of minutes later, the bailiff instructed everyone in the courtroom to rise as Judge Trumbull entered. The judge climbed up to her stand, plopped down into her seat, and greeted everyone. She looked from my attorney to Kerr. "Okay, boys. Any preliminary motions?"

Troy Kerr looked at Giacomo expectantly.

Giacomo argued that any testimony or evidence regarding my use of my gun prior to the incident at Guys & Dolls should be excluded. "Miss Holloway's actions were deemed justified on each count and are therefore irrelevant. The evidence could also unduly prejudice the jury."

Kerr objected, arguing that my history showed I had an unusual propensity for using my gun.

Trumbull sided with Giacomo. "Miss Holloway isn't on trial for those shootings. Any such evidence will be excluded."

Phew.

"Anything else?" Trumbull asked.

When both attorneys indicated they had no further matters, Kerr turned to Giacomo. "I was prepared to fight over the admissibility of the internal affairs report for the shooting at Guys and Dolls."

"That little thing?" Giacomo waved a hand dismissively. "Nyah."

An uneasy look skittered across Kerr's face, giving me no small sense of pleasure.

Trumbull pointed her gavel at Giacomo and Kerr. "You two need to address me, not each other."

Kerr nodded like an obedient child. "I do have one matter, Your Honor. Don Geils pleaded guilty to drug crimes, prostitution, and money laundering, all of which are nonviolent crimes."

It was true. Despite the fact that Geils had come after me with his gun, the prosecutor had decided not to charge him with assault on a federal officer or attempted murder. Geils had no idea I worked for the government when he'd followed me into the VIP room with his gun. He only knew I'd run into his club and put holes in the feet of three of his bouncers. There wasn't enough evidence to make the charges stick.

"If Geils is forced to wear handcuffs during his testimony," Kerr said, "the jury will likely be influenced by that fact. It's bad enough he'll be in his prison uniform."

Trumbull looked to Giacomo for a response.

"Geils owned an unregistered gun and came after Miss Holloway with it even though she'd used only nonlethal shots on his security staff. That's not the behavior of a nonviolent man."

Trumbull seemed to mull things over for a moment. "Tell you what. I'll let them take the cuffs off, but I want his handler standing close by." She returned her gavel to its stand. "We ready to bring in the jury pool?"

The attorneys indicated they were ready.

The bailiff walked down the aisle and opened the courtroom doors, admitting a group of twenty or so people and instructing them to take seats in the gallery. Once seated, the people glanced around the room as if trying to get a read on what the case might be about. None looked particularly happy to have been chosen for jury duty. Several made no attempt to hide their irritation, sitting with scowls on their faces and their arms crossed over their chests, repeatedly glancing at their watches as if we were wasting their time. I happened to agree with them. I could only hope they wouldn't hold things against me. Hell, if it were up to me, none of us would be here today.

When the pool had settled in, Trumbull gave the attorneys the go-ahead to commence the jury selection process.

Kerr took first crack at the pool of potential jurors. He stepped to the head of the aisle, introduced himself, and explained that the case involved allegations of excessive force by an IRS special agent who shot a man during an arrest. At the mention of such scandal, the irritation on the jurors' face morphed to intrigue.

One juror, a white-haired man wearing a red sweater-vest, raised his hand. "You say she's a what now?"

"A special agent for the IRS."

The woman next to him, a curly-haired brunette, asked, "The IRS carries guns?"

It was always the same. There we special agents were, risking our lives every day to collect monies owed by criminal tax cheats, and the majority of people didn't even know we existed.

"Special agents are criminal law enforcement," Kerr explained. "Tax cops, if you will."

"Gotcha," the old man said.

Now that the jurors were on board, Kerr raised a finger. "There's a critical thing we must all keep in mind during this trial. It's called the United States Constitution."

He clasped his hands behind him now and began to pace a few steps one direction, then the other. "The Constitution limits the government's authority and provides all of us protections from abuse by public officials. The fact that someone has committed a crime does not entitle a government officer to violate his rights. Donald Geils, the victim in this case, operated a men's entertainment club and has pleaded guilty to drug and sex charges. He is by no means a model citizen."

You can say that again, I thought.

"Nevertheless," Kerr continued, "he had certain rights, including the right to be free from excessive force."

Kerr stopped pacing and ran his gaze over the jurors. "No matter what you think of Don Geils as a human being, that should in no way influence your decision in this case. Don Geils is not the person on trial here. Former special agent Tara Holloway is."

Former. Ugh.

Several of those in the pool glanced my way. Giacomo had warned me not to smile, as it might come off as a flippant smirk. I tried to maintain a poker face, pleasant but attentive. And innocent, of course.

Kerr asked whether any on the jury pool believed they might have a bias that would prevent them from making a fair and just decision. None acknowledged any bias. In fact, several sat up straight in their seats, much more interested now that they realized they might be picked to serve on the jury for one of the most newsworthy trials of the year. Heck, they were probably thinking over how they could ride my sullied coattails to fame and fortune, maybe get a lucrative book deal or a movie-of-the-week. I could see the title now. *The Tax Woman Cometh.* I hoped they'd get someone attractive to play me. Maybe Emma Stone or Mila Kunis.

Kerr went on to question the jurors more specifically about themselves. Did any own guns? If so, how many and what types? Had they ever fired their guns at another human being? Had any of the jurors ever been fired upon?

This being Texas, the majority of the people on the jury

owned a gun of some sort. Two held concealed-carry permits. None had fired upon another person, though one, a burly man with muttonchop sideburns and shaggy dark hair that hung halfway down his back, had been shot once.

"My hunting buddy got me in the ass last duck season," he said. "Thought I was a bear. Good thing he was only using birdshot or I'd have been a goner."

I wasn't sure whether it would be a good thing or not to have Buns-of-Birdshot on my jury. He didn't seem any worse for the wear, and maybe his laid-back attitude toward weapons would work in my favor.

"I've still got some of the shot in me," the man said. "Had a hell of a time getting through security this morning."

Kerr moved to have the man dismissed for cause.

"I object," Giacomo said. "Taking a few BBs to the butt shouldn't impair the man's judgment."

Trumbull ruled in our favor.

When it was Giacomo's turn to question the jury pool, he asked whether any of them had ever had any trouble with a member of law enforcement. A woman in a too-tight knit dress raised her hand. Giacomo asked her to provide details.

"I was driving down Highway Two-Eighty-Seven one night," she began. "No, wait. It wasn't Two-Eighty-Seven; it was One-Fifty-Seven. Or maybe it was . . . no, it was Two-Eighty-Seven. That's the one that runs through Arlington, right? Anyways, I didn't have my headlights on. I must've forgotten to turn them on, because when I got in my car at the Walmart that Ke$ha song was on. You know, the good one? Anyways, I was singing along as I was driving and didn't realize my lights weren't on."

It took her ten minutes to make her point. She'd been arrested on suspicion of driving while intoxicated but released when a blood alcohol test indicated she was far below the legal limit. I could see why the officer had been confused. The woman wasn't the sharpest tool in the shed. It had probably been hard to tell where dumb ended and drunk began. Still, in case the woman's experience might taint her opinion of law enforcement, Trumbull dismissed her for cause.

Next, Giacomo asked if any of the jurors had ever had a problem with the IRS. Two raised their hands. One woman was angry that she'd been held responsible for taxes on her husband's plumbing business when he'd failed to report his income on their joint tax return.

"How was I supposed to know he'd earned fifty grand?" she said.

Gee, you'd think she might've clued in by the fact that she only worked part-time as a cashier at a grocery store yet they were still somehow able to make ends meet.

Trumbull sent the cashier on her merry, lying way.

Another potential juror had been assessed forty grand in payroll taxes after improperly classifying the cooks and waitstaff in his burger joint as independent contractors rather than employees. "I'm still paying off those taxes," he snapped, casting an angry glance my way as if his tax debt were my fault.

Trumbull dismissed him for cause, too.

Finally, the pool had been whittled down. From among those who remained, Judge Trumbull picked fifteen names, twelve jurors and three alternates. Of the twelve, seven were women and five were men. The man with the birdshot in his butt was among them.

I looked them over, hoping they'd be understanding. I wondered if they realized what power they held.

My entire future was in their hands.

chapter thirty-eight

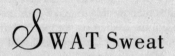

$\mathcal{S}$WAT Sweat

Jury selection completed, Judge Trumbull offered everyone a short break. While Kerr took advantage of the time to speak with reporters, my attorney took a final look at his list of questions for the witnesses and I used the time to produce copious amounts of flop sweat. My gray suit jacket stuck to my back like a scuba suit. Ick.

As the break ended, the leader of the SWAT team, Officer Lamar Thomas, entered the room. Thomas was a tall black man with a military-style haircut and muscles on his muscles. He wore his Dallas SWAT uniform and even I had to admit he looked impressive. He was the one who'd been supposed to lead the raid on Guys & Dolls that fateful night.

Thanks to the break in a water main, the SWAT team had been late to arrive. Given the unpredictable nature of Dallas traffic, you'd think he would've budgeted extra time for a potential problem. If you asked me, he was partly to blame for my predicament. Had the SWAT team been in place as planned, they would've handled the bust, I'd still be a special agent, and my bank account balance wouldn't be so laughably low. I fought the urge to run over and stomp his big toe.

When the jury returned and took their seats in the jury box, Trumbull looked down at the prosecution table. "Opening arguments," she announced. "You're up, Mr. Kerr."

Troy Kerr's opener was essentially an expansion on what he'd told the jurors prior to questioning them, that their job was not to determine whether Don Geils deserved to be shot four times in the leg—*because everyone knows he did!*—but whether I'd abused my authority and used excessive force in my arrest of Don Geils.

Kerr pointed at me. "As the evidence will show, when Tara Holloway fired her first round into Don Geils's leg, he dropped his weapon. But she didn't stop there. She went on to put another bullet in his leg. She didn't stop there, either. In fact, she put a third and fourth bullet into his leg. Four, folks." He formed a gun with his thumb and index finger and aimed it at the jury. *"Bang . . . bang . . . bang . . . bang."* He raised his finger to his lips and pretended to blow away the smoke before taking his seat.

Giacomo stood for his opener. He cut his eyes to Kerr. "Blowing smoke." He turned to the jury. "That's exactly what the prosecution is doing here."

Ooh. Good one.

He stepped over to the jury box and put his hands on the half wall that enclosed them. "Ladies and gentlemen of the jury, I'm not going to insult you by engaging in silly melodrama. You're too smart to fall for corny theatrics. I'm merely going to ask you to do one thing. As you listen to the testimony in this trial, put yourself in the place of Tara Holloway that night." He leaned toward them. "Look through her eyes. Listen with her ears." He crossed his hands over his chest. "Feel with her heart."

He ran his gaze over the jury as he stepped back a foot or two. "The federal government gave Miss Holloway a badge, a gun, and a job to do. It trusted her to do what's right. Now she's trusting you to do the same."

With that, Anthony returned to his seat.

Trumbull instructed Kerr to call his first witness. Kerr called Thomas to the stand.

As Thomas stood in the witness booth, the bailiff looked the man up and down, clearly appreciating what she saw, before raising the Bible for his oath. She swore the man in and he took a seat.

Kerr led Thomas through a series of questions regarding the plan we'd made for the night of the raid.

"Did things go according to plan?" Kerr asked.

"Not at all." Thomas' gaze swung my way before swinging back to the prosecutor. "The team was delayed only a minute or two by a break in a water main. When we arrived at the club, we saw Miss Holloway heading inside. She was supposed to hold the door open for us, then stay outside while the SWAT team made our sweep. We ended up having to break the door down to get in. When we got inside, we found three of the security staff with bullets in their feet and another with a concussion from a strike to the temple. It was then I heard gunshots coming from a room in the corner."

The door to the courtroom opened behind us. We all turned to see Don Geils being led into the room by a U.S. marshal. Geils' black hair was as thick and coarse as ever, though his roots were gray. Looked like the prison store didn't stock Just For Men hair color. His sizable paunch had shrunk a bit. Either prison food didn't agree with him or he spent his time in the yard running from other prisoners attempting to woo him. He seemed even shorter without his stacked heels. He wore the standard khaki federal prison uniform, his hands cuffed in front of him. He walked with an uneven gait I suspected was exaggerated. He limped his way forward until the marshal gestured for him to take a seat in the fourth row.

I forced my eyes away from him. *Worthless bastard.*

"Let's talk about those gunshots," Kerr said, turning his attention back to the witness on the stand. "How many seconds elapsed between them?"

"The second shot came immediately after the first one,"

Officer Thomas said, "but there were two or three seconds between the rest of them."

Several members of the jury glanced over at me as if to gauge my reaction. I hoped I looked nonplussed. In reality, I was scared shitless. Had I fired in rapid succession, the shots would look more like a reflex or impulse. The fact that a few seconds elapsed between each shot made them appear more questionable. Still, when I'd fired my gun that night I'd been beside myself with rage and terror. I'd used every bit of my restraint *not killing* Geils. Then some sort of autopilot had taken over.

Kerr asked Thomas only a couple more questions, then passed the witness.

Giacomo stood, buttoned the coat of his designer suit, and approached the officer. He didn't stop until he reached the divider. The vision was comical. Even seated, Thomas was nearly as tall as Giacomo, and he was half again as wide. They looked like David and Goliath.

The attorney looked the officer over appraisingly. "You are a mighty big man, Officer Thomas."

Thomas chuckled. "You're not the first person to tell me that."

"How tall are you?"

"Six foot four."

"Wow. Weight?"

"Two twenty."

Anthony gestured to the officer's upper arms. "Your biceps are enormous. How much can you bench-press?"

"The same," Thomas replied. "Two twenty."

"Impressive."

I glanced over at Kerr. His expression was quizzical, as if he couldn't understand why my attorney was making his witness look good. I wasn't so sure myself.

Giacomo cocked his head as he eyed Thomas. "Is your size part of the reason you were appointed to lead the SWAT team?"

"My physical abilities were part of it," Thomas said. "Also my leadership abilities."

"Your team respects you? Does what you ask of them?"

"If they didn't do what I told them, they wouldn't be part of SWAT. Not for long, anyway."

Giacomo raised a finger. "You make a good point. The officers who join SWAT, they're a special breed, aren't they?"

"Yes," Thomas agreed. "Very driven. Dedicated. Willing to take risks."

"Do you enjoy leading your SWAT team?"

"I do," Thomas said. "We work together well."

"Lots of planning and anticipation go into the raids?"

"Of course."

Giacomo had the witness eating out of his hand. "It must be extremely satisfying when you make a successful bust."

"There's nothing like it."

"Then it must also be very frustrating when you expect to make a bust, but someone else beats you to the punch."

Thomas didn't respond verbally, but he stiffened, realizing now where Giacomo had led him with his flattery.

Kerr stood and objected. "The defense hasn't asked a question."

Trumbull raised a brow at Giacomo, who rephrased his words. "Obviously, being so dedicated and driven, you'd feel frustrated if you anticipated making a major bust only to be thwarted by the fact that another officer had already taken care of things. Isn't that true?"

Thomas would look like a fool if he argued the point, and the SWAT officer was no fool. "It would be natural to feel a little frustrated, though it's always good to see a criminal get his due, no matter who handles the arrest."

Giacomo left it at that. The seed had been planted in the jury's mind. No need to press the point further.

Giacomo took a couple steps back from the witness-box. "You've admitted that the SWAT team was late arriving at the club that night, correct?"

"Yes," he said, "but only a minute or two."

"Isn't it true, Officer Thomas, that timing is critical in a bust?"

"It can be."

"Being off by just a few seconds can make all the difference in the world, can't it?"

"It depends on the case."

"Sure, sure." Giacomo nodded. "When multiple officers are involved, each counting on the others, it's important that each party do their part exactly as planned, isn't it?"

"Yes," Thomas said, locking a death glare on my attorney. "And Miss Holloway didn't follow the plan."

Giacomo offered him a placating smile. "Ah, but it was you who first failed to follow the plan. Isn't that true?"

"It's not my fault a water main broke."

"No, but common sense tells us that, as the team leader, it is your fault that you didn't allow adequate time for contingencies?"

Thomas had two choices. Argue with Giacomo and come off as defensive and self-righteous or agree and admit he was imperfect, too, like me. He hedged his bets and gave an evasive response.

"I suppose some people could possibly look at it that way," he said.

"You *suppose* it's *possible*?" Giacomo stepped right up to the witness-stand and stood there a moment more, staring right into Thomas' face. "Do I intimidate you, Officer Thomas?"

Thomas snickered. "Not in the least."

Giacomo gracefully tilted his head. "Then why are you afraid to give me a direct answer?"

Ha! There was that hairy ass Daniel had promised me. I glanced back at my father. His lip quirked as he fought a grin.

Thomas shifted in his seat. "Okay, fine. Things would have gone better had I allowed more travel time. Is that direct enough for you?"

"Perfect." Giacomo ducked his head. "Thank you."

Giacomo glanced over at the jury, a nonverbal clue to them that he was about to touch on another important issue. "You mentioned that when you entered the strip club, you found some of the club's staff injured. Isn't it true that you

also found three members of law enforcement critically injured?"

"Yes."

"In fact, an undercover officer from Dallas PD's sex
crimes unit lay unconscious on the floor in a pool of his own
blood. Isn't that true?"

"Yes."

Giacomo returned to the defense table. He pulled a glossy
piece of paper out of his expandable folder and showed it to
me.

Instinctively I gasped and put a hand over my mouth. The
paper was an eight-by-ten color photograph of Officer Aaron
Menger as he'd appeared that night, lying lifeless on the
floor of Guys & Dolls, his head split open, a pool of blood
forming around his head. I hadn't seen the photograph before, and the image brought everything careering back, all
of those sick, frantic feelings of that night. Lying there that
night, Lieutenant Menger appeared as if he might already be
dead. Once again, fireflies flitted around the edges of my vision. I gripped the edge of the table, took a deep breath, and
willed them back.

The jurors' eyes moved from me to Thomas as Giacomo
walked over to show the photo to the witness.

"This is what you found when you entered the prem-
ises?"

Thomas glanced down at the photograph, but his expression remained stoic. "Yes."

"And it's what Miss Holloway found, too, when she entered. Correct?"

"Yes."

Giacomo moved to enter the photograph into evidence.

Kerr objected on the grounds of relevancy. "Whether
another officer had been injured or not has no bearing on
whether the force used against Don Geils was reasonable or
excessive."

"It has everything to do with it, Your Honor," Giacomo
said. "We intend to show that Miss Holloway was under extreme mental distress when Don Geils came after her, and

that distress was caused in large part due to having found one of her partners lying on the floor and apparently dead."

Trumbull allowed the photograph into evidence. "The charges hinge on whether Miss Holloway's actions were reasonable or excessive under the circumstances. The jury needs to see exactly what those circumstances were."

Giacomo thanked the judge and carried the photograph over to the jury. The first juror flinched as she looked at it and quickly handed it to the man next to her. His nose crinkled, but he turned the photo this way and that, taking a good look before passing it on.

Giacomo next admitted a photograph of Nick into evidence. Nick had a black eye and blood all over his face and was hunched over to relieve the pain of his cracked ribs. Thomas acknowledged that when the SWAT team had stormed the place they found Nick on the floor of the club, too, alive but writhing in agony.

Giacomo returned to stand before the witness-box. "When you heard the gunshots, you ran toward the source of the sound and found Special Agent Holloway in the VIP room. Isn't that right?"

"Yes," Thomas said.

"Besides Don Geils and Agent Holloway, who else was in the room?"

"A middle-aged white man and a young Latina woman who I later learned was an undercover DEA agent."

"The DEA agent was unconscious, wasn't she?" Giacomo asked.

"Yes."

"Her top had been removed?"

"Yes."

"As well as her bra?"

"She was naked from the waist up," Thomas said, "if that's what you're asking."

"Exactly. And her chest and neck were covered in fresh bite wounds?"

"Yes. She had multiple bite marks on her upper body."

Giacomo entered another photograph into evidence, this

one of a limp and lifeless Christina, bruises in the shape of teeth marks all over her neck, shoulders, and torso. Her nipples were covered with black squares in the photograph. When my attorney showed me the photo, I instinctively turned my head and closed my eyes. When I opened them, I found four of the jurors eyeing me.

Giacomo led Thomas through a series of questions in which Thomas acknowledged that Wesley Prescott, the john who'd made a midnight snack out of Christina, was also in the room, cowering under a table, when Thomas arrived. In response to my attorney's careful questions, Thomas described the shattered mirror in the room, blown to smithereens as a result of Geils firing his gun at me. Giacomo also led Thomas to describe how I collapsed to the floor, physically and emotionally spent, when the SWAT officer entered.

Giacomo passed the witness. Kerr followed up with couple of questions to hammer the point home that I'd been standing over Geils when Thomas first entered the VIP room. Kerr thanked Thomas for his testimony and dismissed him.

"Call your next witness," Trumbull instructed.

"The prosecution calls Donald Geils to the stand."

chapter thirty-nine

The "Victim" Speaks

The marshal unlocked Geils' handcuffs and followed closely behind him as he limped his way to the stand. The marshal stood at the wall behind the bench while the bailiff swore Geils in.

Once Geils took a seat, Kerr launched into his interrogation. He asked Geils several questions to set the scene, though Kerr chose to focus only on the brief moments prior to the shooting.

"Can you tell us what happened during the raid on Guys and Dolls?" Kerr asked.

"I sure can," Geils said. "I was sitting in my office at closing time, minding my own business, when some of the bouncers got into a little scuffle."

A little scuffle? I glanced back at Nick, who had a death glare locked on Geils. That little scuffle had involved three of Geils' oversized goons jumping Nick and attempting to beat the shit out of him. As the photo Giacomo had entered into evidence showed, Nick ended the night with a swollen lip, a black eye, and several cracked ribs. Merle, too, was glaring at Geils. Another of the bastard's goons had also attacked Merle, who was a disabled veteran. What kind of asshole does that? Still, none of the goons would have attacked Aaron, Nick, or Merle without being ordered to do so by Geils. He ran his club with an iron fist.

"Next thing I know," Geils said, "the girl who'd been working at my club as a bookkeeper comes running inside, uses a handgun to pistol-whip one of my security team, then shoots the other three in the foot. She runs over to the VIP lounge, shoots the lock off the door, and goes inside. I've got a waitress and customer inside the lounge, so I grab my gun and run in after her. When she spots me in the mirror, she turns and shoots me in the leg. I dropped my gun and she steps over and picks it up. She tells me she's working undercover for the IRS and shoots me three more times. If not for the SWAT cop running into the room then, she probably would've emptied her clip in me."

What bullshit. If I'd wanted to empty my clip into him I would've done it.

Kerr stood near the witness-box. "When Miss Holloway shot you, did she fire rapidly?"

"No," Geils spat. "She waited a few seconds between each shot."

How convenient that Kerr didn't ask what transpired during those few seconds. That's when I'd confronted Geils about the bad things he'd done. Of course Kerr wouldn't want to remind the jury of what a loser the alleged victim was.

When Kerr passed the witness, Giacomo stepped up to the box and laid into him. "You've conveniently left out some important details, haven't you, Don?"

Geils merely shrugged.

"When Officer Menger and Special Agent Pratt attempted to stop your customer from sexually brutalizing Agent Marquez, you ordered your security team to go after them, didn't you?"

Geils' gaze shifted up, a clear sign he was debating lying.

Since they were negotiating a plea bargain, there had been no trial and thus no official findings or testimony about the facts of that night.

"You can either admit that you ordered your team of bouncers to get Menger and Pratt out of the picture," Giacomo said, "or you can lie about it and I'll drag each and every one of them into this courtroom to tell us themselves."

Anthony's ass just grew another hair. *Plink.*

Geils scowled at Giacomo. "I didn't know what those two had in mind. So, yeah, I told my security staff to take care of things."

They'd taken care of things all right.

Giacomo continued his questions. "Before Agent Holloway fired on you, you aimed your gun at her back and had your finger on the trigger, ready to shoot her, didn't you?"

It was true. I'd been lucky the VIP room had a mirrored wall or I might not have seen him run in behind me, ready to put a bullet in my back. That mirror saved my life.

Geils' answer was evasive. "She'd shot up my staff."

"So that's a 'yes,' Don?"

Geils sat up in his seat. "Hell yeah, it's a yes. I was afraid she'd kill someone."

I glanced over at the jury. All of them were watching Geils intently.

"And it's true that you, too, fired your weapon?"

"I didn't mean to fire. It was a reflex."

"A reflex," Giacomo repeated, skepticism dripping from his words. "A reflex that resulted in your gun firing because your finger was already on the trigger, ready to shoot, correct?"

Geils stared at Giacomo as if trying to incinerate him with his eyes. The harder Geils stared, the closer in Giacomo leaned, staring right back.

At the prosecution table, Kerr cleared his throat, an obvious signal to his witness to provide an answer.

"Yeah," Geils finally spat. "My finger was already on the trigger. Like I said, I was afraid she'd kill somebody."

Giacomo stood up straight now. "I've got just one more question for you, Don." My attorney glanced at the jury once more before turning back to Geils. "Do you realize how lucky you are that Special Agent Holloway spared your life?"

chapter forty

Hostile Witness

Geils grumbled about not feeling lucky at all to have a bum leg—as if a bum leg was at all comparable to a bullet between the eyes—and was dismissed. The marshal walked beside Geils as he limped his way down the aisle and back to his seat in the gallery.

Kerr called his next witness. "Lu Lobozinski."

Lu had worn her best pantsuit for the occasion, a royal-blue polyester number with flares at the ankles and wrists. She'd paired the suit with her shiny black go-go boots. She'd fluffed her pinkish-orange hair up into a shorter version of her traditional beehive, her locks having finally gained sufficient length after she'd lost them to chemotherapy treatments months ago. She'd also amped up the makeup, her orange lipstick and blue eye shadow at least three layers thick.

After being sworn in, she settled gingerly into the witness stand, glancing about her as if afraid Don Geils might have left cooties on the seat.

Kerr approached the witness stand and asked Lu to identify herself and state her occupation for the record.

"I'm Luella Lobozinski. I head up the IRS criminal investigations office here in Dallas."

"Last spring you hired Tara Holloway to work as a special agent, correct?"

"I sure did. We were lucky to get her. She had some of the highest test scores in her training class. She was the best marksman, too. She's one hell of a shot."

Why was Lu playing up my gun skills here? Didn't she realize that could hurt my case?

"She's known at Criminal Investigations as the Annie Oakley of the IRS," Kerr stated. "Isn't that true?"

"Sure is," The Lobo replied.

Kerr approached Lu with a copy of a document and asked Lu to state whether it was a true and correct copy of the internal affairs report from my last hearing, whether it had been prepared at or near the time of my hearing, and whether it was an accurate report of the findings of the internal affairs officer and director of field operations. She responded affirmatively to all three questions, thus authenticating the document.

Kerr pointed to the last paragraph of the report. "This report indicates that Tara Holloway failed to follow proper procedures when she shot Don Geils in the leg. Correct?"

"That's correct," Lu said.

"What happened as a result of Miss Holloway's failure to follow procedures?"

"I was ordered to terminate her."

"Ordered by whom?"

"The internal affairs officer, the director of field operations, and George Burton, the overall head of Treasury's criminal investigations in Washington."

"After you terminated Miss Holloway for shooting Don Geils in the leg—"

"She wasn't fired for shooting Don Geils in the leg."

Kerr stood there, rigid. "You just said she was terminated for shooting him in the leg. That's also what you told me when I interviewed you two weeks ago."

"No," she said, "that's not exactly what I said. You need to listen better. I said she was terminated for failing to follow proper procedures."

Kerr stammered, trying to make sense of her words. "Wh-h-a—"

"We train our agents to respond with lethal force when confronted with lethal force," Lu continued, unguided. "Failure to do so can be catastrophic. The agent can end up dead and put other agents or civilians at risk. Understand?" She didn't wait for Kerr to respond. "Tara wasn't let go because she shot Don Geils in the leg. She was let go because she didn't shoot him between the eyes."

Kerr's face turned purple. He held up a hand to silence Lu as he tried to gather his wits. "But the report—"

She ignored the hand. "Is poorly written and vague, I know. We're not exactly poets at the IRS. We're numbers people, not word people."

Kerr lowered the report to his side. "Nonetheless, putting four bullets in the leg of an unarmed man would not be acceptable."

Lu was relentless. "Geils was armed when Agent Holloway fired the first shot. At that point he was fair game. As far as the other three bullets, hell, she was under incredibly stressful circumstances. I can't even imagine how it must have felt to be in her situation that night." Lu shot Kerr a pointed look trimmed with thick, fake lashes. "Special agents are human beings, Mr. Kerr, not emotionless robots."

A lump formed in my throat. I knew Lu supported me, but hearing her lay her thoughts and feelings bare like this really hit home.

Kerr did his best to recover his case and his dignity, but he did a piss-poor job of it. He finally decided to cut his losses and passed the witness.

When it was Giacomo's turn to question Lu, the floor wiping began. "Ms. Lobozinski, when you were ordered to terminate Miss Holloway, how did you feel about that?"

"Absolutely furious," Lu replied. "Tara was one of the

best agents to ever work for the agency. Smart. Determined. Resourceful. I didn't want to lose her. With her exceptional weapons skills, I felt comfortable assigning her to the potentially violent cases. I knew she could take care of herself."

The lump in my throat swelled a little more and I swallowed to force it down. I glanced over at the jury box. One of the jurors was fooling with his shoelace while another was absentmindedly chewing on the end of a ballpoint pen. I fought the urge to run over and throttle them. Didn't they realize how important this testimony was? Didn't they realize what this trial meant to me? Fortunately, most of the other jurors appeared attentive.

Giacomo returned to the table and pulled a large folded piece of paper from his briefcase. As he unfolded it, I realized it was the paper target from my firearms test at the end of my special agent training. I'd landed all six bullets dead center. The target had hung on the wall of my office in Criminal Investigations. It probably seemed conceited, but hey, I'd worked hard to develop my aim. I figured I'd earned bragging rights.

When I'd packed up my office, I'd left the target behind along with a buy-six-sandwiches-get-one-free punch card from a local deli. Just one more punch and I'd have earned a free lunch.

Giacomo held up the paper. "Do you recognize this target?"

"I sure do." Lu pointed to my name and the date in the bottom corner. "This was the target from Agent Holloway's firearms test at the conclusion of her special agent training."

Giacomo pointed to the cluster of holes in the center. "What do these holes tell you?"

Lu looked over at me, her blue-lidded eyes filled with emotion. Her voice was soft but sure. "They tell me I've lost an incredibly valuable agent."

The lump resurfaced, joined by the prickly feeling of tears forming in my eyes.

Lu continued on. "If it had been any other special agent

under investigation, I would've agreed with the decision to terminate. But with Tara's marksmanship, she could safely disable a target without having to kill him. Problem was, George Burton and the others simply couldn't believe she's that damn good."

chapter forty-one

Closing Arguments

On redirect, Kerr did his best to make Lu look like a softie who simply felt bad for one of her staff, but when she rattled off the names of several employees she'd happily canned herself he gave up. His case ended with a fizzle, like a damp firework that refused to ignite.

After the prosecution rested, Judge Trumbull dismissed us for a lunch break. "Be back here ready to go at one o'clock."

My entourage surrounded me, sweeping me along to the courthouse snack bar, where they pushed two large tables together in the back corner. The whispered consensus was that things had gone extremely well so far. Still, I didn't dare let myself have too much hope. A conviction would only hurt that much worse if I let myself believe it wouldn't happen.

My mother set a red plastic basket containing a grilled-cheese sandwich and French fries in front of me. "You skipped breakfast," she said. "You need to eat something now or you won't be able to keep up your strength."

I managed to force down a dozen fries and half the sandwich. My father ate the other half while Giacomo helped himself to my remaining fries.

When we returned from lunch, Giacomo presented my witnesses, calling Merle, Aaron, Nick, and Christina to the stand.

Merle testified that he phoned me after realizing Christina had been drugged and seeing the goons jump Nick and Aaron when they went to help her. "One of the bouncers came after me when I went to help. I wouldn't have gotten away from him if Miss Holloway hadn't intervened."

Aaron testified that he'd been headed for the VIP room when one of the bouncers hit him upside the head with a chair. "The next thing I knew, I woke up in the hospital." He described his medical treatment and recovery in detail, showing the jury the still-pink scar on his head from the stitches needed to sew up his scalp.

Nick detailed how, after Aaron hit the floor, three of the goons had turned on him, the other going after Merle when he emerged from the administrative wing of the club. He mentioned his black eye and cracked ribs, lifting his shirt to point to the particular ribs that had been cracked. The women in the jury craned their necks to get a better look at Nick's six-pack abs. One even gestured for him to raise his shirt higher. Trumbull lifted her gavel as if prepared to bang it but then took a gander at Nick's abs herself and changed her mind.

"Officer Menger, Agent Marquez, and I were in big trouble," Nick said from the witness-box. "Way over our heads. I'm grateful Agent Holloway arrived when she did." His eyes sought mine from across the room. "I don't know what I'd do without her."

I blinked back the tears pooling in my eyes and bit my lip to stop it from quivering.

When Christina took the stand, she described the horror of waking up to find herself covered in painful bite marks. She showed the jurors an arched scar that remained across her shoulder blade. Several of the jurors cringed, while one of the females began to weep.

"These types of busts are extremely stressful and dangerous," Christina said. "Officers have to make split-second,
life-or-death decisions. Agent Holloway did what she believed was necessary to protect me and the other agents. No
more. No less."

Christina's gaze met mine and I offered her a small smile
in gratitude, which she promptly returned.

When Christina left the stand, I leaned over and whispered to my attorney, "Are you calling me next?"

"No," he said. "Things have gone well. I don't want to
risk it."

Ugh! Though I knew Giacomo was making a strategic
decision based on his many years of experience as a criminal defense attorney, I felt frustrated by the fact that I couldn't
tell my side of the story in my own words. That I couldn't tell
the jurors how freaked out I'd been by the horrors I'd wit-
nessed in the club that night. That despite Don Geils being a
total scumbag, I hadn't been able to bring myself to end his
life.

That I didn't deserve to be convicted.

Giacomo stood. "The defense rests."

A tremor of terror rippled through me. Had there been
enough evidence in my favor? Had we successfully refuted
Kerr's accusations? Had the jurors gotten a true sense of
what I went through that night?

God, I hoped so. If not, it was too late.

Trumbull motioned to Troy Kerr. "Begin your closing
arguments."

Kerr did his best to minimize the damage Lu had
caused. He stood before the jury box, pleading with the
men and women to convict me. "Regardless of the findings
at the IRS internal affairs hearing, you are charged with
making an independent determination in this criminal pro-
ceeding." Ironic words given that Kerr had admitted my
internal affairs report in order to bolster his case and was
only now asking the jurors to ignore the evidence after it
backfired on him. "The evidence and testimony clearly
showed that Miss Holloway fired bullets into the leg of a

defenseless man. If we allow this type of abusive behavior to go unchecked, the Constitution means nothing. Our rights mean nothing. I'm not asking you to convict Miss Holloway for Don Geils' sake," he said. "I'm asking you to convict her for America."

Jeez. I'm surprised the guy didn't wave a flag and ask the jurors to sing "The Star-Spangled Banner."

When Kerr completed his closing argument, he thanked the jurors and took his seat.

Giacomo walked over to the jury box. He glanced back at Kerr. "Ladies and gentlemen, if you really want to do something for America, you'll allow Miss Holloway, a young woman who put her own life in danger to serve her country honorably and faithfully, to go free. You heard the testimony today. Had Miss Holloway used the force she'd been trained to use, Don Geils wouldn't be sitting over there."

Giacomo pointed over at Geils, who was using his pinky fingernail to dig something from his teeth. I supposed they didn't allow toothpicks in jail. One of the inmates might stab another with it. I wondered how many jabs with a toothpick it would take to kill someone. I'd be willing to try it on Geils and find out.

"Don Geils shouldn't be alive today," Giacomo said, raising his palms. "He should be pushing up daisies, six feet under. *Worm food.*" He pointed at Geils again. "Yet there he sits, alive and well and digging his lunch out of his teeth. His heart is beating. His lungs are taking in air."

Geils glared at my attorney.

Giacomo turned back to the jurors. "To say Miss Holloway used excessive force is entirely illogical. She didn't use excessive force. She used *insufficient* force. Rather than *taking* Don Geils' life, she *spared* it." He let his words sink in for a moment, then ducked his chin in a gracious nod. "Thank you, ladies and gentlemen. We trust that you'll make the right decision."

Would they?

Dear God, I hoped so.

I looked over at them as Giacomo returned to my side.

Several met my gaze, but a few others were looking elsewhere. Hard to glean anything from their expressions.

Trumbull glanced at the clock. It was shortly before five.
"We'll wrap things up for today." She turned to the jurors.
"Be here at nine tomorrow morning to begin deliberations."
She banged her gavel and we all stood as she descended her
bench and returned to her chambers.

chapter forty-two

The Longest Night of My Life

The reporters and their cameramen cornered both Troy Kerr and my attorney as we headed down the steps outside. Both attorneys predicted an easy victory. Obviously, one of them would be proved wrong tomorrow.

Trish LeGrande elbowed another reporter aside and shoved her microphone in Troy Kerr's face. "Given that she fired Miss Holloway, Lu Lobozinski's testimony in support of the former agent was a surprise. What are your thoughts about her statements?"

"It's natural that Ms. Lobozinski would come to the defense of an agent she'd hired," Kerr said. "But that doesn't change the fact that Miss Holloway clearly used excessive force."

"Clearly," Trish repeated, glancing my way.

So much for unbiased journalism, huh?

A male reporter stepped in next. "There's speculation you've got your eye on the bench and brought this case to get the attention of the judicial selection committee."

"Where did you hear that?" Kerr cut angry, accusing eyes to Giacomo before turning back to the reporter.

"I overhead two attorneys in the men's room talking about it," the reporter said. "Another mentioned it in line at Security. Three of the judges in the snack bar were talking about it, too."

Neener-neener.

A red-haired female reporter waylaid Giacomo. "You brought SWAT officer Lamar Thomas down to size. How did that feel?"

Giacomo remained professional, refusing to gloat. "Just doing my job," he said. "Getting honest answers out of people who don't want to give them."

I took Giacomo aside and thanked him. "You were incredible in that courtroom."

He curled his fingers, blew on his nails, and rubbed them on his chest in a gesture of inflated ego. "I am that damn good, aren't I?" He echoed Lu's words, following them with a grin. "Like you."

I smiled for the first time in weeks.

I parted ways with my attorney and entourage on the steps and headed home with my parents, Nick, and Alicia.

Despite feeling utterly exhausted, I couldn't sleep a wink that night. I tossed and turned next to Alicia on the futon in my guest room. I stared up at the ceiling and tried to count sheep. Unfortunately, like my thoughts the sheep went in a hundred different directions.

At 2:00 AM, I slid my feet into my slippers, grabbed my cell phone and keys, and sneaked out of my town house. I looked down the street to see the light from Nick's big-screen television flickering in his living room window. Apparently he couldn't sleep, either.

I sent him a text as I headed his way. *Coming over.*

Ten seconds later he was standing barefoot and bare chested in his driveway, waiting for me in nothing but a pair of faded flannel lounge pants in a Dallas Cowboys print. His breath hung in the frigid night air, but he didn't seem to notice the cold.

I walked straight into his arms. He wrapped them around me, holding on so tight I thought he might crack his ribs again. I would've cried if I'd had the energy. As it was, I was too exhausted to do anything more than stand there and let him hold me up.

After a few seconds, he released me, took me by the hand, and led me inside. Without a word, he swept me into his arms, carried me upstairs, and made sweet, soft, sad love to me. We both knew that even if I won my case tomorrow things would never be the same. This trial would be a scar on my soul.

Afterward, I allowed myself a few minutes in Nick's arms, feeling his chest rise and fall under my cheek, listening to his heart beat. *Thump-thump. Thump-thump. Thump-thump.*

As I lay there, I thought again about how Nick would be affected if I was convicted. Though the thought of him with another women made me utterly sick, I had no right to ask him to wait for me. I didn't want to tie him down, to force him to stay true to me out of a sense of duty or guilt. Breaking up with him would be the hardest thing I'd ever had to do, but I owed it to him to set him free.

Even if it killed me.

When I climbed out of bed, Nick did, too. While I put my pajamas and slippers back on, he slid on a sweatshirt and a pair of sneakers with his lounge pants.

As he walked me home, I said, "Nick, if I get convicted, I want you to move on." As the words left my lips, my heart shrank into a painful ball in my chest.

"You're not going to get convicted," he said, though his uncertain tone told me that he, too, was afraid to let himself have too much hope lest the jury side with Troy Kerr. "And what do you mean, 'move on'?"

"I want you to find someone else."

He grabbed my hand and pulled me to a stop. "Nope. Not gonna happen."

My eyes grew misty, my throat tight. I looked up into his eyes. "I don't expect you to wait for me."

"I've already waited months to make you mine, Tara. I'll wait some more if I have to."

A tear escaped down my cheek and he ran a thumb over the wet trail to erase it.

He looked down into my eyes. "If you're convicted, Tara, I'm quitting the IRS."

"Nick! No!"

"I couldn't work for a government that would treat one of its own that way." He exhaled a long, steamy breath. "I couldn't work for people who could convict you."

"What would you do?"

He shrugged. "I don't know. Run off and join the circus?"

"I can't see you in one of those clown cars."

"Hush, woman," he said, giving me that chipped-tooth smile I never tired of. "I'd be the ringmaster."

We continued on to my door, where he waited while I unlocked it and stepped inside.

"Good night, Nick."

He gave me a soft kiss that turned my heart inside out. "Good night, Tara."

chapter forty-three

$\mathcal{A}$nd the Verdict Is . . .

Tuesday morning brought another case of dry heaves, these even more intense than yesterday's. Today I would know my fate.

But what would it be?

I trembled as I tried to apply my mascara, poking myself in the eye. My lipstick ended up all over my mouth, my blush in wide swaths across my cheeks. When I finished I looked at my reflection in the mirror. Shit. I was the one who belonged in a clown car.

My cat Anne stood in the front foyer, watching me as I packed up to go. She looked up at me with frightened eyes, almost as if she realized something was up. Then again, maybe it was my horrid face that scared her.

The always-aloof Henry had even come down from his usual perch atop my TV cabinet, though he sat off to the side, nonchalantly licking his paw as if to say, *No need to worry. You'll be back.*

"Thanks, Henry," I said. "I needed that."

I gave them each a scratch behind the ears.

Given that we had no idea how long jury deliberations would take, only Nick, Bonnie, and my parents made up my cheering squad today. The others went about their work, though I had strict orders from all to text them the instant I heard the verdict.

I took a seat next to Giacomo, who greeted me with a warm smile. "Ready to walk out of here a free woman?"

"Hell yes," I said under my breath. I just wasn't sure it was going to happen.

The reporters lounged about the benches with magazines and laptops, ready to make productive use of their time while they waited for the verdict.

The jurors trickled in and took seats in the box. A straggler who sneaked in as Judge Trumbull ascended her bench received a cursory admonishment. "What part of 'nine o'clock' did you not understand?"

After the judge gave the jury some standard instructions, they were sent to a nearby conference room to deliberate. We all stood as they exited the room.

Giacomo pulled out his laptop. "You don't mind if I work on a brief while we wait, do you?"

"Be my guest." I stepped back to the gallery to sit with Nick, Bonnie, and my parents. Nick grabbed one of my hands, my mother the other.

With the jury out of the room and my case in a holding pattern, Judge Trumbull handled minor matters in several other cases. Two attorneys debated a trial setting in a mail fraud case while another couple of lawyers argued over the admissibility of an e-mail communication of unverifiable origin.

My mother had brought along some magazines, *Southern Living, House Beautiful, Better Homes & Gardens,* but neither of us could do much more than stare at the pages, unseeing. Time seemed to have slowed, the Earth no longer spinning on its axis but remaining static. Not only had last night been the longest of my life, this morning was following suit.

I glanced at the clock for what must have been the hundredth time. What was taking the jury so long? It had been two excruciating hours. I was innocent, dammit! It shouldn't take this much time for them to figure that out, should it? Then again, this was an important matter. They had a duty to carefully review the evidence before coming to a decision.

Judge Trumbull picked up another file and eyed the clock, too, probably debating whether to break for lunch. She instructed her bailiff to consult with the jury and find out the status of their deliberations.

The bailiff returned a minute later. "The jury is ready."

I tried not to wet myself.

My mother gave my hand one last squeeze. I took my seat at the defense table and watched as the twelve members of the jury returned to the room. My head felt so light and full of air I thought I might faint.

Once they were seated, Trumbull asked the foreman, the white-haired man who'd been wearing the sweater-vest yesterday, whether they had reached their verdict. He announced that they had.

Giacomo stood and I rose, too, on legs so wobbly I had to brace myself with my hands on the table lest I keel over. Nick appeared beside me, putting a supportive hand around my waist, holding me up. I leaned on him, closed my eyes, and silently prayed.

"What is your verdict?" the judge asked.

I held my breath.

"We find the defendant not guilty."

Not guilty.

Not.

Guilty.

I opened my eyes.

It was official now. I wasn't a bad person.

My innocence would be noted in a public record for all the world to see.

My mother let loose a happy cry behind me while the rest of the gallery broke out in murmurs. I was no longer able to stand. Nick lowered me gently into my chair, kneeling next to me, holding both of my hands in his, and looking up into my face with an expression of immense relief.

Giacomo looked down at me and smiled. "Another satisfied customer. I mentioned I charge double for 'not guilty' verdicts, right?"

I looked up at him. "Nice try."

The attorneys thanked the jurors for their service and Trumbull dismissed them.

Troy Kerr walked over and shook Anthony's hand. "Good job."

"Any plans to appeal?" my attorney asked.

What!?! My heart skipped a beat as I jerked bolt upright in my chair. *This nightmare might not be over?*

"No," Kerr said. "I don't see any grounds for taking this further."

I slumped again.

Thank God!

chapter forty-four

My Delivery Arrives

Nick texted everyone the good news, then turned to me. "How do you want to celebrate?"

"Sushi and green tea ice cream."

My parents, Bonnie, Nick, and I went out for lunch. Having eaten little over the last few days, I stuffed myself full of *kappa maki,* California rolls, and green tea ice cream.

Afterward, Bonnie headed home while the rest of us returned to my town house. While I changed out of my suit and into jeans and my favorite Longhorns sweatshirt, my mother and father packed up their things for their trip back to Nacogdoches.

Nick helped them carry their things out to my father's truck.

My mother turned to me before climbing in, fresh tears in her eyes. "I'm glad this is all over."

"You and me both."

She and my father gave me hugs and kisses and drove off.

I turned to Nick, finding myself choking up once again.

"I don't know what I would've done without you through all
of this."

He slid me a sexy grin. "I think I should be rewarded."

I slid him a sexy grin right back. "I happen to agree."

We spent the afternoon in Nick's bed, though, admit-
tedly, a large part of it was spent dozing. The trial had left us
horribly sleep deprived.

Over the rest of the week, my life returned to normal. Well,
it returned to what passed for normal for me these days.

Don Geils and the Department of Justice finalized his
fourteen-year plea deal. Anthony phoned me to let me know
he'd successfully argued to have Geils' $10-million civil
lawsuit against me dismissed as frivolous. That was one less
thing for me to worry about. My new coat arrived from Neiman Marcus, courtesy of the Aberdeens. Jeremy sent me a full
case of cow patties, too, a peace offering of sorts. The media
moved on to new fodder, my trial now yesterday's news.

Each day I fought through rush-hour traffic to go to and
from my job in the audit department in Fort Worth. Nick
and I saw each other in the evenings.

My life wasn't bad. In fact, it was pretty good. Safe. Pre-
dictable. Stable. Still, I still grieved for the life I'd lost. That
crazy, risky, dangerous thrill ride of a life.

On Saturday morning, Nick and I headed over to the firing range in my BMW, my long-range rifle and several
boxes of ammo loaded in the trunk. The morning was ex-
ceptionally chilly and windy, a cold front having blown in
overnight and taking its sweet time moving out of the area.

As always, I hit every target in the bull's-eye. Though
Nick was a good shot himself, he came nowhere close to
matching my precision.

We decided to call it quits after half an hour on the range.
My nipples were so cold and hard they felt as if they might
pop off, and Nick feared his testicles were going to crawl up
inside him.

When we finished, we compared our far-off paper targets
through my father's spare field glasses.

"I might feel emasculated," Nick said as he looked through the oversized binoculars, "if you hadn't made me feel all man last night." He cut me that chipped-tooth grin.

We returned to my town house, where we warmed up with mugs of hot chocolate and stacked empty cardboard boxes around my living room, making it appear as if I had an extensive stock of items to sell at my alleged booth at the Traders Village flea market. I needed to look legitimate. Didn't want the delivery driver for Tokyo Discount Telecom to become suspicious.

Eddie, William, and Tanaka checked in with Nick by phone an hour before the delivery was to take place. Eddie had parked in the lot of a frozen yogurt shop located on the main thoroughfare that led into my neighborhood. William waited in the parking lot of a day-care facility. Agent Tanaka was parked a quarter mile farther down, in the lot of a Presbyterian church. The plan was for all five of us to follow the truck, taking turns in the lead to be less noticeable.

Alicia's in-box at work was already overflowing with clients' tax records, so she'd gone into Martin and McGee today. I was alone as I waited for the delivery, pacing back and forth in my house, trying to force myself to sit still on my couch but having no luck.

Twenty minutes after the estimated delivery time of 2:00, the rumble of a truck engine sounded out front. I took several deep breaths to calm myself. If I appeared overly excited or agitated, I might unintentionally clue the driver in that I knew the products were counterfeits and that agents lay in wait to bust him and his cohorts. Then again, we still weren't sure whether the delivery driver was in cahoots with the people running TDT in Japan. There had been enough evidence for a judge to issue a search warrant, however. Once we followed the truck to its depot, we'd search the place.

I peered through my peephole as the man stepped down from the truck's cab. He appeared to be the same delivery driver who'd dropped off the order at Westside Wireless, the Asian man we'd seen on the video footage. He circled to the back of the truck, opened the cargo bay, and removed a dolly, positioning it upright on the asphalt next to him. He hopped into the bay, disappearing for a few seconds as he rounded up my order. One by one, he loaded six boxes onto the dolly, then wheeled them up my driveway. I stepped back when he made it to my porch and pushed my doorbell.

Ding-dong.

I counted slowly down from ten so he wouldn't realize I'd been spying on him. I pulled the door open. "Hello."

He held out a clipboard. "Are you Sara Galloway?" he asked in a voice tinged with an Asian accent.

"Yep. That's me." *Not.*

He tapped a spot on the paper with his finger. "Sign here."

I signed the board under my alias.

"Where do you want the boxes?" he asked, glancing around.

I pointed to a spot I'd left open in the foyer. "Right here is good."

He rolled the dolly over, quickly stacked the boxes against the wall, and rolled it back out the door.

"Thanks!" I called after him from the doorway. I glanced down the street. Nick sat in the driveway of his town house in a white G-ride, ready to follow the truck.

I closed the door, grabbed my keys and purse, and headed into the garage. I punched the button to raise the door. As it went up, I saw Nick drive by. I climbed into my car and backed out of my drive, following him.

Every nerve ending in my body tingled with anticipation. *This is what I live for.*

chapter forty-five

Call Me Maybe

The five of us followed along at a reasonable distance as the truck made two more deliveries, one at a cell phone shop, the other at a run-down house in South Dallas. The place had burglar bars over all the windows and doors, making the structure appear as much cage as house. I parked down the street and watched through the binoculars as the deliveryman wheeled several large unmarked boxes through the door.

Finally, the driver led us south down Interstate 635, also known as LBJ Freeway, which formed a partial loop around the northern and eastern perimeters of Dallas. Just before reaching Balch Springs, he took an exit and headed into an industrial area. I stayed back as the cars driven by Nick, Eddie, William, and Tanaka converged. The four of them slowed as the truck braked to turn into a truck yard.

The expansive yard appeared to be approximately the size of a football field. Surrounding the yard was a ten-foot chain-link fence with orange plastic strips winding through the links to create a visual barrier. The fence was topped with barbed wire. Not surprising. I'd heard of eighteen-wheelers being hijacked. Trucks loaded with merchandise were probably a common target for thieves.

I pulled to the curb and watched through the field glasses as the driver punched a code on a keypad to activate the electronic gate. The four agents drove their cars into the lot of the small one-story brick building that served as the headquarters for the truck yard. They climbed out of their vehicles and walked inside.

Oh, to be a fly on that wall . . .

I'd reluctantly agreed to keep watch outside. We had no idea how extensive this crime ring could be, and it couldn't hurt to have eyes on the parking lot.

A moment later, my cell phone bleeped with an incoming call, the sound startling me so much I nearly dropped my field glasses. The readout indicated it was Eddie.

I hit the button. "Hey, Eddie."

Eddie didn't reply. All I heard was Nick speaking with another man whose voice I didn't recognize. Looked like Eddie had butt-dialed me once again. When would he learn how to use his new phone? Still, now I *could* be a fly on the wall. A blind fly, maybe, but at least I could listen to their exchange.

"We've got a warrant to search the place," Nick said. "We believe counterfeit goods have been shipped from this location."

"Counterfeit goods?" came the other man's voice, followed by words I couldn't make out.

The rest of the conversation was disjointed. Eddie must have stepped farther away from Nick and the man he was speaking to.

Nick voice came through again. ". . . followed the delivery truck . . . here . . ."

The man's voice followed. ". . . don't know . . . take a look."

There was no noise other than fabric rubbing up against the mic for several seconds before the conversation picked up again.

Nick spoke again. ". . . inspect your truck . . ."

This time a voice that sounded like the Asian delivery-man's responded. ". . . follow . . . boxes . . ."

Frankly, the whole thing was more annoying than in-triguing so far. I probably should have let the men handle the bust.

Though the phone, I heard Eddie shout, "Look out!"

Uh-oh. Look out for what?

Pop! Pop-pop-pop!

Holy shit! Was that gunfire coming from the truck yard? I screamed into the phone, "Eddie! Are you guys okay?" There was no response.

Oh, my God! Had they been hit?

I leaped from my car, opened my trunk, and grabbed the rifle case I'd left in my car after going to the range that morning. In my haste I hadn't put on my jacket, and the cold wind hit me with a relentless force. But a little freezing wind wasn't going to stop me.

Pop-pop!

Yep. Definitely gunfire. A semiautomatic.

The next *pop* was followed by a *blam-blam-blam* that sounded like a government-issued Glock. I wondered how William was taking all of this. Was he scared shitless, re-thinking his transfer from collections? Or was he like I'd been, terrified but thrilled at the same time?

I hung up on Eddie and dialed 911 as I ran toward the yard, fighting through the brisk wind. "There's shooting at a truck yard!" I gave the dispatcher the location as best I could. "Federal agents are on-site serving a warrant."

She asked me to stay on the line while she put out a call for officers in the area to respond.

By then I'd reached the fence. I put my face up to a gap in the plastic but could see nothing. Damn! For all I knew, Nick, Eddie, William, and Tanaka could be lying dead in-side. I fought back a rising panic.

Pop-pop-pop!

Blam! Blam!

Frantically I glanced around for something to climb so I

could see over the fence. Twenty yards away was a gnarled
live oak tree. I ran over, pulled my rifle and a box of ammo
from the case, and began my ascent up the trunk. Who
would've thought all that tree climbing I'd done as a girl in
East Texas would one day pay off?

When I'd climbed high enough to see over the fence, I
found my line of sight blocked by a trailer. I continued upward until I looked down on dozens of trailers situated at
irregular angles, forming a maze of sorts.

At this height, the limbs around me were thinner, sway-
ing recklessly in the wind. I just hoped the one I sat on could
support my weight. Maybe all that green tea ice cream
hadn't been such a good idea after all.

The four agents were hunkered down in the center of the
yard, next to the back bumper of the white truck the Asian
man had been driving. All had their guns at the ready. Luckily, all of them appeared unharmed.

Thank God.

At least a dozen armed men closed in from various directions, creeping toward the agents, using the trucks for cover.
Nick, Eddie, William, and Tanaka were outmanned and out-
gunned.

Sitting ducks.

From my vantage point, I could see the entire yard. It was
like watching one of those maps on a video game with red
dots to warn a player of enemies closing in.

I stuck one leg down between two branches and wrapped
my ankle around them to brace myself. "Send the SWAT
team," I told the emergency dispatcher when she returned to
the line. "These guys are armed to the teeth with semi-
automatics." I took one more look and said, "Tell the cops
not to shoot the girl in the tree. That's me. Gotta go."

chapter forty-six

How Tara Got Her Gumption Back

I hung up on 911 and dialed Eddie. He yanked his phone out of his breast pocket and put it to his ear. "Tara! We're taking fire!"

"I know," I said. "I'm in the oak tree."

Eddie's head swiveled as he looked around, trying to find my location. His head stopped when he spotted me. "Holy shit, girl. That's you?"

"Yeah. SWAT is on its way. There's at least a dozen men closing in on you guys. I can pin them down for a little bit, but I've got limited ammo." My SXR could hold only five bullets at a time. I'd have to use them wisely, as precious seconds could be wasted reloading.

Eddie quickly nudged Nick and pointed up at me. Nick took Eddie's phone. "Tell us what to do."

Don't you just love it when men say that?

I jabbed the speaker button and lodged the phone in the crook of the tree so both of my hands would be free. I loaded my rifle and looked over the yard, evaluating the risks. I put my eye to the scope and took aim at the man who'd ventured closest to the agents. I pulled the trigger.

Bang!

The man's weapon sailed out of his hands. He screamed and scrambled under the closest trailer for cover.

"You've got two men coming up on your left," I said into the phone.

"Gotcha."

I watched as Nick bent down, spied around the corner of the truck, and took out one of the men with a bullet to the shoulder. The other darted around the cab of a bright orange truck, climbed in, and started up the engine. In his haste, he ground the gears before finding the right one, the engine clanging before roaring to life. He drove the truck to the closed exit gate and rammed it. There was an eye-popping screech of metal on concrete as the truck forced its way through the gate.

If the guy thought he was going to get away, he better think again.

"Not gonna happen, buddy." I took aim and shot out the driver's side window. Through my scope, I saw the man throw himself to the floorboards, cowering amid the shattered glass. The truck stalled and rolled to a stop, creating an effective barrier for any of the others who might have thought about escaping.

Another man ran between two trailers, making his way toward Nick, Eddie, William, and Tanaka. He obviously had no idea I was up in the tree, watching him.

Bang!

I shot him in the upper arm. He screamed, dropped his weapon, and took off running. Stupid move. One of his cohorts fired on him as he ran around the back of a blue trailer. He fell to the ground, clutching his arm with one hand, his thigh with the other, screaming, "Don't shoot! Don't shoot!"

Watching the men close in on the agents, I realized their best bet was to get out of the line of fire.

"See that red truck behind you?" I said into the phone.

Down in the yard, Nick's head turned. "Yeah?"

"There's a metal grab bar mounted on the cab. Use it to climb on top of the cab. You'll be safer up there. I'll cover you."

Nick waved for the other agents to follow him. He ran to the red truck, motioning for William to head up first.

Bang! I picked off a third man who'd sneaked too close, putting a bullet in his forearm.

Eddie went up the cab next, followed by Tanaka.

Bang!

I put my fourth bullet in the buttocks of a man who held a gun in each hand like some type of crazed Rambo. He dropped the weapons and grabbed his ass, loping cockeyed to the nearest truck.

I had only one bullet left in my rifle before I'd have to reload. Better make it count, huh?

As Nick scaled the truck, a man came running up the aisle and spotted him. With both hands on the rail, Nick couldn't fire his weapon.

But I could fire mine.

Bang!

The man fell to the ground, a bullet in his hip.

No one messes with my man.

As I stopped to reload, two cop cars pulled up, sirens wailing. Four officers hopped out of the vehicles, though they hunkered down behind the cars as they attempted to get a read on the scene.

I waved my arms and finally got the attention of one of the officers. He ran over and pasted his back to the wide trunk of the tree for safety. He looked up at me.

"I've got the agents on the phone!" I called. "So far they're okay, but they're way outnumbered!"

"SWAT's on the way!" the cop called up to me.

Lying flat on top of the truck cab now, Nick and the other agents had a tactical advantage. The men in the truck yard assumed the agents would be cowering down low and didn't think to look up. The agents were able to get off several shots to keep their attackers at bay and buy some time until SWAT arrived. Nick, Eddie, and Tanaka fired most of the

shots, though William got off two himself. The first rico-
cheted off a side mirror. The second took out a tire, which
slowly went flat. He could definitely use some more practice.

The dark SWAT truck roared around the corner and
drove up the road. The officer at the base of the tree waved
for them to come our way. When the vehicle stopped, five
men poured out, two from the cab, three from the back.

Officer Lamar Thomas jumped down from the passenger
seat and looked up at me, his helmet sliding back on his
forehead. "I don't fucking believe this."

I raised both my rifle and my free hand to indicate sub-
mission. "It's your party now."

"Not so fast," he said, tossing a walkie-talkie up to me.
"We need you to be our eye in the sky."

All of the SWAT officers were male and outweighed me
by at least fifty pounds. No way could these limbs support
their weight.

"SWAT's coming in," I warned Nick through the phone.
"Don't shoot." I looked down at Thomas. "Our agents are on
top of the red truck near the center."

He nodded in acknowledgment.

The SWAT members grabbed their weapons and their
shields and ran to the gate, squeezing past the disabled semi
stalled there. One of the officers peeked through the window. The man who'd been driving the truck was still on the
floorboards, though he raised his hands in surrender. He was
pulled from the cab and cuffed by one of the regular officers.

Another cop pulled out a bullhorn and ordered everyone in the yard to put down their weapons and lie facedown on the ground. None of the men obeyed. One at the
back attempted to scale the fence. With the plastic strips in
the way, he couldn't get a foothold in the links and soon
gave up.

"Two to your right," I told Thomas via the radio as he
stormed in. He got off two shots, taking down both men.
Bang! Bang!
Pop-pop-pop!
I jerked to the left as one of the men spotted me and tried

to take me out. Good thing he was a sucky shot. All he succeeded in doing was putting a few holes in the tree.

One of the SWAT officers ran up behind him, gave him a swift whack in the head with a baton, and the guy crumpled to the ground.

From my perch, I continued to coach the SWAT team until every armed guy in the compound had either been shot, been disarmed, or surrendered. I pushed the button on the walkie-talkie. "Party's over. We got 'em all."

As I descended the tree, Officer Thomas stepped up and held out a hand to help me down.

"Thanks for your help today," he said once my feet were firmly on the ground.

"No problem."

He stuck out his hand. "No hard feelings?"

No hard feelings?

NO HARD FEELINGS?

Was this guy out of his ever-loving mind?

I fought the urge to shoot him point-blank with my rifle, thinking better of it. No way would I go free on that one. "Sure," I forced out between clenched teeth as I took his hand. "No hard feelings."

With all of the adrenaline pumping through my system, I'd forgotten how cold it was outside. Now that the adrenaline had waned, I began to shiver. I returned to my car and cranked the engine on. Luckily, it was still warm. I sat there, enjoying the heater blowing on me full force, while the bad guys were hauled off in multiple Dallas PD cruisers.

Neener.

Neener.

Neener.

Once Nick had finished dealing with the local cops, he glanced my way, walked over, and jerked his head to indicate the yard. "Want to help us search the place?"

He didn't have to ask me twice. I turned off my car and climbed out, sliding into my coat.

The agents and I spent the next four hours going through

all of the trucks and their contents. As it turned out, the counterfeit cell phones were only part of a much broader smuggling scheme. Our search turned up an extensive cache of semi-automatic weapons, knockoff designer handbags, even counterfeit pharmaceuticals, including fake Viagra. Someone was going to be disappointed—actually, two people would be, huh?

Tanaka was thrilled by the find. Given the enormous cache we'd discovered, this seizure would be one of the largest in the history of the Dallas ICE office. He contacted his office, and other agents were dispatched to search the house where the delivery truck had stopped on the way over. Those agents contacted Tanaka soon afterward. Another huge stash of illegal weapons had been found there.

Eddie and William went into the headquarters and seized the computers and paperwork. Nick and I helped them load the equipment and documents into their cars.

"So," I said, turning to William, "you've got your first bust under your belt now. How do you feel?"

He slowly shook his head, his eyes wide. "I feel glad I didn't crap myself."

I gave him a smile. This guy would fit right in at Criminal Investigations.

As Nick walked me back to my car, I felt a spring in my step that I hadn't felt in weeks. I felt happy, satisfied, fulfilled.

I'd got my gumption back.

chapter forty-seven

On My Case

As I sat at my desk in the audit department in Fort Worth late Monday morning, my cell phone rang. The readout indicated it was The Lobo.

I took the call, ready to hear all about how I'd exceeded my authority as an auditor, how I had no business butting in where I didn't belong, how I should've let the agents handle things.

I steeled myself. "Commence the ass chewing."

All she said was, "Come see me," before hanging up her phone.

Great. She wanted to chew my ass out in person.

I told Clyde Hartford that Lu had summoned me.

"You better get going, then," he replied.

I drove to Dallas Criminal Investigations and rode the elevator up to my old floor. When I stepped into the hall, the place seemed oddly quiet. Viola wasn't at her desk, and no agents milled about.

The door to Lu's office was closed. I walked up and tapped softly on it.

"Come on in, Holloway!" Lu barked.

I turned the knob and opened the door.

A chorus of, "Welcome back!" greeted me, along with the kazoo-like sounds of noisemakers. Lu, Viola, Nick, Eddie, Josh, William, and a half-dozen other special agents were gathered in the room. Streamers hung from the light fixture and colorful helium balloons floated in the air. On Lu's desk sat an enormous sheet cake in the shape of a special agent badge with my name written across it.

Did I dare to believe my eyes?

"I . . . uh . . . what?"

Lu held out my Glock and my badge. "You got your job back."

My lungs lurched with a happy sob. "I did?"

"After that stunt you pulled at the truck yard?" Lu said. "George Burton and the others had no choice but to admit they'd been wrong about you."

Nick slid me a cocky grin. "You're that damn good."

I was so elated I felt as if I might float away with the balloons. I sat down in one of Lu's chairs, my smile so wide it hurt.

While the group sang "For She's a Jolly Good Agent," Viola cut the cake and shoved a paper plate bearing a huge frosted piece into my hand.

When the celebration concluded, The Lobo waved for me to follow her. "Come see your new office."

New office? I didn't want a new office. I wanted my old office, the one across the hall from Nick. To my surprise, that's exactly where she led me.

My office had a brand-new desk, new bookshelves, and a new rolling chair, the wobbly one I'd suffered with before now gone.

"What about William?" I asked.

"I never meant for him to stay in here permanently," Lu said. "We had to get the other space painted and rewired before we could move him in. You know how long it takes to get anything like that done around here."

"Thanks, Lu." I grabbed her in a big hug.

When I finally released her, she said, "Enough dillydallying." She pointed at a stack of files on my desk. "You've got several cases waiting. Get to work."

When Lu left, Nick came in with the target from our time at the range last weekend. He tacked it up on my wall where the target from my special agent firearms test used to hang. The old target was now a legal exhibit, part of the official court record of my excessive force trial.

"Have you heard from the Japanese authorities?" I asked. Nick had phoned them immediately after Saturday's bust at the truck yard, and they'd indicated they were prepared to move in on several people in Tokyo.

"They called this morning," he said. "Eleven people were arrested. Nobody's talking yet, but they're pretty sure they've got the men who were at the top of the chain."

"That's good news."

He lifted his chin to indicate my files. "Whatcha got there? Anything interesting?"

I plopped down in my new, much more comfy chair and pulled the stack toward me, eager to see what Lu had in store for me.

The first file was typical, a small, run-of-the-mill case against a dog groomer who'd not only trimmed dog's toenails but trimmed a few thousand off her reported earnings as well.

The second file contained only a phone message slip with the name *Katie,* a local phone number, and a handwritten note in Viola's handwriting. *Whistle-blower. Natural gas company.* Hm-m . . .

The name on the last file blew my mind. "Brazos Rivers?"

"The singer?" Nick stepped up beside me and looked over my shoulder as I opened the folder.

Inside were two front-row tickets for Brazos Rivers' upcoming concert at the American Airlines Center. My first thought was that the tickets were a gift from Lu, but then I noticed the file also contained a transcript of Rivers' earnings that had been reported to the IRS by third parties over the past few years. Royalties. Endorsements. Concert revenues. All in the millions of dollars. According to the information in the file, Brazos hadn't ever bothered to file a tax return or ante up a single penny to Uncle Sam.

At the bottom of the file was an eight-by-ten color photograph of the man decked out in boots, shiny silver spurs, and leather chaps. His chest was bare and hairless. A tattoo of the Texas flag rippled across his toned biceps. A straw hat rested on his head, tilted at just the right angle to cast a shadow across his chiseled cheekbones.

I gulped. Brazos Rivers hadn't been named *People* magazine's Sexiest Man Alive for nothing.

"Give me that." Nick snatched the photo out of my hands. "You're drooling all over it."